Adam Kennedy's previous novels range from the highly successful thriller *The Domino Principle*, which inspired the international hit movie of the same name, to *In a Far Country*, an enthralling family drama set in the 1960s. His most recent titles include the Bradshaw Trilogy: *No Place to Cry, The Fires of Summer* and *All Dreams Denied, Love Left Over* – a collection of bitter-sweet love stories – and *Passion Never Knows*, the first volume of the Kincaid Trilogy. He lives in Connecticut with his wife, Susan.

Dancing in the Shadows

The Kincaid Trilogy
Volume Two

Adam Kennedy

KNIGHT

First published in 1991
by HEADLINE BOOK PUBLISHING PLC

First published in paperback in 1992
by HEADLINE BOOK PUBLISHING PLC

This edition published 2003 by Knight,
an imprint of The Caxton Publishing Group

10 9 8 7 6 5 4

ISBN 1 86019 6063

Typeset in 10/11½pt Times
by Colset Private Limited, Singapore

Printed and bound in Great Britain by
Mackays of Chatham plc, Chatham, Kent

The Caxton Publishing Group
20 Bloomsbury Street
London
WC1B 3JH

For Egon Dumler

One must accept the fact that life has no meaning . . .
then live each day as if that fact weren't true.

Millard Hofer

BOOK ONE

• CHAPTER 1 •

1

In the early springtime of 1934, Roy Kincaid lost his privacy for ever. He found that he was recognized wherever he went. He was suddenly and remarkably famous.

Most of us have no experience with fame. Like great wealth, it's something we know about, read about, dream of perhaps but never experience. Still the word stays alive and electric in our minds. The celebrated, the renowned, though strangers to us, become a part of our lives. Their habits, their triumphs and failures, their idiosyncrasies are known and discussed by those who are obscure and unknown. We are constantly aware of these public creatures.

The wisest people, of course, are neither seduced nor impressed by fame. They realize that the more profound their accomplishments, the less likelihood there is that they will be widely recognized. No serious artist or thinker expects mass approval of his efforts. Significant personal work is seldom destined to be popular.

Kincaid had never attached importance to himself or to anything he did. He did not set out to be recognized or adored by strangers. Neither his appearance nor his background indicated special qualities that might make him conspicuous or enviable. From his birth in Tasmania through his vagabond years as a labourer and merchant seaman he had no objective more lofty than survival.

3

Even jail, he quickly learned, could be a salvation, preferable in every way to the hungry streets of Hobart or Melbourne.

In the winter of 1932, he found himself homeless and stranded in London. No friends, no resources, no alternatives. Or so it seemed. By what sort of miracle then could such a person be caught up, swept along, and transformed? By what process does a sparrow become an eagle? In such new circumstances, how does a man redefine himself? Kincaid had no answers for these questions. Nor did his wife, Sophie. They only knew that the motion picture had created its own new sort of royalty. Round the world, people were enchanted by the faces and voices of young men and women who a short time before had served coffee in diners or changed tyres in Chicago garages; hypnotized by the shadows of these magical strangers who danced and sang and made love on luminous screens in the soft darkness of palace-like theatres. Young men who had driven taxis in Cleveland or New Orleans now owned Bugattis and Bentleys and Duesenbergs. Girls who had grown up in furnished rooms found themselves in splendid homes on Sunset Boulevard with furs in every closet and a servant for every need.

Kincaid, by chance, became one of these chosen people. After he'd finished work in his first film, before it was shown in theatres in New York and London, Paris and Berlin, before any public viewings had taken place, Kincaid and Sophie and their friend Evan Tagg sat together in London and asked each other what would happen after the picture was released. 'Should we hope for a great, loud, and vulgar success,' Evan said, 'or a respectable failure?' Only Sophie had a well-thought-out answer to that question. But she kept it to herself.

These were not theatrical folk, you see. Not these three. Each had a particular rhythm and a unique destiny. Or so they believed. But now suddenly they felt

4

joined in a lock-step they hadn't planned on, headed down a path that was unfamiliar and shadowed.

2

Among the people who wrote columns and articles and interviews in the early years of talking pictures, there were few who were qualified journalists. Just as the actors and directors came from all quarters and learned their professions by on-the-job work, the writers who fed on the film industry as they nourished it, with their opinions and fantasies and prejudices, had shaky qualifications. Among the group were a former madam of a Laurel Canyon brothel, half a dozen failed actors and actresses, numerous drunks, and one morphine addict, a former zoology professor at Columbia University, a bookmaker from Newark, and an overweight exotic dancer from Ottawa whose first job in Los Angeles had been that of pastry chef at the Biltmore.

In this group Gloria Westerfield was a contradiction. She was educated and experienced. She had graduated from Smith, had worked for two years on the *Hartford Republican*, and had then written theatre reviews in New York for the Associated Press before moving west to cover the motion picture business. Still in her twenties, she was attractive, articulate, fair in her treatment of performers, and perceptive and responsible in her criticism of particular films. Her endorsement was thought to be a guarantee of healthy box-office receipts. But she could not be bought, bribed, or seduced. In a community where everything is for sale, her integrity inspired bewilderment rather than respect. Unable to understand or admire her, the studio executives and their underlings simply treated her with caution. Since she was not married and was seldom seen in restaurants or at parties with actors or directors, it was assumed that she was a lesbian. Somehow her name was linked with that of Hilda Becker, a cellist with the Los Angeles Symphony Orchestra, whom Gloria had never met.

Only after the death of Sidney Hostetler, a thin white-haired gentleman who had been an inventive and widely imitated director in early silent films, only then did it come clear that Gloria Westerfield had lived with and cared for this much-admired man who was forty years older than she. After his funeral, when she moved to a house in Cahuenga Pass, lived by herself, wore a mourning band for two years and still refused to patronize the Sunset Boulevard restaurants and night-clubs, the town's hostesses concluded they had been correct all along: she was unquestionably a lesbian.

After viewing *Bushranger*, Kincaid's first film, at a screening-room on the Thornwood lot, Gloria Westerfield wrote the following piece about it.

Julian Thorne is neither a saint nor a philanthropist. Thornwood Studios is as eager to make money as Fox or Warners or Columbia or any other production company in town. But all the same, either by design or by accident, Thorne is capable of giving us an occasional surprise, capable of presenting a film that is not a remake of something we've seen before, perhaps many times before. He has the courage, it seems, to abandon the formula, to risk losing his investment, to make the best possible film from the subject he has chosen, to deliver something new and fresh, a story with believable conflicts and characters who come to life.

Bushranger is that rare sort of film. When it was being shot and publicized last summer and early fall it seemed to defy categorization. It still does. It is set in the last century but it seems sharply relevant today. It takes place in Australia but the characters are somehow familiar to us. It has the trappings of a western but it's unlike any western I've seen. There is no love story, very little kindness or tenderness, and the climax is cruelly tragic. But that conclusion seems implicit from the start. At the finish you know there's no other way it could end. I sat in my theatre seat for ten minutes after the film finished and the lights came on. I knew I had seen something honest and solid and courageous, and I didn't want to lose it by stumbling too soon out into the sunlight.

Who shall I praise first? Thorne of course. He took what could have been nothing more than another tale of gore and betrayal, an Australian Jesse James if you will, and made it a shocking statement about man's inhumanity to man. Without speeches or tears, without moral signposts.

Evan Tagg, a London playwright who is new to films, wrote the screenplay, and I salute him. As in all good scenarios, what is left out is as important as what is put in. He must be given credit for the straight-forward thrust of what could easily have been an engorgement of melodrama and sentimentality.

Tim Garrigus directed. His first step beyond low-budget westerns. And what a bold step he's made. With actors such as Donald Crisp, C. Aubrey Smith, Daisy Bishop, Colin Clive, Geoff Bingham, and Beulah Bondi to work with, with excellent settings and photography, and authentic costumes, he has pieced together a film with a steady throbbing rhythm and painful inevitability. He makes hard choices and makes them work. In this piece of work, Garrigus has moved from competent craftsman to major director.

In a story where cliché and bombast could have taken over, all the performances are restrained and integrated and truthful. And at the centre of it all is the remarkable Roy Kincaid, who plays Ned Kelly. One hesitates to put a hex on a new actor by praising him too much, especially when that actor is totally untrained, new not only to films but to any sort of acting. But I refuse to be cautious. If film acting is the ability to somehow get through and past the camera lens and simply come to life on the screen, then this young man has mastered the art. He is a real and recognizable human being. Terrifying, vulnerable, indestructible, and heart-breaking. Like the writer, Evan Tagg, he seems to know by instinct what not to do. He's only twenty-six years old and I'm convinced he will have a long career. But even if *Bushranger* were to be his only film, he will have made his mark.

Julian Thorne certainly gambled with this production. With the story itself, with the screenwriter, with the director, and the leading actor. I personally guarantee him that his gamble has paid off. *Bushranger* will be a hugely successful picture.

3

Sophie's mother, Margaret Wiswell Cranston, wife to Major William Cranston, had spent her entire life in Northumberland. At Wiswell Towers. Just as her mother and grandfather had, and countless earlier generations of Wiswells.

Sophie, an only child, expected that she, too, would stay on in the family home, raise her children there, manage the lands, and immerse herself in county life. But a few years after the death of her first husband, she had bought a house in London on Green Park and had taken her daughter, Sarah, and her son, Trevor, there to live. Yet always she was in close contact with her mother. Margaret came down by train to London or Sophie visited her at the Towers.

After Kincaid's film opened in London, however, and soon after in every city and town in England, the two women didn't meet for almost two months. At last, near the end of March, Sophie drove up to Northumberland. Her first evening with her mother, they sat in their robes in Margaret's upstairs rooms and talked long after the house had gone dark and quiet.

'I thought perhaps I'd seen the last of you,' Margaret said.

'It's possible. Quite often these days I feel as though I've shed my skin and turned into a new person.'

'You must be terribly proud of Kincaid.'

'Of course I am. I was astonished when I saw the film. I never questioned that he'd be good but I had no way of knowing how very good he'd be.'

'As I told you when I rang you in London, Clara and I saw the film in Newcastle the first day it was shown and we were both stunned by it. Clara's been to Australia, you know, several times, I believe. Travelled there with her father. She's quite an authority on Australian history. Knows all the details of the Ned Kelly story. And the film was totally accurate, she says. Made quite an impression on her. And on everyone else in the theatre that day. A great deal of sniffling and weeping when the poor chap is taken to the gallows. But at the very end, sad as it was, they stood up and applauded.'

Sophie smiled. 'The same in London.'

'Well, I'm extremely happy for him. He's a gifted young man. And I'm delighted for you, too, of course. How have you dealt with all the attention?'

'I haven't,' Sophie said. 'I've been in hiding. Shut up inside our house. And so has Kincaid for the most part. At first he said he wouldn't let all the commotion change his way of life. But he soon discovered that he couldn't step through the door without being approached by a journalist or a photographer. Even with his hat brim turned down all round they recognize him, coat collar up and dark spectacles. They're all very nice of course, terribly polite and apologetic, but the fact remains that they are always there. If we go to dinner or the theatre we have a struggle making it back to our automobile.'

'Sounds dreadful.'

Sophie nodded. 'Even when we're left alone, when people don't actually speak to him or follow us in the streets, there's a great deal of staring, eyes peeping at us from behind napkins or theatre programmes.'

'Won't all of that come to an end after the film has had its run?'

'That's what I assumed. But when I mentioned it to Dorothy, Geoff Bingham's wife, she said, "Don't count on that, my dear. Once you become public property, that's the way you stay."'

'Maybe he should simply refuse to talk with the newspaper people.'

'Oh, but he hasn't talked with them. He's given no interviews since he came home from California.'

'Then how . . .'

Sophie made a limp hand gesture. 'They rehash stories that were printed in California when they were shooting the picture. And they pester everyone who might know him. They've been after Uncle Howard for weeks. And they've tried to contact Sarah and Trevor at school.'

'How dare they do that?'

'They dare, mother. It's what they're paid for, so they'll try anything. I had a serious talk with Miss Endicott at Sarah's school and with John Patterson at St Alban's. They were co-operative, of course. I'm sure they'll do whatever they can to keep the newspaper people away. But the students do have free hours. So one can't be certain that Sarah and Trevor won't be questioned somehow. I'm particularly concerned about Sarah. She'd like nothing better than to see her views on life printed in the newspaper. She's suddenly quite impressed with Kincaid. Quite a change from when we were first married. She wasn't sure then that he was good enough for me. What was that word she used?'

10

'Common,' Margaret said. 'She thought he was unbearably common.'

Sophie smiled. 'No longer,' she said. 'She's seen the film three times, and now, I suspect, she thinks I'm not good enough for him. But I suppose I'll have nothing but surprises in future from Sarah. She's fifteen now, she thinks she's twenty-five, and I'm afraid she'll have to be chained if we're to keep her in Miss Endicott's school for two more years.'

'She's keen to go to California. She told me that when you were there with Kincaid.'

'Of course. Sunshine every day and oranges on all the trees. Dancing on the sand and swimming in the moonlight. She's read every cheap book on the subject and it's all bubbling in her head. And then of course, Evan's out there now. She has a terrible crush on him, you know.'

'Yes, I did know that. But that will go away, I expect.'

'Not so quickly, I'm afraid. Kincaid said Evan got at least two letters a week from her when they were making the picture last year.'

'Evan certainly doesn't encourage her, does he?'

'Of course not. He treats her the way a proper uncle treats a proper niece.'

'How about Kincaid,' Margaret said then. 'How is he responding to all the attention?'

'It's hard to say. As I said, he gets impatient with the press, and he really does hate to be annoyed when the two of us are out together. Also he knows how much I hate the notion of becoming public property, of losing even one shred of our privacy. But on the other hand I know he's pleased that the film turned out well. He's delighted because of Evan, but he's also proud of himself, I think.'

'He has a right to be,' Margaret said.

'Of course he does. I'm thrilled for him. But at the same time . . .'

'Yes . . .'

'I feel like a fool talking about it, even to you. I feel

11

so lucky. I am lucky. But it's as if I have to start all over again now. Kincaid and I have had a short wonderful life together but now . . .'

'Nothing's changed between you, has it?'

'No,' Sophie said, 'not the way you mean. But you see, I've become very spoiled. I don't want one single thing to be disturbed. I want us to stay in our house together, run over to Britanny when we feel like it, fly to the Algarve, drive down to Cornwall. After Toby died I thought I'd never get married again. You know that. Then Kincaid came along, seven years younger than me, from another country, from a whole different life. But I knew from the beginning that he was what I wanted. And thank God he wanted me too.'

'Clara's father used to say, "Don't try to understand luck. Don't question it or try to improve on it. Just enjoy it and be grateful."'

'I agree with that,' Sophie said, 'but even as I say it I feel as if I'm standing in quicksand. You see, I don't want us to spend all our time on ships and planes and trains, I don't want our life to be photographed and dissected. I don't want to share him with millions of ·people he doesn't even know. I don't want to share him at all.'

'You're saying you don't want him to be successful.'

'I know that's the way it sounds but that's not it. That's certainly not it entirely. You know how I am. I've always been ill at ease at huge parties. I don't like gargantuan people or deafening music or wall-size paintings. Is that some sort of childish fear? Perhaps it is. But it's very real for me. Maybe I just want to be safe. I feel threatened by out-sized things.'

'And is that what you see ahead of you?'

'I'm not sure what I see. I can't describe it. But whatever it is, it seems to have no boundaries. This thing that's starting for Kincaid is like walking into a forest. There's no way of knowing how large it is or how one gets out of it once you're inside.'

12

'I'm afraid that's what the future looks like to most of us.'

'Perhaps you're right. But it's never looked that way to me. It's never been that way. And I don't want it to be. I need to know where I am and where I'm going. Even when things were rotten for me I always had choices. I always had a role to play. I've never been a silent witness. I'm no good at that.'

'You think that's what Kincaid expects of you?'

'Of course not. That's my point. He doesn't know what he's getting into any more than I do.'

After a moment Margaret said, 'You probably won't like my saying this, but I think you're asking yourself questions that can't be answered.'

'I know I am. That's what drives me crazy.'

'But all questions don't require answers. They simply answer themselves when the time comes. There's no living person, no piece of meteorological equipment that can tell us whether it will rain or not in Bristol next Thursday. When I married your father and he took me straightaway to India, I had no idea what I was in for but I was in love – or at least I thought I was – so it didn't matter.'

'But you hated living in India.'

'Yes, I did. But India wasn't to blame for that.'

'Are you saying you would have gone to India even if you'd known how things would turn out between you and the Major?'

'Sophie, my darling, there's no way of knowing such things. Not for you, not for me, not for anyone.'

'You have no faith in intuition, then?'

'Of course I do. If you told me you were considering marriage to a certain man but your intuition told you to beware, I would advise you to follow that intuition. But when you tell me you think you see trouble ahead if your husband pursues a public career, I say you must have the courage to wait and see. And to deal with the trouble

13

when it happens. *If* it happens. There is no risk-free life.'

Sophie smiled. 'But one can improve the odds.'

'Sometimes you can. Sometimes you can't. Put yourself in my situation. I'm fifty-four years old. Women my age are supposed to be content with their lot in life, whatever it is. Take pleasure from the children and the grandchildren. Prune the roses and do a bit of needlework. But you know what I'm planning to do. You're the only one who does know. Do you think I know where I'm heading? Do you think I can predict the next five years?'

'No, I suppose not.'

'In that case, would you advise me to reconsider, to settle for what I have, to make a safe choice?'

'You know I would never recommend that.'

'But what if things don't work out? What if I get hurt?'

'You win,' Sophie said. 'You made your case.'

'But it can't help *you* if you don't believe it.'

'I believe it but it still frightens me.'

'Wouldn't you rather be frightened than bored?' Margaret said. '*I* would.'

4

When Evan Tagg returned to England from California he spent several days at his flat in London before going to Northumberland to see his father. On his first day in London he met with Alan Winkler in his office at the *Daily Telegraph*.

'Just what I expected,' Winkler said. 'All brown from the sun and full of yourself.'

'Not exactly. You see before you a humble man. Working for film producers teaches humility if nothing else.'

'Are you rich now? Do you get a share of every ticket that's sold to that bloody film you wrote?'

'Afraid not,' Evan said. 'Screenwriters get free typewriter ribbons and all the coffee they can drink but they *never* share in the profits. They're assigned cubicles like hens at an egg farm and twice each day a pretty girl comes by to collect the pages they've written.'

'You poor sod. You have my sympathy. I read about you in the paper. A house on the beach. Champagne for breakfast. Tapping out a page a day on your typewriter, then resting for the rest of the afternoon. Is that the way of it?'

Evan nodded. 'Privation and anxiety. Night and day.'

'And now that you've got your name on a big picture, they're all clamouring for your services. Am I right?'

'That's right. But no one can have me. I'm the property of Julian Thorne.'

'Nothing wrong with that. When do you start your next script?'

'I've finished it already.'

'Discipline. That's the ticket. Taught you by your editor, Alan Winkler, when you were a brilliant feature writer for the *Daily Telegraph*.'

'That's it. I owe it all to you,' Evan said.

'I told you when that play of yours was produced here in London that I'd never see you in my office again looking for an assignment. Looks like I was right.'

'Don't be too sure of that. I'm in a chancy racket. Up one day, down the next.'

'Get the money while you can and tuck it in your sock. Then you can tell them all to go screw and write whatever you want to.'

'You sound like my agent. That's the way he talks.'

'Good for him. Sounds like a solid chap.' He leaned forward on his desk. 'Now, let's get serious. Tell me about the women out there. A different one every night. Is that the story?'

'Not for me. The same one every night,' Evan said.

'Don't tell me you're married?'

'Not yet. But I will be. The lady has to get a divorce first.'

'I'll be damned.'

'You remember Mary Cecil, the actress who appeared in my play. She's the one. But that's not for publication.'

'You're kidding me.'

'No, I'm not,' Evan said.

'Since when has she lived in California?'

'Since I went there. But we've kept it quiet that we're living together. She's married to a bastard named Alec Maple, and we don't want to give him any ammunition to use against her when the divorce comes up.'

'Do I know Alec Maple?'

'I doubt it. He's a crumb. Used to be an actor. Now he just drinks gin and looks at himself in the mirror. He also used to punch his wife about every now and then but he won't be doing that any longer.'

'So you've changed your address, you've changed your profession, and now you're going to give up being a bachelor.'

Evan nodded. 'The sooner, the better.'

'Can't wait to tell my wife. Cynthia had you pegged for a lifetime loner, a mass seducer.'

'Sorry to disappoint Cynthia. But she read me wrong.'

'What about this new film,' Winkler said then. 'When does that go into production?'

'Good question. Maybe three months from now. Maybe never. It all depends on Kincaid.'

5

When Evan came up from London, Arthur Tagg drove to the railway station in Newcastle to meet his son. On the way back to the Towers they stopped at an inn for lunch. 'Every day while you were away I thought of a thousand questions I wanted to ask you when you came home,' Arthur said. 'But most of them have gone out of my head now that I'm sitting here talking to you.

Remember how I used to caution you and Sophie to keep a small notebook with you to record your thoughts and impressions. I should heed that advice myself.'

They sat at the table for almost two hours as Evan described California in all its intricacy. 'It's an unusual place. Bright and beautiful and totally benevolent. Or so it seems. Like a gorgeous Christmas package under the lighted tree. At least that's how it appears to the people who love it. But the ones who hate living out there say the package is indeed lovely, but it should never be undone. Nothing inside the wrappings, they say.'

'What do you say? Do you like it?'

'I do like it. But my feelings are all tied up with the work I was doing. I've decided that's the best way to deal with the place. Keep yourself busy, don't go to parties, and don't drink the local wine.'

Evan had planned to tell his father about Mary Cecil. He wanted Arthur to know how contented he was. But as they sat together in the car, and later in the inn at lunch, he held back. Something in his father's manner made him hesitate. As always, Evan was conscious of Arthur's caution, his reserve, his reluctance to expose himself to anything new or remotely foreign. Evan felt suddenly unable and unwilling to answer Arthur's questions about Mary, whatever they might be, to analyse and dissect his feelings and his future.

After they left the inn, as they drove west toward the Towers, Evan said, 'I'm sure this will surprise you. It certainly surprised me. I had a letter from my mother a few weeks ago. She's living in California now. She saw my photograph in a Los Angeles paper and she wrote to me.'

When Arthur didn't answer, Evan said, 'I brought the letter along with me. I thought you'd like to see it. It's in my luggage.'

'What did she want from you? Did she want something?'

'No. Nothing like that. She didn't even give me her address or her telephone number.'

'She wants something all right. You can be sure of that. After all these years she's bound to have something up her sleeve.'

'I don't think so. She sent me a picture she'd taken of you and me when we lived in Chicago. You were carrying me on your shoulders.'

'Stay away from her,' Arthur said. 'That's my advice. Don't get tangled up with her. Maybe she'll have the decency to leave you alone.'

'You've got it all wrong, Dad. It was a sweet letter she wrote. Something sad about it. You'll see when you read it.'

'I don't intend to read it. I'm no longer interested in Amy's shenanigans. That's her main talent. A tear in the eye. A little catch in the voice. Making people feel sorry for her. Well, I'm not sorry for her. If she's fallen on hard times, she has only herself to blame.'

'She said she's never forgiven herself for leaving us the way she did.'

'Can't forgive herself, eh? That's a good one. One thing your mother was good at was forgiving herself. Did it take her all this time to figure out she did something wrong?'

'I doubt it. But that's the point. It's more than twenty years since we left Chicago. Seems like a long time to hate somebody. I don't hate her.'

'I don't hate her either,' Arthur said. 'There's no one left to hate. In my mind I buried her. A long time ago. And I suggest you do the same thing. Nobody profits from digging up the past. Especially Amy's past.'

'I'm sorry if I upset you. I thought you'd want to know I heard from her.'

'I'm not upset. I wish you hadn't told me but you had no way of knowing that. If you want to see her that's up to you . . .'

'I told you, I don't even know how to reach her.'

'Oh, but you will. She'll be in touch with you again. I just want you to know that I'd prefer not to hear about it. I closed those doors a long time ago and I don't want to open them up again.'

6

'What's wrong with my father?' Evan said. It was the day after he'd arrived at the Towers. He was having coffee in the morning-room with Margaret. 'He acts like a man who just came home from a funeral.'

'I'm sure he was delighted to see you. He's very proud of you, you know. Awfully excited by the film and everything you're doing in America. He must have told you that.'

'Yes, he did. I don't mean he's acting oddly towards me. It's just that he seems at war with himself. All locked up inside. No light behind his eyes.'

'Did you ask if something was bothering him?'

Evan shook his head. 'I learned that lesson a long time ago. If there's nothing bothering him he thinks you're a fool for asking. If there's something truly wrong he'll say or do whatever he must to conceal it. You know how he is.'

'Yes, I do. He doesn't confide in me any more than he does with you. He never has. But in the past few months he's been particularly withdrawn. I think I know what's bothering him but I can't be certain. Have you talked with Sophie since you came back to England?'

'Just for a few minutes when I rang up Kincaid. We made a date for dinner next week.'

'Then perhaps you don't know that some changes have taken place here while you were away. The Major and I are in the process of getting divorced. I'm sure Sophie must have told Kincaid, and I assumed he'd tell you.'

'Not a word from him,' Evan said.

'Perhaps she didn't tell him.'

'Even if she did, he would likely keep it to himself. He's very slow to pass along information.'

'Well, in any case, now you know. There was a tiresome period of accusation and recrimination but at last William settled down. Or I should say, my solicitor settled him down. So now the necessary papers are being shuffled about, processed, and recorded, and in a matter of weeks, I hope, our marriage will be ended. Are you surprised?'

'I'm not sure. I suppose I am. No one who knows the Major would describe him as an ideal husband but I think most of your friends assumed you'd made the required adjustments through the years. At least I assumed that. I thought you'd decided to stick it out.'

'I had decided that,' she said. 'I didn't institute this divorce business. William did. He accused me of having an adulterous relationship with your father, and demanded that I discharge him. When I refused he told me he was determined to divorce me and that he would name Arthur as co-respondent.'

'No wonder my father's upset. Was all this public knowledge?'

Margaret shook her head. 'After a time William had second thoughts. I was so co-operative I think it scared him off. In any case he announced one day that whatever sins I might have committed he was willing to forgive me. He was stunned when I told him it was too late, that I had decided to sue for divorce whether he wanted it or not.'

'And he agreed?'

'Not at first. But after a long meeting with Tremont, my solicitor, he came away convinced that he mustn't stand in my way. He hasn't been co-operative exactly but at least he's stopped threatening me. Sometimes I don't see him for days at a time. He stomps round the west wing, shoots pigeons from his bedroom window, and takes all his meals in his rooms. An awkward situation for all of us, including Arthur.'

'It seems to me . . . I'm not sure of this, but I think if I were in his shoes I'd be glad to hear that the Major was moving away. He's never made a secret of how he feels about Dad and me. The first time we met him, when he came home on leave from India, as soon as he found out you'd hired my father to tutor Sophie, he raised hell because you'd allowed us to live in the house like members of the family. Isn't that right?'

Margaret nodded. 'And he's been brooding about it ever since. Still wants me to discharge Arthur.'

'Then why would my father give a damn about him?'

'I told you some changes were made here while you were away. I haven't told you all of them and I don't think I should. But Sophie will tell you when you see her. I want her to tell you. I want you to know. But for some reason that I don't completely understand, I wouldn't feel comfortable telling you myself.'

7

When Evan came back to London, he and Sophie had lunch together. After he told her about his separate conversations with Arthur and Margaret, she said, 'Of course he's upset. Your father's been a single man for many years. He's lost his tolerance for drawing-room battles and bedroom wars. He's leaving Wiswell Towers, you know. I'm sure he told you that.'

'Leaving? What does that mean?'

'So he didn't tell you? And Margaret didn't either?'

'Not a word.'

'He's resigned,' Sophie said. 'He wants to leave as quickly as possible but he volunteered to stay on till a new man can be found to take over.'

21

'He must have changed his mind. Otherwise he'd have told me.'

Sophie shook her head. 'He hasn't changed his mind. I talked to Margaret last night. I'm sure he didn't tell you because he knew you'd give him an argument.'

'An argument? Of course I'd give him an argument. Where does he think he's going? He and I have lived with your family since I was nine years old. That's his home.'

'He told Margaret he's sent letters to several schools. He wants to teach again.'

'He's fifty-eight years old, for Christ's sake. And he hasn't taught in a school since he was twenty-five, since he married my mother and went off to America. He knows how these things work. He'll never get a decent teaching job. I don't understand what he's up to. If he'd left years ago because of the way the Major treated him, I could have understood it. But now, thank God, the Major's leaving. Does anyone believe that Arthur's so offended by the idea of divorce that he's breaking all ties with the Cranstons and going off somewhere like an itinerant tinker? I certainly can't swallow that.'

'Neither can I. And neither can Margaret. When she rang up last night she said she hadn't told you the full story. She asked me to tell you.'

'She said the Major threatened to name Dad as co-respondent in a divorce suit. Is that what you're talking about?'

'No. Much to Margaret's surprise, Arthur survived all that. She convinced him that he must stay on no matter how much scandal developed.'

'That's all the more reason . . .'

'Wait a minute,' Sophie said, 'let me finish. You remember that great packet of photographs I sent you in California, the ones that were taken for *Country Life* magazine?'

'Of course.'

'Those pictures were taken by a man named Jack

22

Brannigan. An Irishman, as you can tell by his name, from a town called Letterkenny. When I was introduced to him he told me at once how beautiful I was. Then he turned to Margaret and said, "But as lovely as your daughter is, she doesn't have what you have. Nobody does."'

'The Irish blarney. A womanizer from Donegal.'

'I knew you'd say that. But you're wrong. Brannigan's the last man you'd single out as a ladies' man. He's the same age as Margaret but he looks fifteen years older. One day I heard him say, "God help the man who goes to his grave with no marks on his face, no evidence that he's been alive and active in the world. No one gets to Heaven without a bit of mud on his boots!" Margaret said he told her, "Just because I flatter you doesn't mean I'm insincere. An Irishman sees beauty every place he looks. Only a fool or a selfish bastard denies praise to someone who deserves it."'

'And he has lank blond hair and pale blue eyes.'

Sophie shook her head. 'None of that. Thinning hair and the face of a prize-fighter. Calloused hands and a square hard body with a bit of a belly. But a voice like a cello. Like a warm hand on your cheek.'

'I'd better tell Kincaid about this chap. I think you're in love with him.'

'Not me. Margaret. Silly and giggling and high colour in her cheeks whenever she talks about him.'

'You're not serious,' Evan said.

'Of course I'm serious, and so is she. After he finished his work for *Country Life* and left the *Towers* he wrote to her almost every day. And last summer she went to southern France to meet him. They spent two weeks together in a hotel in St-Raphael.'

'So the Major decided to get a divorce.'

'Not because of Brannigan. He didn't know about him. Still doesn't. The Major thought Margaret was having a do with Arthur. He had the right sin in mind but the

23

wrong sinner. When he threatened Mother with divorce and a public scandal, she hadn't met Brannigan yet.'

'But after she met Brannigan, then *she* wanted the divorce?'

'I don't think so,' Sophie said. 'Not as simple as that. I just think the Major went one step too far. I don't think she ever considered divorce till he pushed it. But once she'd accepted the idea, she couldn't give it up. Then a decent chap came along, someone with a brain and a sense of humour, and there she was, with a man who genuinely likes women, who knows how to talk to a woman and how to listen when she talks. So now my darling, lovely, long-suffering and unappreciated mother is smiling and stumbling about the house and wondering what hit her.'

'And where does my father fit into this love-story?'

'He doesn't,' Sophie said.

'But you think that's why he's leaving?'

'It's just a theory. But it makes sense to me.'

'Does he know about her and Brannigan?'

'No. She's never told anyone except me and Clara Causey. And perhaps Charles Tremont.'

'Then Arthur doesn't know.'

'I didn't say that. I said she hasn't told him. But staff has its own way of knowing. And suspicion is as good as fact below stairs. You see, Brannigan will have no part in subterfuge. As I said, he's written to her regularly since he left the Towers and he makes no effort to hide his identity. Name and return address on the back of the envelope.'

'But Margaret gets letters from all sorts of people.'

'That's true. But Brannigan's name is new on the mail table. And the mail comes first of all to Arthur's desk. He was the only one who knew that Margaret spent her summer holiday in St-Raphael. And I'm sure she had letters from there before she went and after she came home, letters from Brannigan.'

24

'So my father put two and two together?'

'Why not? He's a bright man. And he can't have missed the change that's come over Margaret since last summer.'

'Are you saying he's become jealous of Margaret after all these years?'

'I'm not sure if that's the word I'd use. But there's no question that something snapped somewhere. You saw how he is. A different person.'

'But if he's been secretly in love with Margaret all this time, how did he accept the fact that she was married to the Major?'

'Good question. And it has two answers, I think. One: he knows that Margaret detests my father. He knows – all the staff knows – that they've never had a real life together. And two: you know how class-conscious Arthur is. However strong his feelings might be for my mother, he sincerely believes that he can never be on a level with her.'

Evan smiled. 'As separate as you and me.'

'Exactly. Remember how he used to remind you of that when you and I were growing up together? I thought it was damned annoying when I was fifteen years old. But you believed him.'

'I had no choice. He scared the wits out of me. He never mentioned the word *incest* but there was no mistaking his meaning. Every night I dreamed of hell-fire and damnation.'

'I'd hoped you were dreaming of me.'

'That, too. That's what brought on the hell-fire and damnation.'

'What a waste,' she said. 'We could have ended up married with a dozen children.'

'I don't think so. We know each other too well.'

'I expect you're right. Fiddle-dee-dee.' She lit a cigarette then, studied the trail of smoke, and said, 'Put yourself in Arthur's place. Assume you're in love with a married woman, one who wouldn't be available to you

25

in any case because of a difference in station. So you settle for proximity in place of passion, for warm friendship instead of love. In all respects but one you are married. You depend on this woman and she depends on you. Comfort and kindness and consideration. A series of daily pleasures and rewards. Then suddenly, after many years, the married woman becomes unmarried. This is no threat to you, however, because you know the rhythm of your daily life will not change. Things will move ahead as they did before. Meals will be served, repairs will be made, the estate and its lands will be managed, and the woman of the house will be there with you as she has been for many years.'

'Then the serpent enters the garden.'

Sophie nodded. 'The man from Donegal. Trumpets sound, drums bang, and the lady you love begins to slip away. Telephone calls, mysterious errands, a holiday in France, and a steady flow of letters each addressed by the same abrupt and reckless hand. A secret life developing. Does that seem like a fair picture?'

'Only if we assume that Arthur's in love with your mother.'

'I believe he is but even if he weren't, even if they were only close friends and confidants, the scenario would still hold. Every friendship has its own structure, its rules and its rewards. When one person decides to alter that pattern, the friendship is in jeopardy. And that's what's happening here. At the very least Margaret is changing the rules. From Arthur's viewpoint it may seem that she's about to disappear totally.'

'You make it sound terribly gloomy and romantic. I'm not sure that's what's actually going on.'

'I assure you that's what's happening with Margaret. I admit I'm guessing about Arthur. But I believe it's a good guess.'

Three days after Evan returned to London from Northumberland, Jack Brannigan took the ferry from Dublin to Wales and Margaret met him in Holyhead. They sat in the snug of the Pembroke Inn, looking out across the harbour.

'None of those fine wines from Provence in this cold and grey place, but the barman did find us a decent bottle of claret. Is it good enough for you?'

'Very nice,' she said. 'I'm easy to please. You know that.'

'I don't know that at all. You're damned difficult to please. That's why you've chosen me. Unwilling to settle for a lesser man, an ordinary chap. Only the best is good enough for you.'

She smiled and kissed his hand when he touched her cheek. 'Of course,' she said. 'You're right.'

He turned her face toward him. 'Are you all right then? Are you healthy and radiant, able to survive the beastly winter of your beastly Northumberland? Do you prosper and smile in your bloody castle, with your rotten husband in the west wing and your crowd of servants padding after you up and down the staircase?'

'I don't smile and I don't prosper. I read your letters and I write silly letters to you. But mostly I loll about and miss you so much my stomach hurts.'

'Good. I'm glad to hear that. I intend to occupy your soul like an evil spirit. I want you to have no peace or contentment, no sound sleep and no appetite except when you're with me. I want you to grow pale and meagre till at last your physician says, "Go to Brannigan. He's your only salvation. Bed-rest and wine. Love and rich food. Otherwise you'll waste away and vanish in the wind like a brown leaf." '

'You're never lonely, are you? Your eyes and your

hands are always busy. You start to talk about the most ordinary things and you make them beautiful.'

'That's what you think, eh? You think I lured you to this Godforsaken place to tell you how happy I am?'

'You didn't lure me. You commanded me.'

'Exactly,' he said. 'Pressure. That's my game. Demands and threats. We've got to do better than we've been doing, young lady. I've had quite enough of this love at a distance. Living apart together, that sort of rot. I want you on the premises where I can touch you and look at you and tuck you up in bed at night.'

'That's what I want, too. That's all I want. But the rotten divorce procedure drags on at its own pace.'

'I don't give a damn about the divorce. After it's over, when you get down on your knee and ask me to marry you, I might say no. Did you ever think of that? You've been married and so have I. To hell with all that. I want you, not some bloody contract. I want to live with you, for God's sake. I'll take you to Letterkenny or Dublin or Cork. New York or Buenos Aires. Any place but London. I can't breathe in that dark place. But if you can't come to me, if you won't follow me and cook my meals and mend my socks like a proper wife, then I'll come to that family rock-pile you call the Towers and move in with you. My shoes under your bed, my razor in your bathroom. And a fancy marriage licence framed over your bed.'

'I thought you didn't want to get married.'

'I meant I didn't want to wait. But of course I'll do the decent thing by you. Don't want you to lose your place in the community. No damage to your self-respect. I assume you'll bring me a proper dowry, of course.'

'Of course,' she said. 'That's understood. Men like you are hard to find.'

When they went upstairs to their room he said, 'How long can you stay?'

'I have to be in London on Friday.'

'So you'll be here for five days.'

'Unless you get tired of me.'

'I'm a considerate chap. If I get tired of you I'll never let you know it.'

9

Just before Kincaid and Evan had gone to California, almost a year earlier, the two men and Sophie had had a festive restaurant dinner. Now that Evan was back in London, they went to the same restaurant again. 'We're famous now,' Sophie said. 'We must be reckless and raucous and irresponsible, or people will be disappointed in us.'

During that earlier evening they had anticipated the production of *Bushranger*. With no previous experience in motion pictures, neither Kincaid nor Evan knew what to expect. Now, however, with the picture behind them, they had intricate and hilarious anecdotes to pass along to each other and to Sophie. When they left the restaurant, very late in the evening, Sophie said, 'My ribs ache from laughing. I haven't laughed so much since the last time the three of us had dinner together.'

The following day Kincaid and Evan motored to Oxford to see a soccer match. As he drove through West London, Evan said, 'I was very well behaved last night. Did you notice?'

'I was totally pissed and so were you and Sophie as I recall. If you were well behaved, I missed it.'

'Pissed or not everyone was careful to stay off the subject of Julian Thorne. No mention of what you'll be doing next. Not a word about the future.'

'There's no future to talk about,' Kincaid said. 'Nothing's been decided.'

'Maybe you haven't decided anything but Thorne has.

He calls me from California twice a day. He can't wait to get a go-ahead from you.'

'He hasn't called me. Why doesn't he ring me up if he's nervous.'

'He's afraid to, I think. Afraid you'll say no and that will be it. As long as you haven't turned him down he figures he's still in business.'

'I told him before I left California, before we knew how *Bushranger* would be received, I told him then that I was in no hurry to jump into another film.'

'I think he forgot that conversation. He's got a big money-maker on his hands and he can't wait to start another one. I don't blame him. I think I'd feel the same way if I were in his shoes.'

Kincaid looked at him and grinned. 'You've got the California bug, haven't you?'

'What do you mean by that, you bastard?'

'The bug. You know what I mean. You've been in England less than three weeks and already you're longing back to that house on the beach and pretty little Mary Cecil sitting on the deck in her shorts. Or out of her shorts, however she sits on the deck.'

'I miss her a lot. No doubt about that.'

'Of course you do. And you miss Perino's and the Garden of Allah and the bar at the Beverly Hills Hotel. And your telephone ringing and your name in the *Hollywood Reporter*. You miss all that, Bucko. Like I said, you've got the bug. You'll end up as the C. Aubrey Smith of your generation. Croquet and cricket and white linen trousers. A bit of old England in Santa Monica.'

'I like the money. I won't lie to you about that. I like making a living as a writer. And if the only place I can do that is in California, then that's where I'll be. At least for a while.'

'You know something? You're right. If I was in your shoes I'd feel the same way.'

'How is it different for you?'

'Big difference. You've got a profession. You've educated yourself and trained for it. And now it's begun to pay off for you.'

'Are you saying it hasn't paid off for you?'

'It paid off great,' Kincaid said, 'but all that was pure luck. Like betting on a horse and seeing him come in.'

'Will you stop handing me that modesty crap? Sure you were lucky that Thorne wanted to take a chance with you. So was I. But luck didn't make *Bushranger* turn out the way it did. Hard work and sweat and talent did it. And you did it. You've seen the picture. You've seen how people react to it. Don't kick dirt for me and tell me you're just a lucky bloke from Tasmania. You're an actor now, and a damned good one. And everybody knows it. You know it, too, but for some reason you're pretending you're the lad who came round to deliver the turnips.'

Kincaid grinned again. 'If I'm so bloody important, why don't you treat me with a little respect?'

'You know what I think you're doing?' Evan went on. 'I think you're kidding yourself. I think you had a hell of a good time making that movie but you don't want to admit it for some reason. Are you afraid you can't do it again? Is that the problem? Or is Sophie the problem?'

'She's no problem.'

'Of course she is. Why do you think we didn't talk about where you go from here when we were celebrating last night? I can't answer for you but I'll tell you why I didn't bring it up. Because I knew it would wreck the evening. I've known Sophie all my life. She's always been rich and protected, and she always will be. She could have become a rotten spoiled woman. But she didn't turn out that way. She's a giver, not a taker. She thinks she can fix things. That's her biggest flaw. Stray dogs, hurt feelings, broken marriages. She's determined to set things right.'

'You think she's trying to fix me.'

'No, I don't. You may be the only person she's ever met

31

that she didn't think needed fixing. I assure you, she thinks you're fine the way you are. That's why she's apprehensive about Thorne and California and the film business. It's a big imponderable to her. She's afraid it's going to change her life. But mostly she's afraid it will change you.'

'Did she tell you all this?'

'No. She didn't have to. I know her. And I'll wager you as much as you want to risk that you've heard her say the same things I've just said.'

'You're pretty smart for a writer,' Kincaid said. 'Thorne thinks all writers are dumb. Clever but not intelligent, he says.'

'Don't change the subject.'

'I didn't mean to. You're right about Sophie. But what you don't know is that I agree with her. About California, I mean. It's an ice-cream life out there. The place and the business. It tastes great but it melts quickly. And if you swallow too fast, or if you eat too much, it makes you sick. I'm not crazy. I don't want to make myself sick. And I don't want a sticky mess of melted ice-cream all over my shoes. You're right about something else. When I sat in that dark theatre for the first time and watched *Bushranger*, I knew it was good and I knew I was good. I also know that I can do it again. I'm not scared of it. I know it's tricky work but it's something I can do. Still, it's one thing to take a chance and come up with a winner, the way we did on this picture. It's another thing to say, "That's my life. That's what I'm going to do with myself." I feel good about what we did but I don't want to paint myself into a corner.'

'All right. That makes sense to me. But tell me something. Since you feel that way, since you don't know for sure if you want to make another film, why did you build that beautiful house out there?'

'I had it built for Sophie. You know that. That's why it's a replica of Wiswell Towers.'

'But if you're never going back to California, what good is that house?'

'You're going too fast, Evan. The house is there in case we do decide to go back. If that happens, she'll have a nice surprise waiting for her.'

10

Both Kincaid and Evan were correct in their assessments of Sophie. She seldom felt an impulse to service her own needs. Rather she had a strong sense of the rightness of things. She had a continuing need to solve problems, to correct errors, to set things right.

By nature, however, she was neither competitive nor domineering. All of her major conflicts were internal ones, her heart at war with itself. Where Kincaid was concerned she truly wanted whatever was best for him. With one proviso: nothing must disturb or redefine the structure of their life together. She was fiercely protective of that. Change was the enemy. Or so her senses told her. Still the rational part of her consciousness told her that change was inevitable, that the true and continuing problem was in knowing what could be changed without damage and what must remain constant. Should she encourage Kincaid to plunge into this career that seemed to be his for the taking, or should she continue to resist, to question, to point out the hazards? She asked herself these questions every day and gave herself slightly different answers each time.

In the spring of the preceding year, when she and Kincaid had visited California, when Thorne was urging him to go forward with *Bushranger*, but before any final decision had been made, Sophie had said, 'I know how you feel, darling. At least I think I know. But I feel as if I'm standing at the bottom of a hill and great boulders are rolling down on me. Do you know what I'm trying to say?

I'd hate to see us make a silly decision that might change our lives. Everything's been so perfect for us. I want it to stay that way. I love you and I love England. I need to be in England. The thought of being transplanted to California, of spending time there, of having some sort of synthetic life with Thorne's studio as its centrepiece, fills me with panic. If you ended up being a different person, different from what you are now, it would break my heart. And it might break yours too.'

When she summarized her trip to America in a letter to Margaret, she wrote:

If London is a man's city, as people say, then New York, like Paris, is a woman's city. Or so it seemed to me.

Los Angeles, on the other hand, is nobody's city. Not yet. There's a kind of gangly adolescence about it as though it hadn't yet defined itself, as though no one is certain what final form it will take or if it will, in fact, remain formless, continuing to grow and sprawl, being crowded and cluttered, but lingering still in uneasy transition. Not just a desert outpost, not quite a city. Just an untidy collection of people and ill-matched buildings waiting, it seems, for some master hand to give them order and definition.

I'm being unfair, of course. California, its customs and its residents cannot be judged by standards one has learned elsewhere. One realizes at last that Californians are making it up as they go along. They are benevolent pragmatists structured by two simple concerns. Number one: do I feel good? Number two: is the sun shining today? Ronald Colman, who in his circle is thought to be an intellectual and a sophisticate, said to me one Sunday as we watched a tennis match in his garden, 'This is a place and a state of being that all human beings long for.' When I hinted to him that I longed for quite different things he excused himself and went off to sit with Dame May Whitty on a bench built round a giant gum-tree.

Am I being snide and rudely English? I don't mean to be. Having been too analytical of a place that defies analysis and too critical, perhaps, of a society that recognizes neither the principles nor the practice of criticism, I confess that Kincaid and I had a smashing holiday there. Lying on white beaches, dancing barefoot in elegant clubs, drinking exotic foaming cocktails concocted of gin and syrup and fresh fruits, we seldom looked at our wrist-watches. We always exceeded the speed limit when we drove and barely noticed the women who stroll the streets of Beverly Hills in costumes that resemble underclothing.

We were fêted and accepted on all sides, treated as equals by our inferiors. Our houseman and his wife called us by our first names and the swarthy gentleman who parked our red roadster at the hotel called me 'Honey'. Rudeness is common but seldom deliberate, so people come to accept it. And so did we. If one is confused or offended or feels degraded, one simply smiles. If one is publicly insulted one laughs and orders drinks all round.

When a final decision about *Bushranger* had been made, when it was clear that Kincaid would have to spend several months on location in California it was also decided that Sophie would stay behind. 'I promised the children I'd take them to the Algarve. I always spend summer holidays with them. They count on it and so do I.'

'Don't you think they might like California?' Kincaid said.

'I think they would adore it,' Sophie said. 'California's a seductive place. Especially for young people. All the best things are visible and accessible. There for the taking. Feel the sun, smell the orange blossoms, splash in the sea. Dance in the moonlight, drive in an open car, kiss a pleasant stranger. Los Angeles is not just a place where movies are made. It is a movie. And everyone who lives there is busy acting in it. If you want to eat sausage on a roll you look for a building that's shaped like a sausage. Fish restaurants are shaped like whales. Barristers wear cowboy boots in the court-rooms. It's a great playground. Conceived for children. Inhabited by children. So of course Sarah and Trevor would love it. They might very well prefer it to any other place in the world. That's why I'm not keen to take them there. They're too young to realize that Los Angeles can be swallowed in one gulp. Like a spoonful of trifle. It's a meatless meal. Easy choices, pastel colours, and plastic surgery. And when one dies from boredom it's possible to be buried beside your cat in the pet cemetery.'

In a long letter to her mother Sophie came as close as she would ever come to a clear delineation of her dilemma. After explaining the details of their being separated for the summer and early fall, Kincaid in California and she in Portugal, she wrote:

As you can see, I am my usual calm and peaceful self. How I wish that were true. You know better than anyone how insanely happy I am with Kincaid. After all those years alone after Toby died, I had given up hoping for a good warm life with a man I could love and respect. Then Kincaid appeared. Like a mysterious gift. It seemed to me that no two people had ever complemented each other as we do.

But now he's going away. For several months. And I'm going off too. In another direction. We've discussed it calmly. In great detail. I tell myself that such separations are sometimes necessary. Men have business to conduct. Trips to make. Land to buy or sell in other countries. Holdings to look after.

But then I say to myself, 'What are you doing? You

needn't be separated. You can go with him.' Am I using the children as an excuse when I know in my heart other arrangements could be made? They're old enough to realize that it's important for me to be with Kincaid.

Or I could take them with me to California. Whatever my reservations about the quality of life out there, surely a few months would not destroy Sarah and Trevor. Or me. So why am I taking this position?

I hope I'm not saying to Kincaid, 'Since you've chosen this odd adventure, you'll have to do it by yourself. All domestic pleasures and rewards will be denied till you come to your senses and return to London.' Women do that sort of thing of course – the Lysistrata syndrome – but it's not something I would do. Or would I?

Is it possible that my refusal to go with him to California is not such a simple decision as it seems? Am I hoping to drive an opening wedge in his mind, to plant the thought, before he has irrevocably defined himself as public chattel, that such a definition is unacceptable to me? Am I saying, 'It's my way or no way?' Of course not. At least that's what I tell myself.

Knowing my own feelings, knowing how desperately I love him, how can I do anything but follow him and have faith that no new place or circumstance can alter the way we are together? When I ask myself that question I always give the correct answer. But a moment later another voice speaks up. 'This has nothing to do with love, with your feelings for him or his for you. You have a brain and you have intuition. When someone you care about makes an unwise choice, for whatever reason, you have an obligation to be concerned. You have a duty to try to find the pitfalls and to plot a course around them if you're able to.'

I'm not certain that all of this, that any of this,

perhaps, will make sense to you. Other people's problems often seem to have simple solutions. So I'm not pleading for guidance. I know this is something I must sort out on my own.

During the months they were apart, Sophie sent Kincaid a postcard or a letter almost every day. She told him in detail about where she'd driven to, what she'd seen, the meals, the wine, the weather. She wrote about things and people and places, what Trevor had done, what Sarah had said, a journal of her day-to-day activities. At last, however, after almost two months at Praia da Rocha, she felt compelled to write another sort of letter. She sat in her bed one late night and simply told the truth, as quickly as her hand could write.

God, what a frightful error I've made, thinking you could go off in one direction and I in another, believing I could be separated from you for all these weeks and months and still survive. The bright colours of the Algarve look deadly grey to me. The tiny songbirds seem like predators. The meals, although they are unquestionably delicious, and the excellent Portuguese wines don't appeal to me. I have no appetite, no desire for tennis or swimming, and I sleep badly. Some nights, when everyone has gone to bed, I walk along the beach to the casino, drink cognac, and try to squander obscene amounts of money on the wheel. I bet recklessly but in my perverse frame of mind I still win. The croupiers call me 'the lucky English' but I feel as though I have no luck at all.

All my life I've heard people moan about their loneliness, and I sympathized. I felt that I understood. But I knew nothing about it. Since I've been here I've learned what it really is. It's a void, my darling. Total emptiness.

That night she cried herself to sleep. When she woke the next morning she tore up the letter she'd written and wrote another one, cheerful and informative.

I know you miss me as much as I miss you. But since we're both so busy the time will pass quickly. Don't worry about me. All goes well here and we'll be together soon.

11

When she left Brannigan in Holyhead, Margaret took the train to London where she met with Charles Tremont. That night she stayed with Sophie and Kincaid, and the next morning she took the express train to Newcastle.

'Why are you rushing off?' Sophie said to her. 'Surely you can spend more than one night with us.'

'It is ridiculous, isn't it? But I really do have a number of things to deal with, and the quicker they're dealt with, the better.'

The first morning she was back at the Towers she sent a note to the Major, asking him to meet her at eleven in the library. When her maid came back she said, 'The Major's not available this morning or early afternoon. But he'll meet with you at four if you like.'

'How can he be unavailable? He has nothing whatsoever to do except sit in his rooms and look out the window.'

'I don't know, mum. I gave your note to his man and when he came back he told me what I've just told you.'

He was waiting in the library when Margaret went there at four, standing by the fireplace, glass in hand, buttoned into his waistcoat and jacket like a great oak log. His hair was fresh-trimmed, and his moustache; his cheeks were ruddy and there was an expression round his mouth which on any other face would have been called a smile. He offered to pour her a drink but she refused. Indicating his own glass, he said, 'First today. Not a teetotaller yet, not by a damn sight, but cutting down a bit. That Hemingway chap says you should drink all you can hold before your evening meal but not a drop after. He's probably as wrong-headed about that as he is about military tactics but all the same it doesn't hurt to give the old liver a spot of rest.'

'Well, whatever you're doing, it seems to agree with you. You look well.'

'Working on the memoirs. Going at it every day. Settling a few accounts. Setting matters straight. Giving the old brain and the memory a work-out. Like olives popping out of a bottle. Damned astonishing the things a man can remember if he puts his mind to it.' He thumped his chest. 'Getting the torso in shape as well. Toning up the legs. Indian clubs in the morning and a two-hour walk across the moors after breakfast. And three times a week I take a long gallop on the grey stallion.'

'Well, as I said, you look well.'

'Tried on the dress uniform yesterday and when I looked in the glass I thought I was back in Delhi. Trim and clear-eyed.'

Margaret smiled. 'Maybe you should offer yourself for active duty again.'

The Major scowled. 'Not likely. They didn't value me when they had me. They can bloody well get along without me now.'

'I just came back from London . . .'

'London, was it? I heard you were off on another little journey. Conflicting stories as to where you went.'

'I hope you're not questioning the staff about me.'

'Not necessary. The staff has a great deal of respect for me. A good servant doesn't like to see his master mistreated.'

'Let's not go into that.'

'Of course not. I wouldn't expect that you'd want to.

And there's no need for it, is there? We know all the facts, you and I. And so do the servants. That's why they come to me with information.'

'That's very nice, William. I'm glad the staff loves you. Now, if you don't mind there are one or two things we need to discuss. I saw Charles Tremont when I was in London . . .'

'*Sir* Charles Tremont,' Cranston said. 'Let's give the bastard all the window-dressing he deserves.'

'He wants to make sure,' Margaret went on, 'that you've received all the papers that have come from his office and the court.'

'There's quite a bundle in my desk drawer so I expect I've got everything that was sent along.'

'Then you're aware that the final decree should come through within the next few weeks.'

'I'm sure you've got the dates straight so I'll take your word for it.'

'You know that I've claimed no share of your pension money, or your income from shares, or any other savings or investments you may have.'

'Since you have more money than the Pope I didn't expect you'd be asking for part of my little nest-egg.'

'So much for that,' she said. Then: 'Tremont asked me if you were still living here and I said you were. When he asked what plans you'd made about finding another residence I told him I'd have to ask you.'

'And that's what you're doing now?'

'Yes.'

'The answer is that I've made no plans. This is home, Margaret. This is my domicile. It's where I live.'

'Technically, that's true. Until the decree becomes final. After that, according to the law, you have no residence rights.'

'Ahh, but I'm sure we don't want to discuss fine points of the law. Of course it's understood that this property and all its lands belong to the Wiswells, but since I

41

married into that clan more than thirty years ago I have earned certain rewards, I expect. Right of domicile for example.'

'All that ends when we're divorced. Tremont says I can ask you to leave as soon as the decree is final.'

'Of course you can ask me,' he said, 'but surely you won't force me. As you can see, I keep to myself. Sometimes we don't catch a glimpse of each other for weeks at a time. No reason why we should see each other at all if that's what you prefer.'

'It's not a matter of preference. It's a question of decency and privacy. Some things are simply not done. Divorced people do not go on living under the same roof. I can't imagine that you would want to.'

'But I do want to, Miss Margaret. And I expect to. It's more than fifteen years now since my retirement from His Majesty's service. Every day of that time I've lived here. I have my horses and my dogs and my friends in the county. I have my daughter and my grandchildren, my books and my chair and my bed. Many of my things have followed me to India and back.'

'And I'm sure you'll want to take them with you wherever you decide to go.'

'But I'm not going, you see. I am entrenched. I've captured the high ground. And I defy Tremont and his stiff-necked cronies to flush me out.'

'No one's trying to be cruel to you, William. But you must be reasonable. You have a substantial amount of money in your own name. You can live anywhere you choose. But you cannot continue to live here. I don't want to make this a legal struggle. I don't want to drag it through the courts. But it so happens that the law is very clear. There is a procedure called action for trespass. A person who has no legal right to a house is not entitled to live in it if the owner wants him to leave. This is a civil matter. When a complaint is made and the facts are presented the court issues an order and the person who's in violation must then vacate the premises.'

'Common law and decency are on my side. I would simply ignore such an order.'

Margaret went on. 'In that case an owner can turn to what is called a protective order. This is a criminal matter. It can be ugly but Tremont says it's effective. If I feel threatened by you, if I'm afraid that I'm in physical danger, the court will order you to be removed from my house. By force if necessary. Your insistence on common law or right of domicile won't help you. If you defy that law you'll be put in jail.'

'No one would ever believe I'm a threat to you.'

'You're mistaken. Knowing the facts, anyone would believe it. Your refusal to leave this house is a threat in itself, that great cache of military weapons you have in your rooms is certainly a threat, and in addition to that you threatened to kill me. The details of that threat are in our divorce files in Tremont's office. There is also a deposition from Clara Causey. I told her about the threat the day you made it.'

'That's a damned lie. I never threatened you.'

'Yes, you did. You accused me of adultery with Arthur Tagg although you admitted you had no proof. When I asked what you would do if you had proof you said you would kill me. And Arthur as well. You said it and you meant it. I can tell you what day you said it and what time of day it was.'

He sat solid in his chair and didn't answer. At last she said, 'None of this is necessary, William. Just be reasonable and we'll make a peaceful end to it.'

Still he didn't answer. At last he said, 'If the police come here for me, I will resist them in every way I can. I assure you I'm more than a match for a few county constables. I'm a Sandhurst man, by God. When I'm dead, you can have me carted off. But not before.'

· CHAPTER 2 ·

1

One late evening when Evan returned home he found Sarah, Sophie's daughter, waiting in the corridor outside his door.

'This is a surprise,' he said. 'You're keeping late hours, aren't you?'

'It's not my fault. I've been waiting for you since eight o'clock. It's your fault, not mine, that it's late.'

He unlocked the door and they went into his flat. 'You should have told me you'd be home on holiday.'

'I'm not home on holiday. I came into London just to see you.'

'Does Sophie know you're here?'

'No. And you mustn't tell her. It's bad enough I have to slip past Miss Endicott and her spies. I don't want to deal with mother, too.'

'So you're absent without leave. Is that it?'

She nodded. 'Old Endicott thinks we're all seven years old. I'd like to be permanently absent from that nursery school.'

'If she finds out you've slipped away, you may get your wish. When do you plan to go back?'

'There's a train to Cobham at one in the morning. I'll be in my nun's bed by two-thirty.'

'Good. I'll drive you to the station. Meanwhile, how about a cup of coffee? Or some cocoa maybe.'

'I'd like a glass of wine, please.'

44

He took her coat and draped it across the back of a chair. 'Afraid not, Missy. If we serve the underaged we lose our licence.'

'I have forged identification. I can get a glass of wine in Cobham any time I like. So long as I wear high-heeled shoes and keep my school uniform covered up under my raincoat.'

'Well, that won't work here. I know how old you are.'

'You don't know anything about me. You haven't seen me for months. I wouldn't have known you were back in England if Margaret hadn't told me. After all those letters I wrote you when you were in America . . . what kind of friend are you?'

'Unreliable, I'm afraid. I wrote very few letters when I was over there.'

'But I'm special, aren't I? Aren't I a bit special?'

'Very special. My favourite niece.'

'I'm not your niece and you know it. We're not related at all. That's the best part.' She did a full turn like a model on a runway. She was wearing a tight roll-neck sweater under her school jumper and black pumps with stiletto-heels. 'How do I look,' she said. 'A bit different from the last time you saw me. Right?'

'You look very nice.'

'Don't be such a rat, Evan. Say something sweet. It's hard to look your best in these institutional clothes but I'm doing what I can. You never told me what you thought of the photos I sent you from Portugal. Mother wouldn't let me wear that swimsuit on the beach. Only to sunbathe on the roof. Sometimes when it was just me, I took off everything. I had a great tan. Don't you think I looked good in the pictures?'

'Very nice.'

'Sophie's dressmaker says I have the figure of a twenty-year-old woman. Do you think she's right?'

'I'm sure she knows her business. I'm not an expert on such things.'

45

'Don't tell me that. I've seen how women look at you. Can't I have a glass of wine?'

'No.'

'You really are a rat. You must have had a new lady-friend every week out there in California. I've read a few stories about those actresses.'

'You mustn't believe everything you read. Actresses aren't that much different from other women.'

'Do you think I'm different from other women?'

Evan smiled. 'I don't know. I'll have to give it some thought.'

'Never mind. I know what you think. You think I'm not a woman at all. Isn't that right?'

'I didn't say that.'

'You didn't have to. You have a picture in your mind of Trevor and me playing with the dogs in the garden, and you can't get past that. That's why I sent you those photos. So you'd see how much I've changed.'

'You're obviously dead serious about this so I'll give you a serious answer. I'm sure when you take off your clothes and look at yourself in the glass you say to yourself that you're a woman now. And in many ways you are. But in other ways you're not. You can't fool the clock. None of us can. Do you think I was a man when I was fifteen?'

'Boys are different.'

'That's true. But let me put it this way. Trevor's only a year younger than you. Is he a man?'

'God, no. He's a mess.'

'Don't answer too quickly. He's certainly capable of fathering a child.'

'Trevor? That's disgusting.'

'No, it's not. It's the truth. It seems disgusting to you because you still think of him as a child.'

'I think of him as a mess.' After a moment she said, 'I'm not stupid, you know. I know what you're saying to me. You're saying that no matter how I look, no matter how

46

grown-up I become, I'll always be Sophie's little girl in her pyjamas.'

He smiled again. 'I'm not saying that at all. I'm saying you needn't be in a rush. There's plenty of time for everything. By the time you leave Miss Endicott's, boys will be flocking round you like sparrows.'

'I'm not interested in young boys. Or sparrows either. How old do I have to be before *you* look at me as something other than a child?'

'We'll have to see about that,' he said. 'But one thing I promise you. When you're eighteen or twenty I'll look as old to you as your Uncle Howard does now.'

'God, you're a hateful man. I can't decide whether you don't understand what I'm saying or if you refuse to understand.'

'I'm very smart,' he said. 'I understand everything. Let me see if I've got it straight.' He looked at his watch. 'What you'd like is for me to take you to bed and then get you to the station in time for the one o'clock train to Cobham.'

'I know you're just being clever and horrible, but no, that's not what I want. I just want you to look at me, to notice me, to pretend I'm a stranger. I want you to forget that you watched me grow up and let me be what I am now.'

'That's fair enough. Let's work on that.'

As they drove to the station in Evan's car she said, 'Do you think I'm a virgin?'

'I have to be honest with you. I've never thought about it.'

'Well, in case it matters to you, I'm not. I'm not a tramp but I'm not a little flower either. Haven't been since I was thirteen. I decided I didn't want to be a virgin any longer so one afternoon when I had a free day from school I took a bus to Oakdale.'

'Where you had a friend.'

'Not really. More of a stranger. He was a nice young

man who drove a bakery truck. I've never seen him since.'

'Are you sure you want to tell me all this?'

'Of course. I want you to know all about me.'

2

'I think poor William has gone over the edge,' Clara Causey said. 'Next thing we know he'll be hauling a piece of field artillery up the great staircase and bolting it firmly to his snooker table. What's come over the man? He's always been dotty but now he's being outrageous. What sort of impulse is that, to want to remain in domicile with your ex-wife and her new husband.'

'He doesn't know that part, of course,' Margaret said.

'Ohhh, so you haven't told him about Brannigan?'

Margaret shook her head. 'Discussed it with Tremont at some length and he felt there was no point in adding more fuel to the fire. Not till after the divorce is a *fait accompli*.'

'But now it is.'

'Imminent,' Margaret said.

'And will you tell him then?'

'I suppose it depends on how difficult he decides to be about removing himself from the Towers.'

'Do you really think he intends to gun down the poor constables if they come to fetch him?'

'Six months ago I'd have scoffed at the idea but now God knows what's in his mind. He's always been paranoid, you know. Makes lists of his enemies.'

'But you say he's let up on his drinking?'

'It seems so.'

'Bad sign. Angus used to say a drunken lunatic is not nearly so dangerous as a lunatic who's stopped drinking. Tricky business when that chemistry changes.'

'Watching his diet, he says. Swinging his Indian clubs, hiking every day, and riding horseback.'

'God help us. Doesn't sound like the Major. If Oblomov had been a military man his name would surely have been Bill Cranston.'

'I know you'll think this is an odd question, but is there any chance that I'm being too severe with him?'

'Severe? With him? Why in the world would that thought even enter your head?'

'It doesn't when I'm talking with him. But later, when I'm by myself, trying to set things straight in my mind, when I hear his voice telling me I'm depriving him of his home, the only home he's ever known as a civilian, I start wondering if I couldn't handle all this in a better way. I begin to feel guilty.'

'Guilty? For the love of God, Margaret, I can't imagine what's come over you. There's no one in this county, no one who knows both you and William, no one who doesn't believe you've behaved like a saint toward him. Almost thirty-five years of your life you've been married. Can you even remember when he treated you decently, when he talked to you and listened to you, when he touched your hand or your hair, or kissed you? That's what life with a man is supposed to be about. All William knows or cares about is barracks life. Everything else is foreign to him. Of course he doesn't want to leave your house. He lives in splendour there. You're the only person in the world who would have tolerated him for all these years. He's taken everything you have to give, and offered nothing in return. Except Sophie. And if I didn't know you as well as I do I would suspect that you'd had an affair with some absolutely first-rate, handsome and charming cavalry lieutenant in India and Sophie was the result.'

Margaret smiled. 'Sophie is William's child all right. There's no doubt about that.'

'Of course there isn't. But thank God she's inherited nothing from him. She is vintage Wiswell in every respect. In appearance and character and sensibility. What I'm trying to say to you, Margaret, before you dissolve in a pool of guilt and poor judgement, is this: you have survived your marriage to William. And that's a tribute to you. I know you have scars and wretched memories. Still you've managed to stay the course. But now, when you're still young enough to appreciate it and enjoy it, you have a chance to come to life again. And not just because of Brannigan. Only men believe that a woman must be tied to a man in order to function. I mean you have an opportunity now to belong to yourself again. William has a talent for gloom. Nothing more. After an evening with him I used to be depressed for days. So if you're feeling guilt because you've managed at last to extricate yourself from all that heaviness and the sound of bugles and snare drums, then I say you're not thinking straight. My dear friend, you are on the threshold of some truly wonderful years. You mustn't doubt yourself now.'

3

A casual observer might conclude that Kincaid had somehow become a spectator in his own life, at ease in his mezzanine stall, calmly observing the events all round him, watching the future slowly reveal itself. Such a conclusion would not be totally off the mark but on the other hand the supporting evidence was not as simple as it seemed. Like Sophie, Kincaid was a complex product of his background.

Sophie believed, for example, as people of her class always believe, that all problems have solutions, that what one has learned at home, in classes and books, at university, can be used, must be used, to eliminate barriers and obstructions along the way. Letters can be written, phone calls made, friendships renewed, various handclasps and pressures applied, and at last a solution can be found. What are the values of good lineage, property, and generosity to the church if they can't be used to get one's own way?

Kincaid's life on the other hand had taught him different tactics. Since moments of triumph are rare when one is poor and lacking also in courage and optimism, one slowly discovers the comfort of acceptance. Acceptance with resentment, often with anger, and occasionally with grace. People who have never heard the word *fatalism*, who would not understand it if they did hear it, are the ones who practise it most consistently in their daily lives.

These were the people Kincaid had known. No grand expectations, no great plans. Only in prison had he met people with such plans. An elaborate scheme had put most of them inside the walls and another such scheme, each man hoped, would get him out. But these prisoners were exceptions. The men on the cattle runs and sheep stations of Victoria and New South Wales, the men digging ore or gutting fish, the migrants and draymen, the blokes with brooms and shovels and tattoos on their arms, these grubbers and drunks and street-brawlers whom Kincaid had worked and drunk and fought with along the way were children of chance. Chance was the only constant in their lives. By chance a bit of work turned up, by chance a lorry overturned and crushed its driver. Or a mine flooded. Chance produced a lift on the road, a drink of whisky under a bridge, a woman who would spread her legs for a shilling. Chance brought misery, hunger, and heart-break. And only occasionally a bit of joy. Still it was an ally. Something to rely on. The only thing, if one paid close attention, that was always in evidence.

Because he was very young when he buffeted about Australia and later round the world, Kincaid had made an icon of chance, had given it full credit for the few good turns he'd taken and had assumed the blame himself when things went sour. Needing through the meagre years to cling to something, he had stuck with the belief that chance was an ally that would serve him at last in some quite remarkable way. Ironically, the more he read and learned and educated himself, the more he clung to his pagan faith in tomorrow.

When his fortunes began to turn, therefore, in London, when a slow and sputtering series of events began to bring him into sharp focus, when strangers befriended him, although these individual happenings came, each one, as a surprise, the general sensation of moving ahead was not surprising to him at all. When he was an eight-year-old boy in a New Norfolk orphanage, the thought that had come to him most often was, 'Someday I'll have my turn.'

Chance. Always that. Homeless in London, he became in desperation a busker. No further goal. No plans beyond survival. He saw no advantage, till Evan persuaded him, in being featured in the *Daily Telegraph*. A bit later, when Rosamund Barwick managed to get him released from jail, he accepted her generosity only because it was forced on him by the court. But gradually an unfamiliar warmth inside him seemed to promise a sea change. After a week in the flat above Mrs Barwick's coach-house he knew without question that he had caught a benevolent tide. After he had performed at the Cromwell and the Royal Court he saw for the first time how chance and his own efforts could be blended together.

Thus Julian Thorne was not the surprise he might otherwise have been. Nor was Sophie. The boy from whom gifts had been withheld was suddenly being rewarded. Or so it seemed to Kincaid. Just as he had accepted his earlier misfortunes, he now accepted the good things. If chance had been responsible before, it was responsible now. The aborigine inside Kincaid asked no questions, set no deadlines, and made no demands. That small creature simply smiled and followed what seemed by now to be a well-marked road.

'By God, this is bloody decent of you,' Alec Maple said, 'treating me to a meal here at Juliana's – I assume it's your treat since you rang me and since everyone knows I never pay my own way.'

'Of course it's my treat,' Evan said. 'I invited you.'

'So you did. And will it be a leisurely lunch, preceded by a few lovely beakers of gin, or were you thinking of weak tea, a plate of ham salad, then back to the Street?'

'I'm in no rush.'

'Excellent. Neither am I.'

When they ordered drinks Maple said to the waiter, 'We'll be having several drinks, I expect, so don't drift too far away. And if there's finnan haddie on the menu save a portion of that for me.'

'No finnan haddie, sir.'

'Damn. That's a bad omen. No chance you could nip round the corner to a fishmonger and carry back a bit of finnan haddie?'

'Afraid not, sir.'

'Oh, well, no matter. Perhaps the Bombay will do me. Along with a double helping of trifle with the coffee.'

'Is that your order, sir?' the waiter asked.

'No. God, no. Just wool-gathering. Bring on the drinks with a bit of buttered toast and we'll sort out *la carte* later on.' When the waiter turned away, Maple said to Evan. 'Is that all right with you? I hope so. Hate to rush a splendid lunch. Damned disappointed about the finnan haddie, however.' He glanced round the room. 'Gone to seed a bit, this place. Not what it once was. Maybe we should have chosen Ormando's. You know it?'

'No, I don't.'

'Not far from here. In Old Compton Street. Just off Wardour. They do an excellent lunch there. Maybe we should drink a bit here, then pop over to Ormando's for *linguini*.'

'I don't think so.'

'Ahhh. Resistance. Conflict. Another bad omen. No matter. Let's move right along as though nothing had happened. You have a grave look on your face so I assume you want to have a down-to-earth talk about my wife. How is the old girl? Thriving in California, I expect. Likes nothing better than to strip off her clothes, knickers and all, and brown herself in the sun. Hate the sun myself. Salt air, sea breezes, all that rot. Always thought it was some sort of secondary sex-drive, that urge to strip naked and sunbathe. Are you a sunbather?'

'I like to swim and play tennis so I'm in the sun quite a lot.'

'Of course you are. Keeping trim, toning the muscles, working up a good sweat. I never sweat. Does that surprise you? Never have. No body odour. Shirts and under-drawers and socks never stink. Astonishing, isn't it? I've no need to take a bath but I do anyway. Not often, however, because there's no sense to it. But every now and again women like you to sit in the tub or stand in the shower with them. Have you found that to be true? Odd creatures, aren't they? Obsessed with cleanliness. Wash away their sins. Toilet-water and talcum. Cologne on their nipples. Nasty habit that. Gives you a start when you get a taste of perfume where you don't expect it. Some chap could make a nice fortune selling perfume that tastes good.' He drained his glass. 'I knew a young actress named Jennifer Seaforth who put Drambuie on her nipples. A nice little thing she was and a gifted performer. But she married a man twice her age and went off to live in the Orkney Islands. Every time I see a bottle of Drambuie behind the bar I think of her.' He signalled the waiter for another round.

'All right. Let's get down to cases,' he said then. 'Mary Cecil, that's the topic of the day. My wife. Your companion of the moment. What shall we say about God's sweet creature?'

'Let's get something straight, Mr Maple . . .'

'You can call me Alec. We're almost relatives.'

'I don't want to call you Alec. I'm here because I want to try to work through an awkward situation. I think it's the decent thing to do. I am not here to exchange confidences or anecdotes about Mary. Is that understood?'

'I hope that's not a threatening tone I hear in your voice, Mr Tagg. I react badly to threats. As I recall, I mentioned that to you the last time we spoke.'

'That's right, you did. But you are not being threatened. You're being cautioned. Please don't share your private judgements of Mary with me. My character, your character, or Mary's are not at issue here. No confessions or revelations. You and I are both aware that an unresolved situation exists. If we can have a sensible, unemotional talk about it, perhaps we can find a solution.'

'I can certainly be unemotional,' Maple said. 'Can't guarantee how sensible I'll be.'

'Nor can I. But let's do our best. You know, I'm sure, that Mary and I have been living together in California since last September.'

'Malibu. House on the beach. Seagulls and sandpipers.'

'Since you and I hardly know each other,' Evan went on, 'I want to make it clear that I don't specialize in married women. I don't break up marriages. I had seen Mary on that stage many times but I'd never met her till she appeared in my play last year. Whatever you may imagine, we did not have an affair at the time. Not a flirtation. Not a friendship. Nothing. And after the play closed she went off to Cardiff to see your daughter. Sybil, is it?'

'Yes. Child of my loins but not of my bosom. She wants nothing to do with me.'

'I'm sorry to hear that.'

'No cause for sorrow,' Maple said. 'No tears are shed on either side. The devil is always with us. Must live with that.'

'After I wrote the screenplay for *Bushranger*, when I was about to go to America to work on the film, I heard she was in hospital. So I went there to see her.'

'And not long after that I visited you in your apartment.'

'That's right. Just before I left for California. And at the end of the summer Mary joined me there. Until that time . . .'

'Until that time,' Maple said, 'it was a pristine relationship. Neither of you had ever been drawn to the other. No tender looks. No throbbing hearts.'

'I didn't say that. I was in love with her before I left London but we had never been together till she came to California.'

'And now you're determined to be together till the desert blooms and the seas run dry.'

'There's nothing frivolous or amusing about it,' Evan said. 'We love each other and we want to get married.'

'Gone as far as that, has it?'

'I know you're already aware of everything I'm telling you . . .'

'Not at all,' Maple said. 'How could I be?'

'You know we were together. You even know where we're living.'

'That's true. One has informers in every corner. But the love and marriage scenario is new to me.'

'How can it be new to you? You and Mary have been discussing a divorce since last summer. She's showed me some of the letters she's written you from California.'

'Oldest trick in the theatre. One writes a letter but doesn't send it. Necessary device sometimes.'

'Are you telling me you've had no letters from Mary since she's been in California?'

'Not a line. And the word *divorce* was never mentioned in the weeks before she left London.'

'I don't believe that.'

'It doesn't matter a damn to me whether you believe it or not. I'm telling the truth for once. Why would I lie about it?'

'I have no idea. But if I have a choice . . . believing you or believing Mary . . .'

'You'll believe her, of course. But eventually you'll discover you've been deceived. I don't deny that Mary and I have had a stormy life together. You said you want no details so I won't give you any. We have screamed and yelled, clawed at each other and stayed apart for weeks at a time. But we've never talked of divorce and we never will. I shan't leave Mary and she can't leave me. I'm her armature.'

5

Geoff Bingham had played the principal role in Evan's play, *The Father House*. He had also been brought to California for the role of McBean in *Bushranger*. During rehearsals for the play Evan and Geoff had become confidants and drinking companions, and in California they had seen each other frequently when the production company was together for weeks on location.

Bingham and his wife, Dorothy, had known Mary Cecil and Alec Maple for years. So the day after his luncheon with Maple, as he tried to untangle the conflicts in his head, Evan rang up Bingham.

'Pinewood Studios tomorrow,' Bingham said. 'I'm shooting a dreary film there, long hours with nothing to do but sit in my caravan. So please come to visit me.'

The following afternoon when they met at Pinewood – the first time since *Bushranger* had finished shooting the autumn before – Bingham said, ' "Home is the sailor, home from the sea . . . and the hunter home from the hill." By God, I thought we'd seen the last of you. Drunk with success, seduced by California. You're launched,

57

Cocky. Pots of gold. Fresh underdrawers every day. I'm proud of you. Just what you needed, what you richly deserved after we botched up your beautiful play last spring. Films are the thing now, aren't they? Not for old dogs like me. But for your generation and all the generations from now on. The theatre won't die, God bless it, but it will surely limp and suffer. And I heard a chap talking at the Savile the other day who said we'll all live to see wireless with pictures. Not just voices but faces, talking and singing and acting on a screen right in your library. Lord help us. Science will be the death of us all, you know.'

He led Evan into his caravan and they sat down. 'Can't say you look much different. Your head doesn't seem too big for your hat. And you haven't grown a moustache, bleached your hair, or started to wear spats. Good for you. Also you've finished another scenario, I hear. Smart move. When there's a tail wind behind you it's good to take advantage of it. This new one for Thorne?'

Evan nodded. 'Garrigus directing. And with Kincaid again, we hope.'

'What does that mean?'

'It means that Kincaid hasn't said yes.'

'But he hasn't said no.'

'Hasn't said a bloody word.'

'Not even to you.'

'We talked around the edges of the subject but nothing came of it.'

'Maybe he's waiting for a better offer.'

'There's no offer on the table. Kincaid can write his own ticket with Thorne and he knows it. And it's not a question of money in any case. Kincaid never had money in his life except what he carried in his pocket. Then he married Sophie. Now he can tap into Thorne for whatever he wants.'

'When a chap gets lucky like that he usually goes money-crazy. That's been my experience.'

'Either that or it means nothing to him,' Evan said. 'With Kincaid it means nothing.'

'It doesn't add up, does it? When I was drunk with Garrigus one night in Thousand Oaks he told me Kincaid made a sweetheart deal with Thorne. Negotiated the whole thing himself.'

Evan nodded. 'Once he decides to do something, he goes for the throat. But all that's tied up with where he came from and the way he lived as a boy. Has nothing to do with money. If he decides to go ahead with Thorne it will be for some other reason.'

'Thorne must be suffering. Everybody's kissing his bum trying to get into pictures and he's stuck with a hot chap who doesn't give a damn whether he works or not.'

'Thorne's no fool. He's smart enough to know that Kincaid can't be pushed. So he's counting his money from *Bushranger* and playing a waiting game.'

Bingham was called to the sound stage then. Evan went along and watched him do a scene with a Dalmatian puppy and a nine-year-old girl. When they were back in the caravan Bingham said, 'That nine-year-old girl is really sixteen. She's getting it off with the cameraman unless I miss my guess. And her mother, the blonde with a voice like faulty car-brakes, goes up to the producer's office every afternoon and comes back with her hair mussed.'

At last Evan eased into the subject he'd come there to discuss. He told Bingham about his conversation with Maple. 'Either he's the best liar in England or there's something going on that I know nothing about.'

'Alec's not the best liar in England. I am,' Bingham said. 'He's just an amateur, learning his trade. But he's a devious and clever chap. Always was. That's why he scored so well in *Richard the Third*. I told you that before, I think. Did a top-notch job with that role. We thought he was on his way to the top. But he pissed it all away. Turned his full attention to mucking up Mary's life.'

'But that's an odd thing to lie about, isn't it? If he knows she wants to divorce him, why pretend otherwise? And if he doesn't know, why would Mary go to such lengths to convince me he does?'

'I'm sure you don't think she's lying, do you?'

Evan shook his head. 'Why should she? There's no reward involved. I don't really care what she's told Maple. If she said to me, "I can't get a divorce" or "For reasons that I can't explain, I don't want to divorce Alec, I just want to live with you", if she said either of those things there'd be no problem.'

'Don't fool yourself about that,' Bingham said. 'I expect if there wasn't a problem you wouldn't be here talking to me about it.'

'Maple's an incredible jackass. Damned annoying. I'd like to pick him up and shake him till his teeth rattle.'

'Mustn't do that. He'll set you on fire.'

'You know about that, eh?'

'Eye-witness to it,' Bingham said. 'He set his dresser on fire. Backstage at Birmingham Rep. A nice old gent named Rosewood. And there were other incidents as well.'

'I've never heard of such a trick. How does he get away with things like that?'

'People have asked that question for years. I've never heard a satisfactory answer.'

6

The day her divorce became final Margaret cabled the news to Brannigan. He cabled a reply:

I SALUTE YOU. NOW THAT YOU'RE AVAILABLE DO I STILL APPEAL TO YOU?

Three days later she had a letter from him.

My dear brand-new liberated woman,

I suppose I should now be casual and matter-of-fact, careful not to display my love too recklessly lest you take advantage of me, not only now but in future. The wise men say that love freely given is less attractive and appealing than a prize that must be struggled and fought for. I reject all that. Since I am such a splendid creature, I assume that you are at this moment as exhilarated and full of the future as I am.

As we discussed in Provence last summer, in countless letters, and more recently at Holyhead, you and I have our own enchanting *modus operandi*, no need for social approval or conventional rituals. We are already as married, as joined to each other as we could ever be. Cool and reasonable and grown-up we are, you having been married for more than thirty years to a loutish toy soldier, and myself a scarred veteran of three marriages. We are both well aware that no contract, no ceremony can protect us for ever and ever in sickness and in health, et cetera. We come to each other without illusions or outlandish expectations. Am I right? Of course I am.

Why then, as I write this, are my hands cold and damp? Flushed cheeks. A ringing in my ears. Love, you say. Not true. I've been silly-in-love with you for many months now and all my physical systems have functioned normally. The difference, I'm astonished to discover, is that now, just since I received your cable, I know we can have at last what we only sampled before. Warm feet, your head on my shoulder, coffee in bed every morning. We can be married, for Christ's sake. At this stage in my random life why should that convention, that condition, that odd social exercise have importance for me? I don't know but it does. Perhaps I want the world to know that I'm extraordinary, that you can't possibly survive without me. In short, if you expected me to be matter-of-fact about

61

your new freedom and total availability, I am not. I am ardent, impatient, proud, and disgustingly possessive, dreadfully anxious to tattoo the name Brannigan all over your body.

The following day she received another letter from him.

Those five days we spent in the inn by the harbour at Holyhead are still fresh on my fingertips. But for some odd reason, along with all the good stuff, I can't shake the memory of that haunting tale you told me about Clara Causey's brother, Raymond.

Margaret had told him the story the second day they were together in Holyhead. 'Raymond was still at university then, a handsome young fellow with a friendly disposition. He was twenty that year, just home for the summer. To celebrate his return his father held a great feast for all their friends and neighbours. Among the guests was a young woman who had recently married a man of the county, a man much older than she, who was tolerated but not admired by his neighbours. This young woman, this girl – she was no more than twenty herself – was introduced to Raymond. They danced, I'm sure, and made light conversation as newly-met persons do at large parties. But somehow, in full view of her husband and the other guests, they found their way. Raymond asked her if she liked to ride, and she said yes, that she rode every day. She told him what time she rode out and where she went: to a meadow by the river near a crofter's ruined hut. They met there the following morning and as often as possible thereafter. They were cautious, of course, or so they told themselves, but there was no way they could have concealed the lovely torment they were going through. When her husband found out he hustled his wife away for a long tour of the Continent.

And Raymond's father took him out of Cambridge and forced him to continue his studies in Dublin. Raymond was unable to contact her but she learned where he was and wrote to him as often as she could manage it, tortured, passionate letters. At last, the following spring, she wrote that she was home again in Northumberland and that she had arranged to visit her mother in Wales. She told Raymond she would be at the Pembroke Inn in Holyhead and begged him to meet her there. Her husband, however, was not deceived. When he burst into their room a fight began between him and Raymond. The husband had a revolver and in the struggle it was accidentally discharged. The bullet struck his wife in the head killing her instantly. Her husband then walked slowly down the stairs, crossed the street to the little park just opposite the inn, stood there in full view of the people walking on the paths and put a bullet through his brain.'

I am not a superstitious bastard [Brannigan wrote], as you know. My tastes in music and poetry are not romantic. If I were to attend an opera based on that scenario you described I would leave during the first interval. But because it's a genuine story, involving people you know, and because we were at that same inn together it clings to my memory (as Noel Coward says) and I suspect it always will.

Now . . . we mulled over, and you have continued to mention in your letters, the continuing situation with your former husband (has a nice ring to it), who still shows no inclination to move away from your house, divorced or not. We discussed whether or not you should pursue the legal alternatives suggested by your solicitor. My reaction was, 'Do it by all means. Get the bugger out of there.'

Now I've had second thoughts. Not recommendations, just thoughts. The euphoria that results from your being legally disentangled at last may have softened my usual hard-edge logic. Now that you have won the major battle, perhaps gentility is in order. Not for his sake, for yours. Rather than come at him with the law, giving him something to resist, why not assume that he's civilized – which he surely isn't – that he still has respect for you, perhaps even a speck of affection, and tell him the simple truth, that you're in love with a renegade Irishman, that you're going to get married, and that you think it would be awkward for the Major to be living in a house with his ex-wife and her new husband. No fireworks. No insistence that he do anything at all. Just a reasonable examination of the situation between two people whom one would assume have a bit of residual friendship, if nothing else, after thirty-odd years of marriage.

You have nothing to lose, Maggie. If he insists on being obstinate and wrong-headed, you still have the messy legal alternatives to fall back on. One thing is certain: he *will* leave us to ourselves. If he doesn't we'll put a rocket up his bum and blast him back to India. Or you can come with me to Donegal and I'll show you what life is really about.

All joking aside, you should try the direct approach. Tell him we need our privacy so we can frolic on the snooker-table and dash through the garden in our knickers.

7

When Geoff Bingham met Kincaid for the first time at the film location in California he told Evan, 'He's a bona-fide roughneck, the genuine article. Choose him for your side in a street-fight. He'll punch till he drops, that fellow. Doesn't have to be a thespian, doesn't need to make the moves and learn the tricks. If the camera picks up that silent, bull-headed thing about him, there's nothing more he needs to do. He'll be like that cowboy chap, Cooper. Not fancy. No smart alec stuff. Just a genuine bloke standing there trying to figure out what to do next. Damned appealing that. Can't be learned. If it's not there it never will be there. *Presence*, we call it. Larry Olivier has it, Gielgud doesn't have it yet except when he's doing Shakespeare. I have some of it but not enough.'

Bingham and Kincaid hadn't seen each other since they'd returned to London from California. So when Bingham rang up and asked Kincaid to join him for a drink they arranged to meet at the Garrick bar.

'Riding high now, aren't you?' Bingham said after they sat down together. 'All you chaps, you and Tagg and Garrigus. I must say my telephone's been ringing too. More film work than I can handle just now. Starting to prepare for *Coriolanus* at the Old Vic. Heavy part. Haven't tackled it in years. And we've got a young director – sees himself as a genius – so we'll have to toilet-train him as we go along. But everything will come right in the end or we'll strangle the little twat.'

They reminisced about the filming of *Bushranger*, exchanged anecdotes and work experiences, and at last Bingham said, 'I'm sure you have a busy schedule these days just as I do, but there's a personal matter I wanted to discuss with you. It concerns our friend Tagg. I know you two are friends as well as colleagues, and I've certainly counted him as a friend ever since he and I worked together on his play last year.'

Bingham finished his drink and ordered another round. Then: 'The theatre's an odd place you know. We find ourselves surrounded by eccentric gifted people. An odd lot, the men and women who pull themselves together and step out on the stage eight times every week, always suspended in mid-air, half themselves and half the character they're playing at the moment. Many of us, it turns out, are more at home with the stage character than the real one. A doctor friend of mine once said,

"I treat many actors and I love them. They're a fascinating group. Tolerant for the most part and unusually generous. An actor will give you anything he has as long as it's a voluntary gift. When demands are made on him, on the other hand, he is likely to collapse or disappear." I'm not sure the doctor's right in that judgement but it always comes to my mind when an actor friend begins to tell me the tangled secrets of his personal life.'

'Is that what Evan's been doing? Telling you his secrets?'

Bingham shook his head. 'Not at all. No intimate confessions, if that's what you mean. Evan's not that sort of chap any more than I am. But he knows that I've known Mary Cecil and her husband for years and he came to me to try to make some sense out of Alec Maple.'

He told Kincaid briefly about his conversation with Evan. Then he said, 'I've discussed this at some length with my wife, Dorothy. She's known Alec as long as I have and she thinks he's a hopeless rotter. And of course she knows Mary very well. They're quite close friends. So her reaction was that I should stay out of the whole business. Make no judgements, provide no information or advice.'

'To Evan, you mean?'

'Yes. And I agree with her. But at the same time I feel uncomfortable with the situation. Damned uncomfortable sitting there talking with Evan, seeing that he's bloody confused about what's going on and knowing that I know things he should know. You see what I'm getting at?'

'I'm not sure. But whatever it is, I'm not going to pass along this conversation to Evan. Even if you want me to.'

'Of course not. Don't expect that. This is a private matter, man-to-man, between you and me. I told Dorothy I had no intention of interfering, and I don't. But all the same I wanted to take it up with you. I'm sure Evan has a number of friends but you're the only one I know.' Bingham sat back in his chair. 'The messenger who brings bad tidings to the king will have his head cut off . . . I'm sure you've heard that expression.'

Kincaid smiled and nodded, and Bingham went on. 'That's our dilemma here. That's what we're about. You see, Evan is convinced that Alec Maple is the villain of the piece and, God knows, Maple is a man without qualities if I've ever seen one. I know chaps who would get up and leave this bar if he walked in. Any foul story I might hear about him I would automatically believe. So Evan's right to distrust the bugger. But that's not the whole story. Our little Mary, lovely and dear as she is, is not all she ought to be either. All her friends who used to feel she was wasting herself, even endangering herself, by being married to Maple, have come to realize, just as I have, that it's a marriage she wants. And depends on in some strange way. She not only tolerates mistreatment, she expects it. And Dorothy is convinced she enjoys it. She says, "Mary is a remarkable person and a fine actress but she has a serious flaw: she thinks she has to suffer or she's worthless." And that's true, of course. Mary's not the first woman who got love and screwing and punishment all tangled together in her head, and she won't be the last. Maple is her black prince. He plucked her out of the cradle, so to speak, moulded her and ruined her. When he tells people that she will never leave him he knows what he's talking about. She's told my wife the same thing. Her image of herself and him has never changed. He is the cruel pirate in a black cape and she's the pale virgin being eternally sacrificed. Sounds impossible, doesn't it?'

'Nothing's impossible,' Kincaid said.

'You're a wise fellow.' Bingham leaned forward and rested his arms on the table. 'A stupid woman, one is tempted to say. Self-destructive. Totally lacking in either self-respect or intelligence. Not true in Mary's case. She's bright and sensitive and completely reasonable. Dorothy says Mary discusses herself and Maple as if they were characters in a bad play. Or the subjects of a psychological case-history. An actor must have what we call "a third eye", an ability to step back and observe his own work even as he's doing it. But it seems that Mary also has that ability when she considers her life with Maple. Objective and dispassionate. She's able to dissect it all, label the parts, and draw conclusions. But it's all a clinical exercise. She has no impulse whatsoever, it seems, to improve or correct the situation. Or to disentangle herself from this worthless shit she's married to. Why is that? Dorothy has a theory and I think she's right about it. She thinks Mary is well served by her rotten marriage. In the first place it guarantees endless love and sympathy from her friends and co-workers. And in the second place it exonerates her in everyone's eyes for anything she chooses to do outside the marriage. People say, "God knows, she deserves a bit of kindness and affection," and they forgive her anything. Here's the tricky part, you see. Dorothy and I have known Mary since she was little more than a child, before she met Maple, when she was a promising newcomer. Everyone adored her. She was fresh and lovely, hungry to learn and eager to please. And every man in the company went to bed with her. She wasn't a slut. There was nothing cheap or common about her behaviour. She always looked and behaved as if she'd just left the convent. I've never known her to pursue a man. But I've also never known her to resist one who pursued her. Maple told Evan that he and Mary have "an enlightened marriage". Evan took that to mean that Mary condoned all of Maple's womanizing. But the fact is, they are evenly matched in that regard. If promiscuity were an athletic event one would be hard put to choose a winner between Maple and Mary. I'm not making a moral judgement of little Mary, God knows. I'm telling you this to show you that her marriage is quite satisfactory to her and

68

I'm sure it will continue to be. When Maple told Evan that Mary has never asked him for a divorce, when he said she will never divorce him, I expect he's telling the truth.'

'Evan's not a schoolboy, you know,' Kincaid said. 'Sophie says he's always been a big success with the ladies.'

'I'm sure of it. But all the same everybody's somebody's fool. And from what I saw of him and Mary together in California, and from what I concluded after my conversation with him last week, he's got himself in deep water this time. He's gone daft over Mary.'

'Shall we buy him lunch at Prunier's, get him a little drunk on claret, and tell him the truth about her?'

Bingham smiled. 'I don't think that's the answer and I'm sure you don't think so either.'

'No, I don't.'

'You can tell by my stumbling round the subject that I don't have any bright ideas either. I just hate to see a decent chap like Evan get himself into a tangle. My dad used to tell me that every problem has at least one solution. I think he was right. But in a situation like this I'm against the wall. Damned awkward feeling. Hate to be a helpless bystander.'

'Look at it this way,' Kincaid said. 'He's crazy about her. They're having a great time together. So he'll have to take what comes. Just like all of us do. Nothing lasts for ever.'

'You're a cynical bastard, aren't you? Along with your other talents.'

'I'm not cynical,' Kincaid said. 'I just pay attention.'

8

In 1930, when it had been made clear to everyone that talking pictures were something more than a fad or a technical experiment, when in fact the advent of sound showed evidence that what had been a successful form of entertainment might now become a dynamic international industry, when actors' voices as well as their faces became familiar to audiences, a new weekly film magazine came into being in Los Angeles. It was called *Actors Speak*. Using gossip, rumour, romantic revelations and confessional interviews to fill its pages, selling advertising space to hypnotists, evangelists, and publishers of erotic books, it grew from an original printing of five hundred copies to a printing of twenty thousand three months later.

The magazine was attacked from all sides. Lawsuits were threatened and committees were formed to force a cessation of publication. Ministers preached against it, prominent actors disclaimed it, school officials scolded its editors. But everyone read it. Soon it had national distribution, being sold primarily in cigar-stores and on news-stands in poor neighbourhoods. No one admitted reading it but each week the information it contained quickly became general knowledge.

As the title indicated, most of the magazine's articles were presented in the form of interviews, usually with actors or directors, sometimes with imaginary persons, and often with peripheral figures, actors' families or servants or friends. Readers soon learned that some of the more stunning revelations came from envious relatives or disgruntled servants, sometimes unidentified.

Several weeks after Evan's return to London from California he had a letter from Mary in which she enclosed a clipping from *Actors Speak*.

This clipping is brutally self-explanatory [she wrote]. I don't know how these tacky journalists managed to locate Kincaid's stepdaughter at her school in Kent, but they did. I only hope the magazine won't be floating about London. From what you've told me about Sophie and her family, I'm sure they wouldn't appreciate this sort of publicity.

When Evan unfolded the two pages from the magazine he saw that it was an interview with Sarah, along with a photograph of her in a bathing-suit. In bold black type above the picture, the headline read: KINCAID'S DAUGHTER.

Before the text of the interview began, there was a comment from the editor.

Since Thornwood Studios released *Bushranger* last winter, the name of Roy Kincaid has been on every woman's lips. But Kincaid himself has been unavailable for interviews. Now, however, our man in London, Neal Dyer, has interviewed Kincaid's daughter, Sarah, the voluptuous young woman you see in the picture on this page. She tells us in detail what it's like to be the daughter of an international star.

The interview followed.

You seem quite grown-up for a schoolgirl. How old are you?
I'm eighteen. I'll be leaving this prison in a few weeks. I never should have been here in the first place. The headmistress and I don't exactly admire each other. But my mother's family is quite conservative so they thought I'd be safe here at Miss Endicott's.

Is that what you want . . . to be safe?
Of course not. I want to be independent.

As I look at you, I'd guess that you want to be an actress.
Yes . . . I plan to be. That's one reason I've taken Kincaid's name. He's my stepfather, you see, but I think of him as my father. My real father's name was Black. He was killed in the war. I respect him, of

71

course, although I don't remember him. Also, for an actress, I think Sarah Kincaid is a better name.

Julian Thorne says your father will be starting a new picture soon. Does that mean you'll be going to California with him?
Of course. We're a family. My mother and I wouldn't want to be separated from him.

Have you been to California?
No. But I've read a great deal about it and I can't wait to go there. I expect we'll be living there most of the time from now on. At least I will.

Then you'll be pursuing your acting career?
Exactly. And living my life. You see, my mother's family is quite wealthy and traditional, and since I'm an only child they've been hideously protective. I'm grateful, of course, for what they've tried to do for me but now I'm eager to be my own person, to follow my instincts and make my own mistakes.

What's it like to be the daughter of a man like Kincaid? How did you feel when after only one film he became a celebrity?
I love it. I've seen the film several times and I think Kincaid is marvellous in it. It's great to have a famous father. Some day I hope I'll be as well known as he's going to be.

An American magazine last month said he's one of the ten sexiest men in the world. How do you think your mother feels about that?
I'm sure she thinks she's one of the ten sexiest women in the world so I guess it's all right.

There were rumours that he and Daisy Bishop were having a romance when they were working together in Bushranger. *Did you hear about that?*

No, I didn't.

Do you think your mother heard about it?
My mother's very clever and very beautiful. She doesn't fret much about other people's opinions. Besides, from now on, I expect people will gossip a lot about Kincaid. My mother will have to get used to it.

What if you were married to an actor? Would you be jealous watching him do love scenes with other women?
I'm not the jealous type. Besides, I may never get married. And if I do, it probably won't be to an actor. I've already picked out the man I want. He's a writer.

Is he famous?
Not yet. But he will be.

If you get married and find out your husband doesn't want you to be an actress, what then?
I wouldn't marry a man like that. Marriage isn't a prison, is it? I have to do what's best for me. That's what I expect to do.

One last question. Do you think young women should have love affairs before they're married?
Why not? Men do it, don't they? Anyone can see that men want to make all the rules. That doesn't sound like a good idea to me.

Evan read the pages through a second time. Then he carefully put them away in his desk drawer. He made himself a drink and sat in his chair by the bow window. Wishing there was a way that he could make the article he'd just read, and all copies of it, disappear, he knew that was impossible. His only alternative, he decided, was to go to Sophie and Kincaid and warn them. Sooner or later, he knew they would read what he had just read. Better it should come to them from him.

The longer he sat by the window, however, the more strongly he felt that his best course was to drive down to Cobham and discuss it with Sarah. He knew the magazine's reputation. They could have got hold of her photograph somehow and then simply made up the interview. Or even if they had spoken with her, undoubtedly they had distorted everything she'd said. It was only fair for him to find out her version of the matter before he did anything else about it.

9

Margaret had no quarrel with Brannigan's assessment of her situation. She agreed that attempting to reason with the Major one last time was preferable to an extended struggle through the courts and county authorities. She persuaded herself that circumstances had changed now. The divorce was final. For better or worse, it was behind them. Surely when she told Cranston that she planned to marry again he would give up his maniacal insistence on staying in residence at Wiswell Towers. Still, when she sent a message to him suggesting that they meet in the library the following afternoon, she did so with trepidation. When his answer came back, saying he would meet her but only if she came to his second-floor sitting-room in the west wing, she felt wary indeed.

No one in the household, not even Rose Ball, her personal maid, knew about her involvement with Brannigan. Even the housekeeper, Mrs Whitson, and John Trout, the butler, although they might have been aware of Brannigan's frequent letters to her, had no idea, Margaret was sure, that she'd chosen him to be her husband.

Only hours before her scheduled meeting with the Major it came to her suddenly that Arthur Tagg must be told. Although she didn't expect that Cranston would announce her impending marriage to the staff assembled, she shuddered at the prospect of Tagg's hearing the news from someone other than herself. The following day after breakfast she sat down with Arthur in the morning-room and told him what she planned to do.

'I've wanted to tell you for some time but I thought the decent thing was to wait until my divorce from William became final.'

'There was no reason for me to know,' Arthur said.

'Perhaps not. But I wanted to tell you all the same. You and I have been close friends for more than twenty years. Sometimes I think you and Clara Causey are my only friends. You've been the backbone of this house for me and Sophie and her children, and for the staff as well. I told you all this a few weeks ago when you said you wanted to leave your place here. Now, I'm telling you again. You're indispensable to me, to all of us, and this change in the pattern of my life will in no way affect your work here or my feelings for you.'

'Thank you. But I think my decision was the correct one. I do plan to leave as soon as you've found a proper person to replace me.'

'I'm certain you have your reasons for wanting to go, just as I have good reasons for wanting you to stay. But I warn you, I will use every persuasion I can think of to make you change your mind.'

'I don't like to disappoint you but I don't expect that I'll change my decision.'

'Am I disappointing you?' she said. 'Does the fact that I'm getting married have something to do with your leaving?'

'You'll remember, I offered my resignation some time ago. I've just learned this morning that you're planning to marry Mr Brannigan.'

'I thought perhaps you knew something without being told.'

75

'The morning mail does cross my desk. That's true. And there was no way of missing Brannigan's name scrawled across the back of his letters. But I drew no conclusions from his writing to you.'

She sat silent in her chair for a long moment. At last she said, 'Arthur, this is not a business meeting between an employer and her estate manager. You and I have been special friends for as long as we've known each other. You tutored my daughter, helped me to bring her up through those years when William was still stationed in India. I've depended on you and confided in you. There has been a bond between us, and not just a bond of shared responsibilities. Whether you agree with me or not, whether you want to hear me say it or not, through all those years you have been the principal man, the only man, in my life. We have shared this house and shared our lives. In every way but one, we have lived together. And if you've never guessed it I will tell you now, there have been many times through the years when I wished we could be together in every way. Does all this embarrass you?'

Arthur shook his head.

'I used to get very angry with you,' she went on. 'I told myself that you felt the same toward me as I did toward you, but you seemed determined that I should never know it. No matter what you might say to me now, I know I was right. In any case I'm not asking for corroboration from you. I knew as well as you did that there were walls and moats between us. I knew no way to get past those barriers but it's important for me to tell you now that I wanted to get past them.'

If Arthur had been carried along by her words and the emotions behind them, he seemed suddenly to have worked himself free. He squared himself in his chair, smiled in an angular way, and said, 'You know how grateful I am for the years I've spent here. Because of you, Evan had a foundation to his life that would have been missing otherwise. I know he's as grateful for your kindness as I am.'

'Kindness? For the love of God, Arthur, I'm not talking about *kindness* . . .'

'I hope you'll be very happy in your new marriage,' he went on. 'You deserve to be and I'm sure you will be.' He seemed to run out of words then. He sat stiff in his chair looking down at his hands. As Margaret sat looking at him, her eyes seemed to lose focus slowly. At last she turned her head and looked out through the bright morning window across the gardens.

10

In the short time since she'd last spoken to Cranston he seemed to have undergone a remarkable change. When she explained this later to Clara, Margaret said, 'You remember my telling you that he had pulled himself together, lost weight and cut down on his drinking. Taking long walks and riding horseback. Well, all that self-discipline, whatever inspired it, seems to have vanished. When we met, mid-afternoon, he hadn't shaved or brushed his hair. He was still wearing his slippers. With an old rumpled robe over his pyjamas. His face was flushed and swollen, and he never put down his glass except to refill it. It was beastly hot in his sitting-room but a log-fire crackled in the fireplace. The air was heavy with cigar smoke and perspiration and whisky fumes.'

Determined, however, to have a smooth and peaceful meeting, Margaret had ignored the heat, the odours, and Cranston's appearance, and settled into a chair opposite him. She had even responded to his slurred invitation to have a drink and had poured herself a sherry.

'Come here to gloat, have you? I expect you're carrying your divorce papers with you to show the staff and the neighbours. Telling them you've got rid of the Major at last, is that it? Proud of yourself, are you? Hair curled and lip-rouge on your mouth. All set for a new life, I wager. A flapper's life, is that what you're keen for? Champagne and cabarets in Soho. And a sleek young tango dancer for an escort? Low-cut dresses, black net stockings, and spike-heel slippers with rhinestone buckles. Is that what we can expect from you now?'

Margaret smiled. 'Not at all. I'm a bit too far along the path for that. Besides, I was never one for parties and night life even when I was twenty. No, William, I'm not here to gloat and I don't expect I'll turn into a glamorous new person. Nothing like that.'

'But you're not a frequent visitor here, are you? Not inclined to drop in to pass the time of day. Weeks go by when you never set foot in the west wing. When they mailed me those final papers I said to myself, "Ah, well, it's done. All over now. You've just been legally abandoned by a wife you never had."'

'Very amusing, William.'

'Not amusing at all, by God. It's the Lord's truth.'

'I hope you're not going to turn nasty. I didn't come here for a battle.'

'Came for a bit of praise perhaps. Some heart-felt congratulations for the way you've handled yourself these past months, you and the distinguished Sir Charles Tremont, he who parts the Red Sea several times each week. So I congratulate you both. You've parted the bloody Red Sea and drowned me in it.'

'It's over now, William. I won't be drawn into a discussion of something that's finished and done with.'

'That's Major William Cranston you're describing. Finished and done with.'

'Nonsense. You're still in your sixties. A long way to go.'

'What good is that? When they retired me from the army I was less than fifty. A young man. But I was finished and done with all the same. I'm surprised you didn't put me on the discard list straight away. Arthur Tagg was standing by then, just as he is now.'

'This has nothing to do with Arthur Tagg. I didn't come here to negotiate or defend myself. We've put all that behind us, thank God. I just came to talk to you, in a civilized manner. Just because we're no longer married I see no reason for us to be lifelong enemies.'

'A friendly divorce. That's the new language, isn't it? I read about it every day in *The Times*. New freedoms, new attitudes. You try on a wife or husband like a new coat. Wear it for a season perhaps till it has a few stains and buttons missing, then discard it and find another one.' When she didn't answer he said, 'No answer for that, eh? Did I hit the mark dead centre? Are you about to tell me you've chosen my successor?' When she was silent again he said, 'By God, I'm right. The ink's not dry on the divorce decree and already you're picking out night-dresses for your honeymoon.'

'You're disgusting, William. I meant what I said. I came here in hopes we could forget some of the painful things that have happened these past months, some of the unkind words we've said to each other. But you seem to have an unquenchable thirst for ugliness.'

He took a long drink from his glass, then refilled it. 'So that's what you think, is it? No wonder you couldn't wait to get rid of me. I'm not good enough for you and never have been. You married beneath you and you've had cause to regret it ever since.'

'I've had enough of this.' She stood up. 'Whatever you're thinking, I really did come here to try to make things better between us.'

'I know you did. And I'm glad you came. Don't go. I want you to stay. I promise to be an ideal ex-husband. I'll sit here like a fine gentleman and listen to whatever you have to say.'

'I have nothing more to say.'

'Of course you do. You always have a purpose. You're a purposeful woman.'

Margaret sank down in her chair. 'You're right,' she said, 'there is something I want to say to you. I didn't want you to hear it from someone else. I'm going to be married.'

He clapped his hands. 'By God, that's exciting news. At last Arthur Tagg will ascend to the throne. Let's pull the cord and get him in here. Drinks all round. The queen is taking on a new consort and a commoner at that. Twenty years of loyal service. More than that. He deserves everything you can give him. And I will give the bride away, of course. It's the least I can do.'

'I'm not marrying Arthur. No matter what you think, there was never any thought of my marrying him. He wouldn't have had me in any case.'

'Oh, now, let's not dance round the Major. Why else did he hang about for all those years?'

'I'm not planning to marry Arthur,' she went on. 'I'm going to marry Jack Brannigan.'

'Not Arthur Tagg?'

'No. Jack Brannigan.'

'Who in hell is Jack Brannigan?'

'You probably don't remember him. When the *Country Life* people came to photograph Wiswell Towers last spring, he took all the pictures. He's a photographer.'

After a long moment Cranston said, 'I must be thinking of another chap.'

'I don't think so. There was only one man taking pictures.'

'I only remember that stocky fellow with a square face whose trousers were never pressed. Trout told me he slept in a caravan in the car park outside the coach-house.'

'That's Brannigan,' Margaret said.

'You can't mean it.'

'Yes, I do mean it.'

Cranston put down his glass and stood up suddenly. 'For God's sake, Margaret, you can't marry that sort of fellow. He's not a gentleman. He's Irish.'

'Of course he's Irish. And of course he's not a gentleman.'

Cranston tottered about, unsteady on his feet. He stopped then behind the high-backed chair where he'd been sitting and gripped the top with both hands. 'I don't know why you're telling me this story but I know from the look in your eyes that it's not true.'

'It's true, William. A month from now we'll be married.'

'By God,' he said. He held on to the chair, worked his way round it, and sat down again. Finally he said, almost as if he were talking to himself, 'I knew you were carrying on with Tagg. Now it turns out you were also lying about with an Irish gypsy . . .'

'I was never carrying on with Arthur,' she said. 'I've told you that before and I'm telling you again. For the last time.'

'You're telling me you saved yourself for that Irishman? Is that it?'

She smiled. 'I wouldn't put it that way, but yes, I suppose I was saving myself for him.'

'Sweet Jesus,' he said. Then: 'You'll be abandoned by the entire county, you know.'

'I don't think so.'

'I hope you'll have the decency to live in County Cork or Killarney or wherever the bloody gypsies gather these days.'

'Jack's from Donegal. We're being married there but we plan to live here.'

'I don't believe what I'm hearing.'

'It's my home, William. Of course we'll live here.'

He put his empty glass down on the table beside him and didn't refill it. 'I won't have it,' he muttered.

'What did you say?'

He didn't answer. Finally she stood up, crossed the room, opened the door, then closed it softly behind her.

• CHAPTER 3 •

1

During the three years that Sarah had been at Miss
Endicott's school in Cobham, Evan had visited her
several times. He had become acquainted with Miss
Endicott, who in spite of her militant spinsterhood
enjoyed having tea with personable young men. She was
particularly aware of Evan, who two years earlier had
praised her school in an article for the *Daily Telegraph*.

On this occasion, however, several days after he'd
received the clipping of Sarah's interview, when he went
to Cobham to talk with her and when he attempted first
to pay his respects to the headmistress, he was told by her
assistant that Miss Endicott was unavailable.

'Perhaps I'll be able to talk to her a bit later. After I've
seen Sarah,' Evan said.

'I'm afraid not. Miss Endicott is occupied for the entire
day.'

When Sarah was informed that Evan had come to see
her she refused to talk to him. But when Evan insisted,
when he told the assistant that he had come on urgent
family business, Sarah was at last escorted to one of the
reception rooms.

When they were alone together, Sarah looking pale and
sullen, Evan said, 'What's come over you? I was told you
didn't want to see me.'

'I didn't and I don't.'

'I don't understand.'

'I have my reasons.'

'When I saw you in London you were all smiles.'

'I've learned a few things about you since then.'

'Ohhh . . . so that's it,' Evan said. 'What have you heard?'

'I'd rather not talk about it.'

'Won't I be allowed to defend myself?'

'No. There's no point to it. I'd prefer not to talk to you at all.'

'But I want to talk to you. Did you let yourself be interviewed by a man named Neal Dyer?'

'I don't remember. I might have.'

Evan took the magazine-cutting out of his wallet and handed it to her. 'This appeared in Los Angeles a week or so ago.'

She unfolded the page and read it through slowly. When she looked up she was smiling.

'Did you say those things or did Dyer make it all up?'

'He got it just right,' she said. 'That's exactly what I said. Has my mother seen it yet?'

'I don't think so. I hope not.'

'Why? What's the difference? I want her to see it. It's time she stopped thinking of me as a little girl in a school uniform.'

'Maybe it is. But there must be a better way to bring that about.'

'You think so? I don't. The man asked my opinion about certain matters and I told him. He asked what I planned to do with my life and I told him.'

'Are you saying you don't give a damn if someone else's feelings get hurt?'

'But this article is about me. That's why I like it. It concerns nobody else but me.'

'Not exactly. You told him you've changed your name to Kincaid. That's simply not true.'

'Not yet. But it will be.'

'You told him you were an only child. What was the point of that?'

'Because it was me the man wanted to find out about. Not my odd brother with mud on his boots and frogs in his pockets.'

'Did it ever occur to you that this interview might be picked up by a British newspaper and circulated here?'

'I hope it will be,' she said. 'Any young woman my age would be happy to have her picture in the paper. You see, I'm serious about becoming an actress. So the sooner people come to know who I am, the better. You know a lot about the theatre and the movies. You know that's true.'

'I know nothing of the sort. There are hundreds of girls – thousands maybe, in California and London – who've been photographed in bathing-suits and had their pictures in the paper. But they're not actresses and they never will be.'

'Well, I don't care about that. I see no point in discussing this with you. I don't know why you came down here.'

'There's a simple answer. I was hoping you'd tell me that you'd never given this interview, that you'd never heard of Neal Dyer.'

'Then you made the trip for nothing, didn't you?'

'I hope not. I hope I can still find a way to keep this from Sophie and your grandmother and Kincaid and Trevor.'

'Why bother? It's just a scrap of paper. It can't kill anybody. And even if it could, why should you appoint yourself as a saviour? Are you a perfect person?'

'No. But I care about all the people who are involved.'

'You care about me?'

'Of course I do. You know that. You've always known it.'

'I thought I knew it but I was wrong. If you care about someone you tell them the truth, don't you? You don't lie to them about important things.'

'I don't know what you're talking about.'

'Oh yes, you do. You know precisely what I'm talking about. You just won't admit it. You're about to get married, aren't you?'

'What gave you that idea?'

'Just answer me. Tell me the truth.'

'Am I *ever* going to get married? I'm sure I will.'

'I don't mean that,' she said. 'You're going to marry that actress, Mary Cecil. You've been living together since you went to California and now you're going to get married.'

Evan shook his head. 'She's already married. I couldn't marry her if I wanted to.'

'I know she's married. But she's getting a divorce, isn't she? And as soon as she's divorced she's going to marry you. It's true, isn't it?'

'Who told you all this?'

'Neal Dyer told me. He knows everything that's going on out there in California.'

'I've never heard of him out there. He lives in London, doesn't he?'

'It doesn't matter where he lives. He knows about you and Mary Cecil. And so do I. Ever since he told me I've been reading about her. She's seven years older than you. Did you know that? She's got a daughter older than I am. When I'm eighteen, Mary Cecil will be *forty-three*! Did you ever think about that?'

Evan smiled. 'No, to tell you the truth I never did think about that.'

'Well, I've thought about it. I thought about it a lot.'

'So that's why you didn't want to talk to me today?'

'Why would I want to talk to you?' she said. 'I don't trust you now.'

'Shame on you. No one cares more about you than I do. And you know it.'

'That's right. And you care about Sophie and Trevor and Margaret and Kincaid. Loyal friend of the family. But I don't want you as a friend. I told you that in London. I love you.'

'And I love you.'

'No, you don't. You love me and Trevor together. Sophie's children. That kind of love. You think I'm still a baby, but I'm not. Maybe you're the baby. Maybe that's why you want somebody older than you to mother you. I promise you, when I'm twenty years old you won't think I'm too young for you. But maybe by then I won't care what you think.'

2

When Evan was a small boy his father had said to him, 'You must never feel sorry for yourself. That's a dreadful habit to fall into. It's a temptation, of course. It's always there waiting for us. But that's all the more reason why it must be avoided. It's a career, you see, if we're not careful. Full-time occupation. Every day of your life you'll find some situation or circumstance that could prompt you to say, "Why *me*? Why have I been singled out for this annoyance or this burden?" And from there it's easy to slip into a frame of mind that defines you as a luckless person, one whose future is destined to be as grey and bleak as his present. If you convince yourself that the world is against you, it will undoubtedly come to be true.'

Such counsel, such advice, is easier to give, of course, than it is to follow. But in the case of Arthur Tagg, he himself religiously followed the road-signs he set up for his son.

Arthur had a gift, of course. Or perhaps it was simply a lifelong habit. He used his senses fully. He was a careful observer and an attentive listener. He saw and heard and remembered. When he saw two blind people sitting together in a train coach, laughing and talking, he remembered that incident and measured it against his own experience. Less handsome than one of his brothers, less articulate than the others, he studied himself carefully to discover and to isolate areas of himself that were distinctive and valuable. He focused on these then, when he compared himself with his brothers.

He felt fortunate always that his father was able to clothe him well, to house him comfortably, and to provide him with a solid education. As he sympathized with the ignorance and the poverty he came into contact with, he never failed to feel blessed by his own good fortune. He had been well trained and well treated at university, and though he was not an athlete or a leader of men he was included always by his fellows, and respected and encouraged by his teachers.

Since his days in lower school he had been an attentive reader of history, geography, and sociology. With a great curiosity about peoples and countries other than his own, he had taken pains to inform himself in depth about places he had never seen, to familiarize himself with customs, religions, habits and values that were foreign to most Britons. He accepted without question the fact that life under the Union Jack was not a guarantee of fulfilment or contentment, any more than life in Tibet or Uruguay promised disappointment. Consequently he was not a frenetic patriot. He appreciated England as he did most other elements of his life but he did not believe that there was no other place to live or prosper or raise one's children. When he met Amy, followed her home to America, and chose to stay on there, his father said, 'Unusual fellow, Arthur. More adventurous than one might expect. Keen to see what's just across the wall. Might very well have settled in Prague. Or the Cameroon. Or God knows where. No surprise at all, not to me, that he's living in Chicago. He might even take root there now that he has a son, may never set foot on British soil again.'

His father's prediction might very well have come true if things had worked out differently between Arthur and his wife. Because he was indeed enchanted by life in Chicago, by their flat near the lake on Superior Street, by the money and energy and raw human power of the city. He discovered baseball and American football. He walked for miles beside the lake, up and down Michigan Avenue, Rush Street, and Wabash Avenue. When Evan was big enough to walk he went with his father to Grant Park, Lincoln Park, the Aquarium, and the art galleries. They patrolled the city together.

Unlike many immigrants, however, Arthur made no attempt to turn himself into an American. He continued to walk and talk like a British gentleman. His suits and greatcoats were made by an English tailor in a shop on Wacker Drive. Every two years he sent away to Lock's for a new hat and his boots came from Halliburton's on Jermyn Street. All the same behind that British façade there was a new-born American, a man content with his life, his marriage, and himself.

Then, with no warning, Amy left him, left her son, and went back to the man she had married and never divorced before she met Arthur. Even so, shocked and disbelieving, Arthur felt no impulse to return to England. Chicago was his home now, he told himself, and Evan's home. Also he believed, secretly and stubbornly, that Amy would come back, that the bell would ring one summer evening – he never envisioned her returning in winter – he would open the hall door and she would be standing there.

As he continued to search for her, as his letters came back to him stamped NO SUCH PERSON AT THIS ADDRESS, he went on with his daily routine, walking to his job each morning on Randolph Street, returning each late-afternoon to spend the evening with Evan; through all those worrisome and lonely months he persisted in his belief that he and the boy would stay on in Chicago.

At last, however, one of his letters came back as the others had, but this time, it looked as though it had been steamed opened and resealed. And the letter when he removed it from the envelope seemed to have coffee stains on it. That single homely detail stung him, hurt him in a new way. He had a sharp picture in his mind, suddenly, of Amy sitting in her kitchen with a shirt-sleeved man – was he really her husband, and if not did it matter? – the two of them drinking coffee as she read Arthur's letter aloud. They laughed, of course. Why wouldn't they? There was something amusing, after all, about an abandoned man continuing to search through months and years for a woman who had gone off with someone else. Arthur sat in his chair that night, long after Evan had gone to bed. He found an unopened bottle of bourbon, a long-ago Christmas gift from his employer, and began to drink. At last, he, too, was able to laugh. At himself. But it was an ugly sound. The next morning he made enquiries about a passage to England for himself and Evan.

Whatever misgivings he'd had about returning home vanished quickly after he met Margaret Cranston, after she engaged him to tutor Sophie and to live at Wiswell Towers with Evan. Everything about the arrangement seemed providential to him. He was in Northumberland, many miles from Salisbury, where his brothers lived, indeed he was in a county where he knew no one and no one knew him. Since he'd been forced to make a new start, to separate himself from everything that had gone before, he felt fortunate indeed to be in that far corner of England, warm and snug and appreciated in a fine old house. Although he told himself repeatedly that he was only an employee, that he could become redundant at any time, something inside him felt, from the very first, that he had found the place where he was meant to be. As he took on new duties, as he gradually became, with the Major away, the functioning head of household, he accepted that role with humility and gratitude, did his work conscientiously and neither demanded nor expected special treatment. But the rewards were there all the same. He and Evan were included, made part of the Cranston family. As he carefully warned his son that Sophie was not his true sister, as he reminded himself that Margaret's kindness to him was simply that of a warm and benevolent employer toward a trusted employee, he knew, he sensed, he accepted the fact that other bonds had been firmly put into place, other currents had joined the stream. Without allowing himself to define it or rejoice in it, he knew that he and Margaret were living the warm rewarding life that people hope for but seldom find in marriage. They never kissed or embraced. They went to their separate bedrooms in separate wings of the house each night. But in all other ways they were joined as a man and his wife are joined. In his mind Arthur went no further than assuring himself that he had a permanent position at Wiswell Towers but inside he felt another sort of permanence altogether.

Permanence was the key word of course. Although he had curiosity about other places and other peoples, he was not truly adventurous as his father had believed. Arthur was in no sense a free spirit. As he read about foreign lands, gathered information, and drew conclusions, he did so from the comfort and security of certain solid institutions, his family home, his school, his place of employment. His reluctance to leave Chicago had been a part of that syndrome. So also was his attachment to the Cranstons. It had taken a visceral shock to tear him away from Chicago. Only the same sort of jolt could have brought about his decision to leave the Towers, to leave Northumberland, to leave Margaret Cranston.

He told himself, as he composed his letter of resignation – he was unable simply to announce it to Margaret – that there was nothing personal about it. Simply a recognition of changing circumstances, alterations in the inner structure of the household. Had he been honest with himself he would have admitted that during his tenure there had been many such changes: when Sophie had gone off to school at age sixteen and there had been no more need for him as a tutor; when she married at seventeen and then came home just after the war years with two babies; when Major Cranston was released from military service at the end of the war; and most recently when the Major had tried and failed to have Margaret discharge him.

Through all these adjustments and upheavals, Arthur had stayed smoothly afloat, confident of his abilities and sure of his place. Now, however, the structure and solidity that were emblematic in his mind of his life these past twenty-odd years, seemed to have tumbled. Although his relationship with the Major had always been wary and tentative, although Cranston had made no effort to conceal his dislike for the man who seemed to him both presumptuous and ambitious, Arthur was disturbed by the news of Margaret's impending divorce. He might have been expected to see such an event as a cause for celebration. He knew as everyone in the household knew, that she had had an unhappy and bizarre married life. But all the same, whatever his own relationship with Cranston, the Major's absence from the house would create a vacuum. Circumstances would change. New doors would open. New rhythms. The known disturbing factor might disappear but any number of unknown dragons might slip in through the garden.

Such wool-gathering and anticipation of chaos were nothing compared with the shock that Arthur felt, but carefully concealed, when Margaret told him she planned to marry Jack Brannigan. As he nodded and smiled and wished her well, as he took refuge in cool formality, as he slowly transformed the warm openness that had characterized their relationship from the beginning into a cautious dialogue between employer and employee, he behaved as if he were John Trout, the butler, or Alfred, the groom.

One morning when he was still sleeping Evan's telephone rang. It was Alan Winkler at the *Telegraph*.

'Jesus,' Evan said, 'I know you keep brutal hours but don't force them on me. What time is it?'

'Eight-fifteen. I've been up since six.'

'And now you're ringing up all your friends.'

'Not quite. The truth is I have some news for you. Family matters, you might say. You know a little weekly paper called *Tatler Two*?'

'I've seen it. It's a rag.'

'Of course it is. They put it together in an old garage in Frith Street. Or so I'm told. It's total rubbish.'

'But they sell all they can print, I expect.'

'Exactly.'

'Can I go back to sleep now?'

'Not yet. Someone just put the latest issue on my desk. Shirley Farmer, as a matter of fact. You remember Shirley. She's a great fan of yours. Cried her eyes out when your play closed last year.'

'Good for her. Tell her I dream about her every night.'

'Shirley saw this piece in the paper and thought you'd want to know about it. I think she's right.'

Evan was full-awake now. 'I hope it's not what I think it is.'

'It's an interview with Sophie's daughter.'

'Oh, Christ. And a picture in a bathing-suit?'

'That's right. I guess you've seen it,' Winkler said.

'I've seen it all right. It came out earlier in Los Angeles. I was hoping it wouldn't get picked up here. Do you know this bastard, Neal Dyer?'

'Neal's all right. Used to work at the *Daily Mail*.'

'He's a bastard.'

'He's not a bad sort,' Winkler said. 'Just trying to

'pay the rent like everybody else.'

As soon as he was off the telephone with Winkler, Evan tried to call Sarah at her school. He was told she was attending a lecture and couldn't be reached. When he asked to speak to Miss Endicott he was told she was in a meeting and could not be interrupted.

Ever since Mary had sent him the press-cutting from California, and particularly since his meeting with Sarah at her school, Evan had been poised to tell Kincaid and Sophie what he knew. But each time he was about to pick up the phone, each time he told himself that of course they must know, another cautious voice told him that he must stay clear of the whole business, pretend ignorance and hope that somehow they wouldn't see the interview.

Now, however, he knew he couldn't keep out of it. As soon as he'd shaved and dressed, he rang Sophie's number. When the butler answered he said, 'It's Evan, Oliver. I need to speak to Sophie.'

'I'm sorry. Mrs Kincaid has gone out. Will you speak to Mr Kincaid?'

When Kincaid came on the phone Evan said, 'Sorry to ring you so early. I was looking for Sophie. Oliver says she's out.'

'Drove down to see Sarah. Left first thing this morning.'

'Some problem at the school?'

'I don't think so. She talked with Miss Endicott last evening and she decided to drive down today. Just routine, I expect.'

'I hope you're right but I think you're wrong. I have to talk to you about something.'

On his way over to Arlington Street, Evan had the taxi wait while he picked up a copy of *Tatler Two* at a newspaper kiosk. When he and Kincaid sat down in the breakfast-room Evan showed him the interview. It was identical to the one that had appeared earlier in California but in this paper a photograph of Kincaid appeared alongside the picture of Sarah.

Kincaid only glanced at the article then put it on the table beside him. 'I was afraid this would happen.'

'So you've seen it?'

Kincaid nodded. 'I saw the original version, the one that came out in California. I cabled Thorne and tried to get it killed, so it wouldn't be reprinted here. But it looks as if he didn't get the job done.'

'Then Sophie knows about it.'

'No. I didn't tell her. Thorne's publicity people send me a bundle of that crap every week. Usually I pay no attention to it. But this time the piece with Sarah's picture was right on top. I couldn't miss it.'

'Now what happens?'

'We'll have to wait and see. You said you just bought this copy on the street; a lot of other people will be doing the same thing. We can't buy up every copy in London, so sooner or later Sophie's going to see it. Or somebody will tell her about it.'

'It's a hell of a lot better if she hears it from you, isn't it?'

'That's what I was about to say. But it may be too late for that. Maybe Miss Endicott knows about it. It's a cinch that Sarah knows about it. And unless I miss my guess she'll tell Sophie as soon as she sees her.'

Evan was tempted to tell Kincaid about his conversation with Sarah about the interview but he decided against it. Since he hadn't told Kincaid or Sophie before, there was no point in telling them now. Kincaid believed that he'd known nothing about the interview until Winkler called him that morning, so Evan let it rest there.

'I hope Sophie does find out before she gets home,' Evan said. 'I wouldn't want to be the one to tell her.'

'You won't be. I'll take care of that. This isn't the end of the world, you know. Sophie can handle it. It's not the first time Sarah's acted up and it won't be the last.'

'But this is something new. It's all so damned public. Sophie hates that.'

Kincaid nodded. 'I don't much like that part of it either but I suppose I'll get used to it. And Sophie will have to get used to it, too. If Sarah's changing her name to Kincaid, or pretending she has, and if she keeps passing out pictures of herself in a bathing-suit, she'll be in the papers every day.'

4

Sophie sat with Jane Endicott in her second-floor parlour, a room that was seldom seen by the parents of her students and then only on grave occasions. The two women had talked urgently together for several minutes. Now they were silent. Sophie's throat and cheeks, however, were flushed pink and Miss Endicott's stern face was chalkier and more stern than usual.

'How dare you,' Sophie said at last, 'summon me down here at such short notice and tell me my daughter is in danger of being dismissed from your school.'

'She has been dismissed, I'm afraid. If I didn't make that clear . . .'

'You did make it clear but I don't accept it. If it were as final as you say, surely you would have had the decency to tell me when you telephoned last evening.'

'At that time no final decision had been made. Our committee met only last night and the decision to dismiss Sarah was unanimous.'

'Are you telling me that after a single telephone call from one of your alumnae . . .'

'Lady Crispin, a prominent alumna and a loyal supporter.'

'Both my mother and I are also generous supporters of your school.'

'Indeed you are. And that has made my task doubly difficult. But at last the committee could only conclude that Sarah is out of place here.'

'She's been here for three years. Has she been out of place for all that time?'

'As you say,' Miss Endicott went on, 'you and your mother are respected by all of us. Because of that respect we have tried to make allowances for your daughter.'

'Are you saying she's been a problem ever since she came here?'

'Not in the first year. But increasingly since then. In the beginning she was a sweet child. Intelligent and co-operative. Then, gradually, she became quite wilful. Unwilling to conform. Setting a bad example for the other girls.'

'If she was such a problem, if she behaved so badly, why was I never told about it?'

Miss Endicott attempted a smile. 'Once our young women are placed in our hands we believe it's our responsibility to mould them, to teach them the code they will live by, to correct the habits they may have learned before coming to us. We don't feel it's appropriate to turn to the parents for help. When we fail, the failure is ours. I'm sorry to report that we have failed with your daughter.'

'Please don't refer to Sarah as a failure. In my mind *you* have failed to make your case. You've given me a flimsy story of an interview that Sarah supposedly gave to a newspaper reporter but you won't show me the article you're referring to.'

'I can't show it to you. I haven't seen it and I haven't read it. It appeared in the sort of journal that I would never read.'

'Then how do you know . . .'

'It was read to me over the telephone. By Lady Crispin, a woman of taste and solid moral credentials.'

'I know Roberta Crispin. I know her very well. She's a perfectly decent woman, I suppose, but that doesn't qualify her to sit in judgement of my daughter.'

'The final judgement was mine. Lady Crispin only supplied the evidence.'

'And because of that phone call . . .'

'No, Mrs Kincaid, that was Sarah's final transgression. Not her only one. I assume your mother told you that we voted to expel her once before. Last year it was.'

'No, I did not know that. Why wasn't I told?'

'You were in America I believe. So we dealt with Mrs Cranston. We assumed she would inform you. On that occasion Sarah left school without permission. That means automatic dismissal. But your mother interceded with a great deal of vigour so in the end, after Sarah had spent some days at your mother's home in Northumberland, we allowed her to return to school.'

'I assure you, Miss Endicott, you will see a great deal of vigour and indignation on this occasion as well. I will not accept this story of a newspaper interview till I've seen the evidence myself. I can't imagine why any newspaper would want to interview a fifteen-year-old schoolgirl or how it would be so startling if they did.'

'As I understand it, Sarah was approached because of her relationship with your present husband . . .'

'He is not my *present* husband. He is my *husband*.'

'Of course he is. But he's also an actor, I'm told. In American films. It was this fact, undoubtedly, that prompted the interview with Sarah. But she also furnished them a photograph, a rather daring one, I'm told, of herself in a bathing-costume.'

After a moment Sophie said, 'What did Sarah say when you asked her about all this?'

'She was quite sullen and unresponsive. But she admitted she'd slipped away from the school grounds and met the reporter in a restaurant in the village. She also admitted saying all the things that were attributed to her.'

'She's seen the printed article then?'

Miss Endicott nodded. 'She said Mr Tagg showed it to her when he visited her here not long ago.'

'I see.' Then: 'When you spoke with her last did you tell her she was being dismissed?'

'Yes, I did.'

'What did she say?'

'I hesitate to say. It's not a pleasant thing to repeat.'

'What did she say, Miss Endicott?'

'She looked at me in a saucy way and said, "Thank God!" '

As soon as her meeting with Miss Endicott was over, Sophie said, 'Please have Sarah brought here. I'll take her home to London with me until we can untangle this affair and decide what actually happened.'

'But she isn't here. We discovered she was gone just after I spoke to you on the telephone last evening. We assumed she'd gone home as she did that other time.'

'You assumed? She was in your charge and you're telling me you don't know where she is?'

Miss Endicott looked uncomfortable. 'I'm sure she's at your home in London. She must be there.'

'She left here last night, you say. And I say, she wasn't at my home when I left this morning.'

'Perhaps if you telephone home now . . .'

'That's what I'm going to do. Please ask your secretary to ring the number.'

When the call came through, Sophie spoke to Oliver and to her housekeeper, Mrs O'Haver. Then, while the servants did a thorough search of the house, she talked to Kincaid. When she put the receiver back in its cradle she said to Miss Endicott, 'Sarah's not there. She hasn't been there.'

'Perhaps we should call the police.'

'No, you will not call the police. My family will take care of all that in London.'

5

Through Charles Tremont, the family was put in contact with Harold Mayweather, a private investigator. His appearance was that of a successful banker. Or cabinet minister perhaps. When Evan and Kincaid met with him at the Reform Club he said, 'A simple matter, isn't it? Almost a rite of passage these days. The war brought on these changes. Restless youngsters all round. Eager to define themselves, prove they're grown-ups. Damned disturbing to their parents, of course, but as I say, it's a common occurrence. My office must get twenty calls a week about children who've wandered off somewhere. Usually I send the parents along to one of my associates. Let the young chaps handle these little escapades. But when Tremont calls I take charge myself.'

'Her mother is very anxious that this should be kept quiet,' Evan said. 'No police stumbling about and nothing in the newspapers.'

Mayweather touched his lips with his forefinger. 'That goes without saying. Discretion and silence are the bywords of my profession.'

'We know she hasn't gone to her grandmother's home in Northumberland, and she hasn't come to her mother's house here in London, so there's no telling where she's gone. You may have a difficult time locating her.'

'It's possible. But I think not.' Mayweather patted the breast pocket of his jacket. 'I have her description here, along with the photographs you've given me, so unless she's a very clever lass who's determined not to be found, I expect we'll have her in hand in two or three days. You see, most of these young people who run off want to be found. They're anxious to see what effect it's had on their parents. They want to be noticed. Want to seem important. Once they've accomplished that, they're more than ready to come home.'

'How do you decide where to start looking?' Kincaid asked.

'Depends on what I'm told by the parents. If there's a summer home, I go there first. If there's a favourite aunt or uncle, or a sweetheart or a very close friend, I go to them. In a situation like this one, where the family has no idea where the child may have gone, I go to Brighton.'

'Why Brighton?'

'I can't explain it. But nine times out of ten when a young girl decides to slip away on her own, she ends up in Brighton. They have their hair bobbed, put on lipstick and mascara, and stroll up and down the esplanade, eating sausage-rolls and ice-cream and watching the gulls fly in. No doubt of it. Brighton's the place. I expect your Miss Sarah will be back in her own bed before you know it.'

Early in the afternoon of the third day Sarah, accompanied by Mr Mayweather, arrived at Sophie's house on Arlington Street. She'd been found in a milk-bar on the promenade in Brighton, wearing lipstick and mascara as predicted, with her hair cut as short as a boy's.

That evening after dinner Margaret, who'd come down by train the day before, sat in the library with her daughter and Kincaid and Evan.

'You're very quiet about this,' she said to Sophie. 'I admire you. All the way down here on the train I was afraid I'd find you a total wreck. I'm delighted to see how calm you are.'

Sophie smiled. 'I'm anything but calm. If I seem that way it's because I don't know what to do or what to say.'

'Is Sarah terribly upset?' Margaret asked. 'I assumed she'd come down to dinner.'

'She said she wanted to eat in her room tonight. She and I will have a long talk tomorrow. I was so shocked by her appearance it was hard for me to look at her. We talked briefly but I decided it was better to let the dust settle a bit.'

'She is upset then?'

'Not at all. She came into the house as though she was popping into the Ritz sweet shop for a square of nougat. All smiles. Very taken with Mr Mayweather, it seemed. Laughing and joking together. Home from a great lark.'

'What happens now? Has Miss Endicott reconsidered?'

Sophie shook her head. 'I'm afraid not. I had a long talk with her again today and she is absolutely resolute. She simply won't have Sarah back at her school. It's irrelevant in any case. Sarah made it clear that she won't go back there.'

'But she must be in school,' Margaret said.

'Not there. It's out of the question.'

'There are other schools, of course. But a girl doesn't want a school expulsion on her record. One doesn't want to go through life explaining something like that. Still, once we've arranged for her to go to Webster's or Churchgate, or Eastland perhaps, she'll settle down, I'm sure. This set-back will be forgotten.'

'It's not just the Endicott school she's fed up with. She says she won't go to any school.'

'That's not her decision to make. She'll come round after she's thought it over.'

'I don't think so,' Sophie said. 'If we send her off somewhere she'll simply run away again. That's what she told me and I believe her.'

'I've never heard of such a thing. She's little more than a child. Is that what we've come to? Fifteen-year-old girls making their own decisions? If she absolutely refuses to go to school, what's to be done?' She turned to Kincaid, 'What do you think?'

'I'm not her father.'

'That doesn't matter. You're a sensible man and you're part of the family now. So it's your problem, too.'

'All right. I'll tell you what I think. I expect she's feeling pretty proud of herself because she shook everyone up a bit. She's discovered that if she misbehaves she gets all sorts of attention. That's a big discovery for a kid.'

'But a dangerous one,' Evan said.

'Exactly,' Kincaid went on. 'If she has the idea that she's found a formula that will last all her life, she's in for a great deal of trouble. And so are you, Sophie. If she were my daughter I'd tell her that no one wants to conduct her adult life for her. But until she's legally of age, as long as she's a part of this family, she has certain duties to fulfil, just as we all do. In her case her principal duty is to stay on at school.'

'But what if she runs away?' Sophie said.

'Then she'll be sent back. She must be convinced of that. I don't know a great deal about the British school system but I'm sure there are places that know how to deal with difficult children . . .'

'Of course there are,' Margaret said, 'but we mustn't have Sarah in such a school.'

'I'm sure you wouldn't have to. If she's told that a very strict school will be the final solution she might be less anxious to run away from a better one.'

'It makes sense,' Evan said. 'I think Kincaid's right. If she gets the idea that she can set her own course, no matter what, I think you'll end up with one crisis after another. And each one will be harder to deal with than the previous one.'

'We're not training a horse here. We're talking about a young girl,' Margaret said.

'Not in her eyes,' Evan said. 'We've all read the interview she gave. It's obvious she thinks of herself as a woman. She looks in the glass and says, "I'm no longer a child. Why should I be treated like one?" '

Margaret turned to Sophie. 'You've gone dead silent all of a sudden.'

'I'm listening,' she said. 'You're all trying to put patches on things so they'll work again. And all I can think is that this mess might have been prevented if I'd had the information you people have. Not you, Kincaid, but Margaret and Evan.'

'I don't know what you mean,' Margaret said.

'Of course you do. Don't misunderstand me. I'm sure your intentions were admirable but all the same I wish I'd known that Sarah left school before. When I was in California last year.'

'You're right. I should have told you,' Margaret said. 'And I planned to at the time. But I didn't want to risk spoiling your lovely trip. So I decided to wait till you came home. But by then the situation had righted itself, or so it seemed. Sarah had settled in at school again and it seemed senseless to bring it up. Perhaps I was wrong but it didn't seem so at the time. Sarah was just feeling restless and unloved, as we all did at her age, and she needed to talk to someone. She stayed with me at the Towers, I straightened matters out with Jane Endicott on the telephone, and in a few days Sarah was back in her room at school.'

'I'm not quarrelling with you, Mother. I understand what you're saying. But as Kincaid said, these incidents can be cumulative. Once she'd left school and got away with it, the next time came easier. If I'd known about the first time, maybe I could have prevented this time.'

'Now it's my turn on the griddle, is that right?' Evan said.

'I'm not angry,' Sophie said. 'I'm baffled. When Endicott told me you'd talked to Sarah about that rotten interview, that you'd driven down there to show it to her, I couldn't believe my ears. Didn't it occur to you to tell me or Kincaid so it wouldn't come as such a shock when we read it or heard about it?'

When Evan glanced at him Kincaid said, 'He didn't have to tell me. I already knew about it. It came to me in a bundle of press-cuttings from the studio.'

'And you didn't tell me? Why on earth . . .'

'I didn't want you to know about it. I knew it would upset you. So I took a chance. I thought you might never see it or be told about it. I tried to keep it from being reprinted here in London but it didn't work.'

'My God,' Sophie said. 'I can't believe what I'm hearing. Am I some helpless soul who has to be protected from everything that's not sweet or pretty? It wasn't even a conspiracy. Each of you made separate decisions that I

103

shouldn't be told something that has turned out to be extremely important to Sarah and to me. In the long run it may be important to all of us. I'm not some fragile little creature who weeps and moans about the house. Surely you don't see me that way. Still, you three people, who know me better than anyone does, each of you, individually, decided not only that I could be kept in the dark about this but that I should be. I'm astonished. I'm . . . truly baffled.'

'You've got it all twisted round,' Kincaid said. 'This isn't some great betrayal. When you care about somebody, it's perfectly natural and understandable that you don't want to bring them bad news, especially when it comes from a lousy scandal sheet like the one in Los Angeles or the other one here in London. If you read in a paper that I was a hopelessly ugly man and an embarrassing actor, would you hurry home in a taxi just to tell me what you'd read?'

'Of course not. But this is a different case.'

'I don't think so. It's a different example of the same case.'

'It's different because the article wasn't about me. Or *you*. It was about Sarah.'

'But it's done, Sophie,' Evan said. 'It's all over. Now we have to forget about it.'

'I can't forget it. I'm not even sure she said those things.'

'Neither was I. That's why I went to see her at her school, to show her the clipping and ask if it was an honest interview. She read it over and said it was all accurate.'

'When the article first came out in California, when you saw it, Evan, and you, Kincaid, didn't it ever occur to you that I should see it so I'd have a chance to take it up with Sarah? If I'd been able to do that, don't you think she might still be in school?'

'No, I don't,' Kincaid said. 'She'd have been out, regardless, the minute Miss Endicott knew about the interview.'

'He's right,' Evan said.

'No, Evan, he's not right. But even if he is, I still should have had a chance to participate rather than have everything dumped in my lap after the fact.'

They all sat quietly then, the sinners and the sinned-against, sipping their port and making separate assessments of the extent of the damage and what survival tactics might be appropriate.

6

Kincaid volunteered to go see Trevor at St Alban's. Damage control. Tell him about the interview if he hadn't already seen it. Or try to take the edge off some of Sarah's statements if he had seen it.

'You've never been up here by yourself before,' Trevor said.

'No. Just once with your mother.'

'Good. I can take you round. Show you off. You're famous in this place. *Bushranger*'s a magic word here. You must be tired of people falling all over you. My mother says you can't walk down the street without having somebody come up to you.'

Kincaid smiled. 'I admit I'm not crazy about that part of it. I just keep telling myself it won't last much longer. Once the picture's had its run, once it's out of the theatres, there'll be somebody else to chase.'

'I don't think so,' Trevor said. 'As soon as you make another movie, people will be after you again.'

'We'll see about that.'

They walked down Fishkill Street together, turned left at the bottom of the hill, then left again into the school gardens. When they sat down on a bench under a bent-over yew tree, Trevor said, 'You didn't come up here just so we could stroll round the school gardens, did you?'

'Don't see you often enough. So here I am.'

'That's nice. But I'll bet you came to talk to me about Sarah, about that interview she gave the paper.'

'So you've seen it?'

'First day it came out, I suppose. Half the chaps in the school buy those scandal sheets. They like to read that sexy junk. So do I.'

'What did you think of Sarah's interview?'

'Didn't surprise me. Nothing Sarah does surprises me. How did Mum feel about it?'

'She didn't like it much. Didn't like it at all. It embarrassed her, I think.'

'I thought it would. She worries a lot about what other people think.'

'Did it embarrass you?'

Trevor shook his head. 'Sarah's my sister, for God's sake. And my older sister at that. I know her like my pocket. She was happy to spend time with me as long as she could boss me around but once I started making up my own mind about things she dropped me like a hot brick. That remark she made about being an only child – that's the real Sarah talking. That's the way she thinks of herself. All alone on a platform with people looking up at her and clapping their hands. No room in her life for a/shaggy-dog brother like me. She gets a pained look on her face everytime she has to introduce me to somebody. Usually she just says, "This is Trevor. Isn't he cute?" Then she makes a face.'

'Did you know she wants to be an actress?'

Trevor shook his head. 'She never wanted that before. Not till you and Mum got married. Then when she saw you on the screen and the picture was a big success, she must have thought if you can do it, anybody can. I don't want to hurt your feelings but that's the way she is. She's like one of those lizards that changes colour all the time. Sarah likes whatever's going to benefit her. Why do you think she wants to change her name to Kincaid? Not hard to figure that one out. She thinks it will help

106

her in some way. That's Sarah all over.'

Kincaid smiled. 'Sounds to me as if you're not too wild about your sister.'

'You're wrong. I like her a lot. I might even love her if she'd let me. But I also know what she's like. I know her better than anyone does. She knows that and it makes her cautious. She talks about how generous she is but she only gives away what she can spare. And she can't spare me much of anything. But what the hell, Sarah didn't invent that attitude. I have half a dozen friends in this school with sisters just like her. They're not mean exactly. They're just fully occupied with themselves.'

'She says she doesn't want to go back to school. Do you think she means it?'

'Of course she means it. She never wants to do anything she's expected to do. That's why I don't take her seriously when she says she wants to be an actress. I have a German friend here named Gus, who's from Cologne. His father's an actor in Berlin. I think he's famous there, Gus knows a lot of actors. He says when they're working they never do anything except what people tell them to do. Can you imagine Sarah taking orders from somebody? I can't. That's why she'll never be an actress. Except in her head. She just wants people to look at her. As long as she's the centre of attention, she'll be happy as anything. Not me. What I want is for people to leave me alone. That's why I'll probably be a painter. Nobody gets left alone as much as painters. Their houses always smell of turpentine. They have paint under their fingernails, they don't buy lunch for anybody, and they wear old clothes. I'm sorry you didn't meet my friend, Ben Quigley. He has a big messy house with lots of dogs. His wife likes him a lot and she's not afraid to show it. And he knows everything there is to know about painting.'

'Is he a good painter?'

'No, but that's all right. Everybody can't be good. At least Ben knows what's good, so it doesn't matter too much if his hand can't keep up with his head. He'd make a great teacher if he wanted to, but he's like me, he doesn't want a lot of people hanging about, asking dumb questions. Any picture he looks at, he can tell you what's wrong with it. Not in a bad way. He's not mean or jealous of other artists. Besides, he says there's no such thing as a perfect painting. He likes della Francesca and Ucello the best of all, and so do I. He's already carved a headstone for his grave when he dies. Under his name it says, "He bloody well did what he could."'

7

Late one night, a few days after Sarah was brought home from her Brighton adventure, when Kincaid and Sophie were preparing to go to bed, he said, 'That may be your opinion, and of course you're entitled to it, but I want you to know that I disagree with you. Totally and absolutely.'

She turned to him slowly and smiled. 'What in the world are you talking about? I didn't say anything. Not a word.'

'That's right. You didn't. You're as silent as a stone. These past few days you've had nothing to say.'

'I'm sorry,' she said. 'This hasn't been the happiest time of my life. I'm sure you guessed that.'

'You're still angry because nobody told you about Sarah's interview – is that it?'

'*Anger* isn't the word. As I said the other evening, it baffled me. It still does.'

'We were trying to protect you.'

'Of course you were. But I don't want that sort of protection.'

'You made that clear. We all understood you perfectly.'

'Was I so awful?'

He shook his head. 'Not at all. In any case I'd rather have you awful than completely silent.'

'It has nothing to do with us. I've just had a lot on my mind. A great deal to think about.'

'And what have you concluded?'

'Nothing profound,' she said. 'Except for one thing. I decided that this episode with Sarah may have been a blessing in disguise. If ever I needed an incident to illustrate my feelings about California I certainly have it.'

Kincaid tapped his forehead with a forefinger, 'Very thick skull. I don't understand what you're saying.'

'You understand all right. You must remember my saying I would never want to take Sarah and Trevor to California . . .'

'You said you thought they'd love it there.'

'I'm sure they would. For all the wrong reasons. That's why I don't want them to be there. I don't want them exposed to that fairy-tale life.'

'But they haven't been,' Kincaid said.

'Of course they have. Through you and the film you made. *One* film and already it's had an effect on them. Sarah's never behaved like this before.'

'She's never been fifteen before.'

'It's more than that. Look at Trevor. I know you say he's not impressed by the whole thing and maybe he isn't, not in the way that Sarah is. But I guarantee you, he looks at you differently now. He sees you as an important man.'

'What's wrong with that?'

'Nothing,' she said. 'If it were for the right reasons. But it's not. Can't you see? All of a sudden you're not his stepfather, the nice man who married his mother. You're a movie star. People follow you in the street. Your picture's always in the paper.'

'What are you saying? It's a sin to be well known?'

'No. I'm saying, it's a bore to be well known. And it's confusing to young people. They think being recognized means one is automatically and permanently important. That's not true, and you know it as well as I do.'

'It's all a question of values.'

'Exactly. That's what I've been talking about since the moment we arrived in California. Priorities. That's another word for it. It's what civilized life is all about, isn't it, knowing what's important and what isn't? If you think something truly valuable is worthless and if you attach a high value to something that has no value at all, then you're perfectly qualified to live in Julian Thorne's world. Am I right or am I wrong.'

'From your viewpoint you're right. No question about it. But most people aren't in a position to make those judgements. When you're looking for a job you find yourself in agreement with the man you're working for. Or if you're not in agreement you don't talk about it. Otherwise you find yourself working for somebody else. I've been working since I was six years old. I've never had a job that had any nobility or honour or truth connected with it. It was all commerce. Trading a part of yourself for the money you needed to stay alive. Nobody ever asked me how I felt about the work I was doing. Nobody cared. They just cared if I showed up on time and if I worked hard enough to earn the money they paid me. That's the way the world functions whether we like it or not. Thorne's business is no different. It's just done on a grand scale. There's more money at stake. But most of us do what we're told whether we make fifty cents an hour or five thousand a week.'

'We're not talking about the same thing.'

'Yes, we are. Hunger comes in different wrappings. A man who's hungry to see his name up in lights is no less desperate than a man who has no food for his family.'

'But he should be. That's my point. Otherwise, it's a matter of ego. No cause for desperation at all.'

Kincaid smiled. 'Anyone who says egos don't have to be fed has never spent time on a movie set. Garrigus said the biggest job a director has is keeping all those egos in balance. And he wasn't just talking about actors. Cameramen, grips, wardrobe people, make-up men, property men. Thorne says most of the great performances in his studio take place *behind* the camera. I met an old actor when we were doing *Bushranger*. He told me the biggest triumph in his life was the first time he walked on a sound stage and saw that he had his own folding chair with his name stencilled on it. Another man, an extra, boasted to me that he had once had three close-up reaction shots in a Lon Chaney movie. Then he said, "I never got a call to work with the bastard again!"'

'But you said that most of those people don't even make much money. So why are they doing it?'

'That's the point. I suppose it makes them feel good about themselves. Why does an artist paint a picture he knows will never sell? We have to assume he's got a reason that makes sense to him.'

'I understand all that. I know creative people are a little crazy, but when I talk about the life we saw in Los Angeles I'm talking about ordinary people – women shopping in stores, hotel staff, delivery-men, petrol-pump attendants . . . They're all different from us. Don't you think so?'

'Of course they are. But that doesn't surprise me. Most cities have a personality. Los Angeles is a movie city. Even people who don't work in the industry are affected by it. Some comedian out there said to me, "Everybody in this town has *two* businesses: his own business and show business."'

'Our chambermaid at the Ambassador told me that all the misfits who can't make a go of it anywhere else end up in California.'

Kincaid nodded. 'And some of them end up as millionaires. Jack Warner was a butcher before he came to California.'

'I love this conversation. You're stating my case brilliantly. You feel the same as I do. Sometimes, however, I get the feeling your wavering, that you're tempted to go on being an actor. Then I remember what you said when you came home from America last

111

autumn and I feel good and reassured again.'

'What did I say?'

'I'm sure you remember. You said, "I'm never going off without you again." '

'I remember that. And you said, "I'll never let you go off without me again." '

'That's right. And I meant it.'

He pulled her close to him. 'I'm sure you didn't misunderstand what I meant by that. I meant that whenever I go to California you're coming along whether you want to or not.'

'But I said something different.'

'Not at all. You said you'd never let me go by myself again. To me that means you're coming with me.'

'Since you're not going,' she said, 'I'll never be tested.'

'That's right. If I don't go we'll never be certain what you meant.'

She put her arms around him and said, 'Don't play games with me, you beast. I'm helpless and vulnerable.'

'Of course you are. Like an alligator.'

8

Two days before Evan was due to leave for America his father came down to London to see him.

'It seems as if you've just come home. I thought perhaps you'd be staying longer,' Arthur said.

'Actually I expected to leave a week or so ago. But the project I'm working on has been delayed. There's a chance it may not happen at all.'

'Then what?' Arthur asked.

'Hard to say. You see, Kincaid's the linchpin. The script's ready, the pre-production work has been done, and we've got a shooting schedule, but until Kincaid says yes we can't go forward.'

'And he hasn't made up his mind?'

Evan shook his head. 'If he has, he hasn't told anyone.'

'Seems odd to me. I suppose I don't understand the film business.'

'Nobody does. The rules change every day.'

'If Kincaid decides not to do it, won't they go ahead with another actor?'

'That's a possibility. But in this case I don't think so. The whole thing has been planned for him. I'm sure Thorne could never accept anybody else in the part. So if Kincaid won't do it I think the film's dead.'

'Then he's a powerful man all of a sudden?'

'That's the word. Once it's established that millions of people will pay money to see you, you can name your price. Do whatever you want to.'

'Why wouldn't he want to take advantage of that?'

'Three possibilities. One: he simply doesn't want to make a career of being an actor. Two: he's playing the game. Nothing increases your value to a film studio like being hard to get. Most actors are dying to work. Fifty-two weeks a year if they can. So when one comes along who doesn't seem to give a damn, producers pay attention. Any reluctant actor stands out from the crowd. A reluctant actor who's proved he can bring in millions at the box office is Hollywood's version of God.'

'You said there were three possibilities.'

Evan nodded. 'The third possibility is Sophie. She hasn't told me in so many words but I think she'd be dead set against his doing another film. The first time it was a gamble, an adventure. From now on it's a career. Sophie won't be easy to persuade and Kincaid knows that better than anybody.'

'It's hard to believe that a man who was penniless not long ago is suddenly in such demand. How has he handled it?'

'Very nonchalantly. He knows it can end as quickly as it started. And he doesn't give a damn one way or the other. At least I don't think he does.'

They had drinks together that early-evening in Evan's flat. Then they walked along to Tavistock Place and had dinner in an Italian restaurant.

'I've got a bad conscience, I'm afraid,' Arthur said. 'When you came up to see me at the Towers I didn't tell you that I've given Margaret my resignation.'

'It doesn't matter. I can understand your not wanting to go over that ground.'

'Did someone else tell you?'

'Yes. Both Margaret and Sophie. Sophie told me about the divorce. And that Margaret is planning to remarry . . . I don't remember the man's name.'

'Brannigan, I believe.'

'That's it. Yes. So, big changes afoot.'

'Yes. On all fronts. Sophie and the children seldom seen. You away in California. Margaret's divorce. And now a new master on the premises.'

'Have you met him?'

'Yes, I have. He spent nearly two weeks with us while he photographed the estate.'

'What sort of fellow is he?'

'Seems to be a decent chap. He's Irish, you know. An artistic type. A great talker. His voice rang through the halls every day he spent with us. Carefree fellow. Or so he appeared. Sang a little Irish tune every now and again. A big favourite with the staff. He sat up late every night singing and laughing with the grooms and gardeners, their voices drifting across the way from the staff apartments.'

'You weren't fond of him, I take it.'

'I have no opinion of him one way or the other. He was simply a photographer doing his job. It never occurred to me that I'd ever see him again.'

'But now he'll be moving in.'

'Yes.'

'And you'll be moving out.'

'Yes. However, the two events are not linked.'

'Come on, Dad, let's be honest with each other. The events must be linked. No matter what other changes may have occurred in the house, you're moving out because Brannigan is moving in. Anybody can see that.'

'Did Margaret say that?'

'No. She didn't tell me about Brannigan. Sophie did.'

'Then she must have told you that I resigned before I knew that Margaret planned to marry him.'

'Yes. She did mention that. But she still believes you're leaving because of Brannigan. And so do I.'

'I know you and Sophie have always had storybook ideas about Margaret and me,' Arthur said, 'but they've never been true and they're not true now. The fact is that with so many changes taking place all round I decided to make some changes in my own life. Try some new things.'

'Like what? Sophie said you're planning to teach again.'

'That's a possibility, of course. But I'm a bit long in the tooth, I'm afraid. Most of the public-school jobs go to the younger chaps. Also it's many years since I stood in front of a classroom of cheeky young scamps. So, attractive as the prospect is, I think it's unlikely that I'll earn my keep by teaching.'

'What are your other possibilities?'

'I've always been keen on bookshops. Might give that a try. Or tutor a bit. Or do some translating for publishers – I used to be fluent in German as well as French.'

Evan studied his father and sipped from his wine glass. At last he said, 'You're fooling yourself, Dad. Or perhaps you're just trying to fool me.'

'Self-deception? A cardinal sin. Isn't that what I taught you and Sophie?'

'You certainly did. But it seems to me that you've fallen into the . . .'

'Not possible,' Arthur cut in. 'Faulty reasoning on your part. A mistaken conclusion. Off the mark.'

'All right. I'm going to ask you a question. You won't

like it but I'm going to ask you anyway. Are you in love with Margaret?'

Arthur smiled. 'When you get an idea in your head it really stays with you, doesn't it?'

'This particular one does. But I'm giving you a chance to kill it, once and for all.'

Arthur laced his fingers together. 'I can see how you and Sophie might draw that conclusion. When you were children you saw Margaret and me together day after day. And during those early years the Major was not at home. So I can understand that I became a sort of father to Sophie, just as Margaret seemed like a mother to you. From that point it was easy for you to assume, I suppose, that these two people you both loved also loved each other. I don't deny that there was a strong bond between Margaret and me through all those years. Common interests, shared duties, mutual respect. But the sort of feelings you're talking about were never a part of our relationship.'

'That's all very persuasive, Dad. You've got it all sorted out in your mind. But just saying it doesn't make it true. You're leaving because you can't stand to see Margaret married to somebody else. Isn't that it?'

'But she's always been married to somebody else, hasn't she?'

Evan shook his head. 'Margaret and the Major were never really married. When he came home to stay after the war, why do you think he was so angry with you? There's only one answer. Because he thought you had taken his place. Didn't he threaten to sue Margaret for divorce on grounds of adultery and to name you?'

'You don't believe his crazy accusations, do you?'

'No, I don't. But it was a reasonable perception all the same. The Major, because of his own idiocy, was only concerned with what you two might have *done* together that could humiliate him. But I'm not talking about that. I'm talking about feelings. How you *felt* about her. I didn't imply that you were lovers. I asked if you were in love with her, if you've ever been in love with her, if you're in love with her now?'

'Let me answer that question with a question. You and Sophie are about the same age. You've spent a large part of your lives together. One could easily assume, seeing you together, that you were more than friends, that you had a romantic attachment, one that went beyond friendship. But I know better. If I asked you the same question about Sophie that you've asked me about Margaret, I expect your answer would be very close to mine.'

'I'm surprised to hear you say that. After the lectures you gave me from the time I was twelve years old till Sophie got married and began to have children, I assumed you thought we were on the brink of falling into each others arms. And you were right. We were on the brink. But your lectures helped to hold us back. At least they held me back. Since we're being totally candid with each other, I'll tell you that I have never made love to Sophie. But God knows I wanted to, from the time I knew that such a thing was possible. I asked you if you were in love with Margaret and you said no. If you asked me that same question about Sophie, I would tell you that I was so crazy in love with her I couldn't breathe. When she started to go out with other chaps, those self-satisfied county boys, I would have killed them if I could. Slow torture. Dismemberment. And when she was involved with Hugh Causey, when everyone pretended not to see, I could see nothing else. I was physically ill, weak and trembling. But I knew Hugh Causey's reputation, I knew that affair wouldn't last long. When it ended, I told myself I would avenge her and comfort her. But then it did end and almost immediately she married Toby Black. That was a different kind of pain. I couldn't hate Toby. Nobody could. And I couldn't tell myself it would all be over soon. I knew it would last. So all I felt was dried-out and empty. Till I was twenty-one years old, I told myself that since I couldn't have her I wouldn't have anybody. Seems stupid now but it didn't then. Now I'm thirty-two and I'm not in love with Sophie. I'm sensible now, and moderate, and realistic and philosophical. And aware of my own limitations. But I'll never forget what it was like in that other life, how I felt when I looked at her, when I thought about her. It's a kind of insanity, that kind of love. It usually only happens once, thank God, and once is enough. Now I sit and talk to her, or have lunch with her, and it really is like having a sister. I wonder how this lovely and kind young woman could have caused me so much torment. But she did. And it's not something I expect to forget.'

9

'I didn't believe you when you said we were going to have lunch by ourselves,' Sarah said. 'Are you sure Sophie isn't going to float in here and join us?'

'It's possible, I suppose,' Kincaid said, 'but I don't expect to see her.'

They were sitting at a corner table in Wilhelmina's, a bright, flower-choked restaurant in Adam's Row.

'Can we just talk or is there some scenario you've been instructed to follow?' she said.

'No script. No instructions. I have lunch every day. Today I asked you to have lunch with me. That's all there is to it.'

When he ordered a bottle of champagne and two glasses she said, 'If Sophie has any spies here, she'll murder you. She says I'm too young to drink wine in restaurants.'

'You are. But I fixed it with the head waiter. I told him you're my pet dog. With your new haircut I knew he'd believe me.'

She smiled. 'Very funny. I'll admit it's not a triumph but it looked different in Brighton.'

'Everything looks different in Brighton.'

'I suppose you know about the endless discussions I've been having with my mother,' Sarah said then.

He shook his head. 'I don't quiz Sophie and she doesn't quiz me.'

'Oh, come on. I'll bet she's told you everything we said.'

'You'd be surprised how little we discuss you.'

They ordered their lunch then. When the waiter left them Sarah said, 'Next you'll tell me you never read the interview I gave to that Los Angeles newspaper.'

Kincaid smiled. 'I read it all right. I'm probably the first man in England who did read it. They air-mailed it to me from the studio.'

'And you went straight to Sophie with it.'

'No. Afraid not. I didn't show it to her at all.'

'Why not?'

'To tell you the truth, I thought it was boring. Sophie detests boring things. And so do I.'

'You're trying to get me angry, aren't you?'

'Not at all. People your age say grown-ups never tell them the truth, but *I'm* telling the truth.'

'I never gave an interview before. What was boring about it?'

'That kind of stuff shows up in American newspapers every day. Every young girl in California thinks she's going to be a film actress.'

'And some of them do it.'

'Very few,' he said. 'Almost none. Many of them end up as waitresses or barmaids or telephone operators, a few of them marry, have children, and live in little box houses in the San Fernando Valley. But most of them go back home, to Arkansas or Louisiana or New Jersey, and spend their lives telling their relatives how thrilling it was to be in the movies.'

'I know you're trying to discourage me but it won't do any good.'

'You asked me what became of aspiring film actresses and I told you the truth.'

'Maybe so. But all the same you weren't trying to encourage me. Do you think I'd react the same way if I had a daughter?'

For a long moment Kincaid didn't answer. At last he said, 'I can't be a fair judge of that because I don't have a daughter.'

'But you know what I mean.'

'You mean that since I'm married to your mother my ideas and attitudes about you are the same as hers.'

'It's true, isn't it?'

'In some cases, perhaps. In others, no. The important thing to remember is that I'm not your father and you're not my daughter. We owe each other nothing. You're free to treat me however you like, to give me as much or as little affection as you think I deserve. And I have the same rights in relation to you. I have no desire to mould or restrict your life. It's not my job. If I can help you I will of course, but only if you want me to. I see no reason why you and I should be enemies but we are also not obliged to be friends.'

'But there's no reason why we can't be, is there?'

'None that I know of.'

'That's nice. I don't know any grown-ups that I think of as friends. They're either your own parents or somebody else's parents. There's not much that one can discuss with them. Either they don't listen at all, or they listen so carefully that you know they're getting ready to give you a lecture about something.'

'You'll get no lectures from me. But I won't lie to you either. If you want my opinion about something, I'll tell you the truth. If you're behaving like a jackass, I'll tell you so.'

'What if you're behaving like a jackass?'

Kincaid smiled. 'I can't imagine that ever happening, but if it does I'm sure you'll point it out to me.'

After they'd finished their lunch, when they were having coffee, she said, 'I suppose you think everything I said in that interview was stupid.'

'You want the truth?'

'Yes.'

'All right. In the first place there's no point in talking to a reporter unless it helps you in some way. If you've done something important, for example, and you think people should know about it. Or if you can be helpful to a friend. If you do it just to attract attention, then it's a mistake. In your case Neal Dyer was only interested in you because you know me. People who read his paper don't give a damn about you or your ambitions. They just want inside information about someone you know. In this case, me.'

'But I didn't tell any secrets about you.'

'I know you didn't but that's what they were after.'

'I suppose I shouldn't have said that I'm changing my name to Kincaid. Did that embarrass you?'

'No. But it's silly to talk about it because you can't do it. Not till you're twenty-one. Then you can change your name to Minnie Mouse if you want to.'

'What else did I say that was stupid?'

'Not stupid. Silly. What was the point of saying you're an only child? People who don't know you don't care, and people who do know you wonder why you're lying. If you don't want to talk about Trevor you don't have to. But it's mean and pointless to make a public statement that he doesn't exist. If I put out a story about Sophie and told people that she had no children, wouldn't you feel a bit odd when you read that?'

'I suppose so.'

She sipped her coffee and seemed to make a careful study of the people at the next table. At last she said, 'Were you surprised to find out that I intend to be an actress?'

'I'd never heard you mention it before, but no, I wasn't all that surprised.'

'Do you think I'm foolish to want to do that?'

'Of course not. The theatre's an important place. There's a lot to be learned from a good play. And there's no theatre without actors.'

'I mean, do you think there's any chance I can *do* it?'

'Nobody can tell you that. The important thing is to find out how much you want to do it. What your reasons are. Most actors don't become rich or famous, so if it's those things you're after, chances are you've made the wrong choice.'

'You don't think you made the wrong choice, do you?'

'I never made a choice. I fell into it. I'm not really trained or qualified for it. I'm sure a man like Geoff Bingham doesn't think I'm an actor at all. I could never appear on stage with him and people with his ability. I'd be lost. It's not enough to have strong feelings and deep emotions. How an actor *feels* when he's playing a role is not important. It's how the audience feels as they watch him. That's what matters. Talent is just the starting place. After that comes hard work, life experience, and a bit of maturity. And even that, all of it, means nothing if the audience doesn't like you. Perhaps *like* is not the correct word. I should have said, "if people don't respond to you."'

'Do people respond to you?'

'Judging from the success of *Bushranger*, it looks as if they do. But if I go on making pictures I may find out they simply liked me in that one role.'

'You make it all sound hopeless.'

'I don't mean to. It isn't hopeless at all. If you're doing it for the right reason. But if you don't love the *work* you're better off doing something else.'

'How do I know if I love it enough?'

'You don't. You have to find that out gradually. Until you've studied and read and trained yourself, till you know at first-hand the preparation that has to be done before you can walk on stage in even the smallest role, till you've discovered how to make contact with an audience, how to make them laugh at the right moment and not before, till you've suffered a number of failures and enjoyed perhaps a bit of success, until all these things have taken place, it's impossible to know if you even want to be an actress.'

'Are you telling me I should forget it?'

'Not at all. I'm saying it takes hard work and patience. You can say you're eighteen years old till you're blue in the face but that won't make it true. When you're actually eighteen you'll realize how much more you know, in every way, than you do now.'

'Have you told Sophie the things you're telling me?'

Kincaid shook his head. 'There's no reason to. I'm talking to you as one inexperienced actor to another.'

'All my mother keeps saying is that I must stay on at school.'

'She's mistaken about that. You can run off to Brighton again. You can do all sorts of things with your life. But if you're serious about becoming an actress, you'll want to learn as much as you can. Because all of it will be helpful sooner or later. The more you've learned and seen and experienced, the more raw material you'll have to work with when you finally get a job.'

'I know what you're saying but the thought of going back to Miss Endicott . . .'

'You can't go back there,' Kincaid said. 'They won't have you.'

'. . . or any school like that.'

'There are all sorts of schools in England. But none for you perhaps.'

'What does that mean?'

'It means that if you've decided to follow a pattern of slipping away, of running off whenever the mood strikes you, then you'd best stay away from school altogether.'

'I'd hate to be married to a man like you,' she said. 'You're too sly. I'd never win a battle.'

'I wish that were true. The fact is, I've lost all sorts of battles. In three or four years I expect you'll tell me that everything I've said to you today was clear off the mark.'

'I don't think so. But even if I do, I want you to know that this is the best lunch I've ever had in my life.' She smiled. 'For a minute or so I almost trusted you.'

• CHAPTER 4 •

1

Sam Thorne was two years older than his brother, Julian. When they were boys in Brooklyn, their mother, Helen, often said, 'You see them on the street, you'd swear they came from different parents, from different families, from different countries even. Sam is an exact copy of his father's brother, Nate, but Julian looks like my mother's family. Slim and fresh from the barber-shop. Clever with words and careful about his clothes. Sammy, bless his heart, always has spots on his tie and it's a miracle if his socks are a matching pair. Those two boys can't be related, people say. But people are mistaken. Beneath the surface, my sons are identical. They are one sweet spirit in two different bodies. Bodies as unlike as corn-beef and crumb cake.'

Helen's assessment of her sons was not one that others agreed with. Almost everyone who knew them believed they were as unlike in intelligence and temperament as they were in appearance. And no one who did business with them in Brooklyn, in Newark, or later in California, would have used the expression 'sweet spirit' when referring to either of the Thorne brothers.

As Julian was beginning to exhibit one-reel films in store-front nickelodeons on the Lower East Side of Manhattan, Sam and his friend John Corso had already established an aggressive produce business in Hoboken, buying cheap from New Jersey farmers and Georgia truckers, then sorting, boxing, and carting the goods through the tunnel to restaurants and hotels in New York City. There was muscle and vigour in their operation, chutzpah and intimidation.

When Julian went to work for William Fox, Sam said, 'What's the matter with you? So you're only making nickels and dimes but at least you're working for yourself. Now you tell me you're going for short money from some other duck in the same business. You're crazy, Julie. Get wise to yourself.'

Two years later, when Julian left Fox and joined Jesse Lasky, Sam said, 'You're wasting the best years of your life. You're all over the place. Towel-boy to some schmuck who's half as smart as you are. Now's the time to establish yourself. Look at John and me. A few more years we'll be set for life.'

'A few more years you'll still smell like rotten bananas and keep a baseball bat in your car. Don't kid me about being in business for yourself. You got yourself adopted by the Corso family.'

'So what's wrong with that? You think Carl Laemmle's a rabbi? Look at it this way: people sit down and eat three times a day. They go to a nickelodeon maybe twice a week. So who's gonna get rich, you or me?'

'We'll both get rich, Sam. In five years I'll have my own studio. Making my own pictures. California's the place. That's where I'll be. And you'll be with me. You heard of the Warner Brothers? We'll be the Thorne Brothers.'

'That's right,' Sam said. 'You'll be broke and I'll be supporting you. Maybe I'll smell like rotten bananas but my money will smell good.'

The following summer Julian went to California for Lasky. Three years later he bought a ten-acre abandoned orchard on Beechwood Drive in Los Angeles, put up a stone gate-way with a sign reading *Thornwood Studios* above it, and began to make his own films. 'I need a partner,' he told his brother a few months later, 'and you're it.'

126

'You don't need me,' Sam said, 'You need your head examined. I'm forty-nine years old, for Christ's sake. Marie wants me to retire and you're trying to suck me into a cockamamie business I don't know straight-up about.'

'Business is business, Sam. I'll make the movies. You handle the money. You're a salesman. Any man who can sell cabbage and rutabagas can sure as hell peddle a Thornwood movie.'

'Nothing doing, bubba. I'll stick to what I know. And when you're broke, you and Bella and Rachel can come live with us on Staten Island. I'll take you to the movies every day. We'll play a little handball in the park and then we'll see a movie.'

A few days later when Sam recounted this conversation to Vincent Corso, John's uncle, the old man said, 'You're a smart man, Sam, but be careful you don't outfox yourself. I've kept an eye on your brother through the years. He's made some smart moves. And he's done it by himself. Asked no favours of anyone. Now I think he's got himself in a good position. So if I were you, I'd reconsider his offer. Julian needs your help. Some of the people we do business with think there's a great deal of money to be made in the motion-picture business. There are elements there that look interesting to us. Take yourself, for instance. You're not just a man who knows produce. You also know trucking. I think my brothers and I could become very interested in a business that depends so much on trucking. You follow me, Sam? It could mean a lot to us to have a man we trust out there in California, somebody who knows us, knows how we operate. No contracts. No need for that. Just a hand-shake arrangement between friends. A co-operative venture, we call it.'

Two months later Sam and Marie were living in a house on Green Oak Drive, just ten minutes away from Thornwood Studios. The lessons Sam had learned in the Hoboken produce markets served him well. Informed and courteous, stubborn and insistent, he dealt with

127

exhibitors and exchange directors, with bankers and independent producers, as firmly as he had with truckers and wholesalers. It was a small community and it became quickly apparent to everyone that Julian's brother, Sam, could not be manipulated, outmanoeuvred, or threatened. To buyers and sellers alike he was quick to say, 'Let's not waste time. I see right now we can't do business.'

In those first years of Thornwood, Julian and Sam built twelve sound stages and established a production schedule of sixty features a year; they created their own exchange, and began to buy and build theatres to exhibit their product; they took over part of the Vitagraph operation and the Moseby-Clarion studio on McCadden Place. As the box-office takings flowed in steadily, with money for expansion always available from sources in New York, major actors and directors were attracted to the lot, and Julian, exploring a co-production situation with Gaumont-British, made his first trip to London. Thus began his steady personal transformation. By the end of the following year, during which he made three trips to England, Julian became, in his own mind at least, totally British. His combs and brushes and razors, his shaving-lotion and toilet-water, his soap, toothbrush, cuff-links, tie-pins, cravats, shirts and socks, boots, hats, suits, jackets, trousers, and greatcoats, everything that touched his body was boxed, wrapped, crated, shipped, and delivered to the tradesmen's entrance of his home on Crescent Drive. The interior of that house also was furnished and decorated, with taste and authenticity, from the most arrogant London antique dealers, rug merchants, and fabric suppliers. The gardens of his home were designed and laid out by two gentlemen who had once served the Duke of Kent. The resident gardener was a young man who had been persuaded to emigrate after Julian had admired his handiwork at a country house in Hertfordshire.

The executive offices at the studio were also British in tone and design, and all the young women who manned the switchboard spoke in clipped British accents. One of these ladies, who had been hired by the studio personnel director for attributes that had nothing whatsoever to do with her daily work routine, was put through an intensive four-week training course by a dialogue coach specializing in British accents before she was permitted to take her place at the switchboard. The personnel director, when he visited her at her apartment two evenings a week, insisted that she express her sexual delight in those same newly acquired British speech patterns.

Sam had come to California with reservations. He was a New York City man, Brooklyn-born and -bred. He never walked on grass if he could walk on pavement. He drank no tap water, only seltzer, delivered to his home twice a week. Ebbets Field had a special meaning for him. Coney Island, and the Heights, and Red Hook. And since his marriage to Marie his world had expanded to include Staten Island. Like Hoboken, it was only a ferry-ride away from the magic smells and flavours and street music of Brooklyn.

Marie, when they had discussed the move to California, had shared his anxiety. In Staten Island her three sisters lived only blocks away, with her mother nearby also, in an apartment over her elder sister's garage. Marie depended on her familiar routine, her daily newspaper and the crossword puzzle, her radio programmes, visits from her sisters, short walks to the delicatessen, temple on Friday evenings. 'Small things I like,' she often said. 'You see, I have tiny hands and feet. Small rooms I prefer also. Small windows. Familiar things.' Although she'd grown up in Brooklyn, she preferred Staten Island. 'It's smaller,' she said. Sam, who, except for business, seldom set foot on the island of Manhattan, often accused her of having never been there. 'Of course I've been to Manhattan. Many times,' she said. 'On the ferry.'

'But when you get to the terminal, you never leave it. You buy a seltzer, smoke a Chesterfield, and take the next ferry back to Staten Island.'

All the way to California on the train, Marie sat reading in their compartment, with the lights on and the shades drawn. She never looked out the window except when the train was in a station. When a group of Indians selling trinkets approached the train at the Albuquerque station, she quickly pulled down the shade. 'My God.'

'What's the matter,' Sam said. He was reading the *Brooklyn Eagle*, one of the previous week's papers he'd saved to read on the train.

'I thought I saw an Indian,' she said. 'I must be going crazy.'

'This is Albuquerque, for God's sake. You probably did see one. There are plenty of Indians around here. This is where they come from, some of them.'

'But they don't live here, do they? They don't live among the white people, surely.'

'Why not? Put up the shade. Let's take a look at them.' He reached for the bottom of the shade.

'Don't you dare, Sam. I don't want to see those people and I do not want them to see me.'

'There are Indians in California, you know. Lots of them.'

'Not where we're going.'

'Why not? You think they're all stuck on reservations in Oklahoma?'

'I read some of those articles you brought home. Not a single mention of any Indians hanging out in Los Angeles.'

He reached over and patted her on the knee. 'First time we see an Indian out there, I promise you I'll have a stone wall put up all around that house we'll be living in.'

'*One* Indian I see,' she said, 'and I'm back on Staten Island.'

As it turned out the house already had a wall. A thick

red-brick wall with jagged shards of limestone on the top. That feature, more than anything else, eased their arrival into Los Angeles. 'I was in Forest Hills once with my sister, Rose, and there was a whole neighbourhood of red-brick houses. Most of them had walls, just like this one. Protected community, they called it.'

'There you are,' Sam said. 'You see, we'll be right at home.'

'I never thought I'd like living in Forest Hills, but out here, after that awful train trip, this place looks pretty darned good to me.'

'You'll love it, Marie. Your mama can come visit. And all your sisters. Ten bedrooms we've got in this house. Julie says there's a kosher delicatessen two blocks away and a brand-new temple on Cahuenga, a ten-minute drive from here.'

Sam had been in California for nine years when *Bushranger* was made and released. He had been opposed to making the picture, just as he'd resisted Julian's converting the studio from silent pictures to talkies. 'Gangster pictures we should make. And baggy-pants comedies. Times are tough. Hitler and Mussolini and bread lines in all the papers. People need to laugh. Mae West and Hoot Gibson – that's the answer. A few jokes and string up the bad guys.'

He also objected to Kincaid's contract. 'Who is this bird? Where does he get off, writing his own papers? George O'Brien accepts a term deal. Fredric March does it. Everybody signs up or they don't work. But this nobody Australian from the streets shoves a home-cooked deal down our throats and makes us eat it. You gotta stay away from England, Julie. Every time you hit London you go to pieces. You put on a Derby hat and forget how to do business.'

When *Bushranger* was released, however, Sam was quick to admit he'd been wrong. At his daily breakfast-meeting with Julian he tracked the picture's grosses in every city in the country. 'In New York last week we outgrossed *It Happened One Night*. In Cleveland we kicked the shit out of everybody. In Chicago we were dead even with *The Thin Man* and we're in our tenth week there. It ain't my kind of picture, Julie, I've told you that a hundred times, but it's sure as hell doing my kind of business. Every exhibitor I talk to wants to know what's coming next from Kincaid, and I've got no answer for them. If I tell them we don't even have a commitment from him, they'll think we're running a nut-house here instead of a studio. If I tell them we've got a hot picture all set to go but we don't have a start date . . .'

'I'm leaving for London tomorrow, Sam. You know that. When I come back, we'll have a start date.'

'Maybe we will and maybe we won't. Kincaid's got us by the short hairs and you know it. Two days ago Fred Nitke called me from Kansas City. He said the Paramount guys told him Kincaid's set to do a picture for them. And yesterday in *Film Daily* . . .'

'I know. Justin Gold said Henry French is heading for London to meet with Kincaid. So what? We've got an exclusive with Kincaid.'

'What kind of exclusive? One year from the release date of *Bushranger*, he's free and clear. If he stalls around for a few more months he can make a deal with French or Mayer or whoever he wants to.'

'Maybe he can but he won't. I trust him.'

'Not me. When people start throwing money around I don't trust anybody.'

'Whatever anyone offers him, I'll match it. He won't jerk us around, Sam. I promise you.'

'What if you're wrong? Who do we have for a back-up on the Dillinger project? Who do we use if Kincaid falls through?'

Julian shook his head. 'No back-up. We don't need one. It's Kincaid's picture and he'll make it.'

'I'm surprised you're going back now,' Kincaid said. 'I thought you'd wait around till Thorne showed up.'

'No point in that,' Evan said. 'I see him at least once a week in California. His business in London is with you.'

They were driving from London to Southampton in Kincaid's car. Evan was sailing for America on the *Bremen* that afternoon. 'And to tell you the truth, I'm not keen to see him. He expected that you and I would be talking over the Dillinger screenplay while I was here in London. Every time he rings me up from California, he asks if you've read it yet and I tell him no. I'd just as soon not have to tell him again to his face.'

'Don't worry about it. I'll explain things when I see him.'

'When did you talk to him last?'

'He cabled me yesterday from his hotel in New York. Just before he went to board his ship.'

'Did he ask about the screenplay?'

Kincaid shook his head. 'Once in a while he mentions "our new film", but it's as if everything's been decided and we're going ahead with it.'

'You know something?' Evan said. 'If you want to play games with Thorne that's up to you, but it pisses me off that you're leaving me hanging. You and I are supposed to be friends. You got me involved with Thorne in the first place. I know you don't care if you make the Dillinger picture or any other picture, but I worked my ass off on this screenplay and it's damned important to me. If you don't want to do it I won't try to persuade you, but how in the name of God can you even decide what you want to do until you read the material?'

'That's just the point. Until I've talked with Thorne, until I've settled a few other questions, I don't want to read the screenplay.'

'What other questions? Are you talking about Sophie now?'

'No. I'm talking about me. Until I decide what I want to do and what I don't want to do, there's no point . . .'

'Are you saying it doesn't matter what Sophie wants?'

'Of course it matters. But other things matter, too.'

They drove along in silence for several minutes. At last Evan said, 'I had a professor named Wilton when I was at university. He taught a course in ethics. He used to say that many men are at their best in situations of adversity. He said the true test of a man's character is when he's in a position of power.'

'I'm waiting,' Kincaid said. 'What's the connection?'

'I'm not sure. You probably know the answer better than I do.'

Kincaid grinned. 'You'll get no help from me. If you're about to analyse my character you'll have to work it out yourself.'

'There's a lot I don't know about you but all the same I expect I know more than most people. I know you've had a tough time. Knocking about, looking after yourself. No family. Nothing permanent or reliable in your life. Or so it seems to me. Am I right?'

'If you think I spend a lot of time feeling sorry for myself, you're wrong about that.'

'I don't think that,' Evan said. 'I just meant, you've had a rough time. Harder than most people. Not many alternatives along the way. Not many choices.'

When Kincaid didn't answer, Evan went on. 'Now, all of a sudden, just in the last year, the gates have swung open. When I met you, you had nothing. Now you have everything. Most of all, you have power. That's what everybody wants. Or at least they believe they want it. People eager to help you, to give you things, to be noticed by you. You've just entered a world where you're loved by strangers, a place where everybody wants to be your friend. It's true, isn't it? Am I describing it correctly or not?'

'I don't see things the way you do,' Kincaid said. 'I don't try to figure things out.'

'Of course not. You don't have to. You can just sit back and watch. You're in control. Are you telling me you don't realize that? Maybe it will last, maybe it won't, but for the moment at least, you're unassailable. Let me put it this way. What are you afraid of? Right now. What's your biggest worry?'

'I didn't worry when I had nothing. Why would I be worried now?'

'All right. Let's talk about what I'm afraid of. I'd hate to go hungry. I'd hate to be homeless and have to sleep in doorways or under bridges. I'd hate to be arrested and put in jail. I'd hate to be sick or crippled, with no one to look after me. I'd hate to be deformed or blind or deaf. I'd hate to have a child that wasn't normal or a wife who loved somebody else. Without even thinking about it, I know I'm trying to avoid all those things. So are you. And so is almost everybody. But in your case some of those things have already happened to you. Am I right?'

'No doubt about it.'

'Forget it,' Evan said then. 'I don't think I made my point and I'm tired of listening to myself.'

'You made your point.'

Later on, when they'd reached Southampton and were driving through the streets toward the docks, Evan said, 'Don't get me wrong. If I were in a position where I could make people stand on their heads and sweat a little, I'd probably do just what you're doing. But there's one thing I don't understand. If you really haven't decided whether you want to stay in the movie business, then why are you bothering to meet Henry French?'

'That's easy. Before I talk to Thorne again, before I make up my mind once and for all about what I want to do, I thought it might not be a bad idea to see what I'm worth to somebody else.'

Evan smiled. 'Thorne's right about you, isn't he?'

'How do you mean?'

'He says you're a killer.'

135

Henry French had guest privileges at a club in St James's. Kincaid met him there for lunch two days after Evan sailed for New York. When he joined French at his table, French said, 'There are a lot of snotty bastards in this club. Most of them can't figure out how I wormed my way in as a guest but I don't give a damn what they think. Are you a member here?'

'No, I'm not.'

'As you walked in I noticed the old boys were staring at you from behind their menus. So I guess they're not too constipated to go to the movies once in a while.'

French was thick and compact, dressed like a conservative banker. Bald, with a mahogany sun-tan, and wearing gold-wire spectacles. 'You're not as tall as you look on screen. Nothing wrong with that. Tough to get a tight two-shot with a guy like Cooper.'

After they ordered drinks French said, 'I know you're a busy man and so am I. So I won't waste your time with a lot of talk. I'm not trying to be your best friend. I'm a business man, and I want to do business with you if I can. I can't promise to make you a star 'cause that's already happened. And I understand that nobody's going to lure you away from Julian just by waving money around. But I've never met an actor who didn't want something he didn't have. So let me put it this way: whatever you want that you can't get from Thorne, I can provide it. Paramount can provide it. If you hate Franklin Roosevelt and you want him shot, we can't handle that, but otherwise . . .'

Kincaid smiled. 'I like Roosevelt. I like him a lot.'

'Good. That gets me off the hook there. Now, why don't you tell me what you want?'

'Let's do it another way: why don't you tell me what you have to offer.'

'Well, let's see. I've seen the papers you signed with Julian. A crazy fucking contract. I understand you rigged that whole thing yourself. No agent and no lawyer.'

'We have a solicitor. He read it before I signed.'

'How did you get Julian to sit still for a one-picture deal?'

'I told him what I wanted and he agreed.'

'Well, I have to hand it to you, you people made a helluva picture. A crazy story, a new star, and it paid off. Julian's raking in the money. Do you think you got paid enough?'

'What do you think? How much would you have paid?'

'I won't lie to you. You'd never have got a deal like that from Paramount. I wouldn't have talked to you unless you'd agreed to a seven-year deal. I wouldn't have given you the lead in your first picture, I wouldn't have billed you above the title, and I wouldn't have paid you more than five hundred a week.'

'That settles that,' Kincaid said. 'Now I can enjoy my lunch and not have to worry about talking business.'

'Not a chance. I'm setting you up. Can't you see that? I just told you how dumb I am. Because I play percentages I never would have made *Bushranger*, with you or anybody else. So you ask yourself, "Why am I wasting time with this stupid guy?" And the next thing you know, I've done a fast snow job on you and wrapped you up for three pictures with an option for three more.'

'At five hundred a week, right?'

'If we're talking seriously, here's what I'd propose: fifty thousand dollars for staying home and doing nothing till your contract with Julian expires next December. Then, just for the sake of discussion, let's say three pictures in three years. A hundred and fifty thousand for the first one . . .'

'That's what I got for *Bushranger*.'

'Let me finish. Two hundred thousand for number

two. And two fifty for number three. Plus a hundred thousand a year for exclusivity. And fifty thousand a year for location expenses. Now we're over a million for three years. Have I got your attention?'

'How about co-producer credit?'

'We could work that out.'

'Percentage of producer's share?'

'No problem.'

'Script approval?'

'Within reason.'

'Director approval?'

'Consultation definite. And a maybe on the approval bit.'

'Cast approval?'

'Consultation. Leading lady approval.'

'Final cut?'

'Not a chance. The money gets final cut. Nobody else. Not Jesus Christ himself.'

'I'd want you for executive producer.'

'I'm executive producer on every major picture we turn out.'

'I'd want it in the contract.'

'So would I,' French said.

At the end of their lunch, when they were having coffee in the lounge, French said, 'I think we could work well together. What do you think?'

'I'm easy to work with,' Kincaid said.

'What do you think about the terms we discussed?'

'Very generous.'

'Any other feelings?'

'I've been thinking about it. I haven't discussed any future projects with Thorne . . .'

'The word on the coast is that you don't like what he's got lined up for you.'

'As I said, we haven't discussed anything so I don't know what he's got lined up for me. As far as the terms you and I were talking about, I'm sure I can get the same deal from Thorne.'

'In that case I'd make a better offer.'

'What I'm asking is this: what can Paramount offer me that Thornwood can't. Aside from the money.'

'I don't know what that means . . . *aside* from the money. That's what negotiations are all about. That's what a deal is. *Money*. That's it. Everything else is bull-shit.'

4

The morning after his arrival in London, Julian Thorne went to his outfitter on Jermyn Street and ordered thirty new shirts, twenty ties, and a dozen pairs of silk pyjamas. From there he went directly to the home of Rosamund Barwick for a champagne breakfast. It was an arrival ritual, one they had preserved for twelve years. Their conversation normally consisted of gossip. Bloomsbury gossip and California gossip. Each of them moved and functioned in a world that was foreign to the other and each of them had infinite curiosity about the other's activities. On this particular morning, however, soon after they sat down together, the conversation took a more serious turn.

'I'm a wise old woman, Julian. I know you would never let your first day in London slip past without coming to see me. I also know that today you've got something else on your mind, something more important to you than what the Sitwells are up to or what Virginia Woolf told Noel Coward about her husband. Am I right?'

Thorne smiled. 'You have my full attention, Rosamund. You always have my full attention. Any time I enter this lovely house I leave everything else behind me.'

'Poppycock, Julian. Your mind's as compartmentalized as a honeycomb and every cubicle has a dollar sign on it. You're here to talk to me about Kincaid. So let's get to it straightaway. Have you talked with him since you arrived?'

'Rang him last evening as a matter of fact. He's meeting me at my office tomorrow.'

'And what are your chances? Good or poor?'

'I'm not sure what you mean.'

'Come off it, Julian. Every gossip journal in London is trying to figure out why you haven't announced a new film for Kincaid. And Henry French told Cyril Connolly a week ago that Kincaid would be signing a contract with Paramount.'

'Henry French is a chancy source of information. He'd announce *The Life of Christ* starring Harry Langdon if he thought it would get him some space in the papers.'

'Be that as it may, dear Julian, if there's a problem about luring Kincaid back to California for another film, and if you're hoping that I will intercede on your behalf, I want you to know straight off that I can't do it.'

'I've never asked you to do anything like that, have I?'

'Of course not. But we've always had a special relationship, you and I. Because neither of us makes demands on the other, we are always eager to supply whatever favours or invitations or information we believe might be welcome. Generous. Civilized. "Tis more gracious to give than to receive." Still, the receiving does not go unmarked or unnoticed. Am I correct?'

'You've always been extremely generous with me.'

'And you with me. And I'm sure those impulses will continue. But in this instance, as I've said . . .'

'Are you saying you've already had a discussion with Kincaid?'

She shook her head. 'I've seen him two or three times since the first of the year and we talk occasionally on the telephone but we've never discussed his future plans or his relationship with you.'

'But all the same you seem to have taken a position about his future.'

'Not exactly,' she said. 'The point is that I took a very specific position before, when you were first trying to persuade him to work for you, and in retrospect I believe I gave the wrong advice.'

'To Kincaid?'

'No. To his wife. You remember they were newly married then and Sophie had strong reservations about his following you off into a world neither of them knew much about. We had lunch together one day and she told me how she was feeling. I told her she would be making a serious mistake if she stood in Kincaid's way. With his background, I felt it was essential that he be given an opportunity to make something of himself, to define himself, to be somebody.'

'And now you think that was bad advice?'

'In principle, no. But when I gave it, I had no idea that things would turn out as they have. Surely you must be surprised as well.'

'Very surprised and very pleased.'

'And you have every right to be. But I'm a woman, a woman of a certain age, certainly, but the instincts are still intact. And those instincts tell me that if I were Kincaid's wife, as Sophie is, I would be very hesitant to surrender him to an adoring world of strangers.'

'I can understand that you feel responsible for him. If it weren't for you he might still be in jail. Or back in Australia. Or working in the hold of a ship. You turned his life around. If it weren't for you . . .'

'Don't misunderstand me, Julian. I'm not saying that I delivered Kincaid to you on a platter. Your original interest in him was totally independent of what I was trying to do. When he decided at last to go to California and when he decided later to do *Bushranger*, those decisions were his. I didn't steer him or persuade him. What I did do was to persuade his wife that she mustn't stand in his way. If she asked me the same questions today as she did a year ago, I would answer quite differently.'

'In what way?'

'I would tell her that her relationship with Kincaid must come first, that no amount of attention or public adulation or financial reward could compensate for a wounded marriage.'

'Are you saying that Kincaid can't have a career and a marriage at the same time?'

'You tell me, Julian. What are the odds? And remember, in this instance we're talking about a particular sort of marriage. An unusual man and an unusual woman. You see, all of the things that Kincaid can gain from a career as a film actor are things he doesn't need. Not yet. But a time could come when he truly believes that he needs those things. That would be a day of jeopardy for his life with Sophie. And a miserable day for me if I had helped to bring it about.'

They sat silent then for a long moment. At last she said, 'You sweet lovely man. You don't have the slightest notion of what I'm talking about, do you?'

'Of course I do.'

'No, you don't. And I suppose it doesn't matter. You and Kincaid will have your serious talk about grosses and net receipts and billing and guarantees, and at last some decision will be made. Then later on you'll discover that you discussed all the wrong things.'

5

Some of us undergo remarkable changes as we mature, as we're exposed to new experiences, pleasures and sorrows, as we grow older. Others, it seems, go through no such process. They seem to have sprung to life full-blown, all their attributes and flaws, warts, wens and twitches firmly in place. William Cranston, Margaret's husband and Sophie's father, the tortured Major, belonged to the latter group. From childhood, it appeared, perhaps from conception, he had been structured by self-deception and paranoia. His few triumphs had come from the former, his continuing anxieties from the latter. His faceless enemies made his real ones seem almost inconsequential.

Cranston's late-in-life decision to write his memoirs had been fuelled by a strong desire to expose his persecutors. Each passage he scrawled in his notebooks confirmed his poisoned view of the world and his place in it. Then the entrance of Jack Brannigan into his life intensified a self-pity that was already of monstrous proportions. It also greatly energized his efforts to record his state of mind.

Remembering all the worthless rotters I have known, it puzzles me that I should have been singled out for endless punishment. Since childhood I have tried to be an exemplary person. Surrounded always by destructive, mean-spirited people, I have tried to rise to a higher level. And I've succeeded, by God. Selflessness and nobility were my goals. Kindness and tolerance. Even my own bloody brothers decided from the day I was born, or so it seemed, that I was not up to the mark. Bats and balls were all they knew. My good marks in school were scorned, my attempts at cricket ridiculed. And my parents, too, came down always on the opposite side from me. My work at Sandhurst brought no approval from my family, no kudos for my commission. And when I was posted to India, I sensed they were relieved to have me away. Only my marriage to Margaret brought a sort of mocking approval, approval for her pretty face, her family and lands, her money, but mockery still for me. They were whispering to her, I felt, that she had taken her geese to a bad market when she selected me for a husband.

Whether Margaret's contempt for me sprang from those early contacts with my family, or whether she saved her mean judgements for Delhi, is a question to which I've never found an answer. Surely my treatment at the hands of my commander and his underlings, their assigning me to hateful lackey jobs, must have had some weight in the formulation of attitudes in my own home, those of Sophie as well as my wife's. But Margaret, I've concluded, had her own snotty values to refer to, the cloistered standards of her county. Flocks of sheep, horses in the stables, and overdressed fat women waltzing their drunken squires in great circles. Arrogance of the country folk. Pride of land and shadowy bloodlines. Damned northerners. Full of themselves. Walled in. A chapel inside the walls. Great packets of money to the Church. Self-righteous bastards. Self-involved. Riding their walls and hedges, totting up their holdings and their stores, lording it over their tenants, marking a stranger by his home county, marrying their daughters to the neighbours' sons.

That's it, of course. No matter what my military standing, the weight of my commission, the worth of a man who put everything aside to serve his king, I was branded from the first as an outsider. Not knowing it, I married a place, a point of view, not a woman, and when she left India, taking Sophie with her, using her mother's death as an excuse, it was there, to *this* place, Wiswell Towers, that she returned. More important than her marriage, more precious than her husband was the home soil; the ancestral manor. By God, I was victimized from the start, not by my shortcomings, my failures as man or soldier or husband, but by her birth, the fact of it, the location of it, and her steel-banded ties to the place.

Each of his diatribes to himself, about himself, resembled all the others. Almost daily now, since the divorce talks with Margaret had begun, he had sat in his chair or at his writing table, and repeated the scribbled

144

litany which, in his mind, spelled out his virtues and targeted relentlessly the forces that were raging to bring him down. The themes never varied, the cast of characters was constant, the acts of treachery against his character, his well-being, his destiny, even his right of domicile, were tirelessly delineated and expanded upon. Recently, however, since Margaret had told him she planned to marry again, a fresh theme, a new villain, had come to dominate this catalogue of woes and indignities suffered.

Bloody hell, what a beastly humiliation to have this chap Brannigan foisted off on me at this stage of my life, when I'm unable to deal with him. If he'd been under my command in India, I'd have set him right in a hurry, no doubt about that, the cheeky Irish bastard. I'd have put him through a drill he'd not have soon forgotten, taken some of that mongrel Donegal sing-song out of his voice and the swagger out of his walk.

It's damned ironic. I never expected such sabotage from Margaret's side of the field. Sophie, I expected, would be the problem. When she was growing up, I dreaded the prospect of dealing with the young men I knew would flock round her. But fate and my military duties kept me away when that time came. I was forced to rely on her own good sense, the sound principles she'd learned from me in Delhi, and Margaret's supervision of her. Except for her mis-step with Hugh Causey, she never embarrassed us or herself. And by war's end, when I was mustered out and in a position to oversee my family, our lovely Sophie was married to Toby Black, and a mother already.

I had no fault to find with Toby. A bit too pretty for my tastes, too smooth and gentle, but he'd been a fine soldier from all reports, and his military experience gave him some respect for my position in the forces.

And he died a soldier's death. Something for Sophie and his children to be proud of.

Sophie was no more than a girl, of course, when she was widowed. Still required some supervision from her father, advice about raising her children, that sort of thing. And since we all assumed she'd marry again sooner or later, I knew I'd be responsible for setting up a proper screening process. Wouldn't do to have her head turned by some well-tailored chap who didn't deserve her. While Margaret and her friends were casting about for a suitable husband for her, I set myself up as a committee of one to guarantee that when she married, *if* she married, she'd get what she was entitled to in the way of a husband.

As it turned out her standards were as high as mine. Or so I came to believe. She seemed content to stay on with us here at the Towers, raise her children properly, and live a quiet, decent, widow's life. Even when she decided to buy the house on Queen's Walk in London, I wasn't concerned. By then I was convinced that she was rock-solid, that I'd had a strong influence on her, that her values would be as unassailable in London as they had proved to be during the post-war years at the Towers. What a bloody fool I was. After she reached thirty I was sure she'd never marry again. And then suddenly she was remarried, to an Australian rascal I wouldn't hire as a stablehand, a man without background, education, or profession. It was the greatest embarrassment, the worst humiliation of my life, made worse because I knew that she'd done it only to hurt me. Now I see that it was undoubtedly a scheme between her and Margaret, a childish game designed to best the Major. And they succeeded. I was hurt and shocked. I still am. The fact that the man has suddenly become a public figure, that the name Kincaid is now common currency, in no way alters my assessment of him or Sophie's senseless marriage to him. It's an insult to her mother, to her children, and most of all to me. Kincaid's a common sort and nothing can change that fact.

As one can see here, each time Cranston attempted a frontal assault on Brannigan, he veered off, sought new targets, unable, it seemed, to summarize his anger and indignation, unwilling to crystallize the ugly circumstances of his life and his failed marriage by putting them into words.

At last, however, when the final divorce decree was in his desk drawer, when he knew that Margaret would be married again within a matter of weeks, when he felt defeated, threatened, and persecuted, he stomped round his study, endlessly inspected and polished his guns, stared out the window, drank a great deal of whisky, and finally found a way to absolve himself. He sat down and quickly scrawled the words which he believed would permanently exonerate him, would fix the guilt where it belonged once and for all.

It's Margaret, of course. The flaw is in her. It always has been. She's a woman who should never have married and she knows it now. Her dissatisfaction with India was really her disappointment with herself as a wife. I see that now. She never accepted that secondary role, never felt comfortable in it. Something about the male/female relationship made her uneasy. Having chosen a dominant male for a husband, it was a choice she couldn't live with. She did want to have a child, of course, but once Sophie was born, once that goal was reached, I became redundant in her eyes. Her marriage became an inconvenience. Until her mother's death released her and brought her home to England.

Seen in this light, the whole wretched business with Arthur Tagg comes clear. He was a male convenience. Handled the day-to-day functions of a husband, offered counsel and a certain amount of companionship until the sun went down. Then he went his way and she went hers. And since he was a hireling, he was subservient, of course. By definition. She, herself, was master of the house, as her mother had been. What havoc it must have created in her brain when I came home to stay. By God, I expect the notion of divorce occurred to her that very day. I was a threat to her chain of command. But where does her itinerant Irish picture-taker fit in? He who sleeps in a caravan. If she's divorced me because she wants no part of marriage, why would she take on a ragbag of a creature like Brannigan? To humiliate me, I suppose. But even Margaret wouldn't go to such lengths, would she? After all, if she's married to him she's stuck with the wretched fool. *If* she's married to him . . . perhaps that's the clue. What better way to persuade me to pack up and move on? A new husband is moving in, she says. That begins to make sense. A ruse to speed me on my way. No such marriage planned at all. Simply a great pretence. Along with Arthur Tagg's resignation. But once I'm out of the house, Brannigan will vanish in the bogs of Donegal, Tagg will return to his duties at Wiswell Towers and life will go on, life as conceived and designed by her majesty, Queen Margaret Wiswell Cranston. Well, by God, we'll see about that. We'll bloody well see about all that.

6

Thorne settled himself behind his wide desk, a pink light concealed in the ceiling tinting his white hair and softening his features. 'Well, a great deal has happened since the last time you and I sat down together. As I recall, we had just wrapped *Bushranger*. We both felt good about it, had high hopes for its success, but as with any film, we knew we had to wait for the final verdict from the public.'

He was sitting in his dim-lit office on the top floor of the Thornwood building on Sutton Row in Soho, early afternoon, a soft rain falling in the roof-top garden outside his French windows. Kincaid sat in a deep chair facing Thorne's desk.

'Now, of course,' Thorne went on, 'the verdict is in. It's been in for some time. From the first day we screened the picture, it smelled like a winner. Not only did it open well, it had staying-power. Twenty weeks at the McVickers in Chicago, four months so far at the Roxy on Broadway, and it looks as if it may run for ever at the Palace in San Francisco. Big cities, small towns – it's done well everywhere. We all took a chance and it paid off. I've had big hits before but I've never had one that gave me more personal satisfaction. It's always nice to win but there's a special kick when you bet a long shot and it pays off. So how do you feel about it? Evan tells me you're recognized every place you go in London. He says you don't like that much.'

'I don't like it at all,' Kincaid said.

'Actors either like public attention or they hate it. Most of them love it. A few of them, like Cagney, feel the same way you do. He says he can't stay in a New York hotel any more. He uses a phoney name, comes in the back door and takes the service elevator upstairs, but it does no good. Two minutes after he's in the room the phone starts to ring and strangers are knocking on his door.'

'So how does he deal with it?'

'It's a part of the business. He accepts it. He's like you. He likes his wife. They stay home a lot.' He lit a cigarette. 'You can't blame the fans. They're just regular people. Once they see you on the screen and read about you in the papers, they feel as if they know you. If they're lucky enough to see you in the street or in a restaurant, they want to talk to you, shake hands, tell you how much they like you.'

'I understand it. But that doesn't make me like it.'

'I know it can be a nuisance but people find ways to deal with it. They have to because it doesn't go away. If you never made another picture it wouldn't matter. People would still know you twenty years from now. There are guys in Hollywood who haven't worked for years and they're still recognized every place they go.'

'Maybe I'll have to go back to Tasmania.'

Thorne smiled. 'That won't help. You're big news in Tasmania. The picture did well in Hobart.' He repositioned himself in his chair. 'We both know why I'm here,' he said. 'I haven't been bothering you because the last time we talked you said you wanted to cool out for a while, spend some time with Sophie, and not think about another picture. Wasn't that the gist of it?'

'Pretty close.'

'That was almost six months ago. I think it's time for us to talk now. I assume you agree or you wouldn't be here. I have a lot of things to tell you about the new project I have for you. We also have business details to hash over. Contract matters. But before we go into any of that I have one question to ask you. Depending on how you answer it, I will call California this afternoon and scrap the picture we've been developing for you or I'll give them the go-ahead to set up a shooting schedule. I guarantee you that I am willing to make any deal you want, short of handing over the studio. I said that before, when we discussed *Bushranger*, and I gave you everything you wanted. I assure you, I'll do that again. On a much grander scale. What I'm saying is that no money differences can shoot down this deal. The creative people will be the same crowd we had for *Bushranger*. The only things I have no control over are whatever personal roadblocks you may have. Those you'll have to handle yourself. If you want to go forward on this new film you have to tell me now. If you don't want to, for whatever reasons, as long as those reasons don't include your going to another studio, then I will respect that decision, I'll tear up your contract at the end of the year, and we'll call it a day. So you've got the ball. What's it going to be?'

'What if I told you I haven't made a final decision?'

'I'd say I can't accept that. Last time we talked, you wanted to look at *Bushranger*, see what the public reaction would be, and take some time to decide what your next move would be. I have to look at it this way: if you can't give me a yes now, I could wait six more months and I still wouldn't get the answer I need. You know how I feel about you and your work and your potential, but if the success of *Bushranger* hasn't persuaded you to go ahead, then there's nothing I could say or do that would convince you. I'm sure you have other considerations, family pressures, that sort of thing. We all do. But the final decision has to be yours. It's your career and your life.'

'If you're telling me I have to give you a final answer right now, while we're sitting here, I can't do that.'

'I'm sorry to hear that. Because that is a final answer.' He pressed a buzzer on his desk-top. 'This is a disappointing moment for me. Guys who can do what you can do don't come along very often. But I've got a studio to run and sometimes that has to come first.' His secretary came into the room then. Thorne said, 'Excuse me a moment,' to Kincaid. Then to the secretary: 'I'll be leaving London sooner than I'd planned. The *Britannia* sails for New York tomorrow afternoon. I want to be on it. And send this cable right away to my brother at the studio: KINCAID TURNED DOWN DILLINGER. CALL WARNERS ABOUT BOGART.

When the secretary left the room Thorne said, 'If it was anybody but you, kid, I'd tell you you were making a big mistake. But in your case I'm sure you know what you're doing.' He stood up behind his desk and said, 'I wouldn't want you to quote me, but there's a lot more to life than just making shadows flicker across a movie screen.'

As soon as Kincaid left his office Thorne called his

secretary in and said, 'Don't send that cable to my brother yet. Type it and hold it, and I'll tell you when to send it.'

'I made your *Britannia* reservation but I didn't cancel the tickets you're holding for next week.'

'Good. I'm leaving the office now. If Kincaid calls later this afternoon tell him you don't know where I can be reached.'

'Yes, sir.'

When Thorne came into his office the following morning he asked if Kincaid had telephoned the previous afternoon.

'No, sir. I was here till seven.'

'Hmmmm . . . maybe I guessed wrong.'

'If you're going on the *Britannia* the driver will pick you up at noon, either here or at Claridge's.'

Later that morning, ten minutes before he was due to leave, Thorne's secretary rang through and said, 'Mr Kincaid is here.'

When Kincaid walked into the office he said, 'I wouldn't want you to miss your sailing. I just wanted you to know that I'm ready to talk now. If we can come to terms, I want to make the picture.' He smiled. 'Unless you've already made a deal with Bogart.'

Thorne rang through to his secretary. 'Cancel me out on the *Britannia* and have the driver wait downstairs. Mr Kincaid and I are going to have a long lunch at Prunier's.'

7

The previous afternoon, when he'd left Thorne's office, Kincaid's car had been waiting at the kerb. 'Are you going home, sir?' the driver asked.

'I don't know where I'm going.'

'Shall I drive round for a bit?'

'That's a good idea, Harry. Let's have a nice drive.'

They turned up Charing Cross Road and continued

northwards along Tottenham Court Road. Kincaid leaned back, his head against the smooth fabric of the seat, his eyes half-closed, the streets and pedestrians blurred in his vision as the car rolled past.

They turned west on Euston Road, then along Park Square East to the Outer Circle and into Regent's Park's inner drive. They took the long way round to St John's Wood, then made their way south and west through Notting Hill. Kincaid's eyes were full-open now but he paid no attention to the streets they passed through or the cars and pedestrians that clogged them. He seemed lost in his thoughts, frowning slightly, occasionally stroking his jaw with his fingertips.

At the foot of Kensington Church Street where it meets Kensington High Street, the driver, on the speaking-tube, asked, 'Are we all right, then, sir? Shall we go along the park toward Piccadilly?'

'That's fine. I want to go to the Garrick.'

It was almost four o'clock when he found a corner table in the lounge of the Garrick Club. When he left to go home it was just after six. For all that time he sat alone with one glass of whisky, his back half-turned to the room. The bar and the lounge gradually filled with actors and men of the theatre but Kincaid seemed unaware of the energy and high spirits that surrounded him, colourful accounts of triumph and vengeance.

That evening he and Sophie attended an evening of dramatic readings at St Martin-in-the-Fields, a memorial to Sir Arthur Wing Pinero, who had recently passed away at the age of seventy-nine. After the programme they had a late supper with Howard and Sybil Wiswell, Sophie's aunt and uncle. Very late, when they were at home at last, in their robes, having a night-cap in their upstairs sitting-room, Kincaid said, 'Did you remember I had an appointment with Thorne this afternoon?'

'Of course I remembered. How is he?'

'Suave and benevolent as always. A walking advertisement for Savile Row.'

'But how *is* he?'

'He's fine. Positive, prosperous, and healthy. Bursting with pride about *Bushranger*.'

'I'm not surprised.'

They sat silent then for a while, sipping their brandy, waiting calmly for they knew not what. At last Sophie said, 'And is he also bursting with plans for you? Is he keen to have you back in California Thursday week?'

'He's keen to have me do another film, the one Evan finished just before he came home a few weeks ago.'

'That doesn't surprise us, does it?' she said. 'I'm sure he thinks you have a great future. Everyone does.'

'He's a businessman. He smells money.'

'Of course he does. And do you smell money?'

'I wouldn't put it that way. But I'm getting a sense of the marketplace. I have a pretty clear idea of what I'm worth.'

'What you're worth, or what you're worth to Thorne?'

'What I'm worth as an actor. What I'm worth as part of a motion-picture.'

'I'm sure you're worth a great deal.'

Again they were silent. At last she came over and sat beside him on the couch. 'Hello,' she said, 'my name is Sophie. I saw you in a smashing film, and I thought you were splendid. I'd really like to get to know you better. And I'd like you to know me. As a person, I mean.'

'Sorry, honey, I'm busy now. If you want an autographed photo of me, you have to write to the studio. They'll mail you one if you send along the proper postage.'

'What a rotten man you are. Not friendly at all. Nothing like the person you seem on the screen.'

'I'm sleepy,' he said. 'Let's go to bed.'

'Is that what you say to the young things who ask for your autograph?'

'No. That's what I say to mature ladies like you.'

'Oh, my dear, I promise I'll make you suffer for that.'

'I hope so.'

Later when they were lying in bed, the lamps still lit, Sophie said, 'Why do I feel as though you're playing patty-cake with me?'

'I don't know.'

'Are we pretending your meeting with Thorne isn't important? We have studiously avoided talking about such things ever since *Bushranger* came out. Now you mention it casually, then you distract me with a bit of frolicking in bed and it's off to dreamland. Is that the way it is?'

'I'm sorry about the frolic,' he said. 'I know you'd rather have a polite conversation than carry on like that.'

'You're bloody awful tonight.' She flicked off the lamp. 'I'm going to sleep and dream of the way you used to be.'

He flicked the switch on his side of the bed and the light came on again. He pulled her close to him, her head on his shoulder. 'I don't play games with you,' he said. 'To tell you the truth, I'm not sure how things stand with Thorne.'

'How do they stand with you?'

'I'm not sure of that either. That's what I told him.'

'What did he say?'

'He said I've had six months to make up my mind. He wanted a yes or a no today. I told him I couldn't give him one, and he said, to his mind, that was a no. While I was sitting there he sent a cable off to California, telling his brother that I'd turned down the picture.'

'Now what?'

'Now I expect they'll find another actor and make the picture with him.'

'You already know what I want you to do,' she said then. 'I've never made a secret of it. Are you telling me you're really giving it up? Are you saying that we can be

155

ordinary married people again and not have to scurry back and forth between here and California?'

'That's the way it looks.'

'That's the best news I've had in years.' She flipped off the light again and lay close to him. 'Now I'll sleep like a baby.'

In a few minutes she was asleep, her breathing even and warm against his cheek. Kincaid lay on his back, his arms around her, his eyes open, looking up at a pattern of soft shadows on the carved ceiling.

8

The next morning Sophie slept late. When Mrs O'Haver brought her breakfast it was past ten o'clock.

Ruth O'Haver had been Margaret Wiswell's personal maid when Sophie was a schoolgirl. When Sarah and Trevor were born she took care of them. And when Sophie and the children moved to London she came along, first as governess and finally as housekeeper. She had never been married but she was referred to as Mrs O'Haver. Although there was not a great difference in their ages she always called Sophie, 'child', when they were alone. Or 'Sophie dear'.

'How nice, child,' she said as she brought in the tray. 'You let yourself have a proper night's sleep.'

'That's because I'm contented. I sleep like an infant when I'm happy. I didn't even hear Kincaid get up.'

'He had breakfast some time ago. Up and out early.'

'Out for a good walk, I expect. He never gets enough of Green Park.'

As Mrs O'Haver was leaving the room Sophie said, 'Tell Oliver we'll have lunch at home. At one o'clock. And ask cook to make it an especially lovely lunch.'

It was a lovely lunch indeed but Kincaid didn't come for it. Sophie sat at table alone and toyed with her food. At

156

five o'clock he still had not come home or telephoned. When she asked Oliver to ring the Garrick to see if he was there, he came back in a few minutes and said, 'The porter says Mr Kincaid has not been in today.'

She went upstairs to her sitting-room then and rang up her uncle. When her Aunt Sybil came to the phone Sophie said, 'Nothing urgent, dear. I seem to have misplaced a perfectly good husband. Did he drop in on you perhaps?'

'I suppose he could be with Howard at his club but I don't think so. When Howard came in at lunch-time he said he'd seen Kincaid popping in to Prunier's as he drove down St James's. Thought perhaps he was meeting you there.'

'Afraid not, Sybil. He must have been meeting one of his secret lady-friends.'

'Not likely, Sophie darling. Not the way he looks at you. Howard hasn't looked at me that way since two months before we were married. I expect Kincaid had some business affairs to chat about. Howard said he was with a grey-haired gentleman.'

Only fifteen or twenty minutes elapsed between the moment that Sophie replaced the telephone receiver and Kincaid's return home, but in that short time Sophie felt as though she were being squeezed dry. She felt betrayed and empty, resentful and angry. When she sensed Kincaid's presence in the house she was torn by two equally powerful impulses. One: to run down the broad staircase and confront him. Two: to hide in some dark corner of the upper storeys where she wouldn't have to see him at all. At least not until she had firm control of herself. In a moment, however, he came into the room, all high colour, with the perfume of champagne floating round him, and a pirate's glint in his eye. When he crossed the room and put his arms round her she twisted away and said, 'I don't feel awfully well. I can't talk to you now.'

'What's the matter?'

'Nothing's the matter. I don't need a doctor. I just

need to be by myself for a bit.'

He turned her back to face him. 'You're mad at me. You're angry as hell at me. What's this all about?'

'I can't talk now. I don't want to say things I'll be sorry for.'

'There's nothing wrong with being angry,' he said. 'Go ahead and say what you have to say. What did I do?'

'Never mind what I have to say. I think we should hear what you have to say. When you came bouncing into the room just now, a blind man could see you were full-up with some kind of remarkable news. So why don't you tell me what it is? Then we'll go on from there.'

'You sound as if you're about to declare war. Perhaps you're right. I think we should talk later. After you've calmed down. After you've got hold of yourself.'

'I may never calm down,' she said. 'What if I don't want to get hold of myself?'

He sat down on the arm of a wing-chair. 'I'm trying to figure out what happened to you between the time I left here this morning and a few minutes ago when I came home.'

'Let's talk about what's happened to you. Then maybe you'll realize what's happened to me.'

'Do you think I was in bed with somebody all day? Is that what's got into you?'

'No. I wish you had been in bed with somebody. That I would know how to deal with.'

'You're not making sense, Sophie. Last night . . .'

'All right, *last night*. Let's talk about last night. What was that great performance all about? What you said to Thorne and what he said to you. Was all of it made up or just part of it?'

'It was the truth. I didn't make anything up.'

'Do you expect me to believe that when I went off to sleep last night, smiling like a fool and believing in the tooth-fairy . . . are you really trying to tell me that you

158

didn't know then that you were going to see Thorne again today?'

'That's exactly what I'm saying. I lay there thinking for a long time after you went to sleep . . .'

'And then you woke up this morning and said, "I think I'll stroll over to Thorne's office for a little chat." Poppycock, my darling. You danced all over my head last night. Testing the water. Taking a reading. Trying to see how I'd react when I heard what you're about to tell me now.'

'What makes you think you know what I'm going to tell you now? What makes you think I'm about to tell you anything?'

'Because I'm a witch. I can see through walls and hear the sparrows sing in Bucharest.'

Kincaid stood up. 'Tomorrow we'll talk. I've never seen you like this.'

'Neither has anybody else. Because I've never been like this. Never had this particular experience before. I don't mean I've never been lied to. I'm not saying I've never told a lie myself. But this is absolutely Wagnerian. At what moment in the time I've known you did you decide that you couldn't tell me the truth, that it was better for me to discover things, to stumble on the facts, to find things in bureau drawers?'

'God damn it, Sophie, I've never lied to you about anything.'

'All right, let's test that. Did you tell Thorne that you hadn't decided if you want to do another film, after which he said he couldn't wait, so the deal was off . . .'

'Yes, that's exactly what happened.'

'. . . or did you tell him that you wanted to do the film, that you were going to do the film, and let's sit down and work out the details.'

'I told him that, too. I told him today. I am going to do the film. I spent the day with him getting everything straightened out. That's what I was eager to tell you when I came home a while ago.'

'And how did you think I'd react to that news after the charade we went through last night?'

'That was no charade and you know it.' He walked to a chair and sat down. When he spoke again his voice was very quiet. 'I'll tell you what I thought. I thought you'd react like a grown-up woman does when her husband tells her he has a great opportunity. I thought you'd be happy for me. And willing to sit down and work out the details of the whole business. Willing to go with me to California so we could be together and not strung out half-way across the world as we were last year.'

She was quieter, too, now. 'You think I'm totally selfish, is that it? Just thinking about what's good for me?'

'No. I think you sincerely hate Los Angeles and the idea of spending time out there. But you did spend some time there with me and it didn't kill you. I'm not in love with it either, but if I'm going to work for Thorne, I have to *go* there. It doesn't mean we have to take root there and become natives of the place. Let me put it this way: what if we were having breakfast one morning and I told you I hate living in London, that I hate the whole idea of England, that I only feel at home in Tasmania, in the city of Hobart, what would you say?'

'I wouldn't believe you.'

'Why not? I believe you when you say you can only live in England with occasional trips to Brittany. Why shouldn't I have the same attachment to the country I come from?'

'We have a serious problem to deal with,' she said. 'Why are you trying to create a new one?'

'Because if we take the hateful word *California* out of the picture for a moment, I think you'll see things more clearly.'

'But that's the subject. *California*. That's all we're talking about.'

'No, it isn't. We're talking about whether I work or don't work. We're talking about compromise. If I were as tied to Tasmania as you are to England, I assume we'd try to find some middle ground that would satisfy both of us. If I had a business in Australia that required me to be there six months every year, I assume you wouldn't pack me off there by myself.'

'But you don't have to be in California. Or any place else.'

'Yes, I do. Listen to me, Sophie. I've spent my whole bloody life looking for work, for a place to sleep, for a decent meal, trying to prove to people that I was worth the few shillings they might pay me. So all this is more than just a job to me, it's more than just a bit of money. For the first time in my life, someone's coming to me. Instead of my having to prove I can do the job, I'm being told I'm the only one who can do the job.'

'So you do like all the attention after all?'

He shook his head. 'I'm saying it means something to me to find out I can do something, something that a lot of other people would like to do but can't. I don't give a damn about the public part of it if that's what you're thinking. People love you one day and ignore you the next. That means nothing to me. What's important to me is how I feel about myself. I know we have a lot of money because *you* have a lot of money, and I'm not self-conscious about that. It doesn't bother me one way or the other. I'm glad we have it. But that has nothing to do with my finding out that I can earn money myself. Because of something I do. I don't give a damn about being famous. It never occurred to me that I could be. But now that I've discovered something about myself that I knew nothing about two years ago I can't just walk away from it. Do you know what I'm saying?'

'Of course I do. I know it's important to a man to work at something. I'm not keen to go America. I admit that. And I'm certainly not attracted to California. But it's

161

more than that. What frightens me is the size and the commotion and the ugly power of that whole business out there. I can't take it in. It's like a great machine gone out of control. And for all its public nature, its clamour for attention, for all the smiling and all the glitter, there's something secret and shadowy about it, something not quite clean. Too many surprises, too much compromise. It makes me uneasy. It's like a contest where the rules change every day. I'm a classicist. You know that about me. I like structured things, things that can be analyzed and understood. From what I've learned about the film business, it seems totally pragmatic. If it works it's good. Solve today's problems, meet the schedule, and we'll deal with tomorrow's chaos tomorrow. And your part in it, the actor's part, particularly unsettles me. In almost every job or profession, one must provide a certain type of work. That's what one has to sell. But an actor sells himself. Over and over. His business is to provide his physical self.'

'Like a prostitute,' Kincaid said.

'No. Not like a prostitute. Of course not. I'm not discounting the natural gift an actor must have, the skills he must develop. But all the same I just can't help wishing you'd chosen another profession.'

'I didn't choose it, did I? It chose me.'

'No matter. Whether you chose or were chosen, you're in it. And you seem determined to stay in it. But I can't feel good about it. I feel as if it's going to swallow us up. Angus Bradshaw used to say, "A man with two wives loses his soul. A man with two homes loses his head!"'

'It won't happen to us, Sophie.'

'I know you believe that and I want to believe it too, but I'm still frightened. I can't help it. The whole idea scares me to death.'

BOOK TWO

· CHAPTER 5 ·

1

Mary Cecil cried herself to sleep the night before Evan came back from London. The next morning when she ran across the high-vaulted reception-hall in the Los Angeles railway terminal her eyes were red and swollen. She put her arms around him and kissed him, then buried her face in his neck and said, 'Don't look at me. I look awful.'

He held her away from him, then pulled her close. 'You don't look awful. You look wonderful.' He kissed her again, then he gently kissed her eyes. 'You look as if you've been crying.'

'I have. And I may start all over again. I feel dreadful.'

He led her to a bench a few steps away and they sat down. 'You've got it all wrong,' he said. 'You're supposed to cry and feel dreadful when I go away, not when I come back.'

'It's not that,' she said. 'You know it's not that.' Her eyes filled with tears. 'I feel so rotten. I don't know how to tell you. I couldn't sleep all last night just thinking about it.'

'For God's sake, what is it?'

'It's your car. Your beautiful car.'

'That's nothing to cry about. What about my car?'

'It's gone, Evan. Someone set it on fire in the middle of the night.'

'What?'

'Someone poured gasoline on it and burned it up.'

'That doesn't make sense.'

'It was parked in the carport beside the house. The carport was burning, too. Someone saw the flames and called the fire department. I was sound asleep in our bedroom, at the opposite end of the house. The first I knew about it was when the firemen woke me up.'

'Thank God you didn't get hurt. When did it happen?'

'The night you left Southampton on the *Bremen*. I can't tell you how miserable I felt. When the fire was finally put out, that end of the house was all black and charred and your car was like a great knot of twisted metal.'

'Are you saying someone burned it deliberately?'

'I couldn't believe it either. But the police inspector and the men from the Malibu fire department said it was arson. No question about it. They found two gasoline cans burned up with the car and there's still a stink of gasoline all round. I'm so sorry. I feel awful about it. I slept through the whole mess.'

They walked out to the car-park then and put his baggage in the boot of her Auburn coupé. She manoeuvred through the tangle of downtown Los Angeles to Olympic Boulevard then headed west toward the coast.

'What did the police say when they talked to you?'

'They said Los Angeles has more than its share of nuts and freaks and pyromaniacs so they're never surprised by stupid crimes like this. They asked what we were doing in California and I said you were working for Thornwood. Then they wanted to know if you'd made any enemies since you were here, and I said none that I knew of. So they said they'd talk with you when you got back. Do you know anybody who might do such an idiotic thing?'

'Not in California,' Evan said.

'You're thinking of Alec, aren't you?'

'Don't tell me that thought never came to you.'

'Of course it did. But he's not in California.'

'How do you know? You told me nobody knows for certain where he is at any given time.'

'That's true. But all the same, it would be a long trip for him to make just to annoy me. And since I never heard from him I assume he wasn't here. Or isn't here.'

She had decided not to tell Evan about the late-night telephone calls she'd received while he was away. Now she was tempted to tell him, but instead she said, 'Besides you said in one of your letters that you'd seen him in London.'

'That was weeks ago. When I first got there.'

'All the same . . .'

'I tried to contact him several times later. But I was never able to reach him.'

'He never answers the phone. That's one of his foibles.'

'Along with starting fires,' Evan said. 'Do you know anyone else who's a firebug?'

'I don't think I'd call Alec a firebug. I know he threatens it all the time but I'm not sure he's ever really done it.'

'Geoff Bingham says he set fire to an old gentleman he'd hired as a dresser. Backstage one night. Bingham was in the room when he did it.'

'Maybe he was and maybe he wasn't. Geoff never lets the truth stand in the way of a good story.'

'I'm sure he didn't make up that story.'

Mary didn't answer for a bit. Then: 'I hope you don't discuss me with Geoffie. He's a nasty gossip.'

'He knows we're living together. Almost everyone who was involved with *Bushranger* knows that. And his wife is one of your best friends. You can't expect your name not to come up. He's your friend, too, isn't he? You told me you've known both of them since your first days as an actress.'

'It's true. They're old friends. Actor friends. But that doesn't mean I confide in them. I'm not sure I confide in anyone except you. And my daughter sometimes.'

She took one hand away from the steering-wheel as they waited at a traffic light and touched his cheek. 'I'm so sorry I had to give you such dreary news. And I'm sorry I have a hopeless husband. But can we please not talk about unpleasant things and tiresome people for a while? Ever since you left I've been thinking about the day when you'd come back. I don't want to spoil it. I want to be naughty and reckless and irresponsible, and spend the whole afternoon in our big bed. I need to see if you can possibly taste as sweet as I remember.'

Very late that afternoon they sat on the deck in their robes, drinking wine and watching the sun sink toward the far edge of the sea.

'When did you find out about the new picture?'

'Thorne sent a radiogram to the ship. The day before we docked in New York.'

'That must be a load off your shoulders.'

'Big relief. I went straight to the bar on the promenade deck and got totally pissed.'

'With a beautiful countess from Bulgaria. Sleek black hair, hoop earrings and a gown cut down to her waist.'

'No such luck. I met a man named Webster from Cleveland, Ohio. He manufactures bathroom fixtures. I got drunk with him. When I told him we're about to do a film about John Dillinger he said, "Don't glorify the bastard. He's a bastard."'

'Will Kincaid's wife come out with him this time?'

'I don't know the answer to that. But I expect we'll find out soon. Thorne wants to start shooting sometime in August. We'll have a great deal of location work in Indiana and Illinois and Wisconsin. Then we'll finish up back here in the studio. At least that's the schedule now.'

'Will it be another triumph? Like *Bushranger*?'

'Who knows? It's tough material to write. Farm lads who turn into killers. Country police. Federal investigators. New language for me. I expect I'll be rewriting all the time as we go along. Listening to people. Trying to get it right.'

A bit later, when Mary went inside and came back with a second bottle of chilled wine, she said, 'When you left to go to England, you didn't tell me you planned to see Alec.'

'I didn't tell you because I had no such plans. But once I was in London and I knew he was just a few squares away I thought it might be worth a try. Told myself I might catch him in a reasonable mood. Agreeable. Co-operative. That sort of thing.'

'And did you?'

'Hard to say. His definition of reason is different from mine. But God knows, he can be agreeable as long as the gin continues to flow.'

'Did you meet in a pub?'

Evan shook his head. 'Took him to lunch, actually. At Juliana's.'

'Lovely. Too good for Alec.'

'He doesn't agree with you. He was quite critical of the place. Suggested we trot round to an Italian place he favours.'

'Ormando's,' she said. 'That's his hang-out. Chancy Sicilian food. But they put up with his shenanigans. Let him run up a chit there. So he loves it.'

'In any case we stayed at Juliana's. I had an excellent meal and he must have drunk a half-litre of gin. Beyond that, not much was accomplished.'

'What were you hoping for?'

'As I said, I thought that behind that alcoholic haze there might be a spark of decency. Or if not that, at least a bit of common sense. When he realized that you and I had gone beyond whatever he imagined we were up to, when he knew that we'd decided to make a permanent thing of this arrangement, when I'd convinced him that you and he were a thing of the past, that you wouldn't be coming back to him under any circumstance, when all those facts were spread on the table, I felt there was a good chance that he might have a more civilized and reasonable reaction to the matter of divorce. So I did indeed present all that material to him, as I forked up my gigot and white beans and he slurped away at the Bombay.'

'And what was his reaction?'

'He was highly amused. Thought I was having him on, I think. He seemed to have no objection whatsoever to our living together.'

'Alcoholics are difficult to offend.'

'Is that it? Anyhow I saw no indignation or resentment in his manner. I was not made to feel that I'd trespassed, that I'd played fast and loose with his property.'

'He was amused, you say.'

'Yes. In his elliptical way. He seemed to be taking the position of a producer who was having a new scenario presented to him to see if he found it either believable or commercial. We did not discuss the commercial prospects but he made it crystal-clear that everything I told him was unbelievable. He didn't call me a liar – perhaps he thought that would stop the deliveries of gin – but it was plain that he thought I'd been given false information.'

'From me?'

'He didn't specify. He simply said that you had never discussed divorce with him, never in all your happy years together. He also said that he has had no correspondence from you since you've been here with me in California. No letters about divorce or anything else.'

Mary's cheeks glowed rose from the last blood-orange rays of the sun. 'He's a bloody liar and I think he's drunk himself bonkers. You know I've written to him from here. You've seen the letters. I've read them to you.'

'Oldest trick in the theatre, he says. Write a letter, read it to the audience, but don't post it.'

'Why on earth would I do that? Do you think I did that?'

Evan shook his head. 'I'm simply telling you what he said.'

'You know how much I want things to work for us. It's more important to me than anything.'

'I told him that. I said that if he insisted on being a bastard about the divorce we would simply go on living together.'

'What did he say to that?'

'I don't remember his precise words. But the implication was that he had no objection. Seemed to feel we should get it out of our systems, as the saying goes. He says you'll never divorce him, that you're totally dependent on him. I'm quite sure he used the word *armature*.'

'He would have done. He loves that word. And it does apply in this case. But not as he meant it. The truth is that I've been *his* armature through all these years. Heaven knows where he'd have ended up without me to support him. Financially and in every other way. Of course he doesn't want to give that up. But now he has to whether he likes it or not. Still, it won't be easy. As you've seen, he'll lie and scheme and do whatever he can think of . . .'

'But he wouldn't come all the way to California just to fire-bomb my blue Packard. Or would he?'

She sipped her wine, looked out at the little waves lapping at the edge of the sand, and didn't answer. At last she said, 'What will you tell the police tomorrow?'

'Not much, I'm afraid. If they want a list of my enemies, I don't have one to give them. After all, I'm reasonable and fair-minded. Lovable as well. How could I have enemies?'

If he'd hoped to lighten their conversation it hadn't worked. She continued to stare at the sea. Then: 'You told me your mother lives out here. Is there any chance that she . . . that some friend of hers . . .'

'God, no. She never even came to my mind. People

171

don't go cruising around setting fire to strangers' cars. Not unless they're crazy . . .'

'But you're not a stranger. Maybe she has some resentment . . .'

'I read part of her letter to you. She doesn't feel resentment toward me. She feels guilt. She's not likely to do me some damage that would make her feel even more guilty. We're not talking about a common everyday impulse. You and I only know one person who sets fire to things.'

'I told you. I don't believe all those stories.'

'Maybe not. But the first time I ever laid eyes on Mr Maple, he sat in my flat and told me that his idea of retribution, his kind of vengeance, was to set people on fire. There was no doubt in my mind that he meant it. And no doubt that he could smell smoke when he looked at me.'

'You're not planning to tell the police about that, are you?'

'At first I wasn't but now I think perhaps I should.'

'What good would it do?'

'Probably none. But if they checked passenger lists and immigration records they'd know if he's been in the country, and so would we. You can be sure the insurance people will do a thorough investigation no matter what we say or don't say. That was a Thornwood Studios car. Fully insured. The insurance company will pay all right. They probably have already. But when someone destroys something and it costs them money to replace it, they get very curious about who it was.'

'Oh, God. Is it going to be a big mess? In the newspapers and everything?'

'There'll be an investigation but Thorne can make sure it's not in the papers if I ask him to.'

She turned to face him. 'Please don't tell them about Alec.'

'Do you think he was here?'

'No, I don't . . . I don't know . . . I don't know what

to think. But please don't tell them.'

'If they investigate and find out you're his wife, they'll know about him whether I tell them or not.'

'But they wouldn't know about the threats. And all those stories about his burning things.'

'If you knew for sure he'd been in California, you'd tell me, wouldn't you?'

'What are you saying? Of course I'd tell you. I don't keep secrets from you.'

'It's all right. Everybody has secrets.'

'Not me,' she said. 'Not from you.'

Late that night when they were asleep, the telephone in their bedroom rang. When Evan picked up the receiver and answered there was no response. After a long moment a man's voice said, 'Oh, it's you. You're back then. Well, welcome home.' After the line went dead, when Evan replaced the receiver and lay back in the bed, Mary said, 'Who was that?'

'No one,' Evan said. 'Nobody answered. Wrong number, I expect.'

2

Before his car was burned, Mary had planned to tell Evan about the series of telephone calls she'd had. Very late at night. No answer when she picked up the phone. Even after the fire she expected to tell him about the calls. But when they were together, when their conversation had so quickly turned to Alec, she didn't tell him. She wasn't aware of making a conscious decision about it, she simply didn't say anything.

The morning after he returned, however, when he took her car and drove to the studio, she rang up Burt Windrow. 'Did you telephone here last night?' she asked him.

'Do we say good morning as we learned from our

nannies,' he said, 'or do we begin straightaway to ask questions?'

'You promised you wouldn't make trouble for me with Evan. If you go back on that promise I'll strangle you.'

'There's no need for that, Mary. I didn't telephone you. Did someone tell you I did?'

'No. But there was a call sometime in the night and Evan answered it. I need to make sure it wasn't you.'

'Be reassured.'

'Don't screw me up, Burt. This is important to me.'

'I'm sure it is. No one ever accused Mary Cecil of falling in love casually.'

He had called her first several weeks before, not long after Evan had gone to London. One early morning when she was having breakfast she answered the phone and heard a mellow British voice, an actor's voice. 'Is this the gifted and succulent Mary Cecil?'

'May I ask who's calling?'

'This is the magic fellow who played Laertes when you played Ophelia. It's Burt Windrow come back to haunt you.'

'Why are you calling me? How did you get this number?'

'One has sources of information you know. You must remember that I'm a dear friend of Alec Maple. He is still your husband, isn't he?'

'We're getting a divorce.'

'Ah . . . perhaps I'm calling at a perfect time then.'

'Actually, it's not a perfect time. I'd prefer that you not call me at all.'

'Abandoning old friends . . . is that it?'

'We were never friends and you know it. Whatever we were, we weren't friends. It must be five years since I've seen you or heard your name spoken.'

'Is it that long? The memory plays tricks, doesn't it?'

'I'm going to ring off now,' she said.

'Just give me a moment. Actually I called because I

thought I might be able to do you a service. You see, I've been going through some old papers, throwing things in the dust-bin, and I found a packet of letters from you. I thought perhaps . . .'

'Please throw them out. Better still, burn them. I thought you'd have done that long since.'

'I can do that, of course. But if they were my letters, if I had written them, I would like to have them in my own hands so I could destroy them personally. After all they are extremely intimate in nature. Not the sort of thing one would want floating around.'

'What are you saying exactly?'

'I'm saying that I'll be having lunch today at an out-of-the way spot called Elsie's on the Malibu Canyon road. Only truck-drivers and ranch-hands go there. So if you'd like to meet me at about one, I will buy you a simple lunch and turn over your letters to you.'

Elsie's was half-way between the Pacific Coast High-way and the extension of Ventura Boulevard that becomes Highway 101. Mary arrived there at ten minutes past one. When she went inside, Windrow waved to her from across the room. When she sat down at his table he said, 'One learns promptness if nothing else from a life in the theatre. It's odd, isn't it, how little the public knows about our real nature. We're a disciplined lot. The work demands it. Precise cues and entrances. Maintain the established performance rhythm. No departures from the text or the blocking. Never late to rehearsal. And curtain up on the stroke of eight. God, but you look smashing, Mary. Brown as a nut. Hair bleached yellow-white by the sun. I swear to God, you could play Ophelia today and no one would raise an eyebrow.'

'It's kind of you to say that but I have a daughter who's the proper age to play Ophelia.'

'Of course you do. All the more miraculous that you look so young and radiant.'

'You look well, yourself. Tennis, isn't it? Isn't that your sport of choice?'

He nodded. 'One plays an enormous amount of tennis out here. Perfect weather for it, of course. There's even a bit of money to be made if you're willing to wager on yourself. Very competitive crowd on the courts. Anxious to be the best. Determined to make energy and desire take the place of skill. Eager to lose their money as long as they believe there's an outside chance they may beat you. There are chaps who make a handsome living out here just playing tennis. I'm told I could do that myself if I chose to, but I have other projects in mind.'

'When did you leave England?'

'Five years ago. More or less. Give or take a month or so. It was just after we . . . I'm sure you remember when I left.'

'No, I don't believe I do.'

'No matter. I went off to South Africa. Cape Town, actually. A first-rate company doing *Winter's Tale*, *Importance of Being Earnest*, and one of the Maugham plays – *The Circle*, I think. We had a fine run down there. Good audiences. And a jolly social life. As it turned out, the principal theatre man asked me to stay on in Cape Town after we'd finished our run, and I agreed. Played some lovely leading roles for the next two years until some of my mates who'd gone to America encouraged me to come out here.'

He signalled to the waitress then and said, 'We'll have our food now.' When he turned back to Mary he said, 'I'm sure you're pressed for time so I ordered for us when I got here. Normally this is a steak and roast beef place but they do a nice thing with cold shrimp at lunch-time. So I've asked for the shrimp along with an avocado salad and a pitcher of iced tea.'

He kept up a running monologue as they ate their lunch. 'I had a ripping good time when I first got here.

New boy in town. Great expectations. Parties and yacht trips and interviews and one's picture in the magazines; great glowing promises from studio heads and their underlings. A powerful agent took me on but as it turned out he led to my downfall. Unbeknownst to me he had a passion for a young actress named Laura Barton, who was under contract to Universal. He steered me into a romance with this girl without telling me that she was the mistress of Lionel Tree, who was head of production for the studio. The plan was that I'd take the girl away from Tree, and then my agent would exercise his *droit de seigneur* and take her away from me. But I didn't know that. All I knew was that I'd been fixed up with a lovely girl and we were having a fine time together. Then all at once, everything collapsed. The studio invoked the morals clause and cancelled Laura's contract. She scurried back to Lionel Tree's bed like a deer in a forest fire. But it did her no good. He didn't mind sleeping with her but he made sure she couldn't get a job as an actress. And suddenly all the studios lost interest in me as well. They're a tight bloody fraternity, those buggers. They chew up actors and spit them out like corn-flakes. The only one who came out of the affair without a mark on him was my agent. He dropped me, of course, and last week I read that he'd taken on Laura Barton as a client. So I expect he got what he wanted after all.'

He ate his lunch as he talked steadily. Mary picked at her food, looked at her watch, and listened.

'I did a few small parts but nothing exciting. Nothing that showed what I'm capable of. My old friends from London, Ralph Forbes, in particular, advised me to go home, to do a play or two in the West End, then come back here later. If I'd had the money I would have done that straight away. But as it was, I owed quite a lot to several of my chums so it appeared I was stuck here. Then I had a windfall. A newspaper chap I'd met at Doug Fairbanks' place offered me a job ghost-writing a gossip column for a nasty old drunk named Mavis Castor. It was easy work and decent money so I did it. Next thing I knew, after a few months went by, the old vulture decided to abandon her column – big syndication all across the Midwest – and take over as editor of *Photoplay*. Actually she wanted to hang on to the column and have someone like me continue to write it, but the *Kansas City Star*, the paper that heads up the syndicate, said nothing doing. They sent me train tickets, I went back there for a few days and they gave me a contract to go on with the column under my own name. *Windrow on the Inside*, they call it. Now all those studio bastards who wouldn't give me the time of day are trying to get *me* on the telephone. Whatever they're doing, however much money they're pulling down, they have to see their names in the paper every day or they think they're on the skids.'

Mary looked at her watch again. 'It's nice you're doing well, Burt, and I thank you for the lunch, but I really have to go now.' When he didn't answer she said, 'You were going to bring me some letters. Isn't that what this urgent meeting was all about?'

'Do you believe in fate?' he said. 'I do. I try to plan ahead and make things happen, make something positive out of my life. But when I look back I can see that most of the really good things that have come to me were like summer lightning. Take those letters, for example. You're right . . . that's why I rang you this morning to arrange a meeting so I could give them back to you. Had them all tied up in a packet. Put them on the hall table where I keep my car keys, so I wouldn't forget them. But when I was almost here, when I turned off Ventura into Malibu Canyon road . . .'

'Oh, for God's sake . . .'

'Wait a minute. Let me finish. I pulled off to the side of the road, waiting for the cars to pass by so I could make a U-turn and go back for the letters. Then all of a sudden, I said to myself, "Mary doesn't want those

178

letters. In all this time she's never asked me to return them. So why am I doing this? After all they're my letters, addressed to me, the most beautiful love-letters I've ever received. They remind me of a wonderful time in my life . . ."'

'For the love of God, Burt, what are you talking about? We had a stupid affair. I don't think it lasted a month . . .'

'Three months. A bit longer. There must be at least thirty letters . . .'

'Ten letters . . . thirty letters . . . what's the difference? I can't believe I wrote you that many times, but if I did, I did. I was going crazy back then. Everything in my life was falling apart. Nothing made sense to me.'

'Anyone reading your letters would never guess that. All you talked about was how happy you were. You went into great detail about those lovely afternoons in my flat in Chelsea.'

'I don't want to hear about it. Please. Have a bit of decency. That's a part of my life I'd like to forget.'

'Ironic. I like to remember it and you want to forget it.'

'You never intended to give me the letters, did you?'

'Of course I did. You'd be surprised what a full working day I have. It's very seldom that I break it up for a pleasant lunch like this.'

'What do you really want, Burt? Did Alec put you up to this?'

'He did tell me you were here. And I believe he mentioned you were living in Malibu.'

'God! I feel as if someone's throwing a net over me.'

Windrow smiled. 'You were always tortured. I'd forgotten about that. That's a very sexy quality you have.'

'Why am I sitting here listening to you?'

'I expect it's because of the letters. Once I'd reminded you I still have them, knowing you as I do, I imagine you came up with all sorts of strange scenarios, the various ways those letters might be used against you. Am I right?'

'There's nothing mysterious about what you're doing. It's some sort of blackmail, isn't it? That's why I'm still sitting here. I'm waiting for the second shoe to drop. Sooner or later you're going to tell me what you want, what I have to do to keep those letters out of circulation.'

'Let's forget about the letters for a moment. What would you say if I told you I'm in a position now to help my old actor friends? I assume since you're living here in California that you're available to work in films.'

She shook her head. 'I'm not. Novello wants me for his new play. I'll be going back to London soon.'

'There you are. You see, I didn't know that. I thought if I made some references to you and your stage work in London it might get you some good film roles.'

'That's very kind of you but as I say . . .'

'It's not kindness. For a columnist to stay ahead of the curve he must grant favours and receive information. I'm competing with Parsons and Hopper and Justin Gold and Gloria Westerfield. There's just so much information out there and we all want to get it first. So we depend on our sources. We nurture relationships with people who have inside information. It's like a mathematical formula. They get mentioned in my column and I get exclusive items from them about other people. You're aware of the process, I'm sure.'

'Of course I am. But I don't see how it affects me.'

'Perhaps it doesn't. But on the other hand it might. You're in daily contact with Evan Tagg. He's in daily contact with Roy Kincaid and Julian Thorne. Everything Kincaid and Thorne do is news to people who read columns like mine. Where they go, what they do, what they eat and drink, who they see, who they hate, who they love, what they think, what they say, where they buy their clothes, what sort of pyjamas they sleep in. You see what I'm saying?'

'Yes, I do. And you expect me to supply you with that kind of information?'

'No. I don't expect anything. I'm simply telling you what sort of things are helpful to me in my job.'

'But if I don't supply you with information I'll be at risk.'

'Not at all. We're not talking about pressure or blackmail. We're two old friends having a conversation over lunch. We're not signing agreements or contracts. I like to think of it as an arrangement where two people can help each other. A mutually beneficial situation.'

'And when, under this arrangement, do I get my letters back?'

'Any time you say.'

'I see. That means you've made copies of them.'

'What a suspicious creature you've become.'

'Not at all. I just know the man I'm dealing with. I haven't forgotten you completely, you see. All the rotten things are very clear in my memory.'

'I remember nothing but the good and you remember only the bad.'

After he paid the check, when he walked her out to the car-park, he said, 'I never reveal a source, you know. That's my credo. People have learned they can trust me.'

Mary smiled a great pumpkin smile, 'What a bizarre and ingenuous statement coming from you. It's a wonder you didn't choke on it.'

'Sticks and stones.' As they stood by the door of her borrowed car he said, 'You needn't trust me but I trust you. Implicitly. And because I trust you I'll tell you something no one else in the world knows. It's something that will make our arrangement more productive, I'm sure. Since you have such a low opinion of me, I expect you won't be surprised to learn that in addition to earning my living with this column I have a serious black purpose. I intend to do everything I possibly can to damage Kincaid. If I can muck up his career completely I'll consider myself a total success.'

'Is this a personal thing or . . .'

'Extremely personal. Painful and personal.'

'You know him then?'

Windrow nodded. 'Not well. But well enough. He humiliated me in public. Last year when he came to Los Angeles for the first time. We had a drink together one afternoon at Lucey's, just down the street from Paramount. He almost strangled me. Half the customers in the place looking on. Another thirty seconds and I'd have been dead.'

'Are you saying he attacked you for no reason?'

'No reason whatsoever. At that time he'd never made a film. No one knew him as an actor. I was ragging him a bit, all in fun, and he misinterpreted a remark I made about his wife. Next thing I knew, that butcher's hand of his was around my throat and I was half-unconscious. That night as I lay in my bed with hot towels around my throat, I promised myself I'd get square with that son of a bitch if it took me for ever.'

3

During their luncheon at Prunier's, Thorne had told Kincaid a great deal about John Dillinger and the film they would be making about his life. 'You'll remember when we started to work on *Bushranger* you knew more about Ned Kelly and his family and the uprising at Glenrowan than any of the rest of us. This time the shoe's on the other foot. As it should be. Our research people have put together a file on every word that's been published about Dillinger and Baby-face Nelson and Pretty Boy Floyd, all that crowd. I've read most of it myself, and I've seen to it that Iverson, our art director, Bob Deal in production, and Russ Tunstall, our camera chief, have also read the material. And Tagg and Tim Garrigus, who'll be directing for us again, have turned themselves into historians. Tim's made trips to Indiana and Chicago and Wisconsin, seen where Dillinger grew up, talked to his family, seen the Crown Point Jail that he broke out of, using a wooden gun he'd carved himself. He's been on the grounds at every key point in the story. We think those details are important. We're not just making a cops and robbers show although, God knows, there'll be a lot of shooting and car chases – no other way to tell this story. But behind all the blood and guts we aim to have a social document. This Depression we're going through has done terrible things to lots of Americans. And it seems that the working class, the labourers, the miners, and the farmers, honest hard-working men and their families, have suffered the most. Lost their jobs, lost their farms, lost their homes, many of them, and they don't understand why. Roosevelt's done a lot to make things better but it's a tough job and there's still a lot to be done. Meanwhile all these people who live in the middle of the country feel cut off from what's happening in New York and Washington. Every time something bad happens to a man or his neighbour it seems the banks are behind it somehow. Forced auctions, foreclosures, property taken over. And it's always the bankers who are the villains. Or so it appears. Then all of a sudden along comes this poor kid from Indiana, a farm boy like a lot of Americans, and this guy starts robbing banks. Dressed up in a suit and tie, driving a fast car, he breezes into some small town with two or three of his friends, empties a bank, and a few minutes later he's gone, with ten thousand dollars in his pocket. Breaking the law. No doubt about it. But to a lot of people he looks like a hero. It's an old story in America. Jesse James, the Reno brothers, the Daltons, all of them were heroes to the poor people. Even that snot-nose they called Billy the Kid. Most of the men he shot were bushwhacked, shot in the back, but you can't tell that to anybody who thinks he was fighting for the little guy. So now, right or wrong, we've got John Dillinger, the working man's hero, especially the man who's *out* of work. A man who wouldn't steal an apple gets all switched around during hard times. He admires a man like Dillinger, envies him. There's no question a few people have been shot, and some of them died, but not so many as you might think, considering how many hold-ups have taken place. Even his own men say, "John never shot nobody." So that's the position we're going to take. He's a law-breaker. No doubt about that. But he's not a killer. He's a clever fellow, a ladies' man who takes good care of himself, and people like him. Before he busted out of jail in Crown Point, the sheriff posed for a picture with his arm around him. The FBI's out to kill him if they can, and maybe they will. But whatever happens he'll always be a hero to his own people. What we're going to do is what we did in *Bushranger*. We won't say here's the story of an outlaw or the story of a hero. We'll just lay it out scene by scene, tell the truth as much as we can, and let the people in the audience decide what kind of a man he is. I'm a little concerned about the ending. It's tricky when the story's still going on, when our man is still in the headlines, but that's the way it is so we'll just have to live with it. Evan and Garrigus think we should end with the big shoot-out at that lake in Wisconsin. When the FBI surrounded the hotel, Dillinger got out anyway. We'll end with him driving down a country road with his girl. Not laughing. Just matter-of-fact. Another day, another dollar. Life goes on. He's a desperado. They'll get him sooner or later but they haven't got him yet. We'll end on a high shot. His little car scooting down a narrow road in that beautiful farm country.'

4

'You're as impossible as my daughter,' Margaret said to Clara Causey. 'You both know my age to the very day.

But all at once you seem to have decided that I'm a helpless adolescent. My father used to say, "When a woman wants to get married, she's probably old enough to do so." Well I qualify on both counts. I want to and, God knows, I'm old enough. I suspect that Sophie thinks I'm too old. But that's because she's only thirty-three.'

'I know you're capable of doing anything you want, but all the same I feel terribly remiss. We can't just let you wander off to Donegal all alone to be married.'

'Of course you can and you must. Clara, my dear wonderful friend, there's nothing to be done. I'll simply repeat to you what I said to Sophie. I won't be wearing a virginal white gown. Nor will I carry a great armload of white lilies. If I did I'm sure Brannigan would abandon me at the altar. He assures me it will be a tiny ceremony. All his relatives will be banned. So you mustn't feel guilty about not being there. None of my family will be there either. Sophie and Kincaid and the children will be on a ship bound for America. This time they won't stop in New York, however. Through the Panama Canal straight on to California.'

'For more than a year you've been telling me that would never happen.'

'That's what I believed. And I'm convinced that Sophie believed the same thing. But I was mistaken and so was she.'

'And she's taking Sarah and Trevor, too?' Clara asked.

Margaret nodded. 'Something she swore she'd never do.'

'How did it come about? A change of heart, or was she persuaded?'

'Some of each, I expect. She's always able to see the other person's viewpoint. Not that it lessens her own strength of purpose. She can be as wilful sometimes as my mother was. But on other occasions, when you least expect it, she can bend like a reed in the wind. If someone asks her why she changed course so abruptly, she usually says, "I was being silly. One doesn't have to win all the time."'

'I wish my daughter knew that,' Clara said. 'Nora thinks that every day is a life-and-death struggle. Lose one battle and you die.'

Margaret smiled. 'Nora's a storm-tossed gypsy. There's no one else like her. Sophie's a different sort altogether. She's sociable and flexible and co-operative. Seems to be a peace-lover. And in large part she is. But underneath that silky exterior she's all principle and conviction. She's ferociously British, for example. She truly believes that civilization reached its peak on this island. And it's not just an emotional conclusion. She's a keen student of history. Knows the good and bad, the warts and wens, of our past. But she's pieced it all together and decided there's no better place to be, to spend her life, to raise her children. Those convictions are so strong in her that I'm sure she went to America last year with a closed mind, a preconceived judgement of its shortcomings. Consequently, she saw what she expected to see. Also she spent most of her time in Los Angeles, and although I've never been there I suspect that it's not a total picture of American life.'

'You're right. It's not.'

'You asked me why she's going back there now. For one thing, she doesn't want to be separated from Kincaid as she was last year when he was doing *Bushranger*. She tried to put a good face on it at the time – you remember I visited her for a while in Praia da Rocha – but she was miserable. She made a decision then, I think, that they mustn't be apart like that again. This was before anyone knew what a success he would become so perhaps she felt that any further trips to California might not be necessary. But of course once we'd all seen the film, once we saw the public reaction to it, it was plain that Kincaid's career, if he wanted it, had just begun. The other thing is this: you used the word *persuasion*; we haven't discussed this, Sophie and I, but I think Kincaid may have taken a firm stand about the California business.'

'Does that surprise you? From what you've told me, it's just what I'd expect from him.'

'Exactly. He's certainly able to make up his mind and he's very capable of saying what he's decided. The Major found that out before Kincaid and Sophie were married. But like many strong men, he's also kind. And he's very much in love with Sophie. This may sound strange, but when I first knew him I thought perhaps he loved her too much. Bearing in mind the kind of society in which you and I grew up, it's refreshing to see a man defer to his wife. In Kincaid's case I was afraid he might defer too often. I hoped they wouldn't slip into a pattern where Sophie would make all the decisions. Because she was so young when she married Toby, because of the war, his injuries, and his death, and because she'd had the two children so quickly, only a year apart, she's had to design her own life by herself, to plan for Sarah and Trevor, to manage her money, to deal with servants twice her age, and run a household. By the time she met Kincaid she'd been a widow for twelve years. And Kincaid was seven years younger than she, only eleven years older than Sarah. What I'm saying is that it would have been easy for Sophie, simply out of habit, to have continued as head of the household, maker of rules, solver of problems. And in fact I was afraid that might be happening. So I was delighted last year when I learned that Kincaid had an opportunity to make a career for himself, to establish himself in a profession. I didn't share those feelings with Sophie because I suspected that she was less enthusiastic than I about Kincaid's prospects. It's one thing to marry a successful or important man. It's quite another experience to see your husband, after your marriage, pull himself up by his bootstraps and set off in a new direction. In those circumstances it's easy for any woman, I expect, to feel that if her man was totally contented with her he wouldn't need to scramble about for an activity, a job, a career, particularly one that necessitated his being away from home a great deal. If the family needs money, of course, as most families do, if the man must earn a living, then all these other considerations are academic. But in Sophie's case, where there is as much money available as they could possibly need, one can understand that a wife might wonder, might hesitate, might ask questions. Of herself as well as her husband. Anything that changes the rhythm of a marriage can be cause for concern. You know that as well as I do.'

Clara smiled but said nothing.

'So I come back to my original point,' Margaret said. 'Without knowing what the process was that brought about the decision, I think they've made a good choice. For both of them. Perhaps living in America will only make Sophie more attached to England but there's nothing wrong with that. On the other hand she may find some tolerance for ways of living that she would never have chosen for herself but which seem to nourish a great number of other people.'

'My father always said that the greatest benefit of travel, perhaps the only benefit, is to break that insular membrane we all live in, to consider other alternatives. When I was a very young girl he told me, "The more you see, the more you'll understand. The more you understand, the quicker you'll be to accept new things. And finally you'll be able to accept many things you don't understand at all." '

'That's what I've been trying to say. Your father said it better.'

'What about Sarah and Trevor? How will all this affect them?'

'Kincaid seems to have arranged all that, too. Trevor wants to go back to St Alban's next winter but he'll be in California at least through the autumn. Both of the children are keen to see America. Sarah particularly. Kincaid arranged for her to study acting during the summer with an old Russian actress who lives in Los Angeles. And in the autumn she'll go to a fine girls' school near Los Angeles, where she can continue to study dance and drama along with her other classes. Then, if she behaves herself, we've arranged for her to attend the Ridgewood School in Bexley when they come back to London. Also she'll be allowed to come in on Saturdays for a young people's class at RADA. She's delighted with this programme and Sophie says she's behaved like a lamb ever since it was worked out.'

'How did you deal with Miss Endicott? Ridgewood must have contacted her about Sarah.'

'Of course. But before we spoke to Ridgewood I took a trip down to Kent and spent two hours with Jane Endicott. Jogged her thinking a bit. Refreshed her memory. At last she realized that any negative report she might give about Sarah would be a poor reflection on her school as well. Apparently she was persuaded. She wrote to Ridgewood giving a glowing recommendation of Sarah.'

'Sophie must be very happy,' Clara said. 'All her problems are solved.'

'Let's say she's cautiously optimistic at the moment. I expect she won't be truly content till she leaves California and comes home to London.'

5

The day before Arthur Tagg left Wiswell Towers, when Margaret saw his valises and boxes on the north veranda ready to be taken to the station, she hurried up the stairs to her rooms, sat by the window, and wept. Later, in a letter to Clara, she wrote: 'It was heart-breaking, seeing that tiny cluster of his belongings. Two small valises and some cartons tied with twine. I asked myself, is this all he owns? Is this the sum total of what he's accumulated in his life? Where will he go with these meagre gypsy trappings? Where will he live? What will he do? What will become of him? Is it possible that he'll step into the car tomorrow to be driven to the station and I'll never see him or talk with him again?'

A bit later that morning she sent a note to Arthur and asked him to meet her in the library. When he came in looking as crestfallen as she felt, she said, 'Sit down, Arthur. Let's have a talk.' She poured tea and passed him a cup. Then she said, 'I'm very cross with you. I looked out on the veranda this morning and there were your things waiting to be picked up. It gave me a peculiar feeling. Not a pleasant one. So I decided we should have another chat about it before you disappear across the moors never to be seen again. Is that the way it's going to be? Are you just going to vanish and we'll pretend we never knew each other, that you never lived here?'

'I don't think I'd put it in those terms.'

'I'm glad to hear that. What terms would you use?'

'Just a turning in the road, I suppose. These things happen. Sophie's off to America soon with her husband. My son's already there.' He smiled. 'Migrant workers following the harvest.'

'Oh, poppycock, Arthur. You're not a migrant worker. What harvest are you following?'

He seemed flustered. 'I didn't mean that I . . . I wasn't referring to a particular . . . it's just a figure of speech, I suppose.'

'I know we've discussed this before. You seemed to have a closed mind about it then and I expect you do now. But have you really thought it through? Are you sure you know what you're doing? That it's the right thing to do?'

'Oh, yes. I'm quite sure.'

'But this is your home, Arthur. It has been for more than twenty years. One doesn't simply pack up and leave one's home with no destination. No place to go.'

'But I have a place to go. I'll be using Evan's flat while he's in California.'

'And then what? Will you be off to a bed-sitter in Notting Hill Gate?' As soon as she'd said it, she wished she hadn't. 'I'm sorry. I didn't mean to be sharp with you. But I'm dreadfully upset that you're leaving like this.'

'I thought I was giving proper notice.'

'Oh, Arthur, my dear Arthur, I'm not talking to you as your employer. That's never been our relationship and you know it. We're friends. Close friends. But I feel as if I'm losing that friendship. Ever since you told me you were leaving I've hoped that you would reconsider. I know you've been happy here. You have, haven't you?'

Arthur nodded. 'You've provided a wonderful life for Evan and me.'

'And you have reciprocated in a thousand ways. Is there no chance that you might change your mind? Is there anything I can say or do to influence you?'

'I'm not angry, Margaret. This isn't an emotional decision on my part. Actually I've considered it very carefully in all its aspects and I always come to the same conclusion. If you told me there was no place for me here because of a change in circumstances, I would accept that. When I said that I feel bound to leave for that same reason, a change in circumstances, I was hoping you would accept it as well.'

'You're saying you're leaving because I'm going to marry Brannigan. Is that it?'

'That's part of it, of course. But not in the way you think perhaps.' He paused. 'I don't want to be blunt or presumptuous.'

'Please,' she said, 'be as blunt as you like.'

'You know as well as I do that there's been a certain amount of tension here since Major Cranston retired from the army, and it has increased remarkably in the past year. I think you'll agree that a great deal of that tension was caused by my being here. You and I have discussed it on several occasions, and we agreed that the Major's misconceptions about our friendship were no reason for us to end that friendship or terminate my employment here. Is that correct?'

'Yes. I still believe that.'

'So do I. But as I say, circumstances have changed. Now you're facing a situation where you'll be living here with your new husband, Mr Brannigan, your ex-husband, Major Cranston, and myself as well if I decided to stay on. If we agree that there was tension and turbulence before, one can hardly imagine what these new circumstances might bring.'

'But the Major will not be living here. Our divorce is final now and he must leave.'

'I know. You told me about the legal procedures your solicitor described.'

'The action for trespass has already been put in motion.'

'And I daresay there's been no response from the Major.'

'I believe not.'

'I've known men like Major Cranston before. They're not strong but they have negative power. Their greatest strength is resistance. If he's still in residence here five years from now, I won't be surprised.'

'Is that why you're leaving? Because you believe that?'

'No, Margaret. I'm leaving because I must.'

The following morning, when the car took him to the station in Newcastle, Margaret watched from her upstairs sitting-room. She stood at the window and followed the car down the tree-bordered drive to the county road, then along that road as it curved across the moors and disappeared at last.

Their conversation the previous day had stirred conflicting emotions in her. For the first time since her reckless holiday with Brannigan the summer before, she doubted herself. In spite of the school-girl exhilaration she felt, was she perhaps making a wrong turn? No hint of such a thought had come to her before. Was Arthur, in his way, trying to tell her that, to suggest that to her? Had the excitement of breaking free, of stepping outside her familiar life-pattern, misted her good judgement? Had her refusal to be limited or defined by her age made her forget her true circumstances? Had she convinced herself that she was a young woman still, with a young woman's options? Was she deceiving herself and was Arthur the only one willing to make her aware of it? Each time she looked down on the north terrace, she imagined she saw his pitiful cluster of belongings still sitting there, waiting to be carried away. It was an image that clung to her and upset her out of all proportion to its simple meaning. Was it a stark symbol of souls in transit? Of hers and Cranston's and Arthur's? Of Brannigan's, too, in some strange way? Was Jack making as big a mistake, perhaps, as she was? And what about Cranston? Despised by everyone. How would she react when the lorry came to fetch his military baggage and boxes and crates of guns? When he lumbered down the steps and disappeared in the rear seat of whatever car had been designated to take him to his exile?

As she walked away from the window she spoke aloud. 'What in the world has come over you? Pull yourself together.' She went into her bedroom, sat down at the dressing-table, and brushed her hair, counting the strokes. Then she lay back on the *chaise-longue* and looked up at the ceiling as her thoughts danced back and forth and stumbled over each other. She closed her eyes and consciously tried to relax her body. Fingertips, arches, thighs, one small section at a time. But her mind was beyond any such therapy. It continued to go its own way. At last she gave up all thought of sleep. She allowed her eyes to open and she lay there, powerless, staring up at the ceiling.

When Evan left California to go to London, all the elements of his life seemed to have clicked smoothly into place. The first film he had ever written was a success, he had just finished writing a second scenario, and he was certain he had a strong professional ally in Julian Thorne. He knew no details then of the chaotic affairs at Wiswell Towers, he had no reason to believe that Kincaid would not agree to do the new film, he'd had some communication from his mother, and most important of all, there was Mary Cecil. He hated to leave her in California but the knowledge that she would be waiting there when he came back put a whole different colour on his departure.

In London, facts and events, and his perception of them, told him that his future lay elsewhere. The prime purpose of his trip, to discuss the Dillinger screenplay with Kincaid, was instantly negated when he learned that Kincaid had not read it, was not prepared to read it, and until he had read it, until he had decided whether or not he wanted to do another film, saw no reason to discuss it.

His conversations with his father and Margaret had been disappointments, too. Although he had no affection for Cranston, the Major had been a permanent fixture in that household; the thought of both him and Arthur being absent from the Towers disturbed Evan somehow. He was not offended by the thought that Margaret would soon be married to a man he had never met, but all the same some conservative pocket inside him considered it unseemly. And reckless perhaps. His meeting with Alec Maple had set his teeth on edge; his old friend, Alan Winkler, had seemed stodgy and predictable; and both Sophie and Sarah, in entirely different ways, had appeared nervous and anxious about the future. Even ordinary incidents of the day – an aggressive taxi-driver, a short-tempered newsagent, a slow drain in his bathroom sink – took on new significance, made London a lesser place and his beach-house in Malibu a tender haven in a benevolent land. Heading back there, crossing the Atlantic, standing on the foredeck, his imagination transformed the Atlantic's churning waters into the easy smooth blueness of the Pacific.

This dreamlike, childlike anticipation, however, was turned on its head, first by Mary's swollen eyes and sudden tears, and then by the outrageous news about his car. Then came the extended examination of Maple, his objectives, his motives, his peculiarities, and Mary's surprising defence of him, her insistence that his name must not be mentioned to the officers investigating the car-burning. And had she been entirely candid about her letters to him? Had she truly discussed divorce with him or had she not? And had she seemed distracted since Evan came home or was it only his imagination? Surely when he left for the studio in the morning and when he came home in the late afternoon, there was nothing missing between them, no holding back, no thin transparent shield that slipped between them at certain moments. Or was there?

No matter how much he chided himself and accused himself of imagining difficulties where no difficulties in fact existed, he could not find again the easy rhythm of life and work that he had left when he went off to London. Although he was able intellectually to defuse and scoff at each one of his separate anxieties, he remained unquiet. At the end of each day he felt as if he had been in combat with a room full of great soft pillows, trying to find his way to a door or window and not succeeding. But day after day his most persistent irritant was the memory of that unctuous voice on the telephone the afternoon he came home from England, 'Oh, it's you, You're back then. Well, welcome home.' Several times each day after his return he resolved to tell Mary precisely what the man had said but each time he failed to do so.

7

One afternoon not long before Kincaid and Sophie were due to sail to America, Oliver rang upstairs and said there was a gentleman in the foyer asking to see Mr Kincaid. 'His name is Maple. Alec Maple.'

'I don't believe I know him,' Kincaid said.

'That's correct, sir. He says you've never met.'

'What does he want to see me about?'

'Says Evan Tagg sent him. He indicated it's a matter of some urgency.'

Maple, when Kincaid joined him in the drawing-room, seemed to have groomed himself for the occasion. He wore a dark suit and a sober cravat and seemed to be freshly barbered and shaved. And when he spoke to Kincaid it was with uncharacteristic humility.

'I'm frightfully sorry to disturb you like this. Unannounced and all. I certainly wouldn't have come if I didn't believe it was in your best interest.'

'You're a friend of Evan Tagg, I understand.'

'Not an intimate friend. One didn't mean to imply that. But a close acquaintance. Perhaps that's more to the point of it. We've met several times. Had some good talk.'

'Your name's familiar. Are you an actor?'

Maple smiled modestly. 'There was a time when I was thought to have a bright future in the theatre. Good times ahead, everyone said. But mistakes were made. Careless judgements. Unwise choices. And a patch of illness along the way didn't help. So I drifted away from it, from the make-up and the footlights, and all the rest. Found other interests, as they say. But I've maintained contacts

196

among my actor friends. I'm always welcome back stage. They all seem happy to see Alec Maple.' He glanced at the clock on the mantelpiece. 'I know I've interrupted your afternoon so I won't take a lot of your time. I'll tell you straight away why I've come. You mentioned that you'd seen me before.'

'No. I think I said your name was familiar.'

'Ahh . . . so you did. I'm a member at the Garrick, as I know you are. So I thought perhaps you'd seen me there.'

'I don't believe so,' Kincaid said.

'No matter. In any case it's apropos that I mention the Garrick because it was there that I received the information that I felt should be passed along to you.'

'The butler said that Evan asked you to come here.'

'That's not precisely true. But since I know you two are close friends I twisted the facts a bit in a good cause.'

'I see. What is it you wanted to tell me?'

'An actor friend of mine was told by an American journalist that ugly stories about you are being circulated in California. A whispering campaign I think he called it. A new rumour every week, he says. As though it's an organized campaign to damage your career.'

'What sort of stories?'

'You understand I got this second-hand. But it seems there's a story about your being in prison . . .'

'That's a known fact. I admit that to anybody who asks me. I spent a lot of time in jail.'

'These stories, I believe, are about things that happened while you were there. Ugly. Nasty. Also, there's a story that you're a bigamist. That you have a wife and child in Argentina. And they say your parents are still living in Tasmania, that they're indigent and in poor health but you've abandoned them.'

Kincaid smiled. 'I appreciate your concern and I thank you for taking the trouble to come see me, but you see, I pay no attention to stories like those. I've been reading lies about myself ever since I gave my first interview. Now, since I don't give interviews, they make up stories. Half the things I told them in interviews were made up too. So what's the difference?'

'You don't think these things might threaten your career?'

'As far as I'm concerned I don't have a career. Not yet. My first picture was a good one. If the next one's terrible I'll come back here to London and smoke cigars in my bathtub. So I can't worry about losing something I don't have. And I wouldn't worry in any case. I've never given a damn what anybody thinks of me and I don't give a damn now.'

When he went upstairs Sophie said, 'Who was that?'

'Some bird who says he's a friend of Evan.'

'What did he want?'

'I'm not sure. I haven't figured it out yet. His name's Maple.'

'Evan's lady-friend is married to a man named Alec Maple,' Sophie said.

'That's right. That's who it was.'

'So what did he want?'

'Just a bit of idle chatter.'

'What sort of chatter? What did he say?'

'Nothing worth repeating.'

'What did he *say*, Kincaid?'

He told her then, as accurately as he could, precisely what Maple had said. When he finished she said, 'So it's starting up again. Is this the way it's always going to be? Ugly stories in print? People telling lies about you?'

He walked over to her and put his arms around her. 'No,' he said. Then he kissed her. '*This* is the way it's going to be,' he said then. 'Just you and me. The way it's always been.'

To everyone who knew Sophie well, it appeared that she had capitulated totally. Once the seminal question was settled between her and Kincaid, she applied herself to making plans for their transfer to California. Behind all that industry and concentration was the same questioning and apprehensive person, of course, but that tender creature had been sworn to silence. Once it was clear and accepted that they were going to America for an unspecified period of time, Sophie made it a point of honour not to dull the enthusiasm of her children or Kincaid with her own doubts. She helped herself in this regard by cultivating a fanatic attention to detail, making lists, revised lists, new lists, and last-minute lists, and meeting twice daily with Oliver and Mrs O'Haver, who would be going along, to review progress on their preparations. New trunks and pieces of luggage were ordered, inspected, sent back and replaced. Clothing was laundered or cleaned, new garments were made or bought. Trying to anticipate all their needs, trying to remember from her previous trip with Kincaid what British products she needed but had been unable to locate in America, she overstocked everything, took a year's supply of toilet articles, colognes, cosmetics, shaving-soap, lotions, medicines and shampoos for herself and the children. Beach gear was included, bathing-costumes for everyone, tennis racquets and Indian clubs. Necessary vaccinations and innoculations were researched and administered by family physicians. And careful arrangements were made for the family dogs and cats who would accompany them on the ship. And all this activity, as noted, was performed in good spirits, much like a preparation for *Twelfth Night* at Wiswell Towers.

Miss Glass, who had been assigned by Thorne to organize their previous stay in Los Angeles (she now signed her letters and cables to them by her first name – Jennifer) had been put in charge of the house search. Having summoned the leading estate agents of Beverly Hills and Santa Monica to her Thornwood office, she sorted through the brochures and photographs they gave her and sent the best ones to Kincaid along with her assessment of each property and her personal judgement as to its suitability for the Kincaid entourage.

'How can I choose?' Sophie said. 'They all seem quite magnificent.'

'It's very simple. You simply pick the one that's most magnificent and we'll take that one,' Kincaid told her.

Each day's mail, it seemed, brought a new packet of homes, villas, and estates to consider. After they'd managed to narrow down the group to five, in a few days it had grown to ten again. Or twelve. 'They're all so grand,' Sophie said, 'but perhaps the photos are deceptive. Can't we wait till we get there and see the best ones in person?'

'Of course we can. But if we choose now the house will be ready to move into when we arrive. Straight from the ship to the house with all those tons of whatever it is you've been packing for weeks.'

'And if we haven't picked a house, all of us will have to squeeze into hotel suites till we make a decision. Correct?'

'That's it.'

'Then I must try to choose.'

And she did. She pared the list down to five finalists, cabled Miss Glass for additional data about each of them and when her self-imposed deadline arrived, two days before they were to sail, she made her final tentative definite interim decision, a mammoth Greek Revival mansion on secluded acreage in Santa Monica. The following morning she said, 'I'm ready to cable Miss Glass.'

'Greek Revival?' Kincaid said.

'No. I think the one in Beverly Hills is best.'

She'd picked a rambling Tudor home on a walled estate in Shadow Hill Way. 'This is the one,' she said. 'I promise.'

'I'll tell you what. A few hours won't make much difference. Let's talk it over at dinner tonight. Then we'll cable first thing tomorrow before we leave for Southampton.'

He took her to dinner at Strudwick's, an extremely private restaurant in Adam's Row. It was impossible for Kincaid to be recognized there because the guests never looked at each other.

'You know why I love it here?' Sophie said. 'Because all the customers are so old it makes me feel as if I'm twenty.'

'To me you're eighteen. If you were twenty you'd be too old for me.'

'I know why you're taking me to dinner,' she said then. 'Because I've been so good. So angelic and wonderful. Have you noticed that I spread joy everywhere I go?'

'You spread real-estate brochures everywhere you go.'

'I'm serious. Do you recognize me now as the lady who was determined never to set foot in California again? I'm a different person, am I not? Loyal wife and doting mother. Buying smoked glasses, bathing-costumes, and sun-cream. Checking California temperatures in *The Times*. Giving Sarah and Trevor nothing but glowing reports when they ask for details about Los Angeles. Do you want to know how I achieved this magical transformation?'

When Kincaid smiled and nodded, she said. 'It was a simple trick. I should have tried it before. I said to myself, "If it's good for Kincaid it will be good for me. If it's not good for me I'll make it good. If there's no way to do that, then I'll pretend it's good." '

'You'll like it this time. I don't think you'll have to pretend.'

After they'd finished dinner, when they were having coffee and Armagnac, he said, 'So what's the final decision? Where are we going to lay our heads in California?'

'Shadow Hill Way,' she said.

'Good. I'll send off the cable in the morning.' He took a packet out of his jacket pocket then and said, 'I meant to show you these before we left the house but I forgot.'

'Please. Not another house. I don't want to go through that again.'

'It's a house all right. Remember last year when *Country Life* came to take pictures of Wiswell Towers?'

'How can I forget it? It changed my mother's life. Jack Brannigan took the pictures.'

'That's right. I was still in California doing *Bushranger* then. So you sent me a set of the photographs. I didn't think they were very good prints so I took them to the photo lab at Thorne's studio and asked them to make copy negatives and a new set of prints. After I came back here I forgot all about them. And I guess the lab men did, too, because they've just now sent them along to me. They're beautiful. I thought you'd like to see them.'

He slid the envelope across the table to her and she opened it, took out a number of five-by-seven prints and began to look through them. She studied each one carefully, then went on to the next one. She didn't say anything until she'd put them back into the envelope. Then she smiled at him and said, 'You're a rat. Just when I'm trying to pick a house for us to live in on the other side of the world, you decide to show me pictures of the most beautiful home in England. Bad timing, Kincaid.'

'I know. But I wanted you to see them all the same. It would be great if we could find a place like that in California.'

'Don't torture me.'

'Or if we could just pack up Wiswell Towers, stone by stone, and rebuild it out there.'

'You're really cruel tonight. Here I am, about to settle for a fake Tudor house surrounded by Italian villas, French monstrosities, and California bungalows with thirty-two rooms, and you're teasing me to distraction with beautiful photographs of the house I grew up in. Very naughty.'

He took the pictures out of the envelope again and slowly shuffled through them. 'Some funny things happened when they made these prints. Especially the exterior shots. Did you notice?'

'I didn't pay much attention to those. I know the exterior by heart. I was studying the beautiful rooms.'

He handed one of the prints to her. 'Look at this one. The background's blurred. But look at it closely. It doesn't look right.'

She studied it carefully. 'It's fog,' she said. 'Some days when there's a fog on the moors, it looks that way. Like a low cloud bank. Or the ocean in the distance.'

Kincaid smiled. 'You know why that looks like the ocean?'

'I told you. Because some days . . .'

'No, darling. Because it is the ocean. Remember the piece of land we looked at once when we were driving to Santa Barbara?'

She nodded. 'You loved it and I didn't. And later when we passed by it was sold.'

'I'm the one who bought it. This house you've been looking at is built on that piece of land. Looking out on the Pacific.'

'You mean somebody built a house there that looks like the Towers?'

'Not somebody. I built it.'

She stared at the picture again, then found the other exterior pictures and looked at them. 'It looks exactly the same. It even looks old.'

'That's right.'

'You mean, it's not for a movie or something. You're building it to live in.'

'It's already finished. It's for you to live in.'

'I can't believe it.' She shuffled through the interior pictures. 'And will you try to make the interior look something like these pictures of the Towers?'

'It's already done. These aren't pictures of the Towers. These are interior shots of this house.' He put one of the exterior pictures on the table before her. 'They were taken two weeks ago.'

'That's not possible. How can it be possible?'

'I had all the photographs that Brannigan took. Then I brought over a retired architect from Carlisle who'd done structural work on the Towers forty years ago and had made floor plans. I put him together with an interior designer from Thornwood, they found a contractor and went to work. Now it's done and furnished, with sheets on the beds. And I promise you it doesn't look like a brand-new house. It will look like the Towers as it is now.'

When she stopped studying the pictures she looked up at him. 'You're mad, you know. What did I ever see in you?'

'Madness, I expect.'

'You're a crazy wonderful man. If you ever look at another woman, I'll strangle you in your sleep.'

• CHAPTER 6 •

1

Margaret and her new husband arrived at Wiswell Towers in Brannigan's caravan, great parcels and leather valises strapped on top, tripods, lights, and camera equipment lashed to the outside walls. His personal effects consisted of a box of books, the clothes he was wearing, a corduroy suit wrapped in a roll and tied with cotton rope, a small canvas sack containing shirts and underdrawers, and an extra pair of well-worn boots.

They had spent their honeymoon at the Hotel Russell in Dublin. Margaret had written Sophie a letter from there.

> The bride didn't blush but she wept a bit. It was a lovely simple wedding performed by a poet friend of Jack's who is also a lay preacher. All the legal papers were in order, of course, and we are truly married, but it was a ceremony unlike any other I've seen. The poet's house is like a great barn tucked in among the trees in a forest just west of Letterkenny. One side, to the south, is all glass and sunshine with so many plants growing and blooming that it's difficult to tell where the indoors ends and the garden begins.
>
> We had music, of course. A lady with ginger hair played the harp softly during the ceremony and two Irish fiddlers, one tall and cadaverous, the other looking like Friar Tuck in his monk's robes, played happy

tunes during the drinking before the ceremony and the drinking and feasting after.

There were twenty guests in all, I suppose. (If you detect an Irish lilt in my letters from now on I can only say that it's irresistible.) All of them came early and stayed late, most of the women much younger than I and most of the men my age or older. There was something Shakespearean about the afternoon and long evening, like a feast in the forest with wine gurgling from everywhere, individuals suddenly bursting into song, and the poet's dogs and cats and donkeys either strolling about inside or pressing their noses against the wide window from the outside. It had the flavour of the harvest party each autumn at the Towers. When the servants and gardeners, the gamekeepers and stablemen all frolicked and danced and drank together for half the night. I remember as a girl how I watched from an upstairs window and was terribly envious. Surely you had the same experience. Our parties in the great hall always seemed quite tame to me when I compared them with the gaiety I witnessed in the lower gardens.

Our wedding party, of course did not last half the night. At least it didn't for Jack and me. We drove to an inn on the Sligo highway and spent the night there, with a champagne breakfast the next morning, and then on to Dublin for a week's stay at our lovely old hotel just at the corner of St Stephen's Green. As I write this we are still here, tucked up comfortably in our high-ceilinged room facing the green, overeating outrageously in the French restaurant downstairs, and prowling the beautiful Dublin streets with their bright-painted doors, from breakfast till dusk, stopping in every pub that catches our fancy and quaffing Guinness till we bulge. When I'm home I'll have to restrict myself to soda biscuits and spring water for months.

I am so exhilarated and intoxicated and exhausted

that I've lost all track of the days and often don't know which meal I've missed or whether I had two lunches instead of one. If our lives together were to continue like this, then this letter might very well be my last will and testament. Even Jack, inexhaustible and irrepressible as he is, is showing signs of wear and diminished energy. Last night he was perfectly willing to have a warm bath and retire at two in the morning. Perhaps because I had fallen dead asleep an hour earlier. You needn't read between the lines to see that I am sinfully content. With only a shadowy memory of all past events and no concern whatsoever for what may transpire tomorrow. Doesn't sound like me, does it? In any case, I expect it's not a permanent state. Surely I will become responsible and organized and reliable once again but for now I am simply floating along . . . unsure of a destination, and uncaring.

2

'That automobile was Thornwood property,' Sam Thorne said. 'A brand-new Packard.' He was having his regular morning meeting with his brother in Julian's office. 'Evan was the first man who ever drove it.'

'It's insured, Sam. They won't trouble us about the money. Not with the premiums we pay them every month.'

'I know that. But it's not just the money. It's the principle. I don't like the idea of some crazy bastard thinking he can make a target out of what's ours and get away with it. The police don't know shit about who torched that Packard. Neither does the fire department, nor the insurance detectives. They all came up empty. That bothers me. Next thing you know, somebody'll throw a bomb in my swimming-pool!'

'Forget it, Sam. You've been reading too many detective magazines.'

'I've seen it happen, Julian, and so have you. You may dress like the Duke of Kent now but you're from Brooklyn just like me. Remember how it was with the street gangs? You give 'em an inch and they steal your sister. It's like a germ. If you don't pour iodine on it, it spreads all over the neighbourhood. Let some punk bastard think he's got away with something and it goes to his head. Thinks he's King Kong.'

'You've got King Kong on the brain.'

'I wish we had it on the books. I'd trade three Fred Astaires for one King Kong.'

'Shows what you know about the picture business, Sam. King Kong was a one-shot. Astaire will make thirty pictures before he's finished. And they'll play for ever.'

'Don't try to get me off the subject. I want to know who wiped out that Packard of ours. I'm gonna talk to Tagg again and see if there's something he might have forgot.'

'Then what?'

'Then I'll take a few steps. I have ways to get information.'

'Just don't embarrass me, Sam.'

'Embarrassed is what you should be now. People wrecking our equipment, a car we paid good money for, and getting away with it.'

Evan's office was not in the writers' building at the back of the lot between the Chinatown set and the Midwestern Elm Street set. He shared a suite of offices with Tim Garrigus in the directors' wing of the executive office building. Sam Thorne went directly there from Julian's office.

'I'm still pissed off about that Packard being torched,' he said. 'I don't mean I blame you but there's somebody to blame and I want to find out who it is.'

'I'd like to know myself but I told the police everything I could and they came up dry.'

'Those fucking county cops can't find their ass with both hands. All they know is put on their goggles and drive back and forth on the coast highway.'

'The insurance people didn't find much either.'

'That's 'cause the company paid us off toot sweet. Once they write that cheque the snoop work stops. But I don't give up that easy. Are you sure there's nobody you've met out here would like to take a crack at you? Or your girlfriend maybe? You two aren't married, are you?'

'No.'

'How about an old boyfriend? Jealous maybe. A pissed-off guy.'

'No boyfriends. She's married.'

'There you are,' Sam said.

Evan shook his head. 'They're separated.'

'I knew a guy in Staten Island killed his old lady with an ice-pick after they'd been divorced for twenty years. You know this husband? What kind of a duck is he?'

'You're not going to the police with this, are you? I mean, this is between us. Right?'

Thorne nodded his head. '*My* investigation. Sam Spade Thorne.'

'To tell you the truth, her husband is a nutty guy. He threatened to set me on fire once. He's an amateur firebug.'

'Did you tell the cops that?'

'No.'

'Why not?'

Evan shook his head. 'He couldn't have done it. He lives in London.'

'So do you. So does Kincaid. But you're both here, aren't you?'

'But he hasn't been here. Not so far as anybody knows.'

'OK. That's all I need for now. Forget we had this talk . . . is that all right with you? Don't even tell your lady-friend.'

'She's tired of the whole mess. Doesn't want to hear any more about it.'

'Good. It's better that way.'

John Corso, Sam's former partner in the produce business, had come to Los Angeles six months after Sam. With his wife and five children he moved into a big house on Rossmore looking west across the green acres of the Wilshire Golf Club. A few weeks later he bought controlling interest in a catering company that furnished breakfast and lunch to film units on location. A year later he owned the trucking company that did the hauling of sets and props and gear for all the motion-picture companies in Los Angeles. The former owners complained to police that they had been threatened by business associates of John's uncle, Vincent Corso, but no action was taken.

The afternoon of the day he'd talked with both Julian and Evan, Sam met John Corso in a coffee-shop on Hollywood and Ivar. He told him about the conversations he'd had earlier. Corso listened carefully and dropped another sugar-cube in his coffee. When Sam finished talking Corso said, 'Culver City. That's where we'll get the answers.'

'Who says so?'

'I do. Culver City. That's where the punks hang out. Anything you want done you cruise down Culver Boulevard, Washington Boulevard, Higuera Street, you'll find some kid fresh up the highway from Tijuana who'll do anything you need to have done for fifty clams. Give him a hundred bucks and he'll kill his mother. And the priest who comes to bless her . . . he'll knock him over for nothing. A bonus, you know what I mean? Good will. An investment in the future.'

From the first week they were in California, Sophie, making up a schedule for the servants, for the children, and herself, decided that each Thursday after breakfast, when Kincaid had gone off to the studio and the children had gone down the long slant of steps to the beach, she would write a letter to Margaret. In the third such letter she wrote:

At last we're settled in. Not completely, of course, but much more completely than I'd imagined we would be after such a short time. The children have a young athlete from the University of Southern California who's staying with us to coach them in tennis and swimming, sailing, and volleyball. He's a handsome fellow and Sarah's in love with him, of course, but Charles (that's his name) is accustomed to being admired so she's safer with him than he is with her. Also, he drives off every evening smelling of shaving-lotion and brilliantine so I think he's fully occupied socially.

As for me, I'm still wandering through this magnificent house in astonishment. I sent off photos to you yesterday and when you see them you will surely be as astonished as I am. One feels as though the Towers was plucked off its foundation, loaded on a ship and brought here to California, every door and window and staircase intact. All the pieces of furniture are not identical, of course, not perfect matches of your lovely things, but they're of the same quality and the same period so the spirit is the same in both houses. Going upstairs to bed here is just as I remember it there.

Kincaid says that only the artists and technicians

who duplicate all corners of the world for motion-pictures could have brought off this remarkable feat. In fact, the idea first came to him as he watched the work they did on *Bushranger* and saw how accurately they had reproduced the parts of Australia he knows so well. Then, when I sent him copies of all the pictures Brannigan (my new stepfather) took of the Towers, that crystallized the idea in his mind. How they did the work in just under a year, how they did it at all, is a mystery to me. But thank God it's here. As long as I stay at home I can deceive myself that I'm still in England.

We've found an excellent cook, a Swedish woman named Kristin, and Oliver and Ruth have gathered a fine staff in all departments. Most of them are British and the few who aren't have worked in the homes of English people here.

We have five horses, and beautiful fields to ride through, and a flock of sheep in our meadow. So it's all very much like home.

Kincaid goes to the studio every day. They haven't begun the film yet but all sorts of preparation tests and details must be done. They begin shooting in August and with luck we'll be home for Christmas. In any case we've booked our passage on the *Europa* for 12th December.

Even a careful observer, had he followed Sophie closely through a typical day, would have detected nothing but contentment in her manner. And she was indeed content. That is to say, she had made a contract with herself and she was determined to honour it. She had concluded, as she prepared to leave for California, that she could accept any set of circumstances, make any series of adjustments, as long as the time scheme was in place, as long as there was a stop date, as long as she knew, or felt quite sure she knew, on the day she left

212

England, the precise date of her return. It was not a matter of crossing out days on her calendar. She had no need to do that. It was more a matter of reclaiming her best identity, of knowing when that would take place. Having believed that she could never divide her time between England and America, she now conceded that she could, as long as some structure was in place, as long as she was able to retain control of herself and her life, of her place of domicile and her destiny.

The house by the sea, which Kincaid had conceived as a bridge for her between the life she loved in England and a life she feared in America, and which indeed had greatly eased and made more pleasurable the transformation, that house, for all its beauty and its remarkable power to present Northumberland to her eyes each morning when she woke up, that house, not the pleasure or the miracle of it but the simple fact of it, constantly disturbed her in some unquiet secret part of herself. She was ashamed of that feeling but she could not ignore it or will it away. As she praised her new American home to her mother, as she discovered and admired new details of it each day, she recorded quite different and separate feelings in the diary she had kept since she was a schoolgirl.

Why do I feel as if I've been manipulated? Wasn't it clearly understood between Kincaid and me that after he finished *Bushranger* we would decide together, sometime in the future, if he would make another film or if he would abandon the whole idea of his career as an actor. Because we knew we disagreed about that we decided on a waiting period. We would see *Bushranger* and wait to see what sort of reception it would enjoy, and then, somewhere along the line, we would make a decision.

With the success of the film and with Kincaid's bizarre new status as a public figure, knowing he detested the notoriety and the way it curtailed his freedom of movement, I felt that he was seeing things my way, realizing that such a life was limiting. Not liberating or fulfilling, as people imagine. Although we didn't discuss it – also a good sign, I felt – the fact that he refused to read Evan's new scenario, and had almost no contact for months with Julian Thorne, gave me all the more reason to believe that he had decided against going ahead with Thornwood, and that when he and I discussed it at last we would be in agreement.

But there was no discussion. Not a substantive one at any rate. When he met with Thorne at last, the decision was presented to me as an accomplished fact. Or so it seemed. I suppose I had the freedom to demur, to stay behind as I'd done last year, but once he'd rallied Trevor and Sarah behind him, when even Margaret, in her subtle fashion, was hinting that I must be a proper wife and follow my husband, there seemed to be no forum whatsoever for further discussion.

Did I misread the situation? Did I misunderstand Kincaid's intentions or the things he said? Perhaps I did but I don't think so. There's no mistaking the fact that it was to be our decision, his and mine.

This house, of course, the love and the planning, the consideration of me and my feelings that went into it, certainly put our stay in America in a different light. Margaret says she never heard of a husband doing such a magnificent thing for his wife. And she's right. I'm sure she's right. But there are other things to consider. He and I had seen this land together and I'd told him I didn't like it. But he bought it anyway. And almost immediately he began building this house. Of course he didn't tell me about it because it was to be a grand surprise. And it was, of course. But an even greater surprise and shock was the realization that all this was taking place at a time when I had no intention of returning to America, when in fact I was spending the summer alone with the children in the Algarve. So the nagging question persists: how could he hope to surprise and delight me with something so elaborate when he had no reason to believe I would ever see it?

There seems to be no doubt that he had already decided he would be returning to America. Why then, when he came back to England, did we play an endless charade together, assuring each other that we would decide sometime in the future what our plans would be? Did he tell himself that he couldn't confide in me about his private decision to continue as a film actor without spoiling the surprise of the house? Or did he tell himself that he would save the news of the house to soften the blow when he would tell me at last about his career decision? Whatever his thinking, he had decided, it seems clear, to make me a spectator rather than a participant.

Is that so serious? My God, yes, it's serious. It must have been painful to have been married to a man of my mother's generation, a man who kept his own counsel, made his own rules, set his own schedule, a man who had his life at home and as many lives away from home as seemed appropriate or attractive to him. There was his business, of course, along with all its satellite activities; there was his club, his school-friends, and whatever social life away from home appealed to him. He was not required to be home for dinner. Or to be at home at all. Or to report where he'd been when he did arrive. He provided for his family, hosted dinner parties at home, gave occasional stern advice or warnings to staff or children, donated generously to the Church, and put in an occasional appearance at Sunday services. But his primary responsibility, society agreed, was to himself. He carried the family escutcheon into whatever battles seemed appropriate, and shed the family blood at his own discretion.

But all those rules were known then. And accepted. I believed that Kincaid and I, on the other hand, were playing by different rules. Was I mistaken? It seems so. Or am I imagining all this? Am I creating a sticky situation when I should simply smile and count my blessings? I obviously don't think so or the subject would not be on my mind. How can I not be disturbed if I have reason to believe that this man I'm mad about thinks nothing of saying one thing to me and thinking something else, of promising something he has no hope of delivering, of making plans that don't include me in any way except after the fact.

Being with Kincaid has brought me the only emotional security I've ever known since I realized there was such a thing. I've never doubted him, never questioned anything he's told me. He's given me total faith in the future. Now what, old girl, now what?

4

When he talked with his father in England, after he'd told him about the letter he'd received from his mother, Evan had concluded that his father's instincts were correct. He decided he would make no effort to locate her. Nor would he respond if he heard from her again.

Several weeks after he returned to California, however, another letter from her came to him at the studio. This time her name and address were on the back of the envelope.

Dear Evan,
Last time I wrote to you I think I said I wouldn't bother you again. But here I am, not keeping my word. You can always tear this up though, or throw

it in the fire, and if I don't have any reply from you I guarantee you I can take a hint and I won't write again.

You'll see I put a return address on the envelope this time. That's not where I live, it's where I work. It's the Hook's drug-store, open all night. I'm the book-keeper. Just work a regular eight-hour day-shift, and thank God for that. I don't think I could ever get accustomed to sleeping days and working nights. As it happens, I can get all my book work done in my regular hours, six days a week. By Saturday, though, I'm always caught up so I help Riley, the window-display man, do the windows. Riley's a nice guy. He's fought the bottle all his life but he's got a real flair for working with crêpe paper and cut-outs and other decorating materials like that. He also works cheap because most places, once they've smelled his breath, won't take a chance with him, but Mr Dugan, our boss, thinks he's lucky to have him on the payroll.

Your dad used to say he'd never seen anybody like me for writing letters once I got started. And he's right. I hate like anything to write a letter but once I've got a nice pen in my hand I can keep writing for ever, especially if I'm writing to somebody I like and they like me. So you'll have to bear with me if it seems like I'm rambling on. I just thought of something. Wouldn't it be funny if you got your knack for writing from me? I'm just kidding. I know it's difficult work what you do. You have to have a decent education and talent and the whole works. And some luck, I guess, along with it if you need to make your living at it.

The reason I'm writing again, the main reason, is to tell you how proud I am of you. I guess you won't be surprised when I tell you I read everything I could find in the papers and magazines about you. The schools you went to in England, the newspaper work you did, and your play that was put on in London. I couldn't figure out the title, though. *The Father House*. Does that mean it was a play about your dad? I guess he must have been tickled about that play whether it was about him or not.

Naturally, most of the stuff I read was about the movie, *Bushranger*, and about Kincaid, how the two of you were friends in London when he was just a busker, the articles said. I had to look that word up and the dictionary said a busker is some kind of a street entertainer. We've got some crazy show-offs on the street here in Hollywood but I guess you wouldn't call them buskers. Anyway, I cut out all the pieces about you and saved them in a nice heavy carton. I don't suppose I'll ever lay eyes on your dad again but in case I do he might like to see what the papers wrote about you.

I saw some time ago that you were working on a new script about John Dillinger. I have a cousin, Opal, who lives in Linton, Indiana. I don't have a map in front of me but I think that's close to where Dillinger comes from. And now I see in the papers that Kincaid is going to play Dillinger. That should work fine. I mean Kincaid's got that look, hasn't he? If I was working in a teller's cage and he asked me to turn over the money, I'd turn it over to him pretty quick, no doubt about that.

I see I'm getting ahead of myself as usual. I wanted to tell you that I'd seen *Bushranger* and I cried at the end but I thought it was a wonderful movie. At the beginning, when your name came on, all by itself on the screen, I got some tears in my eyes then, too. I guess I shouldn't tell you that. But it's the truth so why not? I read interviews with screen-writers and every one of them says that nobody ever does a movie the way they write it. Do you feel that way? Because if you do, if you think they ruined what you wrote, I'd better not drone on, telling you how much I liked it. So I won't. If we ever decide to sit down and talk to each other and forget about what happened when you were little, then we'll talk some more about that movie of yours. Maybe this letter sounds like it comes from a different person than the last one I wrote. Well, I feel different. I'm used to the idea of your being grown-up and right here in the same city as me. I've seen some pictures of you so I know what you look like, and I wrote you once before so it's like we already broke the ice. Even though I gave you no address before in case you wanted to write back.

You see, I was afraid to write to you before, afraid of what you might think of me. And I'm still not sure you'd ever want to see me again or talk to me. But at least I'm not scared any more. I just have good feelings about you. Not because you're my kid, but because you seem to be a nice decent guy and I'm proud of what you're doing.

All right. I've run on long enough now. I take my lunch hour every day between noon and one o'clock and you can see from the address our drug-store isn't very far from the studio. So if you want to drop in some day a few minutes before twelve we can stroll down to Thelma's coffee-shop on Hollywood and Wilcox for a sandwich or something. My treat.

Yours truly
Amy Brock

5

As they were having breakfast one morning – a full Irish breakfast was served now at the Towers – Brannigan said, 'I'm a little surprised, Maggie, at the turn of events here as far as the mysterious Major is concerned. Once we arrived I thought he'd be scrambling out the door, carrying his knapsack and shirt-tails flying. But from what John Trout tells me, he's still holed up in the west wing somewhere, sipping whisky and unconcerned.'

'I'm afraid so.'

'I don't like to pass judgement on a chap I don't know, but I have to ask you, what kind of a man is it who wants to stay on in the house of his former wife after she's married to somebody else? I've known some odd crocks in my life but never one who'd put himself in that position. You'd think the man would be humiliated, hanging about where he's not wanted.'

'Cranston has never thought he was wanted anywhere. So this is not a new experience for him.'

'Well, it's new for me, and I tell you the truth, it gives me a rotten feeling, like having a bleeding ghost in the linen closet.'

'I don't like it either, Jack. I hate it.'

'Then something should be done. We're not helpless, are we? What does your solicitor say?'

'It's not his fault. I'm as impatient and annoyed as you are but I've told Tremont from the start that I want to handle this in the most civilized way I can. If we've moved too slowly I expect I'm the one who must take the blame.'

'Not likely. It's the bull-headed Major who's the cause of all this. Someone needs to have a serious talk with him and that's what I intend to do.'

She shook her head. 'That's not a good idea, Jack. I know you're a great believer in direct action but in this case it won't work. You don't know the sort of person you're dealing with.'

'That's my point. We're living under the same roof but I've never laid eyes on the man since I moved in. And if you're worried about me, I tell you I've dealt with hardheads all my life. A bit of reasonable talk can work wonders sometimes.'

Margaret shook her head. 'I appreciate your wanting to help but I promised Tremont we'd follow the legal procedures he described to me. So I think that's what we must do. I'm more frustrated by the whole situation than anyone but I want it handled with as little grief as possible.'

'I'm saying the grief's in the wrong place. It should be on the Major's head and not on yours. He's not suffering. I'd bet on that. He's sitting up there refilling his glass every five minutes and shooting birds through the window. Let's not feel sorry for the Major.'

'I don't feel sorry for him exactly. But I can't help being concerned.'

'Oh, for God's sake, Maggie.'

'I know he has to leave here, Jack. I want him to. I've told you that. It's the doing it that bothers me. The process of turning him out, of turning anybody out of the place where they've lived . . .'

'I can't believe what I'm hearing. Are you going soft on this situation all of a sudden? Are you telling me you're so kind-hearted you mean to maintain a charity wing for retired soldiers and ex-husbands?'

'That's not fair and you know it.'

'I'm not trying to be bloody fair. I want him out of our hair. And so do you.'

'I mean, it's not fair to me to make remarks like that.'

'Don't worry about me being fair to you. You'd best concentrate on being fair to yourself and not fret so much about the bugger in the west wing. You told me yourself that Tremont's people had located a perfect spot for him, didn't you tell me that, an old estate outside Bristol? Comfortable accommodation, good meals, and a retired army officer every corner you turn. Ideal place for him. He can wear his dress uniform to breakfast if he wants to. I expect they'll take away his bloody arsenal but they're sure to let him sleep with his sword beside him.'

'But, you see, there's no point in telling him about that now. Until he realizes he has to leave here, no other place will sound good to him.'

'The bastard's trespassing. Why are we so concerned about his tender feelings?'

221

'It's my feelings I'm concerned about as well. However he chooses to behave, I have to do what seems decent to me. And that's what I'm trying to do.'

'And all the time he's using you. He's playing you like a tin whistle.'

'Perhaps you're right. But I still have to feel good about it when it's over.'

'I'd feel good if it was over tomorrow.'

'So would I, Jack.' She smiled. 'Finish your bacon and sausage.'

'God bless us all,' he said. 'I thought I'd found me a wife. But it looks like I'm stuck with a nanny.'

'Not a chance, my darling. I am not your nanny in any respect, and you know it.'

He sipped some coffee, then set down his cup. 'You're right about that,' he said. 'I know that all right.'

6

One morning after Evan had gone to the studio Windrow telephoned Mary. 'I need to see you,' he said. 'It's quite urgent.'

'It's not urgent for me,' she said. 'And I don't want you to ring me here.'

'You mean, I should ring you at another number?'

'No. I mean, I don't want you to call me at all.'

'What an odd thing for you to say. After that nice lunch we had together, I thought we had an understanding. Thought we understood each other perfectly.'

'I understood you but you didn't understand me. Now perhaps you will. I don't want to see you or hear from you.'

'How odd.'

'And if you're scheming about how you can damage me with those letters I wrote you, you might as well forget it.'

'Oh, yes . . . the letters.'

'Don't play innocent with me. I told Evan about you and the letters. I told him everything.'

'Really? What a courageous thing to do. Well, that takes care of the letters, then, doesn't it?'

'You don't believe me, do you?'

'Of course I believe you. Why wouldn't I?'

'I'm not sure. But I can tell by your voice that you don't.'

'I was an actor, darling. Remember? A man of a thousand voices.'

'Goodbye, Burt.'

'Goodbye, Precious.'

Three days later when Evan came home from the studio, while they were having a drink on the deck, he put an envelope on the table in front of Mary and said, 'What do you make of this? It came to me at the studio today.'

She felt her hands get cold suddenly as she picked up the envelope. 'Who's it from?' she asked.

'No signature. Anonymous.'

'I hate anonymous letters,' she said. 'I throw them away as soon as I see they're not signed.' She took the sheet of paper out of the envelope. There was a type-written paragraph in the centre of the page.

I didn't hear you leave. What time did you get up? I was sleeping like a dead woman. What did you do to me? Whatever it was you must promise to do it again tonight. I'll meet you after the theatre. God, you are wild.

She looked up at him then and said, 'Are you trying to tell me something? Have you made a conquest? Have you seduced some poor little starlet?'

Evan smiled. 'I'm afraid not.'

'Do you think I'm sending you anonymous notes of passion?' She kept smiling but her smile felt awkward to her. Pasted on. A pumpkin smile.

'No. Nothing like that. I just wanted to show it to you because I thought it was peculiar. Just those typewritten lines and nothing else.'

'You're in Hollywood, my darling, where the peculiar is applauded and the outrageous is admired.'

All that evening and through the next day she thought of almost nothing else but the note. It had shocked her memory, brought back scenes and moments she thought she had forgotten. Hastily written notes stuck to the bathroom looking-glass or pinned to pillows. And longer letters. Ecstasy explored, remembered, anticipated. Impressions and feelings crazily jotted down. Another life.

After Evan had gone to sleep that night, as she lay awake in the darkness she realized she had to tell him. It was clear to her now that Windrow was relentless. For reasons she didn't understand he was determined to bend her to his will. Or perhaps he intended to deliver the letters to Evan no matter what she said or did. Every alternative she thought of seemed dreadful to her until at last she concluded that she must tell Evan herself. Also a dreadful thought. But much better than having her letters to Windrow arrive one morning on his desk at the studio. Before she went to sleep she resolved to tell him in the morning at breakfast.

At breakfast, however, she decided that a better time would be that evening when he came home from work. By mid-morning, as she sat alone in their bedroom looking out at the sea, she thought, 'Why am I so nervous about this? Evan isn't a child. There have been other women in his life. And he knows my life with Alec was not a happy one. So why should I expect him to be shattered if I told him about Windrow?' As she sat there, slowly persuading herself, she began to build the confidence she needed. But when she remembered the letters, the tone of what she had written, the language, the animal hunger she had expressed for a man she now detested, she knew that Evan must never see them. Once he had, that impassioned imagery would stay in his mind for ever as surely as if he had been shown photographs.

She took a shower, washed her hair, and got dressed. Then she telephoned Windrow at his office.

'This is a surprise,' he said. 'I didn't expect to hear from you again.'

'Don't play games with me. I need to see you.'

'Another surprise. As I recall our conversation, you made it clear you didn't want to see me or hear from me.'

'I didn't want to. Now I do. I saw that excerpt from one of my letters that you sent to Evan.'

'Now you're playing games with me,' he said. 'I don't know what you're talking about.'

'What's the point of lying about it?'

'Use your head, Mary. Since you've already told him about our brief but delightful friendship, and since you've also told him about the letters, why would I bother to send him anything?'

'That's an easy one, Burt. Because you don't believe I told him anything. And you're right. So I need to see you.'

After a moment he said, 'This is a bad day for me. Deadlines and all that. Why don't you call me early next week?'

'I have to know what you want from me. I need to see you today.'

'Not possible, I'm afraid. Let's leave it this way. Why don't I ring you when things settle down a bit here?'

'I don't want you to call here. Don't be such a bastard, Burt. If you're trying to make me miserable, you've done it. So don't keep turning the screws.'

'You are on edge, aren't you? Let's try this. Why don't you ring me on Friday about this time and we'll try to do lunch.'

'This is only Tuesday.'

'Time flies, when you're having fun,' he said. And the line went dead.

That evening when she and Evan were having dinner at a fish house on the Malibu pier, he said, 'I got another one of those weird notes in the mail today. This time a little message came with it.'

'Still anonymous?' Mary asked, feeling suddenly chilled.

Evan nodded. 'A handwritten note but no signature. Seemed to be a woman's hand. It said something to the effect that she wanted to be a screenwriter and thought perhaps I could help her. That's why she was sending me samples of her writing, so I could judge her work.'

'And did she send you another sample?'

'She certainly did. A longer bit this time. Like an excerpt from a letter. But a bit steamier than before. This lady, whoever she is, either has a great imagination or she's had some unusual sexual experiences.'

'Did you bring it home?'

'Tore it up actually. Not for your eyes, sweetheart. A little raw for me as well, and I thought I'd heard of everything.'

'And she gave no return address? How can you help her in her career if you can't reach her?'

'I think I can guess what her career is. And she doesn't need me to help her there. I expect she's had quite a lot of help already.'

The next day, mid-morning, Mary drove to Windrow's office. His secretary, to Mary's surprise, was a grey-haired woman in her fifties. Framed pictures of small children on her desk. 'Mr Windrow isn't seeing anyone this morning. He's working on tomorrow's column. Perhaps you could call next week.'

'I have to see him today. I'll wait.' She took a chair just opposite his office door and picked up a magazine.

'I'm afraid you'll have a very long wait, Miss Cecil.'

'It's all right. I'm extremely patient.'

226

Almost an hour later the buzzer sounded on the secretary's desk and she went into Windrow's office carrying her notebook. When she came out a few minutes later, Windrow also appeared in the doorway. 'What a pleasure to see you, Mary. Please come in. Awfully sorry you had to wait.'

His office was sleek and bright, like a California patio. All white and peach, pale greens and muted blues. Photographs of sea and desert and palm trees on the white walls. And silver-framed portraits of Harlow and Blondell, Lombard and Cagney and Walter Huston on a table by the window.

'What do you think of my secretary?' he said as they sat down.

'A bit of a surprise,' Mary said.

'That's it. That's the idea. A chap like me, people expect to see a bombshell at my reception desk. Platinum hair and long legs, typing letters with one finger. Plenty of secretaries like that around, eager to be seen, anxious to please, waiting for a screen test or an opportunity to be generous to a film producer. But the heavyweights in this town, Thalberg and Selznick and Henry French, the decision-makers, all those men have secretaries like mine, like Mrs Rawson. Worth her weight in gold, Mrs Rawson. Now, I know it's something urgent or you wouldn't be here.'

'You know damned well why I'm here. I want you to stop sending those bloody notes to Evan. I want to know once and for all what you want from me. What do I have to do?'

Windrow smiled. 'There was a time when that would have been a dangerous question for you to ask me.'

'Don't be cute, Burt. We're beyond that. I'm assuming you're not asking me to step out of my lingerie and join you on the couch. The stakes are bigger than that. Right?'

'For you they are, of course. And for me as well, potentially.'

'I've heard some of the stories that are floating around about Kincaid. I assume that's your doing.'

'Officially I have nothing whatsoever to do with any of those nasty rumours.' He smiled. 'Unofficially, as you're aware, I'm delighted by anything negative I hear about Kincaid.'

'And you want me to provide you with some new material about him. Is that it?'

'Not at all. Fortunately my band of elves is doing quite nicely.'

'Then what is it you want?'

'You mentioned that you were going back to do Novello's new play . . .'

'I said they've asked me. I haven't given a final answer yet.'

'When would rehearsals start?'

'October, they say. I'd leave in two months, I expect. If I decide to do it. What does all that have to do with what you and I have been discussing?'

'A great deal. You're anxious to have your letters back from me. In return, here's what I want you to do. I want you to cable London today that you will indeed do the play. And I want you to book a passage on the next ship to England. If you take a plane to New York I'm sure you'll be able to sail within a week.'

'But I've just told you, they don't need me until . . .'

'I know. But I need you to go now. When you have your steamship tickets in hand I will also give you your letters. When you cable me that you've arrived in London I will send you the copies I had made. I know you're thinking that I may have other copies but let me assure you of something: I never had any intention of using your letters as a weapon against you. Blackmail is not my trade. And I wouldn't have done it in this instance if I hadn't been forced to. You see I'm being pressured from another source. Someone in London has information about me that I wouldn't like to see made public now that

I've become a respected journalist. It's a trade-off, you see.'

'You mean you're forcing me to go back to London in exchange for . . .'

'Exactly. You must have guessed by now what this is all about.'

'I hope it's not what I'm thinking.'

'Who would go to such lengths to get you to leave California and come back to England?'

'Alec,' she said.

'Of course. He knows Evan Tagg is tied here by the new film. He thinks if he can get you to London for a period of time he'll persuade you to come back to him.'

'My God, what a scheme.'

'Alec's always been a bit dotty.'

'But you two were close friends.'

'We still are. Two of a kind, you know. We understand each other.'

'Does that mean you told him about the letters?'

Windrow shook his head. 'I'm sure he never knew about you and me. You see, he doesn't care how I get you on a ship and back to England. That was just his price for keeping silent about a certain episode of mine. It was lucky for me that I had a device to do what had to be done. I'm assuming that you'll use good judgement and do what's expected of you.'

'But what if I do? What if I leave when you say and cable you from London that I've arrived. Once I have my letters in hand what's to prevent me from taking the next ship back to America?'

'Nothing, I expect. But that's not my affair. Once you're back in London, my contract with Alec is finished. If he can't persuade you to stay on, that's his problem, isn't it? Also, you're an actress, darling. If Novello's written a good part for you Alec expects you'll stay on for the play. And so do I.'

Two weeks before *Dillinger* was scheduled to begin shooting, Walter Winchell began his daily column with an item about Kincaid.

Sleepless nights for Julian Thorne. His new picture about John Dillinger, the FBI's most wanted man, seems to be in trouble. His star, Roy Kincaid, is the target of a whispering campaign that could jeopardize his promising career. Thorne says the nasty stories about Kincaid are lies and rumours, but how does he convince Peoria of that?

Later that day Kincaid sat in Thorne's office along with Tim Garrigus and Evan.

'Whether we like it or not we have a situation here that could cause us trouble. We can ignore it, which is what we've done up to now, or we can try to defuse it. The problem is, these stories are spreading like wildfire. All across the country. We're getting letters from everybody. Exhibitors, reporters, and people who buy tickets. They're not angry letters. Not so far. Nobody threatening to boycott Kincaid. Just people who want to know what's true and what isn't. But if the City of Boston, the American Legion, and the Christian Mothers of Cleveland get into it, we could be in for some heavy weather.'

That evening, when Kincaid told Sophie about the meeting, she said, 'Thank God something's going to be done. What gives people the right to circulate such stories? There must be slander laws here.'

'There's no slander involved if you can't identify the person who said it. Everybody gossips. There's no law saying you can't pass along a bit of gossip once you've heard it. No one's saying things about me from a speaker's platform. Nothing's been printed in the papers.'

'But it's organized, sweetheart. It must be. When the same ridiculous stories begin to circulate in New York and Chicago and Los Angeles, even in London, and all at the same time, it's difficult not to believe that someone's behind it.'

Kincaid smiled. 'I told Thorne I think you're behind it. And Evan agreed with me. We know nothing would make you happier than if we folded up the picture before it starts and you and I packed up and went back to London.'

'You're very clever, aren't you? But you happen to be mistaken. And Evan as well. The fact is I would be very angry if someone forced you to do anything. And I truly hate it when people can say terrible things about you and get away with it. That sort of thing must be unusual even for this crazy town. I wouldn't want you to run away to London or any place else. That would be like admitting that everything they're saying is true.'

Kincaid was still smiling. 'I think the answer is for you to go into the streets with a sound truck. You sit inside with a microphone and blast out your message, all the way from Elysian Park to Santa Monica . . . "Why don't you people stop saying those naughty things about my husband?" You'd be in Winchell's column the next day.'

'You don't take any of this seriously, do you?'

'Of course not. It's like trying to walk fast in the mud. I don't mind a good fight but you can't fight with shadows.'

'But you can't just do nothing.'

'Of course I can. That's the best thing to do. Tim Garrigus made a good point during the meeting. He said it's a losing battle when you start answering critics. When you deny the bad stuff all you do is spread it around even further. Most of the people don't know what's been said till you start denying it. When you get all excited about

231

some stupid story, people start to believe it's true.'

'So what's the answer? You just ignore everything?'

'That's right. Nobody's said I should be in jail. So what can they do to me?'

'They can ruin your career. That must be what Thorne's worried about.'

'Thorne's a business man. He's worried about his investment.'

'He's also worried about your reputation. I'm sure of it.'

'The two go together,' Kincaid said.

'Of course they do. That's why I'm surprised that you're so unconcerned. It's true I'd be happy if none of this had ever happened to us, if we could have stayed in London. Sleeping late and having lunch together and taking walks in Green Park. And nipping over to Brittany for a few days whenever we felt the urge. If you'd come to me last week, or six months ago, and said, "I don't really want this sort of public life. Let's give it up," I would have been as happy as a Christmas child. But this is different. I hate to be manipulated and I don't want you to be either. I don't want you to be driven away from this business, silly as it is. I want you to choose for yourself. I don't want some crowd of vindictive, envious people to make decisions for you. You've accepted the Dillinger film. We've all accepted it by coming here. So it seems to me you have to do whatever you can to keep people from sabotaging it. And sabotaging you.'

'You're a tough number, aren't you? If I'd known that about you when you proposed to me, I might have said no. I was only kidding you about the sound truck idea. Now I think you might do it.'

'You're right,' she said. 'If I thought it would solve the problem, I'd do it in a minute.'

232

Even as a very young man, Arthur Tagg had prided himself on his ability to make accurate judgements. He believed that the truth rested somewhere between wishful thinking and pessimism, and he made it a habit, a personal science in a sense, to locate that tiny area of truth and be guided by it. Long after his marriage came apart, when he was able to look at it dispassionately, he concluded that its failure – however guiltless he'd been in that final painful ending – had been directly related to his inability to make his customary clear-headed appraisal of the circumstances. Or of the individuals involved. Most importantly his wife. It had been plain to him, of course, that this young and vital and attractive American girl had been cast from moulds that were unfamiliar to him, that her exposures, her values, her rhythms were very different from his own. Since his habits were strong and disciplined he had tried from the first day he met her to reconcile their apparent differences, to elucidate, to clarify, to be objective. Because time was short and his information about her was incomplete and highly charged, however, he had to choose at last between abandoning his process of judgement and decision, or abandoning her. By then he knew he had no choice. He plunged ahead, subjective and ecstatic, surrendered himself to his senses for the first and only time, and became in very short order a husband, an immigrant American, and a devoted father.

Surprisingly, during his years with Amy, the Chicago time, he never had second thoughts about the departure he had made from his usual pattern of contentment and survival. He simply continued as he had begun with her, moment to moment, sipping the sweet wine of his days, and making no effort to put up walls or fences, to place things in slots or cubicles, to establish fixed routines or set schedules. He lived a sort of life he had not been aware of before, one that he would have summarily rejected if he had known about it. He treasured his wife and their small flat on Superior Street, adored his son, drank a small glass of gin each evening before dinner, listened to the radio, read the *Saturday Evening Post*, and settled slowly and peacefully into a kind of middle-class life he'd known nothing about, one that his schooling had neither told him of nor prepared him for. Feeling a sort of happiness that was new to him, he began to believe, understandably, that he had invented it, that he owned the patents, had memorized the formulas, and would be able to produce it for ever.

In his work, however, in the department store on State Street, he remained his original hand-tooled British self. Sober cravats, starched linen, polished boots. And because his employers catered to wealthy clients with expensive tastes, because much of their merchandise was imported from France or England, Germany or Sweden, Arthur saw at once that his public-school speech which he had feared, when he and Amy arrived in New York, might put him at a disadvantage in the American business world, this precise but pleasant articulation was an asset when he spoke to customers who were familiar with London and Bath, with Provence and Milan and Copenhagen. These people, when they spoke with Mr Tagg of their latest trip abroad, never questioned the quality of the articles he showed them. Or their price. They were never being sold an item, they felt, they were being allowed to buy.

His employers offered to promote him to floor manager. Or perhaps he would like to be a buyer. Arthur gently refused, explaining that he preferred having contact with the customers. So he remained a salesperson with predictable hours. No staff meetings after closing, no extra duties, no travel – nothing, in short, that might disturb the rhythm of his hours at home. There, in his sweater and slippers, he was free to be the man he had become. At the store each day, however, he was a British gentleman whose ability to make accurate judgements of merchandise, of clients, of fellow workers and superiors was critical to his achievement and his popularity among the people he dealt with.

Later, reviewing in his mind that Chicago time, Arthur concluded that his work life there, the choice he'd made to remain during those day-time hours the person he had once been, that unbroken chain of familiarity with those older judgements and patterns and habits, that foundation of behaviour, had shored him up and seen him through when the other, more rewarding area of his life collapsed, when Amy left Evan with a neighbour one afternoon and disappeared. His stubborn dignity, his sense of doing the proper thing, sustained him during the years when he waited for her to come home, when he followed every possible clue in his efforts to find her, wrote letters to questionable addresses, and shamelessly interrogated neighbours and friends for any information they might have which would help him find her.

When he realized that his situation was hopeless, when he knew at last that she had no intention of coming back to him, that contact he'd kept with his old self, with his roots, with England, took him back there. And good fortune brought him to Wiswell Towers.

He saw no connection between his leaving Chicago and his decision to leave the Towers after almost twenty-four years. There was no question that the first decision had been strongly influenced by circumstances, by their effect on Evan and himself. But leaving the Cranston home, deciding to take himself to London, to temporary residence in Evan's flat, had been entirely a matter of free choice. Or so he insisted to himself.

Studying London newspapers and magazines for the several weeks before he left Northumberland, he told

235

himself that he had a pleasant part of his life before him. Still in his late fifties and in excellent health, he was free now to devote more time to himself, to pursue cultural and intellectual interests that had been, to a large degree, neglected during those years when his time had been devoted to tutoring and estate management. He wanted to work, of course, and he would when the proper opportunity presented itself. But for now, he decided, as he perused the journals and the calendars of cultural events in London, he would open up new avenues inside himself.

By the time he arrived at Evan's building in Gordon Square he had carefully pencilled a schedule for himself that would keep him busy for at least six weeks. He began with two days in the National Portrait Gallery. At least that was his intention. But studying each portrait, making notes on his pad, and revisiting many of the rooms kept him there for an additional day. Having learned his lesson about scheduling, when he travelled along Knightsbridge the following morning, bound for the Victoria and Albert Museum he put no time restrictions on himself. He simply noted that the Science Museum, the Geological Museum, and the Museum of Natural History were just there also, the other side of Exhibition Road. He would continue to go there each day, he promised himself, until he felt satisfied that he had thoroughly explored each one of those institutions. He would have a proper tea in that area in the late afternoon and then attend whatever concert or recital was available at the Royal Albert Hall, before going home by underground to Gordon Square.

He kept biscuits and bullion and bits of cold beef and cheese in the flat but at least once a day, often twice, he took his small meals in tea-shops wherever he found himself at meal-time. Many nights he read at home in Evan's deep chair by the bow window. But at least two or three evenings each week he went to the theatre or a concert-hall. And every day, he was up early and out, driving himself relentlessly, like an American traveller determined to see all of London in three days before leaving for a five-day comprehensive tour of Holland, Belgium, France, Germany, Italy, Switzerland, and the Duchy of Luxembourg.

Then one day it happened to be raining early in the afternoon. He found himself in the National Portrait Gallery again, staring at a badly restored portrait of Lord Peter Edward Fernshaw, his eyes barely focused on the painting, and he realized he'd been standing there for a long time, half-conscious. As he turned away from the picture he stumbled a bit and eased himself down on a bench. A museum guard stepped up to him then and said, 'Feeling all right, are you, sir?'

'What? Yes, of course, I'm all right. Just studying the pictures. Giving them a good look.'

'Yes, sir,' The guard moved away but not out of sight. After a few minutes Arthur stood up, strode briskly past the guard to the central corridor, claimed his hat and umbrella, and left the gallery.

The rain had slackened. He opened his umbrella and walked up St Martin's Lane. When he came to a cinema entrance he bought a ticket and went inside. It was warm in the theatre but he shivered as he found a seat against the wall in the rear. The film had just begun. It was a story about New York gangsters, with Edward G. Robinson in the leading role. After it ended, Arthur stayed in his seat and watched it a second time. When he left the theatre he flagged a taxi and went home to Gordon Square.

When he entered the flat there was an envelope from Evan just inside the door. A short note enclosed along with a longer letter.

In haste. I'm sorry but we're very busy just now. I enclose a letter from my mother. Thought you'd like to read it. Hope you're well. More later.

Arthur made tea for himself, turned on the radio and listened to Mahler for a few minutes. Then he switched it off suddenly. 'Not just now, Herr Mahler. None of your bloody tormented music at the moment, thank you.'

He had cheese and biscuits with his tea in the sitting-room. He stayed on in the chair by the window and watched the car lights sweeping across the glass. At last he got up, took his dishes to the sink and rinsed them. Then he undressed, hung his clothes in the closet, and put on his pyjamas and robe. He got into bed with a book, but after a few minutes he closed it, put it aside, and switched off his reading lamp. The room was dark and silent for several minutes. Just the soft swish of cars outside in the wet street. Suddenly Arthur switched the lamp on again. He got up, walked to the writing-table in the sitting-room, found Evan's letter, and carried it back to his bed. He took out Amy's letter, held it in the light and read it through. He folded it carefully then, put it back in the envelope, and switched off the light.

When he woke up early the next morning he was slouched in the chair in the sitting-room, wearing his robe, with a blanket tucked round him. He didn't remember moving from the bedroom to the chair. He stood by the window then. It was still raining outside. At last he closed the shades, walked into the bedroom and got into bed. When he finally went to sleep it was ten in the morning. He slept till seven that evening.

9

Almost two weeks after their meeting in the coffee-shop Sam Thorne and John Corso met again, this time at Sam's house, Sunday afternoon. While Marie Thorne and Corso's wife stayed indoors and talked about the good life on Staten Island, the men sat in rattan chairs, smoking cigars, by the edge of the swimming-pool.

'Did you hear what Fred Allen said about California?' Corso said.

'I didn't listen to him last week. Marie had her cousin and that dumb shit husband of hers over to eat. Otherwise I never miss Fred Allen. Mr Kitzel's the one I like.'

'Mr Kitzel's on Jack Benny.'

'Who's got the friendly undertaker?'

'That's Fred Allen.'

'That's the one I like. What did he say about California?'

'He said, "California's a great place to live if you're an orange." You're not laughing. You don't think it's funny?'

'What does he know? He came out here and made a lousy picture for RKO and now he's putting the knock on everybody.'

'I thought you liked him,' Corso said.

'I just stopped liking him. I'm tired of these New York wise-asses putting the knock on California.'

'You think that's bad, you should hear what Uncle Vinnie says.'

'I like Vinnie. I don't want to hear.'

'He says Los Angeles is a great place to bury a dog. Says it used to be a pretty good place to get laid but no more.'

'So where's a better place?'

'Havana, he says. Any broad who's old enough to graduate eighth grade is too old for Vinnie.'

'You know what I think of that? I think it's disgusting. A man like Vincent Corso with a fine family.'

'I'll tell him you said that.'

'No, you won't. I got too much on you, you little guinea.'

'We got too much on each other, Sam.'

'Take a Jew and an Italian, you got a perfect partnership. Am I right?'

'You got it.'

Sam filled their glasses from a bottle of Chianti. 'On the phone you said something about our french-fried Packard.'

'Yeah. I got some good dope for you. Culver City, like I said. I've got an associate out there, a guy named Omar. Came out from Jersey ten years ago. Everybody calls him the contractor. Some dumb floozie heard a guy call him that in a bar and she asked him if he could build an extra bedroom on her house. He told her he's all booked up but he'd be glad to come around some afternoon and take a look at the bedroom she's already got. He's a bird-dog, this guy. Anyway, like I told you last time, Omar's the guy who's got a line on all the action in Culver City. And he knew all about the Packard. Didn't know it belonged to you and Julian or he'd have backed off. As it was, all he did was pass money along to the Mexicans who did the torch job. He got a call from a nickel-and-dime hustler he knows in Long Beach. Said a messenger would bring Omar a brown envelope. He said two hot-assed Mexican kids would come looking for him. He should open the envelope, give them fifty bucks apiece, and keep the rest for himself. When these two pachucos show up it turns out that Omar knows them. They do little errands for him sometimes. So he asked them what the action was and they said they were gonna torch a Packard in Malibu. Didn't know any names. Just had the address. So Oscar gave them a C-note to split and kept four hundred for himself. Then he forgot about the whole thing till one of my men dropped by to ask him about it. He tried to reach the hustler in Long Beach but his wife said he had a problem and ran off to hide in Mexico. Some place in Sonora, she thought, but she wasn't sure. Later we found out the guy was shacked up with some tootsie in Reno but nobody knew how to find him. When they did find him a week later he was naked and stiff in the desert with a piece of wire around his neck.'

'Shacked up with the wrong tootsie.'

'Maybe. Anyway, Omar made some calls after he found out we were interested in the Packard job. He located the messenger who'd brought him the money and had a talk with him. The kid didn't know much. His dispatcher had told him to go to such and such a place and pick up an envelope, then take it to Omar in Culver City.'

'Who gave him the envelope?' Sam said.

'That's what Omar asked him. The kid didn't know a name but he remembered that he was told to look for a black La Salle parked just outside the Hollywood Bowl entrance on Highland. The car was there all right and the guy behind the wheel handed over the envelope. The kid couldn't see his face but he sounded like a young guy. And he talked like an Englishman.'

'That figures. Evan Tagg's a limey. He's shacked up with a limey broad who's married to somebody else. Also an Englishman. This town's crawling with them. So whoever laid out the five hundred to torch the car must not like those sleeping arrangements in Malibu.'

'That's what Vinnie says. He thinks somebody should have a talk with the husband. Remember Dolph Twilly?'

'Sure. Used to be in Newark.'

'That's right. He and his brother are in England now. They got a big gambling thing going in London. Everybody in tuxedos and monkey suits. Fancy stuff. Vinnie's in touch with them. He says they'll send somebody to talk to the husband. I'm sure he'll be happy to tell us who put out a contract on your Packard.'

10

Four days before she was scheduled to sail for England from New York, Mary Cecil took the eastbound train from Los Angeles. Evan drove her, mid-morning, to the downtown railway terminal.

Both of them were silent in the car as they drove along the coast highway. When Evan turned off the highway to Sunset Boulevard she said, 'Don't you know how difficult this is for me? Why do you have to make it worse?'

'I don't know what you mean?'

'Oh yes, you do. The silent treatment. Silent as a stone. I'd rather have you yell and scream at me than just sit there and say nothing.'

'I don't yell and scream. That's not my style.'

'And this isn't my style. The two of us sitting here like dead bodies in a hearse. Isn't there anything we can say to each other?'

'Last night you told me we'd said everything there was to say. You said we'd talked the subject to death. I think you're right.'

'Is this the way we're going to say goodbye? I'll get on the train like a marionette and you'll stand there on the platform like a stranger, and then the train will put out and that will be it? Is that what I'll have to remember as I cross this bloody country and then cross the bloody Atlantic?'

'You make it sound as if we're planning never to see each other again.'

'We're not seeing each other now, Evan. We're like two blind people. Blind and mute. Going through the motions.'

'You said yourself it's difficult. It is. Nobody likes to say goodbye.'

'We've said goodbye before. More than once. When you were coming here. Or going back to England. And it was never like this. Is it because I'm leaving this time instead of you?'

'Of course not.'

She sat silent again as the car climbed the winding road through the coastal hills. Finally she said, 'You want to talk about the real problem? The real problem is that you think I'm lying to you. Isn't that it?'

'I didn't say that. Did I say that?'

'You didn't have to. It's hanging round you like a cloud.'

'I knew you were considering the play. I encouraged

you to do it. We've talked about it a hundred times. When you'd have to leave. How long you'd be gone. Whether I'd be able to come to London for the opening night. You're an actress. I'd never do anything to prevent you from working.'

'I didn't say you would. That's not what we're talking about and you know it.'

'We've been over all that,' he said.

'Then let's go over it again. It's better than sitting here like two mummies on their way to the tomb.'

'A minute ago we were two dead bodies in a hearse.'

'What's the difference? The result's the same.'

'I didn't accuse you of lying,' he said then. 'I said I couldn't understand why all of a sudden there's such a rush to leave. Three days ago you told me you'd be leaving today. Reservations all made. Tickets paid for. Packed up and on your way. You said you'd had a cable from Novello. Rehearsals start in two weeks.'

'And because I didn't save the cable to show you, you decided I wasn't telling the truth.'

'Nothing of the kind. I showed you the article from that day's issue of *Variety* saying the Novello play wouldn't begin rehearsals until two months from now.'

'And because of that, you thought I should cable Ivor to tell him I'd be coming along then instead of next week as I'd promised.'

'No. I said there seemed to be some question about the dates. So I thought you might want to send another cable to make sure you had the dates right.'

'I know I have the dates right.'

Evan nodded. 'That's what you told me. Several times. That's where the discussion broke down.'

'It broke down because I could see you don't trust me. You think I have another reason for going to London just now.'

'You're putting words in my mouth that I didn't say.'

'I'm talking about what you think, not what you've

said. Can you tell me what reason I could have for lying to you? If I'm not going because of the play, why would I be going? Do you think I have some tender anniversary to celebrate with Alec? Is it possible you think I'm going to London because of him?'

He shook his head. 'I was simply baffled by your refusal to reconfirm the rehearsal dates.'

'And I'm baffled by your refusal to trust me.'

They had a cup of coffee in the station cafeteria while they waited for the boarding announcement. They looked at the morning papers and talked about the items they read there. When it was time for her to board the train they walked along the platform together. At the entrance to her coach they put their arms round each other. 'I love you, sweetheart,' she said. 'I love you, baby,' he said.

She hurried up the steps then and down the corridor to her compartment. As soon as she was inside, she locked the door behind her, sank down on the edge of the bed, and began to cry. As the train pulled out, Evan walked back along the platform to the bar just off the reception hall. He ordered a whisky and drank it. Then another.

He had promised to meet Kincaid for lunch at the Brown Derby on Vine Street. He arrived early and sat at the bar till Kincaid came. When they were sitting in their booth Kincaid said, 'Did she get off all right?'

'Smooth as silk. The train pulled out without a murmur.'

Kincaid studied him for a moment. 'And you pulled into the nearest bar.'

Evan nodded. 'Never had to leave the station.'

'Celebrating? Or drowning your sorrow?'

'Celebrating my sorrow.'

'Shall we both get drunk or do you want to fly solo?'

'Making no plans. Thought I'd sit here with you for a bit, then drive home and do some serious drinking.'

'If you're planning to drive, you'd better go now.'

'No problem. If I'm too drunk to manoeuvre my automobile I will call for one of Julian Thorne's Nubian slaves and have him chauffeur me home. Or maybe I'll enlist Tim Garrigus. He's always happy for a reason to get plastered. We can ring up Carole Lombard and Jean Harlow, and tell them we're free for the afternoon.'

They drank together for an hour or so. Then Kincaid ordered lunch and Evan ordered another drink.

'Here's the problem,' he said. 'The problem isn't what she thinks it is or what she thinks I think it is. The problem, the basic problem is this: that weird off-putting bastard she's married to, that odd fucking warlock really does have some sort of hold on her. Mary has nothing but contempt for him. She detests the bloody fool but he's got her tangled in a knot somehow. It's like he told me. She'll never leave him. Some part of her is tied to him. Unable to cut the cord. I'm not sure she knows it herself. It has nothing to do with her mind or her intelligence. When he sends out signals she simply responds. Like a flower turning to the light. It's sad. Drives me fucking crazy when I think about it. When he told me she'd never asked him for a divorce, never written him a letter about it, I thought the rotten sod was lying in his teeth. But now I believe him. She doesn't want a divorce. She can't divorce him. He caught her when she was a kid, put his tattoo on her, branded her, programmed her, by God, in some remarkable way. She'd never made love to a man before him. I'm sure of that. And no one after till she came with me. She didn't tell me all this but I'm convinced of it all the same. She's a warm and sensitive, intelligent and lovely woman, but she's enslaved by that odd tramp of a ruddy bastard. She didn't have to leave for England today. She knew it and she knew I knew it. But she went anyway. Because Maple blew his magic whistle. He found some rotten scheme to pull her back. When her train pulled out I said to myself, "That's it. I just lost her." But now I'm sitting here, drunk as a fucking monkey, and I know I never had her to start with. A brainy bastard, am I not? Master of motive and nuance, historian of the soul, all human foibles made visible. But I can't understand the simplest things.'

He asked the waiter for a telephone then, called the transportation department at the studio and told them to send a car and driver to take him home. 'Lombard and Harlow will have to make their own plans for the afternoon. Today I'm going to get monumentally pissed all by myself.'

After he left Kincaid sat in the booth alone, drinking coffee. He was about to ask for his check when a tall young woman with brown hair appeared at his table. 'I'm Gloria Westerfield. I don't know if you remember me. I interviewed you last year when you came here to do *Bushranger*.'

'Of course. Sit down. I was just having coffee. Will you have some?'

'No, thank you. I can only stay a few minutes. I was having lunch with Richard Bennett. A fascinating man. But like many fascinating men, he drinks too much. We were just leaving when I saw you sitting here. I normally don't intrude on people's privacy, but since I'd planned to drop something off for you at the studio this afternoon I decided I'd give it to you in person.'

'Glad you did. It's good to see you,' Kincaid said.

'Julian called me a few days ago and said there'd be a press conference at Thornwood on Thursday at five. He said Garrigus and you will answer questions about *Dillinger* and give some details about the production.'

'That's right.'

'Now I'll tell you what I told Julian. If all those reporters and columnists get a shot at you there'll be no questions asked about the film. It will all be about the stories that have been flying around. About you.'

'Julian knows that and so do I. That's the main

reason he asked the press to come by.'

'It's bound to be a tough session. Can you handle it?'

'I don't know. But I guess I'll find out.'

'Have you heard some of the stories?'

'I'm not sure I'm up to date but I've heard a few.'

'When these things happen out here, it's obvious to the professionals that someone's doing a hatchet job. But the average person across the country assumes it's true till they hear or read a denial. When it's a distorted fact, it's a comparatively simple thing to handle. You simply state the true facts and that settles it. The hardest rumours to deal with are the outlandish lies. All you can do is deny those. For example, if somebody says one of your grandparents was a Negro, you can deny it till hell freezes over but many people will still believe it. About you, they're saying you neglect your parents, that they're poor people in bad health living in Tasmania and you don't help them or see them. I assume that's a lie.'

Kincaid smiled and nodded his head.

'But all the same it can be a tough one to deal with. It takes a certain kind of attitude to handle these things. If you take it too seriously, if you're emotional about it, you dignify the rumour somehow, no matter how ridiculous it is. Let me give you an example.

'A year or so ago, the word was out all over town that a very big woman star had just had a baby and the father was Spencer Tracy, who had played opposite her in two films. They were both married so it could have become a career-wrecking situation. So Tracy had to face the reporters. The studio insisted, assuming he'd deny it. But here's what he did. He sat on a chair, gathered all the reporters around him and said: I know why you're here. I know what you want to know. But I'm not going to answer any questions. Instead I'm going to ask all of you a question. Let's pretend, each one of you, that you're an actor like me. You're working with a gifted and beautiful actress you respect and admire. You've worked with her

247

before, she also admires you, and you're genuinely fond of each other. It so happens this film you're doing is a long location job. Let's say it's Alaska. You're away from home and your friends and family so you're with this lovely woman almost all the time except when you go off to bed at night. You get to know each other. Then one night she says to you: "You know me very well. You've met my husband and I've met your wife. We're both happily married people and we intend to stay that way. But I want to have a child with you. No one will know but you and me. It will be our secret. So you mustn't say no. It means everything to me."

'Tracy just sat there looking at us for a while. Then he said, "Just ask yourselves how you would deal with a situation like that, and after you've figured it out you can write whatever you want to about me." He got up and left the room then, and that was that.'

'What happened?' Kincaid asked.

'Nobody wrote a word about Tracy and the baby. And people in Hollywood soon stopped talking about it. Since then Tracy has had the press in his pocket. He always will.'

'It's a great story. But I don't think sincerity and humility will do the job for me.'

'Neither do I.' She took an envelope out of her purse and handed it to him. 'I know you haven't asked for my advice and I'm not sure it would be worth a lot if you did. But I think you're a decent man and I want to help if I can. When I learned about the press conference coming I got out a transcript of that interview I did with you last year. This is a copy of it. I remember after I talked with you, I thought it was the most outlandish, insincere, untruthful, and funny session I'd ever had with an actor. I decided you didn't give a damn what anyone thought of you, that you wouldn't kiss anyone's behind. Look it over. I think it might help you on Thursday.'

• CHAPTER 7 •

1

Alec Maple had had a particularly joyful evening, the
finish to a splendid day. He had slept late, had a long
soak in the bath while he drank his thick Turkish coffee
and his breakfast cognac, and had gone along then to
the barber for a shave and a shampoo. He was proud
of his hair. It had always been a magnet for young
women and it continued to be. He often boasted to
his drinking mates. 'Once they've touched the silken
locks, stroked my hair and run their fingers through it,
the battle's won. Seems they're determined from that
moment to stroke every part of me. And since one
doesn't like to disappoint the tender young souls, one
surrenders everything, makes whatever sacrifice is
required. Generosity is at the core of humanity, after
all.'

From the barber-shop he went to Coram's Fields to
meet a young woman, a student of sculpture from
Iceland, whom he had first met three weeks earlier.
Today they went to a pub on Guilford Street where
Urda, his friend, bought drinks on her generous government stipend. She sipped aquavit, trying to mask her
total absence of intelligence with a vacuous smile, and
Alec drank three pints of Guinness and a bit of Tan-
queray. The two of them, laughing and stumbling in the
street, he laughing and she stumbling, made their way
then to her atelier just off Gray's Inn Road on Wren

Street. Their habit there was for him to remove his clothes and strike a pose on the model stand while she tried to make some progress on the clay figure of him that she'd been struggling with since soon after they met. All her previous work had been concentrated on the figure's pelvic areas and she continued to work there for as long as she was able to resist the true subject. But at last with a Nordic moan, she clutched at herself, pulled off her skirt, took hold of Alec Maple with clay-stained hands, pulled him to the mattress in the corner, rolled him on his back, and straddled him with ferocity. Conquer and kill. When he described these encounters to his pub-mates each day he said, 'But she's the one who's conquered, of course. Impaled and invaded. Turned inside out. No end to her energy, it seems. Body fluids to spare. But at last the lance triumphs. She roars and whinnies like a wild mare, one final squeal and spasm, and she falls like a great oak, quivering but otherwise unable to move. One leaves her then to sleep and recover for the next day's session.'

Late afternoon he attended a Jean Cocteau film at a cinema in Leicester Square, met a critic friend there, and debated the film's merits over drinks later. The critic, a pederast, worshipped Cocteau, man and work. But Alec, as he often did, took the contrary view. 'Awfully precious, isn't it? Symbolic to a fault. Stuffed with obvious symbols. A painting done with water in my view. Invisible. Having us on, old Cocteau. Drawing no proper line between mystery and confusion. Misreading his audience, the bugger. Serving up children's tales, nursery images, to a grown-up audience. The man's a clever charlatan, no more.' His friend made nervous by Maple's energy, and made to feel defensive about his sexual leanings, paid for the drinks before he fled.

Early evening, Maple attended a poetry reading at a private house in Bedford Square. He had not been invited but he announced his name to the butler with such authority that he was presented to the hostess with the same authority, and she, perhaps recognizing him from a previous occasion, welcomed him.

This illustrated one of Maple's credos. 'An aggressive, well-spoken man is seldom turned away.'

When he arrived at Umberto's at nine, he was presented by the owner as a distinguished actor-critic to an American family who were dining there. A stout father and mother in expensive ill-fitting clothes and two nubile daughters who had 'never met an actor before'. When invited to join them, Maple at first declined. He accepted at last but 'just for one drink'. By the time dinner had ended several hours later, the father, drunk and expansive, had invited Maple to Pittsburgh for a long stay in his home as 'artist-in-residence'. The daughters, stimulated by two glasses each of Lambrusco, had gone limp and silly in their admiration for Papa's dinner guest. The younger one, Francine, had rested an innocent dimpled hand on his arm while everyone laughed at one of his backstage anecdotes. The other one, called Sweets by the family, had fearlessly stroked his hair while her mother was away in the powder-room. 'I've never *seen* so much bewful hair on a *man* before.'

The mother, however, an abstainer and a Baptist, her values unchanged by either alcohol or admiration, was constantly alert. Except for frequent trips to the toilet, she monitored every word, every movement, every nuance. Under her watch no hand dared stray from the table-top, no promises of any sort would be countenanced. Like many women whose sensual lives are so far in the past as to be barely recalled, she saw sexual implications everywhere she looked. In a glance or a smile, in the tilt of an eyebrow. And God forbid a tongue should linger overlong on the rim of a glass. Sweets, in particular, she suspected of having some of the jungle instincts of her sister-in-law, a young woman whose languid eyes and soft smile advertised that she had been up to no good and had thoroughly enjoyed it. When Sweets said, toward the tag-end of the evening, 'Maybe Mr Maple could take me and Francine to a matinee some afternoon so we could visit backstage and see what it's like,' her mother answered, 'That would be nice, dear, but you know as well as I do our tour people have got us booked up tight for every minute we're here in London. And the same in Paris, France.'

During the commotion of leaving the table and claiming their coats, Sweets eased up behind Maple and whispered, 'Brown's Hotel. We'll be there five more days.' She took hold of his thumb then and squeezed it with the grip of a stone-mason.

When the taxi pulled up in front of the restaurant, the mother manoeuvred the girls in first. Then she turned to Maple, shook his hand, and said, 'If I ever catch you near my two girls I guarantee you'll spend the rest of your life behind bars.' The father, out of ear-shot on the other side of the taxi, shouted his goodbyes and said, 'Don't forget, Maple, we expect to see you in Pittsburgh. If you lose that card I gave you just remember the name, Bill Nestor. Everybody knows me there.'

As he watched the cab pull away, Maple felt exhilarated and triumphant. Almost every day ended like this for him. Since retiring from the theatre he'd often reminded himself that his art form now was the creative management of his own life, the structuring of days like this one. As he walked home he reviewed the fourteen hours since he'd wakened that morning. There were no cinders and no thorns. No bad memories. He had been admired, lusted after, even loved a bit perhaps, in every corner of the day. Food and drink and good talk, heads turning as he walked along the pavement. And those two delightful girls. His thumb still throbbed from Sweet's kerbside farewell. Perhaps, he mused, with a certain amount of patience and guile he could slip her away from Brown's Hotel for an outrageous hour or two. But there was plenty of time tomorrow to deal with that. For now he was bathed in the splendour of being wanted.

When he unlocked the door of his flat, two strong arms grabbed him from behind before he could switch on the light. And a thick, scented hand covered his mouth. In the darkness a voice said, 'Don't make a sound, Mr Maple. We just want a few words with you. In fifteen minutes we'll be gone.'

He felt a wide strip of adhesive being plastered across his mouth and behind him tape was twisted and wrapped round his wrists. He was steered to a chair then and the light was switched on. The curtains in the sitting-room, which he always kept open, were now closed. Without turning his head he sensed there was a man on either side of him, just behind his chair. Just before him, little more than two metres away, a well-groomed man in his forties sat facing him. Sun-browned skin, black hair turning grey, trim and slender in dinner-jacket and black tie.

'My name is Twilly,' the man said. 'The two men behind you are my associates. We don't know you. Nor do you know us. I am simply performing a service for a friend in America who wants to provide certain information to friends of his. No money will change hands. I'm simply talking about an act of friendship.'

When Maple squirmed from the discomfort of the tape across his mouth Twilly said, 'We'll take that tape off in a moment, once you understand what's expected of you.' He looked round the room. 'Pleasant place you have. Not large or pretentious, but very English. Traditional. I like that. I like almost everything about your country. I admire it. Respect it.'

'You like it because the bobbies don't carry guns,' one of the men behind Maple said.

'That's part of it,' Twilly said. 'It's a non-violent city, London. Reasonable people. I like to think I'm a reasonable man as well. Since I've lived here I've tried to make myself as much like the English as possible. It's a matter of respect for your host country. I buy my clothes from English tailors. I keep my money in English banks. All my people drive English cars. I even try to speak like an Englishman as much as possible. Respect for the language. You know what I'm saying? Americans have no respect of their language. No sense of tradition. Don't misunderstand me. I'm proud that I come from America. But it's still possible to find fault. If you saw my home here, you'd see that many of my tastes are the same as yours. That pleases me because I know you're a cultured man. Married to a successful actress. And you have pets. That tells me a lot about you. I have a house in Surrey with a dozen pets. Dogs and cats and horses. I love animals. So do you, I expect. That's the problem. A man who loves his animals is vulnerable. I saw a man shot to death defending his dog. I was just a boy but I've never forgotten it.' He took out a gold case, opened it, and lit a cigarette.

'Now,' Twilly said. 'Let's get on with our business. We taped your mouth so you wouldn't get excited and wake up your neighbours. But since we want information from you we'll have to remove the tape so you can talk. But you must understand that we'll be talking in a regular tone of voice, just as I'm talking now. If you begin to shout or cry for help the tape will go back on your mouth. Then your bowl of tropical fish will be carried into the bathroom and flushed down the toilet. You understand? After that we'll take the tape off again. If you make a commotion the parrot you have in the kitchen will go out the window. If for some reason you still don't understand, if you still refuse to co-operate, we'll put your little dog in the oven and turn up the heat. After that my cousin, Frank, who's standing behind you, will start working on your fingers. Take the tape off, Frank.'

As soon as his mouth was partly uncovered Maple began to shout, 'If you rotten bastards think you can . . .'

Instantly, the tape was back across his mouth. One of the men walked across the room, picked up the fish-bowl and carried it into the bathroom. The toilet flushed and the man came back with the empty bowl.

'Take the tape off again,' Twilly said.

This time the men were prepared. As soon as Maple said, 'God *damn* you . . .' they slapped the tape on again. The man who'd taken the fish-bowl went into the kitchen. They heard the window being opened, a loud squawk from the parrot, and the sound of the window being pulled shut again. The man was sucking his knuckle when he came back in the room. 'The bastard bit me,' he said.

Twilly had never taken his eyes off Maple. 'The dog's next, Mr Maple. Shall we take the tape off or not?'

Maple stared at him. At last he nodded his head. When Frank pulled the tape off, Maple spoke in a husky whisper. 'Where's my dog?'

'That's better,' Twilly said. 'Your dog's fine. When we got here we gave him a nice piece of meat with something in it to make him sleep. He's good for another hour or so before he wakes up.'

'I want to see him.'

Twilly nodded his head and Frank led Maple into the bedroom. The dog was curled up on the bed, his head resting on his paws. He was breathing evenly, his sides moving in and out like a soft bellows.

When Maple was back in his chair, his mouth and cheeks bright pink from the adhesive tape, his arms still lashed behind him, Twilly said, 'A man named Evan Tagg, who's living with your wife in California, had bad luck with his car. Somebody poured gasoline all over it, set it on fire, and turned it into a cinder. The people who owned that car, a brand-new Packard, are friends of ours. They don't like people burning up things that belong to them. Since you've got a reputation for setting things on fire, and since it's your wife that Tagg is playing house with, your name kept coming up. But some enquiries were made and we found out you were in England when the car went up in smoke. So the next idea was that some friend of yours in California did you a favour, or paid off a debt, or earned a bit of money.'

'What makes you think I have friends in California?'

'We know you do. Los Angeles is crawling with Englishmen. And a lot of them are actors from London. You have friends there all right. Now, before you start to make up a string of lies let me tell you something else. We know the man who put up the money to torch the car was an Englishman, we know what kind of a car he drives. He's not invisible. Someone will smoke him out. But that's not enough for my friends. Since you were involved one way or another, they want you to finger your friend. We're going to stay here till you do. And the longer we stay, the more it's going to hurt.' He looked at his watch. 'Like I said we'll stay as long as we have to but I'd like to be out of here in twenty minutes. So the sooner you start talking, the happier I'll be. We'll put it all down on a piece of paper and you can sign it. Then you can curl up beside your dog and go to sleep.'

Twenty minutes later Twilly took a piece of paper from Maple, read it carefully, folded it and put it in his jacket pocket. 'I'm sure you've heard stories about people like us. Or maybe you see a lot of movies. If you do, you probably think you're getting off easy. And you are. At least I believe you are. I don't think our friends in California are going to send somebody to punish you. I mean, I don't think they intend to hurt you. But that doesn't mean it's over. They may decide you owe them a favour. I might even decide that myself. Nothing's for nothing.'

When they unwrapped Maple's wrists he stayed in his chair. Just before they went out the door, Twilly came back to him and said, 'One more thing. They tell me you're a man who likes to punish his wife. Push her around a little. Put a few bruises on her face. I'll tell you something. I hate to hear stories like that. The idea of a grown-up man putting the muscle on a woman, on his own wife, makes me sick to my stomach. I'd really feel awful if I heard any more stories like that about you. You know what I'm saying? Answer me.'

Maple looked up at him. 'I know what you're saying.'

'Good. You're not a dumb guy. Don't forget it.'

He turned away then and walked through the door to the corridor. Frank and the other man followed him. They left Maple's door open behind them.

2

At the Thursday press conference, after Julian Thorne and Tim Garrigus had made statements and answered questions about the upcoming production of *Dillinger*, about the budget, the projected locations, and the cast, Thorne introduced Kincaid. 'This is the man who's going to star in our film. We're convinced he's the only actor in our industry who can play this part. I believe he has a few words to say. Then you can ask whatever questions you like.'

Kincaid looked as though he hadn't shaved for three days. He was wearing dungarees, dirty tennis-shoes, and a wrinkled sweater. He walked to the front edge of the platform and sat down, directly in front of the journalists and columnists sitting in rows of chairs.

'You people know I don't give interviews very often

so I guess I'd better give you an earful this time. The men here at the studio who care more about my reputation than I do tell me you have some tough questions to ask me. It seems there are some nasty stories going round. Since I don't hang out at the Cinegrill or the Polo Lounge, and since I never read the junk you people write, I don't know what those stories are. But whatever they are, I guarantee you, the truth is a lot worse. That doesn't mean that I promise to tell you the truth, because I don't. But I do promise to tell you something interesting. I wouldn't want you to leave the studio today feeling as if you'd wasted your time.'

A grey-haired man in the first row stood up and said, 'One of the stories we're hearing is that your parents are very poor people, not in good health, still living somewhere in Australia. They could use your help but you have nothing to do with them.'

'I hate to destroy my image by telling the simple truth but this time I'll do it. I have no father and no mother. I'm a bastard twice over. As far as I know I could have hatched out on a rock. I realize I could never have been born if some man and some woman hadn't got together, but whoever they were, I've never seen them. If I met them now I wouldn't recognize them.'

'Who raised you?'

'Nobody. I raised myself. For the first fourteen years of my life the world offered me nothing. I kissed everybody's bum and got nothing in return. So I decided to take what I wanted. Then they gave me something in return. They threw my ass in jail. That was in Port Arthur. Not far from where I must have been born. By the time I was twenty I'd been in eight jails in six countries.'

A young woman said, 'Are you willing to tell us why you were in jail so much?'

'Different reasons. Drunk and disorderly. Burglary. Punching a policeman in Long Beach . . .'

Somebody in the back of the room began to laugh.

'. . . armed robbery and aggravated assault. I must have done some other naughty things but I can't remember.'

More laughter from the reporters. A prissy young man stood up and said, 'We all seem to feel guilt for one thing or another. How do you feel about the mistakes you've made?'

'I didn't make mistakes. I did what I had to do at the time. My mistake was getting caught. Let's face it. Everybody's looking to get rich or get laid. Or both at the same time . . .'

A burst of general laughter this time.

'It's a whore's world. Everybody puts out for somebody. I see nothing wrong with robbing people as long as they're not your friends. People have to eat and everybody's stealing something.'

The young man persisted. 'You're a public figure now. Aren't you concerned that you might be a bad influence on young people?'

'Young people don't give a damn what I say or do.'

An overweight woman with a great feather on her hat said, 'Since you've brought up your prison record I'll say that one of the rumours we hear concerns that time.'

'Prison's a nasty place,' he said.

'The story is that you were a violent prisoner, that you may have killed another inmate.'

'I'll tell you this. I was as violent as I was able to be. A lot of fighting goes on inside prisons. Sometimes I'd go for a week without a fight. Other times I'd be in a fight every day. And every fight I was in, I wanted to kill the guy if I could. Because he wanted to kill me. There weren't any rules in those fights. No referees. We fought till somebody couldn't fight any more and the guards carried him off to the infirmary. Sometimes I got carried off. Usually it was the other guy. Two or

259

three times I never saw the guy again. That doesn't mean he was dead but I can't guarantee that he wasn't. If somebody has to be dead, I figure it's my job to make sure it's not me.'

'What if everybody felt that way?'

'Everybody doesn't feel that way. Most people are scared of their own shadows. I'm not.'

A middle-aged woman with hennaed hair, wearing a low-cut dress, said, 'Some of my readers have written to ask if you're a bigamist. They know you're married but they've heard that you have another wife and child in Argentina.'

'I'm twenty-six years old. My wife and I have been married for almost two years. This is her second marriage but my first. If you want to know if I have a child in Argentina I can't tell you. I might have half a dozen children in Argentina.'

'Are you saying . . .'

'I'm answering your question. I've been a merchant seaman since I was sixteen years old. You've all heard the stories about sailors . . . well, they're true.'

If the laughter had been tentative before, it was out of control suddenly. Even Julian Thorne, who had had a serious look on his face, joined in. Tim Garrigus put his head back and roared.

'I shipped out on freighters. Rust-buckets. They visited a lot of ports. In every port I went ashore with only one thought in my head. And I was happy to find there was always some young woman there who had the same idea I had. I must have gone ashore five hundred times in those years, so figure it out. It's not likely but it's possible that I have five hundred children I've never seen.'

Gloria Westerfield stood up then. When the laughter subsided she said, 'So much for the lies and rumours. Now maybe you'd be willing to tell us the most important thing you've learned about the motion-picture business.'

'That's easy. Everybody's dumb and everybody's crooked. Here's the first law of Hollywood. If you're on the outside you're garbage. If you're on the inside you're king. If you need money all you do is ring up the head of the studio. If the studio needs money they call up the bank. If the bank needs money they send a messenger to the mob. If the mob's short of money we're all in trouble. That means the world's gone broke.'

3

As the time drew near to start shooting *Dillinger*, Evan drove early every morning to the studio and stayed there till seven o'clock in the evening. During those hours he had trained himself to concentrate fully and exclusively on the problems at hand. As he headed home in the early evening, however, the sun dropping steadily, glowing through his windscreen as he drove toward the ocean, all the work details remained in the studio and his questions and confusions about Mary began to hammer in his head.

She had telephoned him when she arrived in New York, the night before she was to sail for England. In their conversation, they pretended, each of them, that there were no questions on the table, no bewilderment or misunderstanding. They spoke only of love and loneliness, of their need to be together, their desire, their dependence. If the words sounded memorized, as if they were being read from the pages of a script, they seemed not to notice. But there was no joy in their voices, no joy on either of their faces when they said goodbye at last and hung up the receivers.

Evan's feelings sling-shotted back and forth among guilt, self-recrimination, anger toward Mary, and anger toward himself. Trying to pin-point the moment where they had veered away from whatever it should be called – the sort of life they'd made together, and the unquiet tangle of doubt and suspicion it had turned into – he seemed to centre always on his return from England, on her apparent uneasiness, on the stasis that seemed to freeze them when the subject of Maple came up. Had she ever given him a sensible answer when he told her about his meeting with her husband? Had she insisted that Maple was lying when he said there'd been no talk between them on the subject of divorce? Evan couldn't remember. But clearly her instinct had been to protect him when Evan had suggested mentioning his name to the fire inspectors.

Was she afraid of him? Or was there something else that frightened her? Whatever the answers, why did she feel she must keep them to herself? And most persistent of all, Evan kept hearing that trained and well-modulated British voice on the telephone the first evening he was back. 'Oh, it's you. You're back then. Well, welcome home.' Not a wrong number. Not a casual hang-up. So who was it? And why was he calling Mary? And why hadn't Evan been more persistent in questioning her about that call? He asked himself that question over and over but found no answer. Nonetheless, he couldn't help thinking that there was a connection between that smarmy voice and Mary's sudden decision to return to London, pretending all the while that Novello's play made it necessary.

In his frustration Evan went so far as to enquire about a passage to England, knowing as he sat by the phone waiting for information that such a trip was impossible now, suspecting at the same time that the answers he needed were no more available in London than they had been in the house in Malibu or in the car as they drove to the railway station the morning she left.

Later he admitted to himself that he had deliberately turned to thoughts of his mother, hoping to find release from his every-evening session of torment about Mary. Was there some connection in his mind between his mother's leaving him when he was a child and Mary's recent departure? If he had asked himself that question he would surely have scoffed at it. And perhaps there was indeed no one-plus-one connection between those two widely separated events. But all the same he found some relief in substituting one for the other. As he reviewed Amy's letter in his mind, as he began to make tentative plans to see her, he found himself somewhat less preoccupied with the tantalizing mystery of Mary.

He had received no reply to the note he'd sent his father with a copy of Amy's letter enclosed. He had in fact had no communication from Arthur since he'd left the Towers and gone to London. Margaret had not heard from him either, according to Sophie. There was some awareness by everyone, however, of the intensive schedule he'd laid out for himself so their impatience with his silence had not yet turned into concern.

Evan's efforts to imagine Arthur's reaction to Amy's letter were fruitless. Although any reaction was possible Evan expected either a negative one or none at all. In light of that he considered whether or not it was some sort of betrayal of his father if he proceeded with a relationship with Amy, or if he even attempted to bring such a relationship into being. He also considered whether or not it was a questionable tactic for him. Did he risk making a lifelong commitment to someone who had previously avoided, in no uncertain terms, making any such commitment to him. Evan, however, was not vengeful by nature. Nor was it his instinct to ask himself if he was in danger of giving more than he might receive in return. His sense of order told him that a child-parent relationship deserved some sort of continuing life, no matter what its past history might be. The thought of going to the studio every day and working there, of being only a short distance from his mother but not seeing her, was disturbing to him and did indeed have the scent of vengeance to it, whether he intended it or not.

One day he rang up Sophie, who he felt would understand the situation he was in better than anyone. But when she came on the phone Evan found himself discussing other matters and never bringing up the subject of his mother. At another juncture he considered laying it all out in front of Kincaid but again he resisted that impulse. At last he told himself that it was a matter that concerned no one but him and Amy, not even his father; he should make the choice that seemed wisest to him and stick with it. Two days later he called her at Hook's drug-store and arranged to meet her for lunch the following day. 'You don't know what I look like but I'll know you, so I'll get there first,' she said. 'You come at one and I'll be there a few minutes before. I'll try to get a booth by the window.' Before she hung up she said, 'I'm glad you decided to come. I'm excited.'

When he arrived the next day at the small restaurant she'd suggested, he saw her wave to him from the last booth at the rear of the room by the window looking out on Wilcox.

She was smaller than he'd expected. Prettier. She wore a soft white felt hat with a navy-blue ribbon round it, a navy-blue, long-sleeved dress with a white collar, and a string of pearls.

'Well, here we are,' she said as he sat down. Then: 'You're taller than I thought from your picture in the paper.'

'I'm about the same size as Dad,' he said. 'Maybe an inch taller.'

'That's funny. I don't remember him being so tall. The memory plays funny tricks on us, doesn't it?'

There was a long silence as they sat looking at each

other. Then Evan said, 'Yes, I suppose it does.'

'Of course everybody seems tall to me. I'm just a little shrimp. Five two or three in my spike heels. I always wear high heels except when I'm barefoot around the house. They say short men never stop trying to compensate. Maybe it's the same for us women.'

'I've certainly met a number of tiny actresses since I've been out here. Do you think there's some connection?'

'I never thought of that. It's hard to tell anybody's size in a movie. All the small people stand on boxes, they say. I walked past Brian Donlevy on the street one day and he didn't look much taller than me.'

They ordered their lunch and drank iced tea and chatted like two old chums about his business, her job, and the characteristics of life in southern California. Finally she glanced at her watch and said, 'Time goes fast, doesn't it? I have to leave in about ten minutes. Takes me five minutes to walk back to the store from here.'

'I've got a car.'

'No. That's all right. I like to walk. That's how I keep my girlish figure.' Then: 'We're not going to talk about serious stuff anyway, are we?'

'I don't think so.'

'We didn't talk about any family matters or anything. But maybe that's better. At least we've had a chance to look each other over. Now you can decide whether you want to see me again or not. No, don't say anything now. Think it over, and if you want to have lunch again just call me up like you did yesterday and I'll meet you here. I like this place. It's a pretty room and nobody gets ptomaine.'

A few minutes later, as she was gathering herself together, she said, 'I'm sorry I'm so nervous. I'm usually not that way.'

'You don't seem nervous to me.'

'Oh, please. Butterflies in my tummy all through lunch. You're not nervous, are you?'

He smiled. 'I guess I was. Not so much now.'

'Usually I'm the life of the party. People say I'm a good talker. I read a lot so I always have plenty of information to spread around. Besides there's nothing sadder to me than two people sitting across the table from each other, chewing their food, and never saying a word, either one of them. Lots of married couples like that, I guess. I didn't even ask you if you're married.'

'I'm not.'

'Neither am I.'

He stayed in the booth when she left, smoking a cigarette and watching her walk up the street. He didn't say to himself, 'There she is . . . that's my Mum' or 'She's got pretty legs.' He just sat there and watched her as she walked up Wilcox, sat there with his chin cupped in his hand and watched her walking away till he couldn't see her any longer.

When he asked for the check the waitress said, 'It's paid for, sir. The lady said to tell you it's her treat.'

4

Three days after the press conference at Thornwood Studios, Gloria Westerfield devoted her entire column to Kincaid.

This is a salute to an actor, one particular actor, a man named Kincaid.

I interviewed him more than a year ago when he first came to town to play the lead in Julian Thorne's film, *Bushranger*. At that time I had mixed feelings about him and I expressed those feelings in what I wrote. I thought he was brash, eccentric, untruthful, and independent to a fault. There was also a tough magnetism about him that I found attractive. Menace is the word perhaps. Many directors, Howard Hawks and Bill Wellman among them, believe that all the great leading men have a touch of menace in their make-up. In that area, on our first meeting, Kincaid certainly qualified.

Actors want to be liked. They feel they need to be liked if they're to continue working, to have a career. They are careful to be attractive and agreeable, to project a polished surface with no rough edges. Since almost anyone may turn out to be a producer, it's important to ingratiate oneself constantly, to offend no one.

Kincaid, on the other hand, has no such instincts. After spending an hour with him I realized that he didn't care whether I liked him or not, and that he had no interest whatsoever in what I might write about him or whether I would write about him at all. He had met with me only because Julian Thorne had asked him to. Since *Bushranger* opened last winter he has given no interviews that I'm aware of.

My opinions of *Bushranger* and of Kincaid's contribution to it are part of the public record. I praised the film highly and Kincaid's performance as well. And I was happy to see that the public shared my views. They seem to believe, as I do, that Kincaid will be an important person in motion pictures, that his success has a solid foundation.

Success, however, sends many messages. And nowhere more powerfully than in the film community. Many people want to share in it, to celebrate it, to emulate it. Others feel compelled to denigrate it, to destroy it if possible. A favourite device with such people is to dig up something in someone's past that will tend to diminish their achievements. If nothing scandalous, immoral, or embarrassing can be discovered, they simply invent something and pass it along as a fact.

Kincaid in recent months has been a victim of this sort of foolishness. In what seems to have been a well-organized programme of slander, a number of outrageous stories about his past, his morals, and his character have been bruited about, both here and across the country. At last Kincaid – surely at the prompting of Julian Thorne, who has an undeniable stake in this actor – agreed to reply to the rumours and gossip.

When he presented himself to members of the press, he made no effort to refute the stories or to defend himself. Instead he indicted and convicted himself of far worse sins than any he had been accused of. He used ridicule and humour as weapons. I've never heard such laughter at a press conference. I've never seen journalists applaud when an interview ended. Not only did Kincaid make ridiculous and irrelevant the stories that have been told about him, he struck a blow against all the careless rumour and gossip we have come to accept as part of our community life in Hollywood.

Several months ago when Samuel Goldwyn was asked to comment on the sexual escapades of one of his important female stars, he said, 'It doesn't matter. With each of Lena's pictures we make more money. She always plays prostitutes, girlfriends of gangsters, or fallen women of some kind. So when she's naughty in her private life, people expect it of her. But if she'd made her reputation by playing nuns and virgins, the public would drop her like a mashed potato.'

If Mr Goldwyn is correct, Kincaid, who played Ned Kelly, the Australian desperado, and who will now play the title role in *Dillinger*, can never again be threatened by character assassination. If he's been naughty no one will be surprised. And if they are he can simply repeat the performance he gave at Thornwood Studios last Thursday.

5

Ten days after Dolph Twilly visited Alec Maple at his flat in London, Burt Windrow was asked to come to Sam Thorne's office at the studio. When Mrs Rawson gave him the message he said, 'What's this all about?'

'They have an exclusive story for you, they said. Asked you to come by at four this afternoon.'

'Call and see if you can change it to tomorrow. I'm supposed to be at Universal at four.'

'Do you know Sam Thorne?' Mrs Rawson asked.

'Julian Thorne's brother. He's a bookkeeper.'

'Not exactly,' she said. 'If we have to change appointments I suggest we call Edgar Ulmer at Universal and reschedule him.'

'What kind of exclusive can I get from Sam Thorne? He probably wants to tell me what their grosses were last week. I can get those figures from *Variety*.'

Mrs Rawson sat back in her chair and smoothed her hair with both hands. 'Do you remember the day you hired me? When I told you I'd worked for twenty-five years in the studios, you said that was important to you. You wanted someone who knows how things work in the executive buildings. That's what I know. When Sam Thorne came here from the East, I was his first secretary. I know the Thornwood operation inside out. If Sam called me twenty minutes from now and asked me to come to his office, I'd get in my car and go.'

'That's because you're his friend. I'm not his friend.'

She shook her head. 'I'm his former secretary. I'm not his friend. I'd go if he called because I'd know it was something important. That's why you should go. Sam doesn't kiss up to reporters. If it wasn't something special he wouldn't have asked you to come in.'

When Windrow was ushered into Sam Thorne's office that afternoon, Thorne remained seated behind his desk. 'I'm Sam Thorne, Windrow. Have a seat.' He didn't introduce John Corso who sat on the couch against the wall. Thorne glanced at his watch. 'This shouldn't take much time so let's get on with it.'

'My secretary said you have some material for my column.'

'I think we told her it was an exclusive story. We figured that was the best way to get you here.' He glanced over at Corso. 'So we could have a quiet talk.'

Windrow heard a solid click then at the door behind him. When his head turned toward the door Thorne said, 'Don't worry about it. That's just so you don't decide to run off somewhere before we finish talking.'

'Are you locking me in here?'

'Shut up,' Corso said. 'Shut up and listen to Sam.'

'We had a mystery here at the studio a few weeks ago. One of our writers, Evan Tagg, was driving a studio car, a brand-new Packard convertible. And one night somebody torched it outside his house. Poured gasoline on it and turned it into a scrap-iron worth about fifty cents. Maybe you saw the item in the paper.'

'I don't think so.'

'It doesn't matter. I'll explain it to you. You see, the Sheriff's department and the fire inspectors gave up on the case but we weren't satisfied with that. We decided to do some investigating on our own. It took some time but we pieced it all together. Do you want me to give you the details or do you want to tell me?'

'What do you mean by that?'

'You know damned well what I mean. If you could see your face you'd know that you're about five shades paler than you were a few minutes ago.'

'I don't know what you're talking about.'

'I promised to give you a story. I'll even give you the headline: Limey columnist goes to jail for arson.' When Windrow didn't answer, Thorne said, 'Tell him about it, John.'

Corso stood up, walked across the room, and leaned against Thorne's desk looking down at Windrow, who suddenly came to life. 'I don't know what you're trying to do to me but it's ridiculous,' Windrow said. 'Do I look like a chap who runs around setting fire to cars?'

'No, you don't,' Thorne said. 'You don't look like you ever had dirty hands.'

'A couple of Mexican kids did the job for short money,' Corso said. 'For a hundred dollars those two pachucos would turn you into dog meat if somebody asked them to. We know who set the deal up, we know who he laid it off on, and we know the messenger who delivered the money to the contractor. And the messenger told us about the bozo who gave the money to him. But he didn't know much. It was a dark night. All he could tell was it was a guy with a limey accent driving a black La Salle.'

Thorne leaned back in his chair. 'At first we decided it was the husband of the doll that Tagg's shacked up with. He's an Englishman named Alec Maple so we figured he had a reason to dump on Tagg. But we found out he was in London the night the car went up in smoke. Still, we thought he might know something about it so some friends of ours went to see him in London. It was a good hunch. These guys reasoned with him a little and he sang like a canary.'

'He even wrote it down,' Corso said, 'and signed his name to it.' Thorne handed him a piece of paper, and he passed it along to Windrow. Before he looked at it Windrow said, 'How do I know Alec wrote this?'

'Because we say so,' Corso said.

When he finished reading it Windrow said, 'Do you

271

think I'm stupid? I know something about American law. Even if it did happen the way you say, there's no evidence that ties me to it.' He tossed the piece of paper on the desk. 'This doesn't mean anything. Alec was in London. How does he know where I was the night the car burned up?'

'You're talking like a lawyer,' Thorne said. 'We're not policemen. We weren't planning to turn this over to the Sheriff's department or the insurance investigators. And even if we did, you may be right. They might not have the evidence to put you in jail. But there's a good chance they'd indict you and bring you to trial. Those newspapers you work for wouldn't go for that kind of publicity even if some sharp lawyer got you off. Am I right? And then there's the Mexican kids. If they take the fall and you get off, their friends are gonna have your picture stuck up on the kitchen wall. You see what I mean? But we're not trying to get you killed. We're not even anxious for you to lose your job or be locked up. But all that's up to you. If you want to take your chances in court along with the other problems I mentioned, then we *will* hand over what we know to the insurance people and let them handle it. Whatever you say, Mr Windrow. It's Burt, ain't it? Whatever you say, Burt.' He held up a file folder. 'We can messenger this over to the insurance people late this afternoon and it's out of our hands.'

'What if you don't send it over to them, then what?'

'Then it's just between us. A personal matter. Just a question of doing what's fair and right. You burn somebody's car, a beautiful car like that, there has to be some compensation involved. Are we starting to understand each other?'

Windrow nodded. 'What do you want from me?'

'Only what's fair,' Thorne said. He looked at Corso. 'There's a Packard agency on the corner of Wilshire and La Cienega,' Corso said. 'A dealer named Serkin. He's got

272

a convertible in his show window, exactly like the one that got torched. We want you to buy that car and turn it over to Thornwood Studios. The papers are all there at the dealers. We told him you'd be over later this afternoon to sign the contract and work out the financing.'

'Jesus, I can't lay out that kind of money . . .'

'Yes, you can,' Corso said.

'It's only fair,' Thorne said. 'We're talking about compensation, remember? Replacement of what was lost. That's the minimum, Burt. Do we understand each other?'

'I understand you, all right.'

'Good.' Sam glanced at his watch. 'John here will drive you over to Serkin . . .'

'It's all right. I have my car.'

'Let me finish. John will drive you to Serkin. After you've signed the papers and John sees they're in order, we want you to drive the Packard to Evan Tagg's house in Malibu. He's at home this afternoon. After you've put the car in the carport I want you to ring the doorbell. When Tagg comes to the door I want you to say, "I'm sorry for what I did to your car. I've just replaced it with a new one." You got that?'

'I heard you.'

'Let me hear you say it.'

'I'm sorry for what I did to your car. I've just replaced it with a new one.'

'You used to be an actor. Am I right?'

'Yes.'

'I thought so. Now, are we on the same track? If you're planning to change your mind or do something fancy after you leave this office, I hope you know how much of a mess that would cause. Not for us. For you. We're being very polite but John and I have handled all sorts of tight situations. We're serious men. You understand what I'm saying?'

273

'I understand perfectly,' Windrow said. 'But that doesn't mean I like it.'

'We don't like it either. But once that Packard burned up it set all kinds of things in motion.'

'You know what Sam's been saying. You got it all straight in your head about the new Packard?' Corso asked.

'It's all straight.'

'Good,' Sam said. 'That takes care of the compensation. Now let's talk about respect. You've agreed to replace the car you destroyed. Now what about the personal damage you caused to me and my brother and our company? When someone destroys our property it's humiliating. Like some bastard robbing your bedroom or rifling through your desk. Makes us look helpless. That's a bad image. Bad for business. Your competitors see you taking it on the chin from some punk fire-bug, they start to think you're fair game. Next thing you know, you got headaches coming at you from every direction. You've agreed to apologize to Evan Tagg, to face up to him like a man and admit you were wrong. Now we have to consider the wrong you did to me and my brother. We suffered from your lack of respect. We were humiliated to have to admit to the insurance company that we were unable to protect our own property. We know you're not a wealthy man. If you were, this would be a simple matter to deal with. A man's dignity is worth a lot of money. When money changes hands in a proper way, it's a token of respect. That's what we're talking about. Some small sacrifice. Some physical evidence that you understand you did a crappy thing. You're an Englishman. You don't understand these things. I'm a Jew. My friend John is a Sicilian. Old cultures. Old bloodlines. Ritual and symbols. That's what we're concerned with here. Do you follow me?'

'I know you're asking me for something. I'm not sure what it is.'

Sam took a piece of paper out of his desk drawer and handed it across to Windrow. 'That's a bill of sale for your car. Your La Salle.'

'I don't want to sell that car.'

'Of course you don't. That's why we want you to do it.'

'It's a brand-new car, for God's sake. I've only had it for three months. Less than that.'

'If it were worthless to you it would be worthless as a symbol. As a gesture. If you gave us something that had no value it would mean that my brother, Julian, and I have no value in your eyes. You only show respect by surrendering something that's important to you. You've injured us. Now you must expect some small injury to yourself.'

'What if I refuse?'

'You can't refuse. You have no chips to bargain with.' Sam handed him a crisp dollar bill. This is my gift to you. Your La Salle is your gift to me and my brother. You respect us. We respect you.'

Corso handed Windrow a fountain-pen. 'Sign the paper and let's go pick up that Packard.'

Very late that afternoon Evan's doorbell rang. When he opened the door there were two men standing there, a tall blond fellow and a heavy-set man in a blue suit and a brown fedora. The tall man said, 'I'm sorry for what I did to your car. I've just replaced it with a new one.' The blue-suited man handed Evan a set of car keys. Then he turned and followed the other one up the wooden steps to the highway. When Windrow tried to open the door on the passenger side of Corso's car, John said, 'I've got a gut-full of you. You can get home on your thumb.'

'What do you mean? Thorne said you'd drive me home.'

'I say you're a punk and I'm taking you nowhere. I hate candy-assed guys like you. You're lucky you're dealing with Thorne instead of me. I'd have left you floating in the bay in six separate pieces.'

Evan went up the back stairway to the carport. He sat in the driver's seat of the new car, turned the key, and listened to the smooth throb of the big engine. But his mind was elsewhere. As soon as he heard the blond man speak he'd recognized the voice. 'Oh, it's you. You're back then. Well, welcome home.'

6

If Sophie was apprehensive about the effect of California life on Sarah and Trevor, and she was, she was delighted to discover how mistaken she'd been. Sarah, after visiting several schools in and around Los Angeles, chose the most structured and restrictive one of all, on the site of an old Spanish convent in Ojai. The school, though it had no church affiliation, was called St Hilda's. The obvious lure for Sarah, as well as for many of her fellow students, was the presence there of Ethel Richmond. Miss Richmond, a tall and straight-backed woman in her seventies, had been the leading actress of her generation in the New York theatre, had retired at the peak of her popularity, and had been the head of St Hilda's drama department for almost twenty years.

Because of her energy, her enthusiasm, and her speaking voice, Sarah attracted Miss Richmond's attention from their first meeting. Making a strong effort to excel in all her dramatic classes and related exercises – voice training, body movement, dance, and fencing – Sarah did indeed excel. To everyone's surprise she also applied herself to her other subjects. French, English literature, algebra, world history, and zoology. After just a few weeks, the headmistress Miss Hollenbeck reported to Sophie that Sarah was an exemplary student.

Trevor, who had chosen to live at home and be a day

student at the Schuyler School in Westwood was also well acclimated, it seemed. Not such a surprise because he had always done good work at St Alban's. But a pleasant development, nonetheless, for his mother. 'I'm glad you've settled in so well at school. I know you weren't keen to leave St Alban's.'

'But I haven't left there, have I? When we're back in England I'll go there again till I'm ready for university. And if we're back here next year I'll have Schuyler to come to. And Mr Grell. And my new friend, Homer Tony.'

The year before, when he and his sister had spent the summer at Praia da Rocha with their mother, Trevor had met an American painter, Ben Quigley, and his wife, Lenore. Quigley had encouraged Trevor to take his drawing seriously and had pushed him into his first experiments with painting. They had corresponded regularly after Trevor returned to England and it was Quigley, when he learned that Trevor would be spending some months in Los Angeles, who sent him to Hermann Grell. 'He knows more about anatomy and drawing the figure than any other man I've met. Whatever you decide to paint later on, you need to have a knowledge of the human figure.'

Soon after his arrival in California, when he'd settled into his new routine, Trevor wrote to Quigley.

Here I am in California. The climate reminds me of the Algarve but everything else is different. My mother was afraid I'd fall in love with the place, become a surf-rider, and never want to return to England, but there's no chance of that. Not for me.

Many of the people I've met here don't seem to know that England exists. Or they think it's a place where everyone is very unhappy because they can't come to live in California. People go to the beach here as if they're going to church. And nobody walks. They take street cars or the little red cars, the trains that go from one community to another, or they drive in automobiles or ride motor-bikes.

As I said, I think my Mum is surprised that I haven't run off to live on the beach in a tent. But I have no urge to do that. Even my sister, who was such a pill last summer, is behaving like a proper human being and that's the surprise of the century. So my mother is walking around with nothing to worry about.

You said you knew about the Schuyler School. Well, it's turned out all right. But it's nothing like an English school. My work is easy because most of it I've already covered at St Alban's but I pretend to work hard so the masters will feel good about themselves and think they're teaching me something.

There are some really rotten fellows in the school. They drive their own roadsters and carry great rolls of American dollars in their trouser pockets. Awfully loud some of them, and eager to tell one about their sexual adventures. Tiresome. But there are some decent chaps as well. We play a lot of tennis and a bit of soccer. And I'm learning to throw and catch a ball, American-style. So all goes well.

The best part, of course, thanks to you, is Mr Grell. What a good man. I don't know how he ever made it out here or why he stays. When he shows up at class it's as if he'd just stepped off the streets of Zurich. Still wears his Swiss suit, all covered with chalk dust. And how exciting it is to watch him draw. It's as if his hand holding the charcoal is not connected to his body. I don't know how long it is since you've seen him but he's quite heavy now. Blocky and solid like a Rodin. But his arm and hand seem weightless, like a dancer making an effortless leap through the air. He keeps saying things like you said to me last summer. 'Never mind genius. You can learn nothing from a genius. Learn to work, to use the materials. Learn your craft, learn the rules of form and perspective and shading. You can't learn to be a great artist – only God can give you that – but I can teach you to be a worker, a craftsman. A genius is another sort of creature. We can admire him, even worship him, but he can teach us nothing.'

They worked out my schedule at school so I'm free to go to Mr Grell's studio in Santa Monica on Thursday afternoons. And I spend all day Saturday there. We're drawing from the model. Sometimes a man. Sometimes a woman. Nude models. Something new for me. The first class I went to, I was sitting in front of my easel with a nice sheet of grey paper thumbtacked to a board all ready to go, my charcoal and chalk and erasers and a piece of chamois in the tray in front of me. Then Mr Grell said, 'All right, dear, we're ready for you,' and a young woman wearing a robe walked up on the model stand, tossed her robe across a chair and struck a pose. I guess my hand must have been shaking. I couldn't draw anything for a while. But finally I saw how matter-of-fact everybody was about the whole thing. There were twenty or thirty people in the class, men and women, all of them older than me, and they were busy as mice, scratching away with their charcoal sticks, blending, erasing, shading, talking to themselves. And once in a while Mr Grell would stand by the model and point to her hip or her shoulder-line or the angle of her neck and say things like, 'When the weight's on the right leg, then you see what happens to the left side of the body. It's a rule of nature. It never changes.'

The model's name was Lucy and everybody in the class seemed to know her. When she had a rest period she put on her robe and laughed and joked with the artists closest to the model stand. And then sometimes she'd stroll around the studio and look at everyone's work. I almost collapsed when she looked at my drawing the first time. But she just studied it for a minute, then she looked at me and said, 'I haven't seen you here before.' She stuck out her hand and said, 'I'm Lucy.' She's very pretty and always wears her hair pulled back tight in a bun. She doesn't look any older than me but somebody told me she's seventeen and she's studying to be a dancer. She models for Mr Grell to help pay for her classes.

In any case, what I started to say was that I got used to the idea of nude models pretty quickly. So now I just concentrate on my drawing and don't notice much who happens to be starkers on the model stand. At first Mr Grell didn't say much to me, but when I thought I was getting pretty good he said, 'Remember what I said about genius? You're trying to draw like Cézanne or Gauguin. I want you to draw, as much as you're able, like Ingres or Degas or da Vinci. *Copy* those men till you can feel in your fingers what they're doing. Then you can go crazy later if you want to.'

I guess you can tell by what I'm saying that I'm having a fine time here. I'm just sorry that you and Lenore aren't close by so we could talk about all the different painters the way we did last summer. If there's any chance you might come this way, Kincaid built us a house the size of a hotel so we've got lots of room for you to stay. My mother knows I'm inviting you and she invites you as well.

One more thing I have to tell you: we have five riding horses here and I've learned to ride western-style on a western saddle. Very different from the way we ride at home. But the best thing is the man who looks after the horses. His name is Homer Tony. Kincaid knew him a long time ago in Australia. They worked on a cattle ranch together when Kincaid was my age.

Homer Tony (almost everybody calls him by his full

name as though it's one word) is an unusual fellow. He's not really tall, not much taller than I am, but he's rugged-looking and very strong. I like the way he looks but some people think he's ferocious. He's an Aborigine, you see. Maybe you know about those people but I didn't. They were natives of Australia like the American Indians were in this country. They have a different look. They're not black but some of their features remind you of Negroes. They make little cuts in their faces in a kind of design that shows what tribe they come from, and when the cuts heal there's a pattern of welts across their cheekbones and on their foreheads sometimes. Some people think it looks weird but I like it.

The reason Homer Tony takes care of our horses is because he's Kincaid's friend. But also he knows more about horses than anybody else in the world, I expect. He can train a horse to do anything. When he's in the paddock they follow him like little dogs. Also he's a great rider. Wild and crazy. With a saddle or without. He did all the stunt riding in *Bushranger*, and they keep after him now to do stunts in other movies but he doesn't like to leave the grounds here.

Here's the thing about Homer Tony. He can't talk. Can't make a sound. When he was ten years old he saw some men kill a woman and they made him swallow lye or some chemical that destroyed his vocal chords and burned out his tongue. So he couldn't tell anybody what he'd seen. There's nothing wrong with his hearing and he's intelligent. You can see that by looking in his eyes. He hasn't been to school but he's learned to write a few words. And he loves to have certain people talk to him even though he's not able to answer.

Kincaid had a nice cottage built for him in a grove of trees down past the stables and he sits by himself down there at night. Listening to the radio mostly. I spend a lot of time talking to him and so does Kincaid. They're really good friends. And he's my friend too now. I'll make some drawings of him and send them along to you later.

Sophie's reaction to Homer Tony had been quite different from Trevor's. The first time she saw him, a few days after their arrival from England, she said to Kincaid, 'Who is that odd-looking man?'

'I told you about him. I had him brought up from Australia to work with the horses on *Bushranger*.'

'And he didn't go back?'

'I asked him if he wanted to stay on for a while and he said he would.'

'Does that mean he'll be here permanently?'

'I hope so.'

A few days later she said, 'We have a wonderful staff here now. Can't we be better organized with the grooms and stable help?'

'We've got Emmett and Carter. And they've taken on a young man to do the cleaning-up.'

'Actually, Emmett and Carter are the ones who've complained. They told Oliver that they feel as though they're not in charge. Your Australian fellow seems to go his own way.'

'Of course he does,' Kincaid said. 'That's what I want him to do.'

'But they say he treats the horses like house pets.'

Kincaid smiled. 'What's wrong with that?'

'Emmett feels it's not the way things should be done.'

'That's for us to decide, isn't it?'

'But I agree with Emmett. There should be some routine followed in the stables just as there is in the kitchen.'

'Homer Tony works from morning till night. We have

thirty head of cattle here and forty head of sheep. He looks after all of them with no help from the grooms. He also knows that he's allowed to handle the horses any way he wants to.'

'But what can Oliver say to the other men?'

'I'll speak to Oliver. If Emmett and Carter have complaints they should come to me.'

'That's no solution. Don't you see, they're afraid of this man.'

'Everyone is when they first meet him.'

'When they give him an order he simply looks at them.'

'What do they expect him to do? He can't talk. And they're not meant to give him orders in any case. He knows what has to be done. No one has to tell him.'

'But he's fierce-looking. You know that. Some of the kitchen help are frightened to death of him. The pantry-girl is afraid to take his meals out to the bungalow. We can't have someone around who frightens the staff.'

'Tell me this,' Kincaid said. 'Has he ever done one single thing to frighten any of them? Has he ever touched anyone or made a threatening gesture?'

'Yes. When Carter was speaking to him a few days ago, he took a riding-whip out of Carter's hands and broke it in three pieces.'

Kincaid smiled again. 'I'm not surprised. I've seen him do that. Two or three times. Each time the person was threatening to hit him. Carter's lucky he only has a broken whip. He could have had a broken arm.'

'All you're saying is what I'm saying. That he's dangerous.'

'Not at all. I'm saying he's kind and gentle. But he can't be bullied or threatened or abused. I admire him for that.'

Sophie sat silent for a long moment. When she spoke again she changed her tone slightly. 'I don't mean to attack your friend. I wasn't speaking for myself. I know how loyal you are to him. But we do have the staff to consider. I really don't know what I'm to say to Oliver.'

'It's not your responsibility. It's mine. I'll speak to him.' He pulled the service cord, then went back to his chair again. When Oliver came into the room a moment later Kincaid said, 'Mrs Kincaid and I have been discussing some staff matters. I understand Mr Emmett and Mr Carter have made some complaints to you.'

'I'm not sure they were complaints, sir.'

'What were they exactly?'

'Observations, I suppose, about the situation at the stables.'

'And what have they observed?'

'I think they believe that the Australian gentleman has not had proper staff experience.'

'He's had none,' Kincaid said. 'Does that mean it's difficult for Emmett and Carter to work with him?'

'I expect that's the gist of it, sir.'

'If we were to discharge Homer Tony, do you think that might set things right? Would that make things easier for Emmett and Carter?'

'They didn't suggest that in so many words, but yes, I believe that would set things right, as you say.'

'I see.' Kincaid slowly took a cigarette out of a silver box on the table by his chair and lit it.

'Will that be all then, sir?'

'Not quite. I'm anxious to settle this matter. Tomorrow morning please tell Emmett and Carter their services are no longer required. See that they're given the proper severance payments and tell them they're free to go. As of tomorrow. Can you do that for me?'

'Yes, sir.'

'Then we must talk to the agency and have them send over half a dozen new men so we can make a selection.'

'Yes, sir.'

'This time I'll speak to the men myself to make sure they understand the situation where Homer Tony is concerned.'

When Oliver left the room Sophie said, 'Well, that takes care of that, then, doesn't it?'

'I hope so.'

She smiled. 'You impress me, young man. You're quite a figure of authority. A commanding presence. Every day I discover new things about you.'

'There's no sarcasm in that remark, I trust.'

'Not at all. Admiration. Didn't you see Oliver's face? I'm sure he has a whole new respect for you.'

'I'm not trying to impress Oliver or anyone else. But I don't want anyone messing about with Homer Tony. He's my friend and my responsibility, and I intend to stand by him.'

'Is that a message to me?'

'Of course not. We've never discussed him before. Not the way we're doing now. You had no way of knowing how I feel about him. What I'm saying now is that he's my oldest friend. For years he was my only friend. He would never ask for any sort of special treatment but all the same it's what he deserves.'

'And I'm to tell the staff they have nothing to fear from him?'

Kincaid shook his head. 'You don't have to tell them anything. I'll take care of it.'

Sophie stood up, crossed the room to where Kincaid was standing, and said, 'Did you read what Gloria Westerfield wrote about you after your press conference?'

'No. I don't waste time with that junk.'

'I thought you liked her. You said she was a cut above all the other journalists you've seen.'

'I do like her. But not enough to read what she writes.'

'Maybe you should. She has some interesting insights

about you. *Menace*. That was the word she used. Thinks you have a great deal of menace.'

'What is that supposed to mean?'

'Ahh . . . but it's very important. It explains why women are fascinated by you. It means that underneath your calm and silent exterior, there's a mean, angry bastard waiting to burst out.'

Kincaid smiled. 'She's right about the *bastard* part.'

Sophie put her arms round him. 'I think she's right about all of it. I'm starting to be a bit frightened of you myself.'

'That's ridiculous.'

'No, it's not. I like it.'

7

Mary posted a letter to Evan as soon as her ship arrived at Southampton.

> God, but it was a miserable crossing. The weather was not miserable. I was. I never left my stateroom. Took all my meals there. Never went on deck. I thought if I isolated myself I could find a way to sort through the tangle we seem to have got ourselves in. That terrible drive down to the railway station haunts me. How could two people who love each other as we do find themselves in such a frustrating turmoil? Each time I remember the confused look on your face I begin to weep. I want you to know that whatever went wrong I'm sure it was my fault. I will take all the blame. I'm not certain just what I did or what you think I did, but I'm convinced that I said or did something stupid. It all started with the things Alec told you when you saw him here in London and it went on from there. And the business about the car upset you terribly, I know, just as it did me. But we let those things go all out of proportion.

I won't write more now. I have to get some things sorted out first. Then I'll send you a long letter. I know you're busy at the studio so I hope you haven't been as tortured as I've been. I promise you, all this foolishness we've been going through will soon be settled and we'll be together again the way we were. Novello's play doesn't matter, nothing matters except us. I cannot be estranged from you. Any other havoc or chaos I can deal with, somehow, but not that. Please don't think bad thoughts about me. Just be patient for a bit longer and I promise I will deliver myself to you, all bright and smiling and gift-wrapped. No stormy skies and no serpent in the garden. I love you and I miss you terribly.

As soon as he finished reading her note he sent her a cable.

WE'LL BE FINE. DON'T WORRY. MY FAULT. NOT YOURS. ALL MY LOVE.

He believed that message. And the more he thought about it, the more he thought about her, the more he believed it. Her absence, he concluded, had put things in their proper perspective. He told himself the things that had disturbed him could be put aside, must be put aside, and they would be. Looking forward to the long letter she'd promised, he began one of his own to her. Before he could finish it, however, and post it, he heard from her again.

I can't believe the ugly things that are in my head just now. No one could ever have convinced me that I could have such terrible thoughts about you. I was so upset at first that I couldn't write to you. I thought there was no point to it in any case. I knew it would be torture for me to say the things I'm going to say

287

now and I wanted to avoid that pain. I decided simply to forget that you exist, to put every thought and memory of you out of my mind. But at last I knew I had to tell you what I know. I couldn't bear the thought of your going smoothly along, thinking you'd got away with something dreadful.

What kind of man are you, Evan? That question has been ringing through my brain ever since I found out what you've done. What sort of secretive, manipulative, merciless bastard are you? I've spent my entire adult life in the theatre. I thought I'd had complete exposure to chicanery, conniving, selfishness, and cruelty, but that education, I've discovered, was only partial. Now, alas, it's complete.

In my note from Southampton I told you that I had some things to settle here in London. I was talking about Alec, nothing else. I knew I had to thrash out the divorce situation with him so I could come back to you free and unencumbered.

I lied to you when I said I'd insisted on a divorce from Alec before I came to you in California. I also lied about the letters I said I was sending to him. I hate to lie but I thought in this case it was justified. I was so ecstatically happy being there in Malibu with you, so drugged with contentment, so sensitized to every detail, every nuance, every moment. That sort of abandonment, losing myself in you, was a new and hypnotic experience for me. I didn't want it to end and I didn't want to risk diminishing it, diffusing it, altering it in any way. I didn't want our lovely evenings to be spoiled by discussions of Alec, his quirks and his unpredictability. So I nailed him up in a closet and forgot about him. He was no longer a problem, no longer my husband, he didn't exist. Childlike behaviour? Of course. But I'd never been a child in love before. So I continued to tell you white lies about the divorce and I continued to forgive myself. I rationalized that the longer I was away from Alec, living openly with you, the easier it would be to convince him at last that you and I are permanently together, that there was nothing to be gained by his playing dog in the manger, that divorce was inevitable. So the sooner he co-operated, the simpler things would be. If one says there's never a defence for lying, then what I'm saying means nothing. But the central point is this: when I arrived in England I had only one objective, to go at once to Alec and tell him that somehow, as quickly as possible, I planned to divorce him. With his co-operation or without it.

And that's what I did, Evan. The first full day I was back in London. Alec sleeps late so I went at nine in the morning so I'd be sure not to miss him. As it turned out it wouldn't have mattered when I arrived because he doesn't go out now. He hasn't been outside his flat for days. When I saw him, when he told me why he's afraid to go out, I was physically ill. As I write about it now, I feel suddenly nauseous.

Perhaps you know everything I'm about to tell you. I'm certain, since you arranged it, that you know some of the details. But there's no way you could know it all without hearing it from Alec and seeing what's become of him.

You've met Alec. Two or three times. You've talked with him. You've seen what he's like. I should say what he used to be like.

Alec is a vain man. He never concealed it. He celebrated it, in fact. It was his armature. His friends accepted it, as I did, and his enemies hated him for it. But it was a fact, a hateful but central characteristic. His hair, his teeth, his nails, their care and public presentation, were of vital importance to him. He would spend three days in a dozen stores selecting a shirt. His long scarves were knitted or crocheted to his finicky specifications. When he bought new boots he deliberately aged and tortured them, then applied thirty coats of shoe-cream so they looked old but beautifully preserved. Everything he wore was selected to preserve his image. Each article of clothing had a history. Each outfit was a careful combination of old and new. A patched suede jacket, faded corduroys, a sweater that cost sixty pounds, and hand-made boots from Jermyn Street. And the silk kerchief in his breast pocket once belonged to John Barrymore. That sort of thing. A hopeless dandy and peacock. But that was Alec Maple. Still I never fully realized until I saw him yesterday that his ridiculous vanities, his self-absorption were the glue that held him together. If you and your horrid friends set out to destroy him, I assure you, you have succeeded. If you saw him as he is now you would not recognize him. I recognized him, of course, but I couldn't believe what I saw.

There was no answer when I knocked on the door of his flat. At last I tried the knob and the door opened. There was an ugly stench in the place as if the windows had not been opened nor the loo flushed for days. The window-shades were drawn and only one small lamp in the far corner was lit. Just before I switched on the ceiling light I heard him say in a hoarse whisper, 'They ruined me, Moo. Look what they did to me.' He had called me Moo when we first met, but not for more than twenty years now.

He was sitting in a wing-chair just opposite the hall door. He hadn't shaved for ten days or two weeks, however long it had been since they left him there. His beautiful hair which had been shampooed once a day through all the years I'd known him was matted and thick and stringy, clotted, it seemed, his face looked grey and stained, he smelled of urine and sweat, and his lips were badly infected by the surgical tape they'd plastered across his mouth. Those twisted strips of tape were still lying on the floor by his chair. And his little dog whined by his feet.

My stomach turned over at the sight of him and from the stink in the room. I went past him to the water closet and was sick.

When I came back to the sitting-room I opened the curtains and the windows. By daylight, the flat looked even worse. Scraps of food and cartons and soda bottles scattered across the floor. I gathered up a great bag full and put it in the kitchen in the dust-bin. Then I forced myself to sit down in the chair facing him. He told me then about the men you'd sent there and what they'd done to him.

Good God, Evan, what sort of mind do you have? What kind of conscience? And how do you have connections with such men? You know how I feel about Alec. He's a worthless person. I have nothing but contempt for him. But when I saw him sitting there like a broken toy, like the victim of a street accident, I thought to myself, 'For the love of God, this is a human being.'

Was it all about that bloody car? Was that it? Just because your car was destroyed? Or was it some sort of vengeance because of me? Whatever it was, what good did it do? What was in your mind? Do you know what those three men did?

I'm not saying that they beat him or strangled him or tortured him physically. Apart from taping his mouth and his wrists, I don't think they injured him or even touched him. They did something worse. They frightened him almost to death. They humiliated him, destroyed his dignity, caused him not to recognize himself. He hasn't lost his mind. I don't mean that. He's simply lost himself. All the bravado and guile and sly tricks he's always used, his image of himself as a reckless freebooter, all those crutches for his self-esteem were kicked out from under him. He said, 'I wet myself', like a child at the kitchen door, like a totally numb and defeated old man in a rest-home.

And it was all so senseless, Evan. He knew nothing about your car being burned. He wasn't able to tell them anything. Finally when he was afraid for what they might do to his dog, he says he just made up a name to give them, a name he'd never heard of. And that seemed to satisfy them. After they flushed his tropical fish down the toilet, opened the window and turned his parrot loose and almost drove Alec out of his mind, all they got was a fake name of somebody who might have poured gasoline on your car and burned it up. What good did that do them? What good did it do you? I assume they sent the name along to you since you're the one who hired them. They told Alec your name and how much money you were paying them.

I'm sure Alec will pull himself together after a while. He'll go outside again and start to clean himself up and visit his pubs. But he'll never be the same person he was. Some people might say that's good. God knows, he's never been a paragon of virtue or honesty or anything valuable. But Jesus, he deserves better than this – to be tied in a chair and treated like an animal.

I thought I knew you. If someone had told me you could be responsible for something like this, I'd have said they were crazy. But now I could believe anything about you. I can't tell you what this has done to me. I had turned myself over to you completely. Now I feel lost. And suddenly I'm afraid. Will I come home some night and find strange men in dark suits waiting for me? It's a thought that haunts me.

You won't hear from me again. And please don't send me any of the things I left in Malibu. I don't want to be reminded.

• CHAPTER 8 •

1

Evan found Mary's letter when he came home one afternoon from the studio. He read it at once, as soon as he was inside the house. Then he slowly read it through again. He put the letter down then on the kitchen table and walked outside to the deck. It had rained that day. The sand looked dark and heavy and greyish-brown. There seemed to be no horizon line where the sky and the ocean met. The tide was edging in slowly, but there was no surf, no sound of waves folding in on the beach. He stood there at the railing for a long time. At last he went inside, sat down at his desk and wrote out a cable message.

STUNNED BY YOUR LETTER. DON'T KNOW WHAT YOU'RE TALKING ABOUT. LETTER FOLLOWS. I LOVE YOU.

He went to the telephone then to call in the message but before he finished dialling he replaced the receiver in its cradle. That night he stayed up very late, sitting in his chair by the seaside window listening to the gulls and the night-birds, and the sound of the rain which had begun again. And the onshore wind rustling the fronds on the date palms just beside the house. When he went to bed at last the wind had picked up and the rain was slashing

293

against the windows. The timbers in the house creaked and groaned, and a bedroom shutter began to slap against the siding till Evan got up and secured it. When he finally went to sleep, first light had begun to leak into his bedroom.

It was late when he woke up. He rang the studio and told his secretary he'd be working at home all day. Then he drove down the highway to the Malibu pier and ate a fisherman's breakfast. By the time he got home it was almost noon, the rain had stopped, and the sun was slanting down through the cloud cover.

He picked up his pen and a clip-board, went out on the deck, and began a letter to Mary. He wrote without pausing. All the thoughts he wanted to put down had crystallized in his mind as he lay in the dark the night before.

I knew when I came back to California from London, when you met me at the station in Los Angeles, that something had gone wrong for us. I understood, of course, that you were upset by what had happened to my car. And so was I. But there was something else disturbing you. I didn't want to question you. I thought it would all come out when we'd had time to settle in a bit. But the tension, whatever was behind it, stayed with us.

You seemed angry when I told you about my meeting with your husband. Not angry with him, I felt, but angry with me, as though you didn't believe what I was telling you. As though you thought I was lying. Now, of course, in the letter I've just had from you, you tell me you were lying. And the reasons you gave were understandable. But still I wonder why that would make you so angry or impatient or ill at ease with me.

Then there was the matter of the fire investigation. I couldn't help thinking that you knew something about it that I didn't know. And when I suggested that the police should be told about Alec's penchant for lighting fires, you were adamantly opposed to any mention of him. I honestly didn't believe that he had made a long secret journey from England to America to destroy the car I'd been driving but all the same the force of your opposition surprised me. It made me wonder if he had indeed been here and you knew it. If all this seems fanciful to you, perhaps you can imagine the bewilderment I felt when I read your letter yesterday. You seemed to be describing an ill-conceived episode from a screenplay I would never want to be associated with.

But let's get back to us, to you and me, to what was happening from the time I returned from England till the day you left to go there. I'm trying to recall and examine specific events, but quite apart from such things there was a climate between us, an atmosphere, that seemed new to me. You were loving and affectionate as you've always been but something was changed. Was it your concentration, something as subtle as that? Did it mean something that you often seemed totally inside yourself, that your eyes wandered off sometimes in mid-sentence, that you began to misplace your keys, your lipstick, your hairbrush almost every day, and that such tiny unimportant incidents seemed to make you angry or unduly critical of yourself.

Admittedly, I may have been absurdly sensitized by what I perceived as a change in our life together, something gone off, gone awry. And you, perhaps, were also disappointed or confused by the way things were going. But, however one describes it, we seemed to be surprising each other, thinking to ourselves, 'Who *are* you? Suddenly, I don't know you.' The laws of the theatre require that once that line is spoken between lovers, the audience has every reason to believe they're in for heavy weather, just as Chekhov believed that when a revolver is introduced in Act One, it must, without question, be discharged in Act Three.

I'm thinking about the letters I received at the studio, ostensibly from a young woman who wants to write scenarios. I showed you those letters only because they seemed odd to me and I thought they might amuse you. But they didn't. Nothing like it. I sensed that you thought I was using the letters in some mysterious way. Did you think I connected them with you? In any case they seemed to make you uneasy. I've turned that episode over in my mind a hundred times, trying to discover what it was that you seemed to take personally. And just the other day as I was cleaning out my desk I found those two letters, glanced at them again and found what I think may have unsettled you. In what is presented as a sample of her work the woman who wrote to me offers what appears to be a letter from a woman to her lover. In her description of their sexual joy, she uses the word 'wild'. It occurred to me suddenly, having never really noticed it before, that that word is a lovely part of your own sexual vocabulary. I can't count the number of times I've heard you say it. Did you pick up on that word even though I did not? Did you imagine that such a coincidence would lead me to believe that you had sent those letters for some reason? I assure you that thought never entered my mind. Nor do I see it as even a remote possibility now. I bring it up only because it was one more thing that seemed to throw you off and cloud the atmosphere around us.

Then came your abrupt departure. And your apparent unwillingness even to discuss the reasons for it. And the rotten time we had on the way to the station that morning. After you left I kept asking myself if I really knew you, if we really knew each other. Then, just a few days ago, the note you sent from Southampton arrived. And all our problems, whatever they had been, seemed to be solved. I wanted to believe that.

But in that same note you said the Novello play was unimportant, that it didn't matter to you. If that's true, I asked myself, then why the great rush to leave here and go to London? Nonetheless, you know from the cable I sent that I was eager to put all the difficulties and misunderstandings behind us and find a way for us to be together again as soon as possible.

Then came your strange letter, your last letter to me, as you made clear in the final paragraph. That letter is incomprehensible to me. As if I had picked it up on the street with no knowledge of who sent it or to whom it was addressed. And the more I studied it, the more peculiar it became. At last, however, as I lay in bed last night thinking about it, as I began to place it alongside all the things I've just outlined here, it began to make sense. I concluded that you had decided to leave me long before I knew anything about it, perhaps when I was away in London. You used the Novello play as your excuse. Did you assume that I would see through that at once and conclude that you had another reason for going? I did have that impulse and you sensed it, of course, that last morning, but I wanted very much to believe you so I told myself I did believe you. But always those words I'd heard from Alec, that you would never leave him, that you could never leave him, kept coming back to me. And he was right, wasn't he? That's what this letter of yours, in its convoluted, comic-strip fashion is trying to say, isn't it? But why did you feel you had to invent a damaged, wounded, possibly deranged Alec? And where, in God's name, did that idiotic story come from, that I hired some shadowy characters to question him, tie him up, and drown his goldfish? Are you trying to convince me that such a thing really happened? Or has Alec just made you believe it took place? He is an actor, you know, and a borderline psychopath as well. You must know that such a thing never happened, or that if something remotely like that did happen I could not possibly have been involved in it. I would swear that you know these things. So I'm left with my original conclusion, that you need some sort of crutch, some device, to justify your kissing me goodbye. So the alleged suffering of poor Alec, allegedly caused by me, gives you, at least in your own mind, that justification. What outrageous poppycock, Mary! If we're going to give each other up, can't we have a little class about it? Do I have to conclude that you never felt any attachment to me beyond a temporary one? Do you have to pretend that I caused some psychological cruelty to be practised on your husband? And all this because some nut burned up a car that wasn't even mine? Let's use our heads. You asked in your letter how it is that I have connections with such men. The answer is that I don't. And even if I did, why would I think that Alec torched the car when you and I both assumed, once we'd discussed it, that he had not been in America, could not have been in America when it happened?

I hate the thought of our breaking up, Mary. I particularly detest the idea of its happening in this clownish idiotic way. Don't you realize that these trappings and stage-dressings aren't necessary? I'm a grown-up. I knew you were married from the start. I knew you'd never given me any guarantees. Don't you know that all you had to say was, 'I'm sorry. It's not going to work.' I wouldn't have liked to hear that but I would have accepted it. Just as I accept the charade that's taking place now, even though it disgusts me. When you loved me I didn't have to be a saint or a god. Now that you've decided not to love me any longer, why is it necessary to turn me into a comic-book felon? You're better than that, Mary.

Since you've decided that all this is a melodrama about a destroyed Packard I feel obligated to provide you with the final scene. But it's not a fantasy like your story about my cruelty to Alec. This actually took place. The physical evidence exists. One evening a week or so ago two men came to my door. One was a tall blond fellow, the other one shorter, heavier, Italian-looking. I'd never seen either one of them before. The tall one handed me a set of car keys and said, 'I'm sorry for what I did to your car. I've just replaced it with a new one.' They turned and walked away then, up the steps to the highway. When I went out to the carport a few minutes later, there was a new Packard sitting there, still smelling of the showroom. Just like the one that was burned. In every detail. Except for the small dent you had put in the front fender of the other one.

There's a missing piece to the story that you don't know about. When I'd just come home to California from England, I answered the phone one night and a man's voice said, 'Oh, it's you. You're back then. Well, welcome home.' It was a British voice. A trained voice. Like an actor. When you asked me who it was, I said it was a misdial. Do you remember that? In any case the man who gave me the keys to the new car was the same chap. The same voice. Unmistakable. So the mystery of who burned the car and why he did it may be more complicated than we thought. Maybe you're the only one who knows the answer. Also the guy came down to the side door, the way we always do. He didn't come to the upstairs door, the way people do who haven't been here before.

You asked me not to send you your things but I'm sending them anyway. I don't want to be reminded either.

'I hope I haven't broken some local laws of etiquette,' Sophie said. 'I didn't consult with Kincaid about this. It's just that I like the things you've written about him, I had an impulse to tell you so, so I invited you to lunch.'

'I'm delighted,' Gloria Westerfield said. 'And you mustn't fret about etiquette out here. The social ethic is much like the work ethic. If it works, it's good. Only the British colony here have strict social rules. More rigid than in London, I imagine.'

'Much more. Mayfair is as relaxed as Madeira compared with an evening at Ronnie Colman's or Audrey Smith's. I am not a leader of London society – Kincaid wants none of it – but I do know it bears little resemblance to the Santa Monica version.'

'Your husband doesn't like parties?'

'Detests them. Most of all, I think, he detests the people who do like parties. He humours me from time to time. He doesn't mind going to the Rathbones or the Hardwickes and he knows Jimmy Whale is an old club friend of my Uncle Howard, so we see those people occasionally, but for the most part we poke about here at home. Actually, I'm surprised the English group wants anything to do with Kincaid. He makes fun of their fierce cricket and croquet competitions, and he certainly has his own mode of dress. But they do keep inviting us and I keep writing polite notes saying I'm sorry we can't come. I expect we'll be banished at last.'

'I don't think so,' Gloria said. 'No one is more socially desirable out here than the people who are too busy to show up.'

It was a lovely late-summer day and they were having lunch on the shaded terrace outside the morning-room. Sophie told her about Sarah and Trevor, what their lives were like when they were in England and what adjustments they had made since coming to California. 'I always forget how flexible young people are. Especially my children's generation. They were born just after the war, and all the changes that were taking place between then and 1930 seem to have infected them. Did something to all of us, I expect. It isn't that there are no longer any rules or restrictions. There are, of course. But people don't seem to be so conscious of them. None of us seem afraid that we'll do the wrong thing. Not so influenced by other people's opinions.'

Gloria nodded. 'It's slightly different in America, of course. The frontier spirit is still very much alive here. People take pride in flaunting the rules, defying the moral code, whatever that is. They define themselves that way, I suppose. But I do agree with you. I was eleven years old when the war ended so I did all my growing-up in that time period you're talking about. It was unquestionably a time of change. Particularly for us females. When women threw away their corsets once and for all, a lot of old ideas went with them.'

'The most interesting thing to me is that not just young women like us were affected, or children like mine, but older women as well. Take my mother, for example . . .' Sophie stopped talking suddenly. Then: 'Am I being ingenuous? I told you I don't know the rules of the game here. Now I must ask you a rude question. I'm not about to become a story in your column, am I? It never occurred to me that you would see this as anything other than a social invitation. Was that a foolish assumption?'

Gloria smiled and shook her head. 'Not at all. When I accept an invitation, as I accepted yours, everyone concerned can be sure that it will have nothing whatsoever to do with my work.

'That's a relief. I don't usually chatter like this. I'm not addicted to ladies' luncheons.'

'Neither am I. As a matter of fact, I've drawn such a firm line between my business and social lives that I have very little social life at all.'

301

'Well, from now on you will. The two of us can have lunch together whenever you like.'

'That's a nice offer,' Gloria said, 'And I promise you, I'll take you up on it. I've only visited England twice, but coming here makes me think I'm there again.'

'That was Kincaid's idea. He built this house so I'd feel at home. I was very much opposed to his becoming an actor, did you know that?'

'No, I didn't.'

'Not in favour of it at all. And part of that concern was my aversion to living in America. That's why this house is an exact replica of my family home in Northumberland.'

That evening at dinner Sophie told Kincaid about her luncheon with Gloria Westerfield. 'What an interesting young woman she is. We sat on the terrace chattering away like school chums till almost four o'clock. I think I've made a new friend. I certainly hope so. She's awfully keen and well brought up and easy to be with. I'd never guess she was a journalist or any sort of public person. She seems quite shy, actually. Bears no resemblance to the newspaper people you've described to me. In any case, I can't remember when I've talked so much. Told her all about the children and our house in London. And I told her a great deal about Margaret, her divorce and all.'

'You may open the paper tomorrow morning and find out you're famous.'

Sophie shook her head. 'No. We went into that. Rather specifically as a matter of fact. She makes a clean separation between her friends and the people she writes about. Got the impression she doesn't have a great many friends. That surprises me. She's so nice. And she's certainly a handsome thing.'

'Too tall.'

'She is a bit taller than you, isn't she? You men are so conscious of that.'

'I was kidding. I don't give a damn how tall she is. Besides, you know Evan's motto: he says they're all the same height lying down.'

'That's not his motto. I've never heard him say that.'

'Of course not. You're pretty tall yourself.'

'Shame on you. What's come over you? Next, you'll be telling naughty stories at the dinner-table. I'll have to put you in quarantine for a month before we go back to England.'

'England? Where's that?'

'Don't tease me, you rotten movie-star. You know very well where England is.'

'That's right. I do. That's where they grow beautiful women like you. Rosy cheeks, slender waists, and small bottoms.'

'You're really outrageous tonight. It's the company you keep. All those grips and juicers and stunt chaps . . . am I getting the language right?'

'All except stunt chaps. None of those around.'

'Bad company. Playing card games all day and telling off-colour stories.'

Kincaid grinned. 'I've stepped up in class. You should see the company I kept in Australia. Or some of the types I shipped out with when I was a seaman.'

'But you like that sort. Those were happy days, you told me.'

'You mustn't believe everything I say. I just say whatever I think will make you feel good.'

'I'm glad to hear that. It would make me very happy if you told me you weren't going off to Chicago to put on those funny clothes and pretend you're a gangster. Before we left London, I asked a dozen people if they'd ever heard of John Dillinger and they all said no.'

'If you ask them that a year from now you'll get a different answer.'

'Cock-of-the-walk. Getting a bit cocky, aren't we?'

'Of course. People think I'm the world's greatest

303

fellow. Otherwise you wouldn't have asked me to marry you.'

She left her chair, came round the table, pulled an empty chair close to his, and said, 'Did I really do that? I suppose I did. What did I say? What were my exact words?'

'I don't think we should go into that.'

'Why not?'

'No one likes to hear precisely what they said at any given moment.'

'I do.'

'You remember, I'm sure, that I have a perfect memory. Like a recording apparatus. When you ask for your exact words, you're in danger of getting them.'

'Please,' she said, 'what did I say?'

'All right. But remember, you forced me to do it.'

'Bloody hell, Kincaid, get on with it.'

'You said – and these are your precise words, remember that – you said, "I'm quite a lot older than you are and you'll probably turn me down, but all the same I want you to say you'll marry me. Before you say no, let me promise that I'll take very good care of you. Whatever I lack in beauty, I'll make up for with money . . ."'

'You're really quite impossible, aren't you?'

'All this is word for word. Just what I promised.'

'I see. So the thing that convinced you was when I mentioned the money.'

'You didn't let me finish. You went on to say, ". . . so I can buy you anything you want. You'll be the most pampered man in England. And furthermore I'll make no demands on you. We can have separate bedrooms if you like. And if you fancy the upstairs maid . . ."' As he talked, she picked up a water goblet from the table and slowly emptied it in his lap.

Later that evening, when they were sitting in bed, their heads propped up on pillows, she said, 'I didn't ask her directly but I got the impression that Gloria lives by herself. She says she's not married and she doesn't seem to be living with anyone.'

'The gossip is that she prefers women.'

'I don't believe you.'

'It's not my story. I didn't make it up.'

'Who says that?'

'I don't know who says it. One can't help hearing such things. People talk.'

'I think it's disgusting. What a town this is.'

'There are also lesbians in London, you know. Even a few scattered about in Northumberland, I expect.'

'I'm not talking about that. I'm talking about ugly gossip.'

'Maybe it's not just gossip. What makes you so sure?'

'Because I'm a woman. Don't you think I can tell? I'd wager a thousand pounds she's not.'

'A thousand pounds isn't so much. I'm not sure you're convinced.'

'You're impossible tonight. What's come over you?'

'I'm still trying to recover from that cold water in my lap.'

'Next time I'll try cognac.'

'You're vicious,' he said. 'You should have told me that when you asked me to marry you.'

'Seriously,' she said then. 'She's interviewed you once or twice. You've sat and talked with her. Have you ever for one moment thought she . . . I detest that word.'

'You mean, do I believe the gossip?'

'No. Forget the gossip. I mean do you honestly think she's a woman who wants nothing to do with men?'

'Seriously?'

'Seriously.'

Kincaid shook his head, 'If she's not interested in men I would be very surprised.'

'Then you don't believe the gossip?'

'Not for a minute.'

'Now we're making some progress,' she said. 'Here's

my next question. Why don't we introduce her to Evan?'

'Why would we do that?'

'Because he's a single man and she's a single woman, the ages are right, and I think they'd like each other.'

'Evan's living with Mary Cecil.'

'No, he's not. She's gone back to London.'

'That doesn't mean they've broken up,' he said.

'I think it does. But even if they haven't done yet, they will.'

'The voice of the witch.'

'I mean it. I never thought that arrangement would last.'

'It's lasted almost a year.'

'Trust me, my love, Evan is available or he will be soon.'

Kincaid shook his head. 'If I've ever met a man who doesn't need a procurer, it's Evan.'

'All men need procurers. Left to themselves, they make impossible choices.'

'I didn't.'

'But you didn't chose me,' she said. 'I chose you. That's what you've been talking about all evening.'

'I'm trying to have some fun here and you keep getting factual. So here's what I think. Whatever Evan's status is, I think matching him up with Gloria is a rotten idea. Evan never met a woman he didn't like and I'm sure he'd like Gloria. But I don't think she'd go for him. And if she did I'd try to talk her out of it.'

'You're not serious.'

'Of course I'm serious. You've been talking about what a sensational woman she is. I'm saying I agree with you. I think she's too good for him.'

'I don't think anyone's too good for Evan. And I'm surprised to hear you say that.'

'Why? I think he's a great guy. I'm sure he thinks I'm a great guy. But that doesn't mean he thought I was a good choice for you.'

'Of course he did,' she said. 'I've never heard him say a word against you.'

'Neither have I. But that's beside the point. After you and I slipped off to Brittany and got married, do you remember how long it was before we saw Evan?'

'He was working on his play.'

'Poppycock, Sophie. Nobody works day and night for weeks at a time. You have meals, you go to the theatre, you have drinks with your friends. But he didn't do that. He's like a brother to you. You think he couldn't have found time to see you if he wanted to? Of course he could have done. But he didn't want to see you because he was afraid you'd guess what he thought about me. I was a guy from the streets when he met me, living in a flophouse. And the next thing he knew, I was married to the silver princess. Of course he didn't jump up and down and clap his hands. Why should he? In his shoes I'd have probably felt the same way.'

'What are you saying? Do you think there was something between me and Evan?'

'Of course I do. You grew up together. There'll always be something between you. I don't mean you meet twice a week in a hotel in St John's Wood, but you're *connected*. When I say I think Gloria Westerfield's too good for him, does that make you think there's something going on between her and me?'

'Of course not.'

'There you are. That's my point. Evan was entitled to make a critical judgement of me in relation to you and I'm entitled to make one of him.'

'But you don't know Gloria the way Evan knows me.'

'That's right. I'm not able to judge her or make a list of her attributes. It's all instinct. You think she's splendid. I think she's splendid. It's all the same thing.'

'I'm not so sure of that,' Sophie said. 'Maybe I should keep her away from you.'

'Not necessary. I've got my hands full with you. Besides, she's too tall for me.'

3

One morning at breakfast Jack Brannigan said to Margaret, 'I'm going upstairs to talk with the Major today.' When she didn't answer he said, 'I thought you'd be up on your feet cracking me on the head with the teapot. Are you speechless? That's not like you.'

'I don't know what I can say. You know how I feel. Since you hadn't brought it up for a while I thought perhaps you'd decided that patience is the answer.'

'Patience may be the answer when you've got an agreement. But we've got none with him. You've got a legal divorce, Maggie, but no agreement. The man in question is locked in upstairs like a stone lion. Or a stone jackass is more like it. He's making fools of us. He's constantly on our minds, while there's nothing at all, it seems, in his cranium. He's invisible but the house moves to his rhythm. Even the staff walk around wall-eyed as if they're expecting him to start rolling cannon-balls down the great staircase.'

'I know how you feel,' she said. 'You know I do. But what good will it do if you talk to him? What will it accomplish?'

'I don't know the answer to that. Nobody does. But at least after I see him there'll be an answer. Some kind of a first-hand report, if nothing else. And that's a great deal more than we've got now.'

'You know I'm going down to London to see the solicitors next week. Can't this wait till then?'

'Of course it could if there was any point to it. But whatever Tremont says, whatever he advocates, sooner or later somebody has to talk to this ruddy nuisance. What's in his head now? What are his intentions? Or does he have any intentions at all? If we know something more concrete than we know now, won't that help Tremont to effect that protective order? We can't just keep dangling it in the air. Sooner or later it's got to be processed and put into effect. Then if he still won't budge, the constables can roust him out and carry him downstairs in a potato sack.'

'I've been hoping that wouldn't be necessary,' she said. 'I have bad dreams about that happening.'

'But it is necessary, Maggie, unless I can talk some sense into him. The bad dream is what we're living through now.'

'If you're expecting to have a sensible discussion, you'll be gravely disappointed. He can't discuss anything. He either sits there in a stupor or he rants and raves. I don't know what he's capable of. I'm afraid to have you go up there.'

'Don't fret about me. I've gone up against the best of them in Letterkenny and Donegal Town. But I promise you I won't lay a hand on the old goat upstairs. I don't want to put him unconscious. I just want him to respond to my magnetic presence and my overpowering logic, and nod his head when I tell him to pack up his kit and make himself scarce.'

Brannigan scheduled his visit for just after lunch. 'Before he's dead drunk or back in his bed,' he told Maggie. 'I want to have his full attention.'

When Brannigan knocked on the door of the upstairs sitting-room and the Major opened it, it was clear to Jack that he did indeed have Cranston's attention.

'If I don't invite you in,' Cranston said, 'I expect you'll keep pounding on the door till I have you removed.'

'I can't be removed. I'm in residence.'

'I can have anyone removed, by God. I'm master here.'

He stepped back from the doorway. 'I'll give you ten minutes of my time. I'm a busy man.'

'I'm not busy at all,' Brannigan said, 'so I intend to stay for as long as it takes to talk some sense into you.' He walked to a chair and sat down.

'By the clothes you're wearing, I'd take you for a stablehand but since you're a cheeky bugger I assume you're the present husband of my former wife. I'm surprised she hasn't fitted you out with a proper lounge-suit.'

'Let's get something straight, Cranston. When a damned fool insults me it doesn't bother me at all, but I won't stand for any remarks about Margaret.'

'I'm in my own parlour, sir. I'll say what I like. I was married to Mrs Cranston for more than thirty years. I earned a few rights in that time.'

'You have no rights at all when you speak about Mrs Brannigan. That's her name now.'

'And a shanty Irish name it is. I'd offer you a drink but I don't keep beer. And even the grooms don't drink Irish whiskey on these grounds.'

Brannigan didn't answer. He sat in his chair and looked at Cranston. 'No answer for that, eh?' Still no answer from Brannigan. 'A gift of gab the Irish have. Or so they say. I say that's all they have. Along with a touch of larceny in their hearts. I've heard men say they'd rather trade horses with a Jew than an Irishman. What do you say to that?' Cranston poured himself a drink, gulped down half of it and sat heavily in the chair facing Brannigan. 'Well, since talking's what you're good at, let's hear what you have to say. What are you waiting for?'

'I'm waiting for a moment of silence. I'm waiting for your insulting tongue to stop wagging.'

'By God, I'm warning you. I've thrown bigger men than you through windows for talking to me like that.'

'If you lay a hand on me, Major, you'll find out you've

never seen a bigger man than me.'

'I've never seen a rag-tag Irishman I couldn't handle.'

'Now you're looking at one.'

Cranston finished his drink, poured another one, and didn't answer. Finally Brannigan said, 'I'm sure you accept the fact that you and your wife are divorced and she's now married to me.'

'Everybody knows that by now. And God help her.'

'I agree. She's too good for me. But we're married all the same, and I intend to do my best for her. I want her to be content.'

'I've washed my hands of her. What do I care if she's contented or not?'

'But I care. That's why I'm here. And I'm afraid Maggie won't be happy . . .'

'Maggie, is it? Have you turned her into a gypsy, too?'

'. . . she won't be happy till you agree to leave her house.'

'I've heard that song. More than once. From her and her snotty solicitor.'

'She has a legal right to the privacy of her home.'

'*Her* home. Of course it's her home. Margaret owns everything here. She's a Wiswell, by God. Child of privilege. Thought she owned me, too, but she found out different. I've got some rights as well, sir. I'm no one's chattel.'

'Some time ago,' Brannigan said, 'you were served with an action for trespass.'

'Damned foolishness. I ignored it. How can a man be a trespasser in his own home?'

'You just admitted that Margaret owns everything here.'

'But I was her husband. I've earned a right of tenancy.'

'Are you saying you intend to stay on here indefinitely? Is that your plan?'

'I'm saying I've earned a right of tenancy.'

'You can say whatever you like but the law doesn't agree with you.'

'Damn the law. You notice there's been no enforcement of their bloody action for trespass. There's such a thing as common law as well. I'm well informed in these matters.'

'Let me put it this way: Margaret has been patient up till now. She doesn't want to humiliate you. She's still hoping you'll listen to reason and leave peaceably.'

'She can hope whatever she likes. It's no concern of mine.'

'But now,' Brannigan said, 'she's reached the end of her patience. She's going down to London in a few days to meet with Sir Charles Tremont. A final meeting. She'll authorize him to seek a protective order that will be passed along to the chief constable of this county.'

'Who's to be protected?' Cranston said. 'I'm the one who bloody well wants protection.'

'I believe this has been explained to you before. But I'll go through it again. A protective order is designed to protect a citizen who feels endangered by another person. In a situation where threats have been made . . .'

'I've made no threats. Who says I've threatened anyone?'

'Tremont has depositions from Margaret and two other people swearing that you threatened her life and the life of Arthur Tagg as well. That material will be turned over to the authorities . . .'

'Damn the authorities.'

'That won't work this time, Cranston. This is a criminal process we're talking about. Much more serious than what you refer to as your right of tenancy. You could face a jail sentence. Margaret knows that. That's why she's been reluctant to bring this action. But now she's going ahead.'

'I'm a retired military officer with a fine record of service. No authorities will send a squad of constables

312

to carry me out of my own home.'

'That's precisely what they will do. First they'll serve you a paper fixing the date for you to quit your residence here. Then, if that's ignored, they will send people to escort you off the grounds.'

'They'd better send a full platoon if they intend to lay hands on Major William Cranston. I'm a soldier, by God, more than a match for a few country constables with night-sticks. I'm trained in the art of combat. Skilled with firearms. Not to be jerked about or treated lightly by minor functionaries.' He drained his glass, then fixed a glare on Brannigan. 'And not to be manipulated by a lower-class Irishman with his eye on the spoils of marriage. But you must have a few tricks up your sleeve. I'll grant you that. Nobody ever questioned Margaret's intelligence. So either she's gone off her head altogether or you have some black-ass gypsy powers of persuasion.'

Cranston tugged himself up from his chair, took a key from the pocket of his waistcoat, and made his uneven way to one of the gun-cabinets. 'I can see by the way you carry yourself, bouncing about on the balls of your feet, that you're not a military man. No posture, no bearing, no sense of command.' He unlocked the case, opened the door and took out a heavy repeating rifle. 'And no knowledge of weapons, no experience on the target range, no skill in those areas.'

'That's true,' Brannigan said. 'In Donegal we only shoot rabbits and British soldiers. Usually with a scatter-gun.'

'If you'd been in my command you'd have been whipped for a remark like that.'

'If I'd been in your command I'd have been executed for shooting my commander.'

Cranston tottered toward Brannigan, holding the rifle across his stomach with both hands. 'Every weapon I own is combat-ready. Cleaned and oiled. All sights and firing-pins properly adjusted. You see this piece? Not a

313

long-range weapon. But deadly accurate. Scared to death of this particular gun, the rag-heads were. They'd seen it in action. Seen what it can do to a man's head. Explode it like a melon.' He stood in front of Brannigan, the rifle not pointed at him but held at the ready. 'I keep them all properly loaded. Ammunition in all the chambers. A weapon that's not loaded is no weapon at all. That's what I taught my men. I never coddled the buggers, but they had respect for me, you can be sure of that.'

'If it's all the same to you I wish you'd stop waving that toy around and put it back in the case.'

'Makes you a bit jumpy, does it? I expected it would. I'm doing you a service, you see. Showing you what you're up against. You Irishmen think your mouth is a weapon. But I'm a Sandhurst man. I know what a real weapon can do. I know when to use it and how to use it. I'm glad to see I've unsettled you a bit. That was my intention. Give you something to dwell on. Make you think twice perhaps before you come up my staircase uninvited and start to tell me what I must do. If you're dead-set on making all my decisions for me, it's good for you to see what you're up against.' Still he didn't point the gun at Brannigan but when he repositioned it in his arms it was angled toward Brannigan's mid-section.

'You're not threatening me are you, Cranston?'

'Not at all. You're telling me what I must do. I'm suggesting to you what you must not do.'

'But you're the one with the gun in his hand.'

'That's right. Something to keep in mind.'

'To me, that's a threat. Now Tremont will have four depositions instead of three.'

When Brannigan went back downstairs, crossed the house, and joined Margaret in their upstairs sitting-room he said, 'The man's a bloody maniac, Maggie. Out of control. We can't wait any longer. Tell Tremont to put things in motion. We have to get him away from here.'

At last Evan had a letter from his father, the first since he'd returned to California from London.

I remember that I always cautioned you and Sophie, when I was instructing you in English composition and the niceties of social correspondence, that it was absolutely necessary to make as early a response as possible to whatever letters you received from friends or family. You can see that I am a poor practitioner of my own teachings.

What is my excuse? I have none. The central truth is, I suppose, that I have been a bit bored with myself these past weeks and I saw no point in passing that boredom along to someone else. Does a bored person write boring letters? It's a conclusion I might not be able to defend but I made it nonetheless.

Don't be alarmed. I am not despondent. Perhaps I exhausted myself during my first weeks here in London. I was like a child at the fair. But after a time I realized that I had begun to turn pleasure into a burden. 'Today you will enlighten yourself and broaden your mind. Enjoy yourself or else.' That sort of thing. I seemed to meet myself coming and going from the British Museum, the National Gallery, and the Royal Albert Hall. So I ground to a halt. All that looking, listening, reading, and note-taking was followed by a period of sloth. Does that surprise you? It surprised me, since I've always believed that the hand activates the mind, that one's mental keenness has a direct connection with one's level of physical activity.

I found myself sleeping late, eating peculiar food at odd hours, spending the afternoons in cinemas, listening to inane programmes on the wireless, and reading great stacks of mystery-thrillers written by cretins. And I became a dreadfully poor housekeeper, Evan.

Your tidy flat became, I'm afraid, a sorry mess.

Are you saying to yourself, 'My poor old Dad's gone bonkers?' Understandable conclusion but not true. I would be lying to you and to myself if I didn't admit that there was more than a bit of trauma involved in my leaving Wiswell Towers after all these years. Why else my frenetic museum-going and cultural gluttony once I came to London? If I'd planned carefully and objectively I would have realized that such a result, or a similar one, was inevitable. One cannot go from a fully involved life of many colours to a self-serving existence, alone in a city of grey and umber, without having withdrawal symptoms. So, since I am not as unusual a specimen as I would like to believe, I suffered my share of anxiety.

I'm telling you all this not to elicit sympathy but to explain, at least in part, why you've had no word from me. Also to report that my not-so-fierce demons have been tamed now, I trust. I've left your delightful flat and taken a bed-sitter in Oakwood Court just off Holland Park. A private home owned by a certain Dora Collins and her brother, Luther, who share the first two floors. A tailor named Elster occupies the basement flat with his collie dog, and I am the top-floor resident, with treetops outside my windows and a gas fire that will undoubtedly keep me warm when the weather changes.

I am also employed now. Salesperson and accounts-keeper in a small but select bookshop on Kensington High Street, walking distance from where I live. My employer is an elderly gentleman, Everett Smith-Justin, who is civilized but forgetful, and who seems to see himself as a character from Charles Dickens. He is Pickwick, Uriah Heep, and Mr Dick by turn. Sometimes all three in the space of a few moments. Many of his clients are his age or older, and along with the books they purchase they require a great deal of attention, advice, reassurance, and general conversation. I am able to provide all these things, I find, in a manner that seems to satisfy them.

So I've begun a new life, you see. It's an interesting experience at my age, having suddenly a small circle of acquaintances none of whom knows anything whatsoever about one's life, one's past, one's sins, or one's pleasures. I take a perverse joy in providing no biographical information to anyone. So I'm seen as a man of mystery. I think perhaps people assume that I've lost all my loved ones in a railway accident and that I'm still too stricken to talk about it. In short I am discovering the rewards of anonymity. I recommend it to everyone.

You're no fool, of course, are you? Your perceptions are as keen as any I know. I'm certain you are reading studiously between the lines. You needn't. I will be candid with you. These are not the triumphant hours of my life. I assume that these circumstances and my attitude toward them is temporary, that the fog will lift and I'll find myself somewhere else with new attitudes and new aspirations perhaps. But I'm not sure that such changes, if indeed they come to pass, are in my control. I suppose it could be said that I am in limbo. If it's not energizing and rewarding, it is also not painful. Not yet.

I've thought rather a lot about the talk we had concerning your mother when you were in London last. I'm not sure I gave you good advice. Perhaps I was just repeating to you the things I've told myself all these years. If I had an opportunity to see her again, even if I very much wanted to, I don't think I could. As I've considered such a possibility, I've been able to find no solid ground. For years I've taken refuge in anger. But anger, like passion, changes through the years. As we arrive at more realistic assessments of our own worth, the past crimes committed against us become less heinous than we've always believed. Vengeance and retribution, even forgiveness, gradually take on different colours.

If a characteristic of my present state is that I am somewhat less sure of my convictions than I once was, then this apparent confusion in my mind about your mother is just another illustration of it.

I suppose what I'm struggling to say is that if you have an opportunity to meet Amy, to get to know her perhaps, or if you want to create such an opportunity, don't imagine that it would be in any way a betrayal of me. If I were you, if I were in your position, I expect that I would be unable to resist such a chance myself. There is no need for me to know what you decide to do one way or the other, but whatever course you choose, I want you to know, in case you haven't guessed it already, that you have my love and my blessing.

As a child Evan had seldom wept. It was simply not a part of his system of sorrow and pain, of pity or con-dolence. He accepted that about himself. And he did not weep now as he put down his father's letter. But he marked the day in his memory. In the time it had taken to read those words Arthur had redefined himself, had come to life in a way that Evan had never hoped to see.

5

Almost every day, when he was not at the studio for war-drobe tests, make-up tests, matching shots with stunt doubles, or story conferences about the *Dillinger* script, Kincaid put on his old ranch clothes, Australian gear of the kind he'd worn on the cattle station near Glenrowan, saddled up his quarter-horse, and rode out across the pastures, through the groves of gum-trees and along the stone walls that bordered his land on the bluff above the sea, with Homer Tony.

Except for that one occasion with Sophie, he had never tried to define or explain his friendship with this mute and savage-looking, carved-out-of-stone creature, a man close to Kincaid's own age who seemed old enough to be his father. Their history together was formed of dust and grit, sweat and grime, rope-burns and strained muscles, rain-drenched days and nights in the open, foul water, tasteless food, harness straps and hackamores, dirt and stink, storms and floods, freezing rain and blistering sun, fist-fights, knife-fights, three-day-drunks, Glenrowan whores in soft beds and fat Aborigine girls on their backs, laughing, with their legs in the air in shaded groves or on hot summer sand.

It had been a life of few words and limited choices. Everything tactile, concrete, warm or cold, wet or dry. No chance to plan, no voice in the work strategy or the day's decisions. They had been victims together. Wild and untamed, accustomed to pain and disappointment and punishment. Cruel jokes, humiliation, and work till they dropped. Working always together in a world without mirrors, a world of hard, stupid men and brute animals. Each of them saw his own discomfort and struggle and dead-tired stumbling only on the sweat-streaked face of the other. Without saying it, they knew they were two hopeless souls connected, like tandem prisoners in leg irons.

Sensing this connection, marking it as an absolute truth in his life, Kincaid was both unable and unwilling to describe or defend or explain it, either to himself or to anyone else. Sometimes when they sat in Homer Tony's cottage with the radio never turned off in the kitchen, Kincaid talked about whatever was on his mind, and his friend listened, his tiny black eyes with no light in them focused unblinking on Kincaid's face, understanding everything, laughing wild at the funny parts and making a deep almost soundless groan, more an exhalation of air than a sound, when Kincaid was angry or disappointed about something. Most of the time, however, they were silent together with only an occasional bit of profane cowhand lingo muttered by Kincaid, making them both smile, reminding them of thousands of days and hours that had been stored away in the dust and commotion of those young years.

No one but Homer Tony ever heard Kincaid say, 'I don't know what I'm about, you know. Half the time, when I shave in the morning, I look at this mean fucking face of mine and I think, "What the hell are you doing here? You belong somewhere else, with mud and blood and guts and cow-shit. You're an Aborigine bastard just like that worthless lazy Homer Tony."'

Homer Tony had a lunatic laugh, like a dingo on a dark night, and he laughed hardest and longest when Kincaid called him ugly names. He always pointed his finger at Kincaid while he was laughing and rocking back and forth, as though he was saying, 'You're the ugly, lazy, worthless Aborigine bastard. It's you, not me.'

Kincaid's monologues, when the two men were together, usually took the form of reminiscence. Homer Tony never tired of stories about the cattle station, about the liars and bullies and thieves, storms and floods, stampedes, injuries and death, grisly practical jokes, and easy women. Almost every story, or some part of it, made him laugh and shout and slap the table with an open hand. Later Kincaid would remember him that way. Laughing. And he laughed hardest when Kincaid insulted him. 'When you laugh, you bastard, you're uglier than most people are when they're crying' or 'If I was as ugly as you I'd wear a saddle blanket over my face.' And always Homer Tony poked his finger at Kincaid, a signal they both understood. 'Not me. You're the ugly one.'

When Kincaid talked about something serious, Homer

Tony listened carefully as though he understood every word and every nuance. And he did. When Kincaid said, 'Look at me. I'm the luckiest son of a bitch in the world,' Homer Tony sensed all the fine shadings of that remark. When Kincaid talked about hard times and unemployment, men all across the country and in Europe and Australia being out of work, he understood that very clearly as well. And when the subject was Thornwood Studios, production problems, and difficult people, Homer Tony had his weeks of involvement with *Bushranger* to refer to. He knew.

'A lot of people think I'm rich and I guess I am. I'm not blind. I can look around me and see what I own and how I live. That makes me feel fortunate but I don't feel rich. It's nice while it lasts, like the sun shining through the bunk-house window in the morning, but you can't expect it to go on for ever. At least I don't. The sun keeps slanting around to the south and pretty soon it's shining through some other window. The funny part of it is that in my gut I don't feel any different about myself than I did when we were sweating our balls off on the cattle run. You can't feel rich unless you're born rich. I was born poor and I still feel poor. I'll always feel poor. Whatever I manage to stow away, I'll always expect some stiff-necked bastard in a blue suit and white collar to show up one day and take it all back. And you know something, maybe that wouldn't bother me at all. Maybe I'd feel better about myself, feel more at home, if that happened. Maybe I'd say to myself, "Now you've got back to where you started." I don't mean that I don't deserve what I'm getting, the money and the way I live now, and all the good stuff. I think I deserve to have any bloody thing I can lay my hands on. Not because I'm some special bloke but because anybody deserves to have what he's able to get. I used to think that meant you had to steal what you wanted. Or you had to work yourself crazy twenty hours a day. But now here I am, sitting on my ass most of the time, not doing much of anything to put myself forward, and people keep throwing money at me and wanting to be my friend, and I think to myself, "What did I do? What button did I press?" But I don't have the answer. I just know that for some reason, all of a sudden I've got it good. And if things like that are going to happen to somebody I don't mind if they happen to me. I don't mind being the lucky duck for a change. But it doesn't make me think I'm any different from what I was before. In my gut I'm an Aborigine, for Christ's sake. Just like you. I always thought if I got out of this world without getting shot or hung it would be a miracle. I still think that.' When he heard those words Homer Tony patted himself on the head. 'No, not you,' Kincaid said. 'If somebody put a gun to your head they'd take a good look at that ugly face and throw the gun away. You're too ugly to kill. You're so ugly you may live a thousand years.'

One afternoon in August they sat on the stone wall that ran along the bluff-edge of Kincaid's land with the cliff falling away sharply on the ocean side and the waves thundering in heavy against the rocks two hundred feet below.

'I don't think I told you this before,' Kincaid said. 'When I first saw this land, before I bought it, this wall was already here, running all along the cliff-edge. Looked as if it had been here for a hundred years, thick and solid, almost five feet high. But down there,' he pointed to the north, 'near where we built the house, there was an opening in the wall, six or eight feet across, like a gate. Except this opening led nowhere. Three feet past the wall it's a straight drop to the rocks down there at the back of the beach. The wall hadn't crumbled away there. And it wasn't as if somebody had hauled the stones away to use some place else. The original wall had been built like that, with that opening left in it, just at the edge of the cliff.'

When Homer Tony nodded his head Kincaid said, 'You know what I'm thinking about, don't you? The way the tribes in Victoria and New South Wales built their walls. They always left an opening like that so the good spirits could get in and the bad spirits could get out.'

Homer Tony kept nodding his head and smiling. 'Sophie was with me when I first saw this land. She hated that open space in the wall. Said it scared her. So when I bought the place the first thing I told the stone-masons was to build up the wall there. Fill in that opening.'

Later that afternoon when they were drinking a beer in Homer Tony's bungalow, Kincaid said, 'Remember, I told you I'd be leaving for Chicago before too long? Well, now it looks as if we may go later. Tim Garrigus has an idea that he'd like all the Chicago scenes and the country road stuff shot in bad weather. Rain and snow, and cars slipping and sliding in the slush when they leave town after a bank robbery. And I think he's sold Thorne on the idea. So we may do all the interiors here in studio before we go east. That means it'll be six weeks or two months before we go. And if we hit the bad weather Tim's hoping for, God knows how long we'll be stuck in Chicago and Wisconsin and Indiana. We'll probably be lucky to finish up by Christmas. For a while I thought maybe you'd like to tag along with us out there, hang around and be my stand-in, but the more I hear about Chicago, the more I think it's a bad idea. It's a monster city, they tell me, all glass and concrete and petrol fumes. Not a blade of grass or a horse-turd any place in sight. Doesn't sound great to me. How does it sound to you?'

Homer Tony stared at him for a long moment as if he were trying to decide what answer Kincaid wanted to hear. At last he solemnly shook his head. 'That's what I thought,' Kincaid said. 'I thought you'd rather be here with the horses, riding the pastures with Trevor, and keeping an eye on the ocean just in case a couple of mermaids get beached down there.'

Homer Tony laughed and nodded his head and with his hands he outlined the shape of a mermaid in the air.

'God help any mermaid that you get your hands on,' Kincaid said. Homer Tony kept smiling and nodding his head.

6

The day before Margaret went down to London to meet with her solicitors, Brannigan drove his caravan to Holyhead in Wales and boarded the ferry there. On his way to Dublin, where he had contracted with a publisher to spend a week photographing the River Liffey.

Since the key members of Sophie's London staff had travelled with her to America, Margaret spent two nights at Brown's, and on the morning of the third day she took the express train north again to Newcastle where Clara Causey and her driver met her at the station.

Before Margaret's departure for London the two women had arranged by telephone that she would stay at Wingate Fields for a few days on her return. It was also a time when Clara's husband, Ned, had gone to Scotland to do some shooting on Hugh's estate. 'So we'll have the place to ourselves,' Clara had said.

After dinner the first evening, when the two women were having coffee in the library, Clara said, 'You're really in a state, aren't you?'

'I've been trying to hide it.'

'I can see that. And you're quite good at it. But I know all your quirks and I've never seen you quite like this. If I didn't know you so well, I'd think you were on the verge of tears.'

'You're one day late. Last night in London, I cried myself to sleep. Haven't done that since Sophie's poor Toby died. I didn't recognize myself in the looking-glass this morning. Great puffs under my eyes. But I think I'm all cried out now.'

'I'm not so sure of that.'

'I couldn't wait to get here so I could sort it all out with you. You always have such a clear head.'

'Only with other people's problems. With my own I'm just as confused as everyone else.'

'That's some consolation but not much,' Margaret said. 'You see, I seem to have arrows flying at me from all directions. I hate to admit it, even to you, but it's starting to get the best of me.'

'It's all that business with the Major, isn't it?'

'It's not just that, but that's the central calamity. All the other headaches seem hinged to that one.'

'I know you met with Tremont in London. What does he say?'

'What he's said from the start. Since his first meeting with William. He says he's irrational, undependable, and paranoid. After just one meeting he said that. It took me ten years of marriage before I was able to admit those things to myself.'

'But what does he advise?'

'There again, he's been consistent. He's always advocated taking a tough approach. He still does. He insists that William will respond to nothing else. And he's right, of course. But I've held back, trying to avoid an ugly confrontation. Hoping for some miracle, I suppose. I can't bear the thought of our home being turned into a psychological battleground. When I said that to Tremont he said, "But that's what it is now. Two adversaries in opposite wings of the house." He says we must move ahead and implement the protective order. He believes we've waited much longer than we should have.'

'Will you agree to it?'

'I have agreed to it. Whatever rational intelligence I have left has always agreed. It's my coward's heart that holds me back. I'm simply not vengeful. I'm not

325

vindictive by nature. The code of Leviticus is not my code. God knows, I have enough reason to be angry with William. And I'm very bored with his behaviour. Also, I'm embarrassed to tell you, there's something about him that frightens me.'

'He's irrational. That's always frightening.'

'I know that. I know all his faults, you see. But still I don't want to hurt him if I can avoid it. And I certainly don't want to destroy him. I'm afraid he'll fight like an animal if the authorities come to remove him from the house. God knows what he's liable to do. And I couldn't bear to see that.'

'But that's outside your control, Margaret. Cranston has choices. He has had all along. If he's determined to make a martyr of himself or just a plain damned fool, that's not your responsibility.'

'I realize that. But I can't feel good about it.'

'You have a choice, too,' Clara said. 'You can simply let him stay on in the house and try to pretend he's not there.'

Margaret smiled. 'I don't have that choice. Brannigan would never stand for it.'

'You can't blame him for that.'

'I don't blame him. I can see everybody's point of view. That's my weakness. I can even see William's point of view.'

'In that case I think you should get a new prescription from your optometrist. We all like to tell ourselves we're generous and unselfish but that's an irrelevant characteristic when a dog is determined to bite you or a taxi's about to run you over.'

'You're right, of course. As I said, my brain is in good working order. I just have an emotional imbalance that's making me stagger a bit.'

'Have you told Brannigan everything you're telling me?'

Margaret shook her head. 'I haven't let him see how

truly upset I am. Jack's a man. And most men when they're faced with a problem are determined to solve it. He and Tremont are as different as night and day but they're in total agreement about how to deal with William.'

'Then that makes three of us,' Clara said. 'If you're trying not to be cruel, the cruellest thing you can do is to let the situation drag on as it has done. It simply postpones Cranston's facing the inevitable, it's slowly turning you into a nervous wreck, and if you're not careful it could do some serious damage to your marriage.'

'I know that. Sometimes I think it already has.'

'How do you mean?'

'I'm not sure. I don't mean that we're having arguments or sleeping in separate bedrooms. No chance of that happening with Brannigan. But I can see he's disturbed by the whole rotten business with William, just as I am. And he's doubly disturbed, I think, because I seem to be holding back. Jack's a possessive fellow. I'm sure he's asked himself more than once why I'm being so considerate of a man who's behaving like a fool, a man I was unhappily married to for more than thirty years. I expect Jack believes our marriage won't truly begin till we have the Towers to ourselves, till William has packed up his firearms and gone somewhere else to live.'

'You can't fault him for that either.'

'Of course not,' Margaret said, 'and I don't. Don't misunderstand me. I can't imagine a better life than I'm having with Jack. That, more than anything else, was what was in my mind when I told Tremont to go ahead and do whatever must be done. But I can't help feeling . . . I don't know.'

'I'm sorry. I've been questioning you like a barrister. I'd love to be helpful if it's possible, but I don't mean to pry.'

'Oh no, you mustn't feel that way. That isn't why I

hesitate. My thoughts are so jumbled, I'm not sure what I'm thinking . . .'

'Let's not talk any more tonight. I'm sure you're tired from your trip.'

'No, Clara, please. My silliness has nothing to do with you. I was so anxious to talk to you, and there's so much ground to cover it's all getting tangled in my head.' She smiled. 'Let's have a bit of brandy. Then if my tongue doesn't behave properly I'll have something to blame it on.'

A few minutes later, as they sat with fresh coffee and snifters of brandy, Margaret said, 'I was trying to say some things about Jack. And I must be careful so you won't misunderstand. You know what he's like. Free and open. Nothing hidden below the surface. Nothing's changed about him since our wild courtship in Frejus. He's warm and responsive and kind and funny and ardent – that word doesn't express it . . . He's able to be a husband and a friend at the same time. There's nothing about him or about us together that I'd want to change. At the same time I can't help feeling sometimes that his life with me, our life together at the Towers, is not what he wanted it to be.'

'In what ways?'

'Silly ways. Unimportant ways. For one thing he's not comfortable with the staff. Consequently they're not at ease with him, I'm afraid. He's never lived in a home with servants. He's accustomed to doing for himself. He likes to cook and scrub pots and run the carpet-sweeper. I've never seen him ring for Trout or Mrs Whitson. When he gets dressed for breakfast that's the outfit he wears till bedtime. I think he feels as if the house belongs to the staff and he's a temporary guest there. One afternoon when we were sitting in the music-room and the maids were padding about doing something or other, he said, "Where in hell do you go when you want to be private?" Another day, when we'd driven to Carlisle and were coming home up the drive, he said, "I'm a clochard at heart. What am I doing in a place like this? The butler's morning-coat cost three times as much as my entire wardrobe!"'

'But that's his sense of humour, isn't it?' Clara said.

'Of course. So I pay no attention when he says things like that. But sometimes I look at him and he seems to have drifted off, lost his concentration, and I can't help wondering where he's gone to. When we first came home I invited a few neighbours in, just two or three at a time, perfectly nice county people, and Jack seemed to enjoy it. He laughed and told stories and was very warm and entertaining. But one day he said to me, "Did you notice how your friends looked at me? Like I was some bloke you'd brought in to trim the rose-bushes. They seemed bloody interested in my corduroy jacket, too, I noticed. I thought that skinny pouf, the one who looks like a plucked chicken, was about to ask for the name of my tailor."

'That night when we went up to bed Jack said, "You know what I love about you, Maggie. You haven't tried to make me over. One of my mates in Letterkenny, the day we were married, took me to one side and said: Next time I see you, you'll be wearing a boiled shirt and patent-leather slippers and a bit of velvet on your collar. A high-class woman like her don't want a bundle of rags like you slumpin' about the premises."'

'But he's joking, isn't he? You said he jokes about everything.'

Margaret nodded. 'It's true. But I've noticed that the things he jokes about most often are things that bother him. He's determined to be his own man, you see. Wherever he goes he presents himself as a man from Donegal. Take him or leave him. I think he told himself from the first time he saw the Towers, when he was doing the photographs for *Country Life*, that such a life in those surroundings was not for him. But now it is his life and it's giving him problems. He still wears the same jacket and trousers almost every day, however, and he comes down to dinner in his old slippers. But while he's promising himself that he'll continue to be the same vagabond he's always been, I think he feels some changes may be necessary. Although he has nothing in common with any of the county people he's met and would never spend ten minutes with them by choice, at the same time he doesn't like it when they look down their noses at him. He's independent but he's also proud. He doesn't like to be shunned or rejected, even by fools. I expect he thinks it's a reflection on me as well. One night he said, "I think your stiff-necked friends think you've made a bad choice. They think you've picked a sorry specimen for a husband." And he wasn't joking when he said it.'

'What did you say?'

'What could I say? He's right. I know how they feel so I don't see them any longer. You know the Good-pastors and the Marbles and Victoria Weeks. They can't imagine anyone marrying outside the county. And to marry an Irishman . . . they think he's a buffoon. And that bothers him.'

'What's to be done?'

'I don't know. So I've tried to ignore it. I'm afraid that anything I might say or do would only bring it into sharper focus. You know what I'm saying? It's like having a good serious talk with your husband about your bedroom life together. Very seldom productive. Very often disastrous. I can't say to Jack, "You must dress the way you wish and behave as you always have, and to hell with everybody else." The fault truly isn't with him. It's with this place you and I grew up in. You love it, I know, as much as I do. We no longer notice how insular it is, like a strange reptile feeding on itself. And how self-satisfied and in-turned all the people are. Even the servants are infected by it. They seem determined to preserve all the superficial behaviour they've observed in us through the years.'

'It's not easy, is it?' Clara said. 'Could you ever live any place else?'

'Of course I could. Jack's lived all round the world and I wouldn't hesitate to go any place he wanted to go. I've told him that many times. But if it came to making such a decision, choosing a place to go, the idea would have to come from him.'

'Why is that?'

'I know him very well. If I said, "Let's leave the Towers and go live in Greece or Montreal or Provence", he'd think I was doing it just for his sake and he wouldn't have that. Or even worse, he might conclude that being married to him had destroyed the life I once had here . . . you know what I'm saying?'

'Yes, I do. I wish I didn't but I do. I'd like to be able to tell you that I think you're imagining all this but I'm sure you're not.'

'No, I'm afraid I'm not. When I watched him leave for Dublin a few days ago he sat there behind the wheel of his caravan like a schoolboy off to a soccer match. Or a prisoner released from jail. Have you ever seen a young stallion break out of his paddock and run free across the moors? That's all I could think of as Jack's caravan speeded away down the long drive to the road.'

BOOK THREE

BOOK THREE

• CHAPTER 9 •

1

During the last week in August a neighbourhood cinema near Lincoln and Fullerton on the north side of Chicago was showing *Manhattan Melodrama*, a film about gangsters, starring Clark Gable.

After the first show, among the crowd spilling out of the theatre into the summer heat was a well-built man wearing a grey fedora with a black ribbon round it, a dark vest and trousers, and a white shirt open at the collar. Suddenly the man broke away from the two women he was with and ran toward the alley that was just beside the theatre. He was quickly surrounded by half a dozen men firing pistols. He stumbled up the alley, fell to his knees, and rolled over on his back. John Dillinger was dead.

Two days later the key people associated with Julian Thorne's production of *Dillinger* assembled in the conference room just beside Thorne's office. Kincaid and Evan Tagg were there, along with Tim Garrigus, Russ Tunstall, the cameraman, Bob Deal, the line producer, Loren Iverson, the art director, Leon Dart, head of publicity, and half a dozen other people from key departments.

When everyone was settled round the long table, a thin cloud of cigar-and-cigarette-smoke hovering above their heads, Thorne said, 'I want you to forget the rumours you've read in the trade papers the last day or so. The word is that we're going to abandon our picture. It's all over, they say. He's just another dead gangster now and who gives a damn? Or they say somebody will have a quickie Dillinger film out inside two months. This morning in *Film Daily*, Justin Gold said J. Edgar Hoover had telephoned me and made a personal request that we abandon the whole project. Not true, any of those reports. The real story is this: not only are we going ahead, we're going full steam. Before this happened I was convinced we had the makings of a great film. Now I guarantee we've got a blockbuster on our hands. It's a fine script that Evan has put together for us and now we have what we didn't have before – a dynamite ending. But here's the pressure: we have to write that new ending and shoot it within the next three weeks because everybody in the country knows Dillinger was shot on a hot summer night in Chicago. And everybody who reads a paper has seen pictures of the Biograph theatre and that neighbourhood. So that's where we'll shoot it. Right there. Just like a newsreel. Less than a month after the real thing happened we'll have our death scenes in the can.'

'Are you sure we can move that fast?' Bob Deal said. 'I've had production crews in Chicago before, and the police and the local authorities broke our balls with delays.'

'My brother, Sam, is on top of that. He's got connections there. It's already been worked out on the telephone. All the papers will be signed in plenty of time so we won't be held up. The important thing is that we mustn't hold ourselves up. So Tim, we're putting you and Bob and Russ and Loren on the night plane tonight. And we've booked a dozen more seats for whatever people you need to take along. We've reserved rooms for you in the Drake and a production office at the Knickerbocker. The rest of us will be there within a week or ten days. By then Evan will have laid out any summer exterior shots we have to add for the last section of the film before Dillinger gets shot. We'll shoot those right after we do the night shots for the final scene. Then we'll go back to our original schedule. Shooting pretty much in sequence from the top of the picture.'

'That means the original schedule's ass-backwards now,' Iverson said.

'That's right, Loren. Instead of doing all the interiors here and then going east for the exteriors, we'll reverse it. Only now we'll shoot as many interiors as we can manage on the actual locations before we come home.'

'You're gonna give me fits, Julian,' Tunstall said, 'trying to squeeze our big lights inside those country banks and farmhouses.'

Thorne smiled. Ten thousand dollars worth of dental sculpture. 'You're a genius, Russ. You told me so yourself. Just remember, we don't need a Gregg Toland look. And it's not going to be a pretty Paramount picture. We're dealing with tough times, unlucky people, hard lives. If it looks a little rough the way you shoot it, that's perfect. *Bushranger* had rough spots in it and they worked. They'll work in this film, too. We'll see some shots from *Manhattan Melodrama* when Dillinger's watching it in the theatre. That's a slick picture. When the audience sees those clips they'll say to themselves, "That's just a movie. This Dillinger film is the real stuff."' He looked at Garrigus. 'I know what you're thinking, Tim. You had your heart set on shooting all the exteriors in sloppy winter weather. I liked the idea, too, but we're screwed on that. We don't have a choice. We have to get the summer stuff now. And once we're set up in Chicago we have to stay there and keep shooting. But I guarantee you, you'll see all the nasty weather you want before we get back. The good news, as I told you last night, is that we got Ann Dvorak to play the Hungarian woman in the red dress, the one who was with him in the theatre. I wanted Stanwyck to play the other woman, Sally Wick, but she wouldn't buy it. So I talked Daisy Bishop into doing that part – you'll have to be very nice to her in Chicago, Tim – and Stanwyck will do Lola, the part we'd set Daisy for at the beginning.'

'I still don't know how you managed that switch.'

'I promised Daisy I'd borrow Joel McCrea to play opposite her in *Flower Girl*. She's got a big yen for him.'

'So's my wife,' Iverson said.

When the laughter died down, Thorne said, 'The telephone lines are going to be hot between here and Chicago these next few days. We'll be making it up as we go along and we're bound to have some headaches. But let's be patient with each other. You all know what you're doing or you wouldn't be here. This time I'm just asking you to do it faster. We're planning on a release date just after Christmas. Before the kids go back to school. I promise you, we'll end up with something to be proud of, the same as we did last time.'

After everyone else had left the room Kincaid and Evan and Garrigus stayed behind with Thorne. 'Let's talk a little bit about story,' Thorne said. 'I've sent all three of you every bit of printed stuff our research people could get hold of, and we'll screen the rough newsreel footage as soon as our cutters can put it together. There's no dialogue to speak of in the final sequence at the theatre but the action shots have to be perfect. Before we shoot, we'll know every move that was made outside the Biograph that night and that's the way we have to shoot it. Just like it was.'

'How about the women who were mopping up his blood with handkerchiefs and selling it piece by piece? Are we going for that stuff, too?' Garrigus said.

'Let's shoot everything. In the cutting-room we can get rid of whatever we don't want. But let's have it on film so we'll have a choice. This was an execution. They didn't even try to take him alive. Dillinger never fired a shot. We want to see all that, without leaning on it. He's not an innocent guy but maybe he should have had a chance to surrender and face trial. Still, we're not making judgements. We're just laying it out, letting the audience decide, the same as we did in *Bushranger*.'

338

'What about those two women he was with?' Evan asked. 'What do we know about them?'

'Not much. That's what I was coming to. We've got our ending and that's great. But we've also got two women we don't know what to do with, and we can't slough them off. For months before he got killed Dillinger was out of sight somewhere. Everybody thought he'd be with his old girlfriend, Lola, the one from Crown Point, but instead he turns up with these two mice that nobody ever heard of before, the one from Hungary who may have fingered him by wearing that red dress, and the other one who looks as innocent as Mary Pickford and says she's from South Dakota. It's a tricky story problem. We have to tie the three of them together but we have to be careful about details. If we make up a fancy story line and two weeks before release date one of them starts telling the real story, we look like stupid ass-holes and the picture could suffer because of it.'

'Where are the two women now?'

'That's something else that Sam's working on. The older one, the Hungarian, is being held because they say she's an illegal alien. Her papers aren't in order. But the people Sam's been talking to say the police are protecting her. Nobody knows for sure who they're protecting her from or why.'

'What about the other one? The pretty one?'

'Floating around, I guess. The police talked to her but the word was she didn't know anything. Didn't even know the guy she was with was Dillinger. Or so she says. Sam's people think she can be located if we put out the right bait.'

'Like what?' Evan said.

'Like money. These aren't debutantes we're talking about. For five dollars you can stay all night and they'll cook you breakfast in the morning. But all the same the money tease didn't work with the Hungarian. One of Sam's friends visited her in jail and showed her five grand in hundred-dollar bills. All she had to do was talk to us for an hour and tell us what she knows about Dillinger.'

'And she didn't buy it?' Garrigus asked.

Thorne shook his head. 'Laughed in the guy's face. She's a tough monkey, I guess. He asked her how much she wanted if five grand wasn't enough and she told him to go screw himself. Sam says it looks as if there's a detective from East Chicago who's calling the shots for her. Nobody knows why.'

'So that leaves us with the girl from South Dakota,' Evan said.

'That's what we're working on. When they locate her, they'll throw some money at her and see what happens. Meanwhile, let's see what kind of a rough story line you can work out. We've got a tough lady who knows her way around, an innocent-looking kid from Hicksville, and the most wanted fugitive in the world. So who's doing what to whom? People who sat behind them in the theatre said the three of them were laughing, eating jelly-beans, and having a great time. Like I said before, we have to keep it simple so we don't get caught out later. It may turn out that it's better to ignore them than it is to guess wrong and make fools of ourselves. Or we could get lucky and the little milk maid might give us some straight information. I have a good hunch about it. One way or the other I think we'll get what we need.'

Julian Thorne's wife, Bella, kept herself busy with her home, her daughter, Rachel, her needlepoint, her work with the Fairfax Avenue synagogue, her charities, her regular radio programmes, and writing long letters to her sisters in Jersey City and Baltimore. She was tenderly supportive of her husband and proud of his achievements but she had never, from the beginning, involved herself in his work. She never criticized his films, his London wardrobe or his acquired Mayfair speech, and never asked him questions about the studio or its operation. And Julian seldom volunteered such information.

Their evenings together at home would have provided a stranger with no hints about Thorne's means of livelihood. One could guess by the quality of the furniture, the carpets, paintings and wall-hangings Bella had selected that theirs was a family of means, but there were no signed photographs in silver frames, no pictures of Julian with the mayor or the governor or Samuel Goldwyn. Even in the relaxed atmosphere of the den or the billiard-room there were no framed posters, no plaques for excellence in film-making or civic endeavour. The activities of both Julian and Bella had earned such awards, many in fact, but they were all carefully packaged and stored away.

Nor did they entertain on a grand scale. Not in their home. Sam and his wife came for Sunday dinner every few weeks. And women friends of Bella's came occasionally with their husbands for cocktails or Sunday luncheon served on the terrace. But it was not a meeting-place for colleagues and associates in the motion-picture industry. When Julian hosted a business dinner, entertaining actors and directors, or exhibitors, or managers of exchanges, he took a dining-room for the evening at Luchino's in downtown Los Angeles.

Bella was always beside him, of course, when her presence was required or when her absence would have caused questions to be asked, but it was well understood and accepted by those whose business or hobby it was to count the quirks or read the whorls of the local rich and prominent that Bella Thorne was a woman who preferred to stay at home.

Sam's wife, Marie, shared Bella's views. She said, 'When Sam was selling asparagus and bananas and celery I never asked him when he came home at night about the condition of the green beans or how many truck-loads of Idahos he sold before lunch-time. And that was a business I know something about from working in my uncle's vegetable store on First Avenue. Now Sam's in a business, or a racket, whatever you call it, that I don't know squirts about, so why should I stick my nose in? What am I supposed to know about grosses and completion bonds and above the title? Those are just words I hear bouncing off the wall sometimes. Nothing for me to get steamed up about.'

On this occasion, however, the evening of the day he'd had a long meeting about the Dillinger film, Julian said to Bella as they had a glass of tea together before going up to bed, 'I hope I'm guessing right about the Dillinger film. I'm not sure.'

'At least he's dead now, the poor man. Everybody knows that. So you don't have to worry about a lawsuit.'

'That's the point right there. He's dead now.'

'That's what I said. Dead men can't sue.'

'But here's my point. We have a story about a real man who's a law-breaker, a dangerous renegade. And to many people he's a hero. Because he robs banks.'

'Nobody with a bank account thinks a bank robber is a hero.'

'But there are thousands of people in this country, millions of people, who've never had a bank account in their lives. So they think it's not a bad idea when some poor bastard decides to steal a few thousand from a bank.'

'Robin Hood,' she said.

'Exactly. But here's the question. You take this man who's reckless and dangerous and he's a hero. A good idea for a film. But what happens when he's dead?'

'Then he's dead. Kaput.'

'But he's not reckless or dangerous any longer. And maybe he's not a hero either. Maybe he's just a dead jail-bird who got shot in an alley.'

'Robin Hood's dead,' she said. 'But that didn't stop Douglas Fairbanks. You told Sam you did well with that picture.'

'I did,' Julian said. 'Big grosses.'

'Well, there you are.'

342

After the production meeting in the conference room with Julian Thorne, Evan walked through the studio streets toward his own office. As he passed the executive office building he saw Sam Thorne step out of a black limousine. A stocky man with thinning dark hair got out on the other side and the two of them walked into the building together.

Evan spent the rest of the day at his desk. His secretary brought him coffee and a steak sandwich at lunch-time. He began to flesh out the characters of the two women who'd been with Dillinger, tried to imagine their relationships with each other and with him.

Making pages of notes and facts and suppositions, keeping it simple as Thorne had suggested, sketching out possible scenes that might include the daily activities of three such people, a man and two women friends, one of them a sweetheart perhaps, Evan was intrigued by the notion that at least one of the women might not have known her companion was Dillinger. Or perhaps neither of them knew. But if the Hungarian woman, Agnes Szepy, had actually set him up for the government agents by wearing a bright-red dress, then she surely knew him from the start or had somehow found out who he was.

Evan experimented also with the time structure. How long had the three known each other? Had Dillinger met the young woman, Sally Wick, more recently? What if she had met him the afternoon of the day he was killed? Or what if she had been a waitress at the resort in Wisconsin where Dillinger and his men had had a bloody gun-battle with government agents? Or could she be Agnes Szepy's daughter? Or a younger sister? Or was the Hungarian woman a procuress perhaps? Had she furnished Sally's tender services to Dillinger? And what was her connection with the detective from East Chicago? Evan looked at his maps and saw that East Chicago was just across the state line from the city of Chicago, in Indiana, Dillinger's home state. Did that mean something? Newspaper accounts had said that at least two East Chicago police were with the Federal agents outside the Biograph. But no Chicago police. Could something be made of that? Also, since Dillinger made no effort to surrender, did he know somehow that Melvin Purvis and his men were there to kill him, not to arrest him? And how did the two women feel about his death? Was Sally in love with him, perhaps?

Evan spent the afternoon shuffling pages, wondering, guessing. How much should he tell? How much should he imply? One had to be careful not to give too much importance to relationships that would probably end up as no more than ten minutes on the screen. In his scenario till now, Lola had been the only continuing woman in Dillinger's life. Was there some point to be made about the man if it was found he'd abandoned Lola for Sally just before his death? Or was it a mistake to build up the script relationship between Agnes and Sally and Dillinger? Maybe the critical fact was that on his last evening alive he was laughing and eating jelly-beans with two women he barely knew and didn't give a damn about. What if the East Chicago police had furnished him Agnes's house as a place to hide out and had then used her to betray him? But why would the police help him in the first place? Evan looked at his maps again. East Chicago seemed to be in the same county as Crown Point. Dillinger had made a dramatic escape from the Crown Point Jail using a wooden gun he'd carved in his cell. There was a famous photograph of his jailer there, his arm around Dillinger, both of them laughing. Had there been some complicity on the part of Lake County police? Had money changed hands? If so, could Dillinger have come back later, after the Wisconsin shoot-out, to blackmail those same police?

'Find me a safe-house or I'll write to the *Chicago Tribune* and tell them the true story of how I broke out of Crown Point.'

'Back-plot,' Evan decided, 'I can't get into that. That's a script in itself. But I can know it. I can understand why Szepy and the police are behaving the way they are even if I don't spell it out in the script. The iceberg below the water line, that sort of thing.'

As he worked through the afternoon Evan was aware that this process of exploration was his strength as a writer; not structure or plot or dramatic effects, but relating people to each other, allowing them to reveal themselves, seeing them struggle and squirm, rebel and compromise, and become the story. And if the ones whose conflicts were most severe also loved each other, so much the better.

Before he left his office late in the afternoon he rang up Julian. 'I've had a good day,' Evan said. 'I think I know half a dozen low-key ways to tie up Dillinger with the two women so it doesn't throw the rest of our story out of whack. But nothing we come up with will be half as good as what we might find out from Sally Wick if we can talk to her. I've made some good guesses, I think, but even two or three solid facts would pin the whole thing together.'

As he walked toward the parking lot where he left his car every morning, Evan passed the executive office building and saw Sam Thorne's limousine still standing there at the kerb. As he kept walking past the building he had a visual reprise of Sam and his stocky friend getting out of that car earlier in the day. Suddenly Evan realized where he'd seen that man before. He turned round, went back to the building, went inside, and climbed the marble stairs to Sam's second-floor office. The secretary talked with Mr Thorne briefly on the phone, then waved Evan in. 'You just caught him,' she said. 'He's about to go home.'

Sam was leaning back in his desk chair with a big smile on his face. 'I just talked to Julian so I know why you're here. You're gonna light a fire under me.'

'Why would I do that?'

'So I'll round up that girlfriend of Dillinger's . . . what's her name?'

'Sally Wick.'

'That's it. My brother says you're frothin' at the mouth. Anxious to get her on the griddle.'

'That's right. It's important.'

'Trust me, kid. I'll hand her to you like a Reuben's cheesecake.'

'I know you will, Sam. But that's not why I came up to see you. I wanted to ask you about that gentleman I saw you with earlier today. A heavy-set guy in a navy-blue suit.'

'Half the guys in this business are heavy-set guys in blue suits.'

'The two of you were getting out of your car late this morning.'

'That's John Corso. In Jersey they used to call him Johnny Cello. Cause he's built like one.'

'So he's an old friend of yours?' Evan said.

'My best friend. John and I were in business together from the time we were sixteen. Buying and selling. Did damn well with it, too. Then I came out here to show Julian how to make money, and the next thing I knew, Johnny showed up.'

'Is he in the film business?'

'Let me put it this way. Without him we got no film business. He's put together the biggest trucking operation in Los Angeles. We can't make movies without wheels and Corso owns the wheels. Then last year he bought out a big chain of laundry and dry-cleaning joints. So now he's got a lock on that. Services all the studios and all the restaurants and hotels in town. He's got it licked. And if you ask him he'll tell you I taught him everything he knows. Except how to eat. He worked that out for himself.'

After a moment Evan said, 'You remember the talk we

had, after those guys came to my house and left a brand-new Packard in the carport?'

'Sure I remember. Damndest thing I ever heard of. Only time I ever knew of the insurance company getting screwed. We got full payment on our policy for the car and then you got a brand-new car for yourself. If I could pull off a scam like that every day I'd be out of the movie business in a minute.'

'Why do you use the word *scam*?'

'It's just a word I like. Use it all the time. I hear about a dozen scams every day.'

'You remember I told you that two men came to my door and one of them handed me the car keys, then they turned around and left . . . well, one of those men was your friend Corso.'

'You're jazzin' me.'

'No, I'm not. I'd never seen him before that day. Then I saw him with you this morning and I knew it was the same man.'

Sam shook his head. 'Johnny never gave anything to anybody. He sure as hell wouldn't hand over the keys to a brand-new Packard.'

'Maybe it was the other fellow who handed me the keys.'

'Doesn't matter. Corso doesn't make deliveries. He's got twenty guys who run errands for him. You want to do business with him you go to his office. Or the ice-cream store on Beverly Drive. Besides, like I said, there's a hundred guys in this town look like Johnny. A thousand maybe.'

'I don't have an explanation for it, Sam, but I know what I saw.'

'I can't see what you're all worked up about. If somebody handed me a brand-new car I wouldn't look a gift horse in the mouth. You know what I mean?'

'Sure, I do. But I don't like mysteries. When somebody burns up a car I'm driving that makes me mad. When a stranger hands me the keys to a brand-new car with an owner's certificate in my name in the glove compartment, then I start to wonder. I want to know what's going on. Maybe somebody plans to burn my house down next.'

'Not a chance. The guy paid you back with a new car. So now the deal is closed. You can bet on it.'

'What if I had a talk with your friend Corso?'

'I'm not telling you what to do, kid. But if you're asking for advice I'd say John's a busy man. And one thing he hates is people asking him questions. I already told you you're talking about a case of mistaken identity so why don't you let it go at that?'

After a moment Evan said, 'Maybe you're right. I guess that's what I'll do.'

'You look disappointed. I guess I wasn't much help. Like I said, Corso's my friend but he's not a guy you want to get pissed off at you.'

'I gathered that.'

'I'll tell you what,' Sam said suddenly, 'if you know the name of the agency that sold the car . . . do you know it?'

'The Serkin agency. Wilshire and La Cienego. There's a medallion on the back bumper.'

'Al Serkin. I know him. He's the world's most honest man except when he's selling cars.' He leaned forward, forearms on the desk-top. 'Here's what you should do. If it was me I'd take the direct approach. Go straight to Al. Tell him somebody gave you this car and your lawyer says you have to find out who it was so you're sure you're not driving a hot car with a phoney registration. Serkin will help you out. He'd better. I must have bought thirty studio cars off the bastard and he tries to dick me every time.'

Just before Evan left his office Sam said, 'I'll give Al a ring and tell him you're on your way. Let me know what you find out.'

Albert Serkin had the haunted eyes of a man who knew he'd made at least one enemy every day of his working life. But he wore tailored clothes, gold-rimmed glasses on a ribbon, and he spoke in the measured tones of a Pasadena cleric. As soon as Evan came into the showroom Serkin hurried out of his office and took him back inside.

'Sam Thorne tells me you're driving one of our new four-door convertibles.'

'That's right.'

'No problems with it, I hope.'

'No. I just have a question. This car was a gift to me and I need to know who bought it. My lawyer's afraid it might be stolen.'

'That's quite a gift, especially from someone who didn't identify himself. But in any case I told Sam I'd do my best for you so I'm sure we'll be able to give you a name.' He asked his secretary for the card-file of new car-buyers. 'Since you're driving the car I assume the registration's in your name. T-A-G-G. Is that correct?'

'That's right. The bill of sale is also in my name.'

'Are you sure of that?'

Evan nodded. 'It was on the front seat of the car when it was delivered to me.'

'That's unusual. Let's have a look.' He started to flip through the small file-box. 'The buyer and the owner are usually the same person so we make up our file cards from owner's registrations. But we also keep a copy of the sales slip which shows the actual buyer as well.' After a moment he looked up and said, 'That was T-A-G-G?'

'That's right. Evan Tagg.'

'Your name's not here. We don't have a card for you. Are you sure it's one of our cars?'

Evan nodded. 'Your medallion's on the back bumper.'

'Let's have a look at it.' They walked across the showroom and out into the parking area. A tall white-haired man, his skin as brown from the sun as tobacco, left the showroom and trailed a few steps behind them. When Evan pointed out his car Serkin said, 'My God, that's a handsome machine.' He walked round it carefully, then leaned down at the rear of the car and studied the medallion on the back bumper. He took his glasses off, bent close and squinted at it.

When he straightened up he said to the white-haired gentleman who was now standing directly behind him, 'Take a look, Marvin. Tell me what you think.'

Marvin squatted down, carefully easing his trouser creases, and inspected the medallion. When he straightened up he said, 'The medallion was taken from another model, Al. Probably a '32. This is not our automobile. We didn't sell it.'

The next morning Sam Thorne rang up Evan in his office. 'How'd we make out with Serkin?'

'It's not one of his cars. He didn't sell it.'

'Where did it come from then?'

'He has no idea.'

'I'll be damned,' Sam said. 'Well, now it's really a mystery, isn't it?'

'I'm not sure. Let's just say there are some strange things going on.'

'So what's your next move?'

'I don't have one. There is a question I'd like to ask you, though.'

'What's that?'

'It's about John Corso. Have you ever heard him mention a man named Alec Maple?'

'Who's Alec Maple?'

'An Englishman. A strange bird who lives in London.'

'I'll tell you one thing straight off. Johnny's never been to England or any place else except New York, New Jersey, and Los Angeles. His idea of a long trip is having one of his drivers take him down to Long Beach. I guarantee you he doesn't know this guy Maple.'

'I just thought he might have mentioned him.'

'Not to me,' Sam said, 'and I'll tell you something else. If he had I wouldn't tell you.'

While he was in Dublin, spending every day on the banks of the Liffey, Brannigan stayed in a small hotel called Bratton's, just off St Stephen's Green. Neal Bratton, grandson of the original owner, Timmie Bratton, and a five-time grandfather now himself, held forth behind the bar just off the foyer while his wife, his daughter, his son and daughter-in-law cleaned the lobby, made the beds, swept the floor in the ten small rooms, and prepared breakfast and supper for the hotel guests and certain regulars from the neighbourhood, many of whom came to eat with all good intentions but never got beyond the bar. The midday meal was available only to those select few who were invited to eat in the hotel kitchen at a long table with the family. That included his son Terry's three children and his daughter's two little girls.

Jack and Neal had been chums since they were boys in Donegal. Neal had spent each summer with his mother's family on their small sheep-farm near Letterkenny. At the age of six the two boys had shouted to anyone who would listen, 'It's Bratton and Brannigan, fresh from the farm. We'll do you no good, but we'll do you no harm.'

When he was behind his gleaming bar of brass and burled wood and Jack was on his stool at the end, Neal would offer ribald accounts of their lives together to whoever would listen.

'We're as different as night from day, this lad and me. I'm a spotless Catholic, mass every morning and giving generously to the parish, helping out at the church suppers, selling my kisses for next to nothing at the harvest bazaar, doing my bit and more of the world's work, loving father of three, grandfather to five little angels, a generous son to my mother and Da while they lived, and a faithful loving mate and protector to just one delicious lady for all my grown-up life. Sadie the lady, we call her, and that she surely is.

'So I'm an exemplary fellow, you see, not only by my own exacting measure but in the eyes of Father Connell, the nuns of the parish, the stout boyos who roll in my barrels of beer every morning, my loving children, my adoring wife, and the handsome ladies of the neighbourhood who admire my strong neck and muscular forearms. I'm blessed, you see, receiving Heaven's rewards while I'm still earthbound. And if I ever blaspheme may I fall stiff and dead on these slats behind my bar. I present my case in all modesty and humility knowing as I speak that I've fashioned myself into a God-fearing and extraordinary man. When I look at my darling Sadie I think to myself, "Would this fine example of womanhood have chosen any man who did not possess a flawless character, the singing voice of an angel, the arms of Vulcan, and words of love sweet as cherries." Of course she would not, and did not.'

At some point there was often a light flutter of applause from the bar customers assembled, and sometimes foot-stomping and wedding bands tapped against glasses, or knuckles knocking in rhythm on wood. Neal would then make a scathing comparison between himself and some friend at the bar. The regulars knew that his most ruthless words were stored up and applied to Brannigan whenever he was in Dublin. So Bratton's bar on those nights was the only place to be. By the second night of Jack's stay this time the word had got round, all bar-stools and standing spaces were taken, and Bratton disappointed no one. After a particularly laudatory self-portrait in which he positioned himself as a peer of Shaw, as superior to St Patrick, and dangerously close in significance to the Deity, he turned on Jack Brannigan.

'Now if you will,' he began, 'those of you with strong stomachs, consider this hapless creature crouched here at my bar like a flaming gargoyle. I tremble with fear when I tell you that I have known this fellow, more accurately I've been *exposed* to him, throughout my life. And my greatest pride lies in the fact that I have never been influenced or infected in any way by his pagan beliefs and nasty habits. If he were less pitiful, I would certainly have cut him loose long since, but when I was just a boy of six or seven years I could see that only his exposure to me might save him, only my example could lift him, albeit slightly, out of the low corridors his instincts propelled him through. When I look at him now I hesitate to say that I have influenced him in any way, because I know that if I'm able to point out some improvement he's made in himself as a result of my example, even those of you who are half-drunk or half-asleep will say, "Great God, what must he have been like *before*?"

'He's a fallen angel, you see, my friend, Brannigan. I say he's my friend not out of pride but to buoy his spirits. Because the sweet Lord knows he has no other man in the world who calls him friend. As a tiny boy he was a passable scamp, I suppose, but even then the good wives of Letterkenny called their children inside when he toddled by. It's a story with a touch of sadness to it. Or so it seems. A poor unfortunate blighter, you may say to yourselves. But no. We're speaking of a man who had absolutely nothing to start with. No humour, nothing in his character of diligence, no gift of speaking. But mark this. This wandering soul, this Jack Brannigan, has managed, by an aimless waste and scattering of his pitiful natural resources, to dissipate even the things he never had. Starting with nothing, he's ended up with less than that. His working life has been a shambles of low energy, poor concentration, and lost opportunities. He's taken a crack at a hundred different jobs of work and failed at each one. Then one day someone hung a camera round his neck and since then he has called himself photographer. But as often as not, after a long day of shooting quaint street scenes through the window of a public house, it turns out that there was no film on the spool in his camera-box.

'His personal life I hesitate to mention. His sweet mother and father, being people of pride and character and good taste, turned him away as soon as he was able to walk about and locate the public water closets by himself. I won't speak about his toilet habits, however, even in this low company. Suffice to say that one of his unfortunate wives kept a double padlock on her bathroom, with the keys round her neck on a cord. You notice I say *one* of his wives and I make the sign of the cross when I say the words, because here is a man who in the course of his shabby travels here and there has married every woman who asked him. When I demanded to know one day exactly how many wives had taken his name he blushed and said, "I've never had a skill for mathematics." God bless us all. I'm happy to say I've never met most of his wives. One can scarcely imagine what sort of desperate soul would look at the creature you see here sagging against my bar, would study him closely in a strong light and say to herself, "*That* is the man for me." It's almost a biblical scene, fraught with moral judgements, about the wages of sin and man's highest destiny, peopled by scores of weeping women who have chosen badly. What can be done for a man like this, you may ask, this capsized schooner of a man? I say his presence here has value if only to remind each of us how fortunate we are. In gratitude for that, I'll stand drinks all round for my non-paying customer, Jack Brannigan, the man who left Letterkenny under a cloud and returns there now at his peril and only under cover of darkness.'

On the third day of Brannigan's stay in Dublin, Neal Bratton, leaving the hotel bar in the charge of his son, Michael, spent the day prowling the banks of the Liffey with his friend. At lunch-time they had Guinness and shepherd's pie in a pub called Diogenes in Pearse Street.

'We're lucky buggers, Jack,' Bratton said. 'It's a mean fucking world out there. Men who can't find work, their families going hungry. Poor little bastards not old enough for school yet with their hands held out on O'Connell Street. They're sleeping in the parks now, all sorts of people, thin ragged blankets pulled round them, and the police letting them stay there. The priest says the church house and the annexe are full to bursting now with the homeless from our parish. And many more expected once the weather turns cold. Sadie's been handing out more food through the kitchen gate than we serve in the hotel, and a good number of the men you see gathered in my bar of an evening don't have a penny in their pockets. I pretend to keep a careful tab of their drinks but I know it's useless. There'll be no miracles coming soon for Ireland.'

'Nor any place else,' Jack said. 'I've talked to seamen just come home from New York or Hamburg or Marseilles, and things are no better there, they tell me. No jobs to be had and people lining up outside churches or soup kitchens waiting for whatever they can get to line their stomachs.'

'Where does it end, Jack?'

'If you've been reading about that fat clown in Italy or the chap with a Charlie Chaplin moustache who's yelling and screaming to the German people, getting them stirred up against the Jews and the English and the French and anybody else he can think of, you probably think, as I do, that we're sure to have a bloody war again.'

'It's an ugly thought. We've only had peace for sixteen years.'

'Every twenty years, they say, somebody finds reason to start a war. Then the young men who are sleeping in St Stephen's Green and all the other parks will be killed in the trenches.'

'No trenches this time, they say. Aeroplanes and motor vehicles. Faster ways to die, they've found.'

'We'll have to die at home,' Jack said. 'We're too long in the tooth for this one.'

'For the last one, too, they told us. Only fit for home duty. And all the while we were aching to fight and do our bit.'

'The Lord was watching over you, Neal. Otherwise you'd be lying in the Argonne Forest long since with pretty French jonquils blooming over you.'

'Like I said, we've got the luck, the two of us. I sit in the kitchen there in the hotel with my children and the little ones all round me, and Sadie ruling the roost telling us how to behave, and I think to myself, "Somebody's looking after me, and thank God for that." '

'It's Sadie. She's the one looking after you. The priest and the man in the sky saw through you long ago.'

Bratton shook his head. 'You were an altar-boy just as I was. How you turned out to be a heathen atheist is a mystery to me.'

'I'm not an atheist. I'm not even an agnostic. I'm just withholding judgement.'

'It's blasphemy, Jack. You're at it again. Let's have another pint, you godless bastard, before a bolt comes down on you and takes me as well.' He signalled to the barman.

Brannigan grinned and put a hand on his shoulder. 'You've got it all twisted round, Neal. When we give up the ghost, you and me, we'll be going to the same destination. Only you'll march through the main gate where the harps are playing and I'll be sneaking in the back way along with the kitchen staff.'

'God help us, you may be right. It's like I started to say before: while half the world goes to bed hungry and good men hang themselves in desperation from the rafters in the cow barn, you poke about here and there with your bloody camera, taking pictures of painted doors and old men without teeth, and people pay you decent money to do it. Then you hop in your caravan and journey back to your fine house in Northumberland where that handsome woman is waiting for you. If I weren't such a fortunate man myself I'd envy you.'

The day before Jack was to leave for England, after he'd completed his assignment, he and Bratton walked along the paths of St Stephen's Green and sat down at last on a bench by the pond where the swans were swimming. 'Last night Sadie asked me about your fine new wife and I didn't have a thing to tell her. I'm not nosing into your affairs, Jack, but do you realize you haven't made a single mention of her since you've been here?'

'No. I didn't realize that.'

'God help us, you are going home, aren't you? You're not about to tell me you've had the shortest marriage in history, are you?'

'I wasn't about to tell you anything. That's why I said nothing.'

'I'm not sure what that means,' Neal said, 'but all the same I don't like the sound of it.'

'It won't be the shortest marriage in history. I assure you of that. If it's left to me I'll never leave her till the pennies kiss my eyelids. But all the same . . .'

'Ahhh . . . now it's coming.'

'Not what you think,' Jack said. 'You met her, Neal. And Sadie did as well. The first time I brought her to Ireland. You saw the quality of her at once, just as I did. As soon as I laid eyes on her. It's there for anyone to see. And if I told you she's ten times the woman she seems to be, I wouldn't be lying to you. I'm not about to squeeze out a tear or two, slobber on my necktie and tell you I've married a woman who's too good for me, but all the same I can't get it out of my head that I'm a disappointment to her. Not as a man. I don't mean that. And not as a husband. I treat her like the treasure she is and she treats me the same. But still I can't help feeling uneasy. You've seen the pictures I took of her house. You know the kind of place it is . . . like a second home for the Queen. But

I'm a misfit there, Neal. Like a visitor from the bogs. When we went there after we were married and I was standing in the great hall looking about, she said, "Don't fret about this place. It's not a museum or a palace. It's just a place to live. And it's yours now as much as mine. You needn't adjust to it. We'll let it adjust to you." Pretty words. And she meant them, I don't question that. And she feels that way still. But it's not so simple for me. I walk through those rooms and corridors and see myself in those gold-framed mirrors that are ten metres high, and I think, "This bloke must be looking for the kitchen. Looks like he was sent by the butcher to deliver a joint of mutton."'

'Come off it, Jack. I can't believe what I'm hearing. I've never seen you in a spot where you didn't feel at home. Sadie says you're never seen a stranger. If you ask my advice, I'd tell you to squander a bit of money on some decent clothes. There's no law that says you have to go on wearing baggy corduroy trousers and your old tweed jackets with patches on the elbows. Freshen up the label, man. You've stepped up in class. You have to dress for it. That's why those tailors make so much money. They take blokes like us, strip us down to our underclothes, measure all our extremities, and the next thing you know, we're togged up and looking like proper gentlemen.'

'It's not that easy. After I'd met a few of Margaret's friends, after they'd looked down their noses at me and sniffed at me like I was the tinker's dog, I decided I'd better get some new togs. Even sneaked off to Carlisle one afternoon and had some measurements done. When I took off my pants and jacket the bloody tailor stared at them like they were the burial garments of a leper. Then he looked me over and said, "I assume you'll want to order some proper undergarments as well. And we'll furnish you with a decent bootmaker."'

'I lay in my bed that night and thought about what I was doing and the next morning, first thing, I drove over to Carlisle again. I went to that candy-ass tailor and cancelled the order I'd made the day before. If he didn't like it I told him he could kiss my bum.'

'Good for you.'

'I'd decided the night before that if I was going to be a misfit I might as well be dressed for it, in my own clothes. I could have twenty new suits of clothes and I still wouldn't look right to certain people.'

'So to hell with them. That's what I say.'

'And I say the same thing. But I feel bad for Maggie.'

'You're daft, Jack. Does she feel sorry for herself? Is she trying to make you over into a fox-chaser who talks through his nose? Does she walk round with a long face?'

Brannigan shook his head. 'That's not her way of doing things. If she was unhappy I'd never know about it.'

'You're getting old, Jack. Your brain's starting to go soft. When a woman's unhappy, her poor sod of a husband is the first one to know. Sadie says that's why most women get married. So there'll be somebody round the house to take the blame.'

'Not Maggie. She takes all the blame to herself.'

'Then stop punishing yourself and count your blessings, you damned fool. Ever since you got here I've been telling you what a lucky bastard you are so don't make a liar out of me by crying on my shoulder. I'm ashamed of you. Half the people in the world are on their ass, not knowing where their next meal is coming from, and you're sitting here with a belly full of beer and a fat cigar in your mouth worrying about being an embarrassment to your wife. All wives are embarrassed by their husbands, so why would you be the exception? I guarantee you, if the time comes when Margaret doesn't want you hanging round, you'll be the first to know.'

359

Kincaid and Sophie sat silent as they finished their dinner. At last she said, 'Let's have our coffee in the library. It's easier to talk there.'

'I think we've talked enough already.'

'No, we haven't. You're upset. And so was I a moment ago. It's important for us to understand each other. And that's impossible unless we talk. We mustn't have a silly fight about this.'

When they were sitting in the library she said, 'You're right. The reason we made this move to California was so you and I could be together and have some sort of normal life while you're working. And you certainly made it easier for me by building this marvellous house. I'm delighted with the way things have worked out here. We have a good staff, Sarah and Trevor are settled in and doing well in their classes, and I have more than enough to occupy me. I've accepted a situation I never thought I could – that we would have a permanent place to live in California whenever you came here to work. But now, just when things are organized and going smoothly, you want us to pick up everything and move to Chicago.'

'Not exactly. I'm talking about the two of us going to Chicago. No servants, no pets, no children. Just you and me.'

'Don't you think I'd love to do that? I hate the thought of my being here and your being half-way across this monstrous country for weeks. Months maybe. You don't know how long you'll be gone, do you?'

'It's a tough schedule. We hope to be back the end of October but it could be mid-November. It depends on how many interiors we're able to shoot on location.'

'That's what I mean. It could be ten or eleven weeks.'

'Exactly. That's why I want you to come with me.'

'And that's why I can't come. We're looking through opposite ends of the telescope on this. Don't misunderstand me. I love it that you want me along. But this house can't run itself . . .'

'Of course it can. Oliver and Mrs O'Haver are running it now and they'll continue to if you're away.'

'I wish that were true but it doesn't work that way. Staff function well when the head of the house is in residence. Not so well when they're left to themselves. Can you imagine making a film without a director?'

'For Christ's sake, Sophie, we're not talking about the movies.'

'You're really angry, aren't you?'

'No. I'm mystified. The reason you're in America is so you and I don't have to be separated the way we were last year. Now it turns out we're going to be separated anyway.'

'But that's not my fault,' Sophie said. 'You don't blame me for that, do you?'

'I don't blame anybody. This isn't a court-room. I just thought we'd worked things out but you say we haven't.'

'That's not fair, darling, and you know it. This isn't a contest. I'm not castigating you because you have to go off on location. You must go. I know that. It's your work, your responsibility. But I'm trying to make you see that I have responsibilities, too. And it's not just this house. Perhaps it would go along all right for a few weeks. But I simply can't pop off and leave Trevor and Sarah in limbo.'

'They're not in limbo. We've only seen Sarah once or twice since she went off to Ojai and Trevor's so fully occupied we're lucky if we see him once a day.'

'That's true. But they depend on my being here even when they don't see me. Children don't mind at all if they're too busy to spend time with their mother but they become very cross and unsettled if the situation's reversed, if Mummy is suddenly not available for them. Also, it's not just the children. Let's be honest about it. When Tim Garrigus was here the other night he and I talked a great deal about location problems. He gave me quite an education on the subject. He said you people would be in good hotels for as long as you're in Chicago. But after that, when you're following Dillinger's trail through Indiana and Illinois and Wisconsin, you'll be living in whatever accommodation is available. Country hotels and rooming-houses. And staying only two or three days in each place. You'll be up at six in the morning, into the car, and gone for the day. Home in time for dinner perhaps, if the day's location is not too far from where you slept the night before or where you'll be sleeping that night. He says it's like fighting a war, and I say that's no place for wives. By that I don't mean that I can't survive a bit of inconvenience and discomfort. I'd be happy to if it meant we'd be together.'

'I'd be back every night. We'd have that time.'

'I know that. That's what makes it so difficult to be rational about the other fourteen or sixteen hours in the day. But we have to be. What in the world would I do with myself, sitting in some strange bedroom all day? Also, you can't convince me that it wouldn't be a distraction for you. As you're trying to do your work I'd hate it if you had to think of me all the time. If you had to wonder if I was warm enough or if I'd been able to find a decent place to have lunch. Have I painted an accurate picture of what the life will be like?'

'I can't tell you. I've never seen that part of the country. I don't know what to expect.'

'But you know the location routine. Tell me this: if I'd been here when you made *Bushranger* would you have wanted to have me with you on location?'

'I'd have wanted you to be there,' he said, 'but it wouldn't have worked. It was too rough. Dust and dirt and sleeping in trailers. But this time it won't be like that.'

'Garrigus said it could be worse. At least you had nice California weather for *Bushranger*. In the Midwest where you're going now he says the weather can be cold and brutal from October on.'

'Look, you make a hell of a case. Sounds like it was all laid out by a barrister. For months you said it didn't make sense for you to come to California. Now you're saying it doesn't make sense for you to come with me to Chicago.'

'It doesn't make sense. You have to admit it.'

'Who says it has to make sense? I don't care if it makes sense. Your father said it didn't make sense for us to get married. But we're married, aren't we?'

She got up from her chair then, came over and sank down on the floor by his chair. She put her arms round his legs and rested her cheek against his knee. 'I feel so rotten about this,' she said. 'I told you I don't want us to fight about it, and I meant that. I'm just trying to sort out what's best for everybody, trying to use my poor brain. If you say I must come with you I'll come. You know that. And I won't be a baby about it. I promise you. I'll take along a bag of books and my woollies, and everything will work out. I'll be a darling wife who doesn't complain and everyone will envy you.'

He put his hand on the soft waves of her hair. 'Too late for that,' he said. 'Everyone knows you're a shrew and nobody envies me at all.' He felt the weight of her head and the warmth of her cheek against his leg as they sat there silent in the dim light of the library with the logs burning low in the fireplace. They felt drowsy and connected and very permanent but they both knew she wouldn't be going with him to Chicago.

5

Margaret came home from her trip to London and from her visit with Clara Causey several days before Brannigan was due back from Dublin. Her first day at home she sat at her desk in the morning-room and wrote to Sophie. She told her in some detail about her meeting with Tremont and their decision to put the protective order in motion. She also told her as much as she knew about Brannigan's talk with Cranston, and went into some detail about her concerns and trepidations relative to Cranston and his volatile behaviour.

She made no reference whatsoever to the extended dialogue between Clara and herself about Brannigan. It had been one thing to examine it slowly in Clara's empathetic presence, quite another to try to clarify matters that were persistently unclear in a letter to her daughter. Her decision for silence was not simply a choice of secrecy. Nor was it specifically related to Sophie. After her long and involved dissection of matters with Clara some instinct told her that enough had been said. She didn't regret discussing it with Clara but she felt displeased with herself all the same, as though her words had put her at risk, as though she had objectified and crystallized, made permanent perhaps, a perceived condition that would vanish if left to itself.

There was another matter, however, that she was eager to pass along to her daughter. She had also planned to share it with Clara, but after the discussions about Cranston and Brannigan the story of her meeting with Arthur Tagg in London seemed cruel, somehow, like an addendum, an afterthought, spoken at a graveside. But she told that story now to Sophie.

I saw Arthur Tagg in London. Quite by chance. As I've told you, I've heard nothing from him since he left the Towers. Nor has he communicated with John Trout, Mrs Whitson, or anyone else on the staff. At first I was very concerned. Then I found myself getting angry. Whatever his feelings may have been on leaving, there ought to be some *politesse*, I told myself, some acknowledgement of the fact that he had shared a substantial portion of his adult years here with us. I began to feel like an abandoned pet, a summer cat left to her own devices after a London family packs up and returns to the city.

I did not seek him out, however. I made no plans to find him when I was in London. And even if I had I'm sure I would never have been able to locate him. He's left Evan's flat, you see, and has set up house in a bed-sitter, address unknown to me, but somewhere in the vicinity of Holland Park.

After lunch with Sir Charles in St James's Square my head was ringing with legalese, complications, implications, and two glasses of lovely Bordeaux, so I decided to walk back to Brown's. It was a soft summer afternoon; the pavement was not crowded. I turned into Jermyn Street, bought an expensive silk cravat for Jack, then walked up St James's to Piccadilly. As I waited there for the light to change a bus marked Kensington Road stopped at the kerb just in front of me. I stepped on it, like a schoolgirl on a lark, and when the conductor came to me I said 'Kensington High Street Station.' I had a vague notion that I would walk back through Kensington Gardens and Hyde Park to Park Lane, then find a taxi to take me to my hotel.

It was a pleasant bus-ride. I took a front seat on the upper deck and drank in the details of the streets as we sped along. By the time we reached my stop, however, I had lost my enthusiasm for a long hike through the park. So I crossed Kensington High Street and strolled along looking in windows and occasionally glancing about for a taxi.

I came to a bookstore then, very traditional, fine old leather-bound books displayed in the window. So I went in. A gentleman came forward to help me, and it was Arthur.

I was surprised, of course. He was the last person I had expected to see. But the sensation was more profound than that. It was a pleasantly warm day and I had been walking but all at once I felt chilled and my hands went damp and cold. And Arthur's face, poor man, went quite red. In the years we have known him I had never seen him blush before.

How can I tell you what this meeting was like? I can only say that it was a very unsettling few moments. I'm not sure how long I was inside the bookshop. It was not long. Nor do I remember the precise words that were exchanged between the two of us. But till the day I die I'll never forget the first thing he said to me. After we'd unquestionably recognized each other he said, 'Is there some particular book I might find for you?'

In a sort of nervous monologue after that I asked him why we hadn't heard from him, what news he'd had from Evan, how long he'd been working there. Then I told him you'd gone off to California with Kincaid and the children, and that all the staff at the Towers were keen to have some word from him. Then I picked up a book from a stack in the centre of the room and bought it without looking at the title. As I prepared to leave I asked if we might know his London address and telephone number and he gave me a card with those of the shop. I asked him then, shameless hussy, if he could join me for tea at Brown's when he left work. He said no, he could not because he had to stay on that evening. When I suggested that he join me later for supper he said that, too, was impossible. Continuing to humiliate myself, I said that I would be in London the following day and if there was any time when he might be free . . . He said he was sorry but he would be in Golders Green for the entire day. A book fair of some sort.

I actually stumbled as I left the bookshop. I felt

as though I'd witnessed a traffic accident or had seen a dog run over by a lorry. Thank God I found a taxi just at the kerb. When I got in and told the driver where to take me he said, 'Are you feeling all right then, mum?' I must have been as grey as the street. I slumped back in the seat and wept like a child, all the way to the hotel.

If this sounds like a tale from a demented woman, that's precisely how I felt when I was alone in my hotel room. I drew a warm bath and sat in it for a long time, trying to relax and trying to understand those strange and painful few minutes with Arthur.

I'm still trying, Sophie. If I ran into you in the street and you pretended not to know me, I could not be more stunned than I am now. If he'd been angry or insulting or vengeful it would have destroyed me. I would have asked myself what I'd done to deserve such treatment. But I could have dealt with it somehow. This, however, was much worse. When a friend of more than twenty years, a dear friend you have worked with, lived in the same house with, someone you've respected and admired and loved and treated always with kindness and affection and consideration, someone who has quite literally shared a vital portion of your life, when that person looks at you one day with only the slightest spark of recognition, more accurately when he looks at you as though you were invisible, as though you were *dead*, how can you understand or accept or endure that experience? I don't know the answer to those questions. I'm simply doing the best I can.

6

Before Kincaid left for Chicago, Sophie decided she would like to have a dinner-party for the family. 'On your last night here,' she said. 'Sarah will come down from Ojai, I'll capture Trevor and see that he has a good wash, and I thought I'd invite Evan. How does that sound?'

'I thought you'd want to drive me up to Oxnard to a low hotel and lock me in a bedroom for three days.'

'I'd love it. Let's do that instead.'

'We'll compromise,' he said. 'I'll keep you in our bedroom upstairs those three days. Then on that last evening we'll have Oliver help us down the stairs so we can have dinner with Evan and your kids.'

'How lovely,' she said. 'That's what we'll do. And if you want some of your chums from the studio to come to dinner we'll ask them, too.'

Kincaid shook his head. 'I'll see enough of those clowns for the next few months.'

When Sophie rang up her daughter to tell her about the dinner-party Sarah was delighted. 'We'll have a feast,' she said, 'with lots of champagne. You and I will wear long gowns and the men will wear tuxedos.'

It became a festive occasion indeed. Crystal and silver and great banks of flickering candles. Bowls of flowers on every table and sideboard in the dining-hall. Before dinner they drank champagne in the music-room and Trevor, looking splendid and suddenly quite tall and lean and grown-up, lifted his glass and said, 'I propose a toast to all of us and to our first family party in Towers West. As Tiny Tim said, "God bless us every one." '

It was an evening of jokes and stories and anecdotes, laughter and singing and hilarity. Sarah did impersonations of all three of the Barrymores, Trevor sang risqué songs he'd learned at St Alban's, Kincaid told outrageous tales about seamen and prison guards and cattle stations, and Evan repeated every backstage story he'd ever heard, while Sophie orchestrated and conducted the entire evening.

They left the table and the dining-hall at last like a

troop of children rushing for the Christmas tree. 'And now,' Evan had announced as they were about to get up from table, 'we will have the event of the season. The great Kincaid will play a championship billiard match with his always dangerous challenger, Trevor Black, starting almost at once in the billiard-room. Best two out of three. The loser must polish the winner's boots each Saturday for three months.'

After the first match, won by Kincaid, Evan was sent to the library to fetch the cognac decanter and Sophie trailed along after him. 'Let's sit down for a minute. I've had a letter from Margaret about your father and I think you should know about it.'

After he delivered the cognac to Kincaid in the billiard-room Evan came back to Sophie. 'No bad news, Sophie. Mustn't spoil such a triumphant evening.'

'Arthur is apparently in fine health if that's what you mean, so there's certainly nothing to fret about in that area. But mother has seen him and she . . . perhaps you've had a recent letter from him.'

'I have actually. Ten days or two weeks ago, I expect.'

'Did he mention that he'd seen Margaret?'

'I don't believe he did.'

'He must have written you before he saw her in his bookshop.'

'Oh, she found him there, did she?'

Sophie nodded. 'But quite by chance.' She told him then, about the contents of her mother's letter. Without going into detail about her mother's feelings, she did say that Margaret had been upset by Arthur's behaviour. 'She said he treated her as though she were an absolute stranger. Not a handshake, not an embrace, not even a smile. At least that's the impression she gave me in her letter. Doesn't that seem strange to you?'

'You know Arthur as well as I do. No one ever accused him of being demonstrative.'

369

'But for the love of God, Evan, he has feelings, doesn't he?'

'I'm sure he does. But he manages not to show them.'

'But Margaret isn't a casual acquaintance. She's . . . I don't know what sort of label I'd put on their friendship – you and I have discussed this many times – but it was certainly real. And valuable to both of them. Now he seems to have forgotten she exists.'

'I expect he just wants to give that impression.'

'But why would he do that?' Sophie asked.

'It's human nature, isn't it? When your life makes a sharp turn, when you lose something or give it up, sometimes it makes things easier if you tell yourself you never had it in the first place.'

'But he was standing there talking to her, just as you and I are talking now. She told him she'd like to see him, for tea or for dinner, whenever he was free, and he made no response. He treated her like any other customer who'd walked in from the street. Can you explain that?'

'No, I can't. But it doesn't surprise me. I have great difficulty explaining my own actions sometimes.'

'You really don't want to discuss this, do you?'

'I can't discuss it. Not in a sensible way. Because I can't look into my father's brain or his heart any more than you can see inside Margaret. It seems to me the critical change took place in stages. When your mother broke up with your father – that was number one; then she found Jack Brannigan; and when Arthur packed up and moved to London, that was the third act curtain. I can't imagine that Margaret didn't see that and accept it. Big decisions were being made all round. Major adjustments. Your mother's a bright woman. I'm sure she didn't expect that things would toddle along just as they had before.'

'You think Arthur hates her now?'

'I'd be surprised if he does. But it's possible, I suppose. Since I've never known how he felt about her, it's impossible for me to know how he feels now. But as I said, when circumstances change many other things change as well.'

'I must say, you seem dreadfully matter-of-fact about all this. Do you know something you're not telling me?'

Evan smiled. 'Of course. I know all sorts of things you don't know. But not about Margaret and my dad. I know almost nothing about them and neither do you.'

'That's not true. I feel as if I know everything about them. At least the important things. And when I hear what I've just heard from Margaret, that he treated her like a stranger after all the years . . . I don't know what to say. I find it terribly upsetting. Did he say anything in his letter to you?'

'About Margaret?'

'About anything. Did he seem different or bitter or upset about his life?'

Evan shook his head. 'As a matter of fact, in some way it was the best letter I've ever had from him. He seemed to be saying that he's discovered at last that there are things in the world that can't be conjugated or categorized or worked out by logarithms. It always seemed to me that he was determined never to make a mistake. Now I think he feels differently.'

'Did he say he'd made a mistake? Do you think he wants to go back to the Towers?'

'No. He didn't say that at all. I just got the idea that he's stopped looking for guarantees, that he's starting to live one day at a time.'

'I don't see what connection that has with the way he treated Margaret.'

'I don't either. But there may be a connection in his mind.'

She sipped her brandy then and studied him over the rim of her glass. 'Time slips by, doesn't it? It occurs to me that you and I have seen very little of each other the past year or two.'

'I've been here in America quite a lot.'

'You seem quite philosophical about the changes in Arthur's life. How do you feel about yours? Have you also changed a great deal?'

He smiled. 'I don't keep a close watch on myself. No bureau of weights and measures. You're probably a better judge of all that than I am. What do you think?'

'As I said, I haven't seen you much . . .'

'Therefore . . .' he said.

'Let me put it this way. Ever since I met you when I was ten years old, even when we were having our childhood wars, I've always felt that if I were up against the wall, if I was in any sort of trouble, the person who'd be most likely to help me out, to share the risk, to stand in the rain with me and get wet, was you. There was nothing mawkish or sentimental about it. It was just a strong feeling left over from my childhood.'

'And now?'

Sophie laughed softly. 'You think I'm going to drop a fire-bomb on you, don't you? Well, I'm not. You seem to be saying that change is inevitable, that it's all out of our hands. I can't go along with that. Certain things in me will never change. Not if I can help it. I don't believe in love that stops. If I care about someone they're not required to pass muster once a year. When you're inside the enclosure, you're in for good. You know what I'm saying?'

'Exactly.'

'But I won't lie to you. As we've been talking these past few minutes I felt a pronounced chill in the room. The thing I remember most about growing up with you is that we cared about everything. Animals and birds and ideas and plants and people. We were angry little brats. We saw cruelty and carelessness and injustice everywhere we looked. And we raged against it. We detested the people who didn't notice or didn't care, people who said, "That's life. That's the way things are. Some things can't be fixed." You used to say, "That's not life. That's not

the way things are. There's nothing that can't be fixed."
How do you feel about that now?'

'Same as I did then.'

'I'm glad to hear you say that. I'm not stupid and I'm not a child. I know it's a pragmatic world. And you're working and living in the pragmatic centre of it. But it would really wreck me if I said to you one day, "You've turned into a pragmatic bastard," and you just smiled and said, "That's the way it is. Everybody changes." Do you think that's likely to happen?'

'I certainly hope not,' he said, 'but I guess we won't know for sure till you call me a pragmatic bastard. You think that's likely to happen soon?'

'No.'

'Good.'

Trevor won two out of three in his billiard tournament with Kincaid.

'I think he let you win,' Sarah said.

'Did you let me win?' Trevor said to Kincaid.

'Not a chance. You know me. I hate to lose. So from now on we play snooker. I'm a killer at snooker.'

'You're a killer at billiards, too,' Trevor said. 'I think you did let me win.'

Kincaid grinned and shook his head. 'Where I come from, if you throw a match, if you let the other bloke win to set him up for the kill later on, they break a cue over your head. I've known pool hustlers in Hobart who had knobs all over their skulls.' He bent his head down in front of Trevor. 'Take a good look, sport. You won't find any bumps on my noggin.'

When Evan said good-night to everyone and went out to his car, Sarah walked along with him.

'You look great tonight,' he said. 'Like the rich women of Lisbon. A sleek black gown and your hair pulled back in a bun.'

'Least is best,' she said. 'Isn't that the way of it?'

'Sometimes.'

'Most times. I'm learning a lot, you see. Like a sponge. Soaking up all sorts of things. Watching people. Listening. Using my head. Learning patience. Learning the laws of the theatre. Of performing. You mustn't force yourself on the audience. They want to discover you. They want to come to you. You must allow them to do it. Am I right?'

'Of course you are. I'm impressed. But still it's not an easy thing to do.'

'I know that. But it's getting easier all the time. I never stop practising. I have a sign up in my room at school: JUST BE THERE. Nobody taught me that. I discovered it for myself.'

'I told you, I'm very impressed.'

'Good. I'm glad. That means I'm doing the right thing. I'm sure you've noticed that I've changed my attitude toward you as well.'

'Oh . . . how's that?'

'You know what I'm talking about. I've stopped chasing after you. For now I'm concentrating on my work. I'm learning to live inside myself. Meanwhile, I'll see you when you're around, when you come to the house, but more important, you'll see me. You already know how I feel about you so I don't have to keep telling you. And I won't be coming to your house at night, begging you to go to bed with me. I'll just be going ahead with my life, learning things about myself, making myself as beautiful as I know how, and finally, when I'm seventeen or eighteen, you'll discover me. It will probably come as a big surprise to you. I know what I'm like underneath this plain black dress and when the time comes you'll know too. Then you'll kick yourself for wasting time with all those other naughty ladies.'

She kissed him on the cheek. Then she turned and walked across the stone driveway to the house.

· CHAPTER 10 ·

1

As soon as he found out he'd be leaving for Chicago sooner than planned, Evan called his mother and arranged to meet her for lunch the next day. 'Musso's at twelve-thirty,' he said. 'This time it's my treat.'

'I was a little worried after you called yesterday,' she said. They were sitting in the front booth by a window looking out on Hollywood Boulevard. 'You seemed to be in such a hurry. I thought maybe you were in some sort of a mess.'

Evan smiled. 'It seems as if I'm always in a hurry these past few weeks. But I'm not in a mess.' He explained to her then the situation with the Dillinger film. The production meeting with Thorne had taken place just the day before. 'So now we're all working long hours and getting ready to leave for Chicago. I wanted to make sure I'd see you before I left so that's why everything seemed in a rush when I called yesterday.'

'It was funny you telephoned when you did because I was just about to call you at the studio. How long will you be in Chicago?'

'Three or four weeks I expect. Then we'll be on the move around the Midwest for a couple more months. If everything works out we'll be back here sometime in November to wrap the picture.'

'Chicago,' she said. 'That brings back some memories, doesn't it?'

Evan nodded. 'I'm anxious to see the place again. We'll be staying at the Drake. Just a few blocks from where we used to live.'

'I loved that neighbourhood. I suppose it's changed a lot by now. I used to take you over to the lakeside in your baby carriage and sit there for hours looking out at the water. And on weekends in the summer, Arthur and I took you to Oak Street beach so you could crawl around in the sand. You were always brown as a berry in the summer.'

They ordered sauerbraten and potato pancakes for lunch. While they ate she encouraged him to talk about his work; she sat silent for the most part and listened. At last, however, as they were having coffee, she said, 'When I wrote you those two letters I promised myself I wouldn't get all serious and down in the mouth about things that happened a long time ago. And when we had lunch the first time I felt the same way. Let bygones be bygones and all that. But yesterday, after I talked to you on the phone, I had a change of heart. I thought, my God, we can't just pretend that everything that happened didn't happen. Suddenly I wanted you to know something about me, where I came from, how things were between me and your father. But maybe you know all you want to know. Maybe you've already made up your mind about everything. I'm sure Arthur doesn't have a high opinion of me and he can't be blamed for that. So if you feel the same way he does . . .'

'I'm not sure how he feels. I know you two broke up when I was not very old but I was too little to remember much about it.'

'He never talked about me? Never showed you snapshots we took on the beach or in the park in the summer?'

Evan shook his head. 'Until we met for lunch not long ago I had no idea what you looked like. If he had photographs they must have been lost when we went back to England.'

She stirred her coffee slowly, looking intently at her cup as she did it. Finally she said, 'I guess I know how he feels. If somebody did to me what I did to him I know how I'd feel.' She looked up then. 'So maybe he was right. Maybe it's better just to leave things as they are. You're grown up now and you're making a good life for yourself so what's to be gained by dragging up the past? I just like being able to see you like this and you don't seem to be holding any grudges against me so why look for trouble. Am I right?'

'I don't know. It depends on how you feel about things.'

She smiled. 'That's the problem. I have mixed-up feelings. I don't want to take the risk of having you turn against me. And at the same time, if we like each other, and if we have a chance to see each other and sit and talk like this every so often, it doesn't seem right if we have to steer clear of certain subjects, if we have to pretend that things are one way when the truth is they may be some other way altogether.'

She sipped from her coffee-cup. 'I guess it sounds as if I want to tell my side of things so you'll think it wasn't all my fault because Arthur and I split up the way we did?'

'There's nothing wrong with wanting to tell your side of it, is there?'

'Maybe not. But that's not what I'm thinking about. Because it was my fault. I'm to blame for what I did and I'm to blame for the way I did it. In a way I'm afraid to tell you the way things were, especially since it seems that Arthur never told you much of anything, but I don't feel right about not telling you either. I think it's a part of your life you have a right to know about. I was your mother and then I stopped being your mother. I've never been able to explain to myself exactly how that happened. But I feel as if I have to try to explain it to you. Does that make any sense?'

'Of course it does.' He signalled to the waiter for more coffee.

'Where shall I begin?' she said. 'I won't give you my entire family history. There isn't much to tell in any case. My family name is Wheaton. W-H-E-A-T-O-N. Both my parents were from France, from a tiny village in Vaucluse called Venasque. My father's name was Emile Huiton but the spelling was changed by the immigration officer when they arrived in New York. My father was the chef in a famous restaurant in Lyon until a wealthy American came there one day and persuaded him to come to America, to work at a restaurant in New York. So that's where I was born and grew up. My father was very successful. He went from one fine restaurant to another, to whatever place offered the most money. We lived in a beautiful apartment in Abingdon Square and I went to day-school at a convent not far from our home. My parents were fanatic Catholics. My mother had intended to be a nun until she met my father, and I'm sure she thought that's where I would end up. But it didn't work out that way. When I was seventeen I met a boy named Dieter Brock, whose father taught German at Columbia University. They lived on Hudson Street, not far from my parent's building, and Dieter worked in a candy-store on Sheridan Square after school. He was eighteen, very handsome, and he said funny things and sang songs all the time. The girls from my school stopped in there every day to buy candy and chewing-gum, and to stare at Dieter. I was too timid even to look at him but he wasn't timid at all. The next thing I knew I was meeting him secretly on Saturday and Sunday afternoons. We went to Central Park together or took the ferry to Staten Island. We were desperately in love. From the beginning all we talked about was getting married. He took me to meet his parents and his sister, Ona, and they were very nice to me. Then somehow my parents found out what I'd been doing. My father gave me a terrible lecture about Germans and

Germany and the Lutheran Church, and my mother said, "If you marry outside the Church your father and I will never lay eyes on you again."

'From then on my father took me to school every morning in his carriage and Mother came to fetch me in the afternoon. I was not allowed to leave the house in the evening or at weekends. But my best friend, Mildred, took notes from me to Dieter and brought back his notes to me. He told me he was working out a way for us to get married, that he'd met a lawyer from New Jersey who could arrange for the necessary papers, and it would only be a matter of two or three weeks till he would come for me at my school and we would run off together to Atlantic City. It all seems so strange to me as I tell you about it now, like an odd Cinderella story, but at that time, to an innocent cloistered child like me, it was a matter of life and death. I lay awake at night in my bed, I trembled whenever our doorbell rang, and I suffered through the day if there was no note from Dieter. At last one morning in the cloakroom Mildred said, "Dieter will be outside the school at noon, when we start our lunch hour." I don't know how I got past those next three hours. I mumbled and stuttered in my classes and stumbled when I walked. But when the noon bell rang I raced through the corridors, into the basement, and out through the fire exit to the street. He was waiting there in a carriage.'

She smiled faintly and sipped from her coffee-cup. 'It all seems like a tale from another century, doesn't it? And it is, of course. Thirty-five years ago. A different world from today. I knew nothing about life. In the confession booth I was speechless. Since I knew nothing whatsoever about sin, I believed that everything I did or said or even thought was drenched in sin. But on that afternoon as we journeyed by train to Atlantic City I sincerely believed I was going where I was destined to go with a sweet beautiful boy I was meant to be with.

'After our marriage ceremony we stayed in a hotel that night and most of the following day. When we got off the train in New York that evening, my father and Mr Brock were waiting for us. Dieter said, "It's not what you think, Dad. We're married." But my father struck him in the face, took me by the arm and half-dragged me through the station to his carriage. The next morning my mother took me to Baltimore to my aunt's house and ten days later, when we came back to New York, we went directly to the west side docks and boarded a passenger ship. That night we sailed for France. Six months later I met Arthur, a few months later we were married, and the next year you were born.'

'And what became of Dieter?'

'After my mother went back to New York I was left with my father's sister in Neuilly. I was to finish my classes at a school for young women near her home. Some weeks after my mother left I had a letter from Dieter's sister telling me that he had been sent to a university in Buenos Aires. She also said that my father and her father had arranged to have our marriage annulled. I've never seen my parents since that day and we haven't written to each other.

'After I met Arthur when he came to Paris for the Exposition, when we realized we were in love with each other, I left France and went to Chicago, where no one knew me, and your father followed me. We were married there and you were born there, and we expected, Arthur and I, to spend the rest of our lives there. But it wasn't meant to be. When you were three years old, our doorbell rang one afternoon while you were having a nap. I opened the door and Dieter was standing there. He said, "Don't close the door. I have to talk to you."'

'How did he find you?'

'Mildred, my schoolfriend in New York. She was the only person I'd stayed in touch with and I'm sure she believed she was doing me a favour. I guess she couldn't imagine that I wouldn't want to see Dieter. But I didn't want to. And that's what I told him, standing there in the doorway. I told him I was married to a fine man and had a child. I asked him please not to come back, that it would only cause trouble. It was hard for me to be so abrupt with him but there was no other way. I was happy with my life and I didn't want to do anything that would spoil things. It upset me seeing him all of a sudden like that but I never doubted that I'd done the right thing by sending him away.'

'Did you tell Arthur about it?'

'No. I'd never told him about Dieter because it was a closed chapter as far as I was concerned. And I was sure when I shut the door that day that I'd never see him again. But I was wrong. A week later when I was in the park with you he came and sat down on the bench beside me.'

Evan smiled. 'And I was asleep as usual.'

'That's right. You slept through everything. You were always a good sleeper.'

'So he hadn't gone away then?'

Amy shook her head. 'And when he sat there talking to me I understood why. He said our marriage had never been annulled. That the Catholic Church had annulled it simply because we'd never been married in church. But since it was a civil ceremony we were still legally married. That's what he told me that day in the park, and I sat there like a person in shock with my world tumbling down around me.'

'So he wanted you to come back with him?'

'He didn't put it that way at all. He wasn't trying to ruin things for Arthur and me. He said it just wasn't fair for me to think I was married to Arthur when I wasn't. Legally, it made me a bigamist and you an illegitimate child. He told me he wanted to do the decent thing and help me out if he could. He said the two of us could explain the situation to Arthur, and then Dieter and I could be divorced, and Arthur and I could get married

381

again. It all seemed completely logical to Dieter because he didn't know your father. I tried to imagine myself explaining to Arthur that I'd been married before I met him, and that by some oversight I was still married, but if he'd just be patient I could probably be divorced in a few months and then he and I could get married again. It sounds almost funny when I talk about it now but at that time, for days after that talk with Dieter, I was like a crazy woman. Not crying or thrashing around the room. Just sitting in the flat staring at the walls. Or down by the lake with you, gazing out across the water. And every evening I sat through supper with Arthur and we listened to the radio and read the paper and fed you and bathed you and put you to bed and then went to bed ourselves, just as though everything was perfectly normal and peaceful. But all the time I felt as if I was standing at the edge of a cliff with a strong wind blowing. Dieter had said he'd be in Chicago for ten more days. Then he had to leave to go to a job here in California. With every day that went by I got more crazy. A hundred times, I suppose, when we were sitting in the living-room after supper I felt like blurting everything out to Arthur. But I couldn't do it. I was sure that if I told him the truth he'd leave me. I knew he'd hate me for being a different person from the one he'd thought I was. I couldn't decide whether he'd take you with him when he left, or if he'd just go off by himself and never see either one of us again. No matter what happened I knew there was no way out for me. Finally I decided that I would go away myself and take you with me. I'd leave a letter telling Arthur the truth, exactly what Dieter had told me, and then you and I would run off somewhere and start over. I'm sure you can tell by what I'm saying that my mind wasn't working at all. I was stunned and confused by seeing Dieter again. And heart-broken by the things he'd told me and the choices I had to make. I wasn't much more than a child myself then. Twenty-one or twenty-two. Cut off from my parents. No close friends to turn to. I started remembering things the nuns had taught me; it seemed I had earned some sort of divine vengeance, that the happiness I'd found with you and your father was being taken away from me and there was nothing I could do about it. Maybe you'd be better off without me, I thought. Craziness. I see that now. But that's the way my mind was working. You'd be better off with your father than you would be with me. What kind of life could I give you by myself? How would I support you? How would I explain to you when you were older why I'd left Arthur? Every question that I couldn't find an answer to made me more depressed.'

She had met with Dieter the day before he was to leave for California. They sat in the coffee-shop on the street floor of his hotel on Dearborn Street.

'My God, you look awful,' he said. 'Are you sick?'

'I wish I could die. I think I'm losing my mind.'

'I didn't want to ruin things for you. I just thought you should know . . .'

'It's not your fault. Maybe it's not anybody's fault. It's just hopeless,' she said.

'No, it's not. You haven't done anything terrible. He'll understand if you explain it to him.'

'He'll never understand. And I can't explain it to him. I can't do it. I'm going away. It's the only thing I can do. I'm leaving.'

'That's crazy, Amy. That's no answer.'

'I'm not asking for advice, Dieter. I'm telling you what I have to do. Don't make it harder for me than it already is.'

'But you can't just go off without . . . you can't just disappear.'

She started to sob then. 'I can't do anything else. If I stay here I'll mess up everything. I want Evan to have a happy life. He's still a baby. In a few years he won't remember me.'

'I think you're making a mistake.'

'I don't care what you think. I'm doing the only thing I can do. Do you think I like it? I hate it. It makes me sick. But if I stay here I'll kill myself.'

'Where are you going? Do you have any money?'

'I called the train station. I have enough to get to Kansas City,' she said.

'Then what?'

'Then I'll get a job and support myself. Just like everybody else.'

That afternoon when Dieter's train for Los Angeles left the station in Chicago, Amy was in the seat beside him, a ticket to Kansas City in her handbag.

Sitting across from Evan in the booth at Musso's, Amy had tears in her eyes. 'You see,' she said, 'it still hurts. Not the way it did that day and for years after, but it hurts all the same. It always will, I guess.'

'Then you and Dad never talked about it. He never knew why you left?'

'We didn't talk about it but he knew. Before I went to the train station I went back to our flat and left him a letter. I told him I was married to somebody else when I met him and now I was going back to my husband.'

'Was that what you'd decided?'

'No. Nothing like that. But I didn't want Arthur to think I might be coming back. I didn't want him to start looking for me. I thought it was better if everything ended all at once. Maybe I wanted him to hate me. I certainly hated myself. Anyway I lied to him. Told him I was going back to Dieter. Then later the lie came true. I did go back to Dieter. I got off the train all right in Kansas City. I found myself a job and lived in a boarding-house, and every few days I had a letter from San Diego, where Dieter had gone to work. I was miserable in Kansas City. I worked all day six days a week and sat in my room by myself all evening till I went to bed. I had a little picture of you in my gold locket and I looked at it all the time. Then one day the chain must have broken and I lost the

384

locket. When that happened I felt as if my last link with Chicago and you and your father had been broken. I must have said something like that in a letter to Dieter because he wrote back and asked me to come to San Diego. He said, "Maybe you'll start to like me again. If you don't we can get a divorce. No matter what happens you'll be better off than you are now." '

'So you went?'

She nodded. 'And I don't regret it. I'd have gone to pieces if I'd stayed in Kansas City. Every day I spent there I had to fight myself to keep from going back to Chicago. I was desperately lonely. I thought of nothing but you and Arthur, cried myself to sleep and dreamt of our little upstairs flat, spent hours on Sunday, my day off, trying to find some solution, trying to see some way that things could be changed or fixed. But I kept seeing Arthur's face, looking deceived and bewildered and unforgiving, and I knew all over again that there was no going back.'

'And was it better after you went to San Diego?'

'Yes, it was. The simple fact of my leaving Kansas City made it better. The distance made it better. And Dieter did everything a human being could do to turn my life around. He tried to pretend that our parents had never interfered with our marriage, that we had gone on smoothly together. He was determined that we would be a contented married couple like any other. And we were in many ways. But you and your father were always with us. There was no way we could avoid it. We were young and we did all the things that young people do. But inside I felt very old. I hated the feeling but I couldn't shake it. That last day I spent in Chicago wouldn't leave me. When I went out to meet Dieter that morning I left you with a neighbour, a sweet woman who looked after you whenever I had to go on an errand or if Arthur and I went out for an evening together. I left you there that morning, you were sound asleep as usual, and that was the last time I saw you. When I came back a while later to leave a letter for

Arthur, I didn't go next door to see you. I couldn't. But all the same every moment of that last day was tattooed on my brain. At last, several years after I left, I wrote to the neighbour and asked if she knew where you were, you and Arthur. Dieter knew I wrote to her. He encouraged me to do it. But when she wrote back, a cold, two-sentence note without salutation or signature, she said, "Your husband and your child don't live here any more. They went home to England." That was the last news I had of you until I saw your name and your photograph in the Los Angeles paper last year.'

2

When Alfred Bridger of the county police arrived at Wiswell Towers to interview Major Cranston, the Major, in full dress uniform, received him in his upstairs sitting-room. Bridger declined a drink but accepted a cigar, and came directly to the point.

'My office has a great deal of respect for you, Major Cranston, but we have our work to do. Rules and regulations. Proper procedures. I'm sure that as a military man you appreciate all that. The details must be respected.'

'Procedures and details . . . the backbone of any operation. My men had those principles drilled into them.'

'Exactly. Knowing your background, I was sure you'd be co-operative. Do your bit to help us out.'

Cranston wagged his head and cracked his knuckles.

'We've been advised that certain civil papers were sent to you some time ago. These papers required a response but none has been received. I assume you have a solicitor . . .'

'No, I don't. No need for one. I have better uses for my money. Also I've read quite a lot of law myself. A keen eye for the tricky points.'

'Then you must realize you're in violation of a number of court orders.'

'No, I don't acknowledge that.'

'We sent a certain Constable Durham here to talk to you a week ago and you refused to see him. Isn't that correct?'

'If you're referring to that chap in a blue uniform I did not see him. I'm a retired officer, sir. I don't sit down to tea with enlisted men.'

'He was sent here on official business just as I am.'

Cranston smiled. 'We never gave him a chance to state his business. But I'm giving you every opportunity to state yours.'

'Good. Since you don't deny that legal papers have been served to you at this address, let's put aside the legal terms, the dates, and precise violations and go straight to the heart of the situation. When you and Mrs Cranston were divorced recently her solicitor filed an action for trespass against you . . .'

'Bloody ridiculous on the face of it.'

'Since the house is in her name, since you are no longer her husband, since she has remarried and you no longer have right of domicile, the court has ordered you to quit the premises. You ignored that order.'

'It's no damned business of the court where I live.'

'In this case it is. Your wife then asked for and obtained a protective order from the court, demanding that you leave the premises because she believes you represent a physical threat to her.'

'Nonsense. Bloody nonsense.'

'Not at all, Major. This is a matter for the criminal division. Your wife has given a deposition stating that you threatened her life. Two other depositions support her statements.'

'Damned lies. All of it.'

'You have a right to retain counsel and defend yourself. What you do not have a right to do under this order is to remain in this house. You have been given two separate dates for quitting the premises. Both have been ignored. In addition to whatever charges may be brought against you, you are now in contempt of court. As soon as I'm back in my office this afternoon, a final date will be fixed and delivered to you. If that order is ignored by you, a squad of constables will come here and take you into custody.'

'By God, we'll see about that. I'm getting damned tired of this flood of legal papers and empty threats and bullying by petty county officials.' He stood up and stomped across the room to his desk. 'You talk about trespass. You and your like are the trespassers.' He opened his desk drawer, took out a military revolver, and held it in his hand. 'Fully loaded, sir. Protection against vagrants, poachers, and trespassers. In the hands of a trained marksman, and I am certainly that, this piece is a bonafide discouragement against trespass.' He pointed the gun casually toward Bridger. 'If anyone's to be escorted from this house, I'm the one who'll do the escorting.'

'I'm a representative of the law in this county, Major Cranston. I assume you're not threatening me with that revolver.'

'Not threatening you. Showing you off the premises.' He turned and pointed to his gun-cabinets. 'And if you're sending a squad of men to take me into custody I hope you'll warn them that it's a well-armed, well-trained officer they've been sent to fetch.'

Bridger stood up. 'As I said, we've given you every consideration in this matter out of respect for the Wiswell name and your military rank. But now you're forcing us to move quickly and I assure you we will.'

Cranston crossed to the door and opened it, still holding his revolver at the ready till Bridger disappeared down the corridor.

Half an hour later Brannigan joined Margaret in the drawing-room. 'Good news or bad news?' she said.

'Just what we've come to expect, I'm afraid. Mr Bridger

thinks the Major belongs in a clinic.'

'Did he persuade him to leave?'

'Not exactly. The Major produced a revolver and persuaded *him* to leave.'

'Oh my God, what does that mean?'

'It means they'll be sending a squad of men to take him off the premises.'

'Oh, they mustn't do that, Jack. We can't have that.'

'It's not up to us, Maggie. When Bridger reports him as a dangerous man, that's another charge altogether. Has nothing to do with you or me.'

'But I can't sit here and watch a squad of police . . .'

'That's right. And they don't want you to. Bridger will let us know when they're coming and I'll see that you're driven along to Wingate Fields.'

'What an awkward, ridiculous situation. How did I get into such an awful corner?'

Brannigan put his arm round her. 'Because you lost your head over a reckless Irishman. Because you married me.'

3

The day after Thorne arrived in Chicago with Kincaid and Evan, the three of them, along with Tim Garrigus, sat in a top-floor suite looking out across Lake Michigan. It was late in the afternoon. 'I've been on the phone with my brother half the day. Why he's sitting in Hollywood solving problems for me here in Chicago, while I'm running the studio out there by long-distance telephone, is a mystery to me but that's the way it's working out. The good news is that Sam's friends here seem to have made a deal with Sally Wick, the girl Dillinger was with at the Biograph. Sam talked to her on the phone this morning. But it's a tricky situation. The girl's scared to death. Doesn't want to see anybody. Wants to disappear.

Doesn't want her picture in the paper, wants to go back to South Dakota and hide. The police don't want her for anything so she's free to go but she doesn't have a dime. So when Sam talked money with her she caved in. Five grand to talk with us for an hour. Another five if she tells us anything we can use. She could be jerking us around just to get her hands on some travelling money. We all know that.'

'If I talk to her for five minutes,' Garrigus said, 'I'll tell you if she's blowing smoke or not.'

'You're not going to talk to her,' Thorne said. 'Neither am I and neither is Evan. That's the problem. Like I said she doesn't trust anybody she doesn't know.'

'What good does that do us?' Evan said. 'If we can't talk to her . . .'

'Sam tried to lean on her but it didn't do any good. She's staying in an apartment on Fullerton Avenue, upstairs over a candy-store. It's not far from the Biograph. An old Irish lady who runs the store is looking after her. She'll count the money downstairs before anybody goes upstairs to talk to the girl.'

'So who's gonna talk to her?'

'Kincaid,' Thorne said. 'She saw him in *Bushranger* and she thinks he looks like a regular guy. Maybe she thinks he's a hood, like Dillinger, I don't know. Nobody takes notes or pictures, nothing gets written down, and she talks to nobody except the guy who's going to play Dillinger. That's what she told Sam.'

'Maybe she's got a big yen for you, Kincaid,' Garrigus said. 'Give her a tumble over the candy-store and she'll talk like a magpie.'

'That's your specialty, Tim,' Kincaid said. 'Why don't you go and tell her you're me?'

'I'm too good-looking,' Garrigus said. 'Nobody would ever mistake me for an ape like you.'

'How about it, Kincaid?' Thorne said. 'It wasn't my idea. It was hers. I can't force you to do it but it's the only chance we've got to get some inside information. I think it's worth a try.'

'So do I,' Kincaid said.

'Show her my picture, will you?' Garrigus said. 'Once she gets a look at me she'll ditch you at the candy-store and zip down here to the Drake looking for Garrigus.'

'Why don't you come along and wait downstairs in the car?' Kincaid said. 'Then she won't have so far to go.'

'We set it up for three tomorrow afternoon,' Thorne said. 'My driver knows where the place is. He'll take you there and wait for you outside. He's a hard-nose, one of Sam's friends. He'll carry the envelopes. Five grand in each one. After he turns over the first one to the Irish woman she'll take you upstairs to the girl.'

'Who decides if she gets the second five thousand?' Kincaid said.

'You do. We're not trying to chisel her. If she's on the level, if she talks turkey to you, let her have the money. Just give a nod to the driver and he'll turn it over.'

The next afternoon, just before three o'clock, Kincaid stood in the candy-store on Fullerton while Mrs Keeley, the store-keeper, took the packet of bills out of a brown envelope and counted them. When she looked up she said, 'It's all here, all right. My understanding is that there'll be five thousand more after you've talked to the girl.'

Kincaid nodded to the driver and he went back outside. 'That's right,' Kincaid said to the woman. 'The money's in another envelope out in the car. If Miss Wick goes through with her part of the bargain she'll get the full ten thousand.'

'She knows that. She'll talk to you all right. I ain't sure what kind of information you're after but if you're lookin' for a bit of smut you won't get it from Sally. She ain't some kind of a two-bit doxy. She's a good kid. If it was just money she's after she could have made a bundle talking to some of them reporters that's been tryin' to get their hooks on her. But she's having none of that. She don't want her

391

name in the papers. Don't want to see her picture on the front page. That's why she's talking to you people. 'Cause she knows the whole town won't be reading every word she says. The man on the phone guaranteed that.'

As they went up the narrow stairs at the back of the shop, Mrs Keeley said, 'You look like a decent enough guy but I learned a long time ago not to put any faith in the way a man looks. I asked Sally if she wanted me to sit in the room with you two while you talk, but she said no, I should just mind the store downstairs like I always do. But don't let that put any ideas in your head. Any loud noise or commotion and I'll be back up these stairs like a cat. Just 'cause I'm a woman don't think I'm easy-handled. I'm a tough old mick. I can do whatever needs to be done. And right now I'm looking after this young gel you're about to meet. Do we understand each other?' She turned on the landing to face him and Kincaid smiled and nodded his head. 'By my watch it's 3.15. At a quarter after four I'll be leaving.'

Mrs Keeley unlocked the door with a key, swung it open and said, 'Here he is, Sally, that movie fella that wants to talk to you.' When Kincaid stepped through the doorway she pulled the door shut behind him and locked it with a key.

It was a small room with one window looking out on an air-shaft, a sink and a hot-plate in one corner, a single bed against the wall, and two straight chairs. Sally Wick stood on the far side of the room by the bed. She was small, very slender, brown hair cut short, wearing a simple cotton dress, an over-size sweater round her shoulders, and sandals on her feet. As soon as the door clicked shut she looked at Kincaid and said, 'It's really you, ain't it?' She had a light sing-song voice, a country voice. 'I told that man who called me up from California that I wouldn't talk to nobody but you, but I figured they'd try to stick me with somebody else anyhow. I'm accustomed to people saying one thing and doing something else. Have a seat

392

there. Those chairs ain't much but I reckon it beats standing up. I'll just sit here on the day-bed if that's all right with you.'

They sat facing each other for a moment. Finally she said, 'I read *Photoplay* and *Silver Screen* whenever I get the chance and most of the articles say that all you actors look different in person than you do on the screen. Taller or shorter, or your hair a different colour, or something. But anybody who saw you in *Bushranger* would recognize you in a minute. You look just like that part you played. I cried my eyes out when they hung you right at the end and you said something like you knew all along it was bound to happen. Talk about cryin', I thought I'd drown myself. That was the saddest end I ever seen in a movie. The thing is you don't really look like an actor. Does it make you mad if I say that? You look like any other guy that might be tending bar or standing around outside of a pool hall.'

Again she was silent. Then: 'I'm nervous as a chicken. I guess you can tell that. I just rattle on like I been doing when I'm nervous. I thought you'd come in here firing questions at me so you'd be sure to get your money's worth. But so far you haven't said anything to speak of.'

'I'm not much good at this,' Kincaid said. 'I'm not a big talker either. I don't usually ask a lot of questions.' He stood up, turned his chair around and sat on it with his arms resting on the back.

'That's the way my brothers and my dad always straddled a kitchen chair,' she said. 'Country-style. Either that or tilted back against the wall, gettin' brilliantine from their hair on the wallpaper. Round grease-spots like that on every wall in our house in South Dakota.' She pulled her dress down to cover her knees. 'I read in a magazine that you did some time in the pen.'

'That's right.'

'Is that why they picked you to play Ned Kelly? Is that why you're gonna take the part of John Dillinger?'

393

'I don't think so. I don't think that matters one way or the other.'

'It would matter to me,' she said. 'If I was going to make a movie and there was a waitress part in it, I'd look for somebody who knows what it's like to wait on tables. Somebody who could clear four or five places without a tray.'

The expression on her face didn't change but there were tears on her cheeks suddenly. 'I'm sorry,' she said. She went to the sink, rinsed her face with water, and dried it with a towel that hung from a nail in the wall. When she sat down again, on the other chair this time, she said, 'I promised myself I wouldn't do that. But ever since that night it's just been happening to me. All of a sudden I start to bawl like a baby. I hate to do it. My mom said she never saw a kid that cried as seldom as I did. But you know . . . too much has been happening and I can't get caught up with all of it.'

She brushed her hair back with her hand, squared herself on the straight chair and said, 'I didn't forget why you're here. I'll try to tell you everything I know. But if I don't seem to know very much, don't think I'm lying to you. Everything I know about John Dillinger, almost all of it, I read in the papers after he was dead. The man I knew called himself Frank Taylor, like I told the police. I never called him anything but Frank. Agnes Szepy called him Frank, too. Everybody around the neighbourhood called him that. So when we talk about him that's what I have to call him. You know what I'm saying?'

'How long did you know him?'

'Since the beginning of summer. Just before Decoration Day, it was, sometime the last week in May. I'd been in Chicago for six months or so. At first I lived in a little flat on North Avenue with a girl named Opal, who I'd met on the Greyhound bus when I came to Chicago from Yankton. She was from Minnesota, a farm kid like me, trying to get out of the sticks and find out what's going on

394

in the big city. So when we got to Chicago we pooled what little money we had and rented this flat. Opal got a job first thing, working as a barmaid in a German restaurant not far from where we lived. I tried to get a job there myself but they said I was too skinny. So after a week or so I ended up selling tickets at a movie-house on Oak Street. Things went along pretty good for a while. But after three or four months Opal moved out. She said a man she'd met at the restaurant had an apartment he never used on Chestnut Street and he'd offered it to her to live in. She also said she was quitting her job at the restaurant so it wasn't hard to see what was going on, even for a dumb bunny like me. Anyway, I couldn't pay for the flat by myself and I couldn't find a new room-mate so I had to move. The only decent place I could find was a room with a hot-plate like this one, with the toilet down the hall. It was up in this section, on Lincoln. But two days after I moved in I lost my job cashiering. I had a rough couple of months then, moving from one crappy room to another, taking whatever waitress work I could find in restaurants and bars and coffee-shops. If you didn't know it already, I'll tell you now. Nobody wants a waitress around if she doesn't have a big chest. You can be cross-eyed or bow-legged but if you don't stick out in front they don't want you serving beer or handing out coffee.'

'You're a very pretty girl.'

'I'm not crying the blues,' she said. 'I know I'm just as much a woman as anybody else. But when they measure by the pound, I come up a little short. Or with a tape measure, the same thing.'

'How about the other woman who was with you at the Biograph that night? Agnes Szepy. Did you know her before you moved to this neighbourhood?'

'No. But I met her pretty soon afterward. She was a regular at the coffee-shop where I was working so we talked a little whenever I waited on her. And later when I waited tables in a Polish tavern on Glenmont she came in there. Had a ginger brandy every afternoon. Just one good drink and then she'd be gone. She was always dressed up and smelling of nice perfume. She wore pretty clothes. Dark colours mostly. Even in the summer. The only time I ever saw her wear a red dress was that night at the movies with Frank and me.'

'You two became friends then?'

'Not exactly friends. We just knew each other a little. She was always nice to me but she was never what I'd call a friend. She must be old enough to be my mother for one thing. And she's a foreigner. She speaks English all right but it sounds different from an American talking. But like I said, she was always friendly. Once when she knew I was looking for a place to live she offered to rent me a room in her house on Coolidge Street. Four floors she's got there. Room for an army. I was about to take her up on it because it's a nice place and the price was what I could afford. But the fellow I was working for then, a good guy named Dennehy with a family at home and never putting his hands on the waitresses, he told me to steer clear of Agnes's place. He said, "She's always looking for young girls, if you know what I mean. That's her business." And he was right. The only man living in her house was Frank. And that was just temporary, I found out later. Every room at Agnes's had a young woman living in it. And all those girls had a lot of visitors, if you know what I mean. So I turned down her offer but she didn't seem to mind. She was still nice and friendly every time she came into the tavern. I said it was a Polish place because all the customers were Polacks but Dennehy was the man who owned it. And he's a mick. Straight over from Galway.'

'You say Dillinger lived in Agnes Szepy's house?'

'For a while he did. When I first met him. But later on, when me and him was together, we lived in the downstairs of another house that Agnes owned, on Greene Street, just off Parkside. That was the best place I ever lived in my life. A big bathtub like a boat. And a walk-in closet. And we had our own yard with a gate and a fence in back. Frank used to joke about that. He'd say. "In the front and out the back. That's my style. If someone chases me I'm over the back fence and gone." At the time I thought nothing of it. Just a joke. I knew he carried a gun but he said he had to because he was a labour man, a union organizer, and I knew from things I'd seen in South Dakota that could be a rough-neck job. Besides, here in Chicago, I've seen lots of guys with guns bulging under their jackets.'

'How did you meet him?'

'Agnes,' Sally said. 'She came into Dennehy's with him one day and they sat back in a corner. When I went for their order Agnes said, "I brought you a new boyfriend, Sally. He's a hick from Indiana. Likes farm girls." I remember he looked up at me and said, "Agnes talks too much. And she never gets her facts straight. I'm from Kentucky, not Indiana." He held out his hand and said, "I'm Frank Taylor."'

'Did he have a moustache then?'

She nodded. 'He had a moustache from the first time I met him. I thought he was a businessman at first because he always had a good shave and a haircut and he wore a nice suit and a grey fedora hat even in the hot weather. When it was really hot he just wore a vest. But always a white shirt and a tie and that grey hat. You've seen his pictures. He was a good-lookin' fella. Not real tall but he had a good build and he looked swell when he smiled. But he wasn't my type. At least I didn't think so when Agnes came by with him that first time.'

'How about later?'

'Later it was different.' She smiled. 'He came in by himself one night, just when I was getting off work, and he said, "I'm going to the late movie at the Essex. George Raft. You want to come along? I promise not to bite you or steal your shoes." So I thought, what the hell, I'm crazy about George Raft so why not? Besides there was some nutso Italian kid who'd been hanging around pestering me to death so I thought it might cool him off if he saw me with an older guy in a suit like Frank. So we went to the movie and then we had some ice-cream later, and he walked me back to my place and didn't make a pass or try to paw me or anything so that was that, I figured. I didn't see him for about two weeks, then he showed up again and we went to a different movie every night for a week. And we drank coffee in all-night diners and talked a lot. Mostly I talked and he listened. Nobody had ever listened to me that way before. I got so I couldn't wait till I finished work so I could see him and tell him everything I'd been saving up. Then one night he told me he was moving out of Agnes's house and into the apartment on Greene Street. "I know you're a nice decent girl," he said, "but I like you a lot and I'd like you to come live with me if the idea doesn't scare hell out of you." It did scare hell out of me in a way but I did it anyway. And I'd have done it even if I'd known who he was. When I read the articles they've been writing about him since he was killed I don't recognize that guy they're writing about. I know he robbed banks and all that but I don't think he ever killed anybody. Even the guys who ran with him, men in his own gang, say he never killed a man. That's what I read.'

'Do you think Agnes knew who he was?'

'I don't want to talk about her. I'm afraid to.'

'Some of the papers are saying she set him up. They say she wore that dress so Melvin Purvis could spot her and be sure the man with her was Dillinger.'

'I don't know anything about that.'

'Can you tell me if you've talked to her since that night?'

Sally nodded. 'Two days after that she called me. I think they were still holding her for questioning . . . is that what they call it?'

'That's right.'

'Anyway, it seemed like to me there was other people

398

in the room when she was talking to me.'

'Do you want to tell me what she said?'

'She told me to go home to South Dakota and not talk to anybody.'

'What did the police tell you?'

'Pretty much the same thing. But it wasn't the Chicago police. It was a detective from East Chicago named Rostov. He said he was a friend of Agnes.'

'Did the FBI question you?'

'No. I thought they would but they didn't.'

After a long moment Kincaid said, 'Does it scare you to talk to me like this?'

'I said I would and I'm doing it.'

'I know you said you would but nobody's forcing you to. I'm the one who decides if you get the full ten thousand dollars and I've decided. You're going to get it. So if you want to call it off right here, I'll leave you alone.'

'I want to do what I promised.'

'They grow tough ladies in South Dakota, don't they?'

'Sometimes,' she said. 'Not always.'

'I don't know what you were told about this movie we're doing. Did somebody tell you about it?'

'The man who called from California said they want to make it as close to the way it happened as they can. The guys who talked to me before, the ones from Chicago, don't know nothing about movies. They just know how to get things done. When those torpedoes come into his place once a week, Dennehy takes them in the office and gives them an envelope full of money.'

'Like I'm doing?'

'No. This is different.'

'You're right. It is. Let me tell you what's going on. The script for this movie is already written. Everybody in the world knows the ending now. We can't change that. And we're not trying to blame anybody. We don't want to indict Melvin Purvis or a detective named Rostov or Agnes Szepy or even John Dillinger. This will be a film about things that happened, not what caused them to happen. And it certainly won't be a film about you. Your life with Dillinger this past summer is a movie in itself. But that's not the movie we're making. Nobody expects a film called *Dillinger* to be a love story and this one won't be. Only you and I know what's been said here this afternoon and anything we use won't have your fingerprints on it, I promise you. We're not trying to tell the world things they don't know about Dillinger. We're going to put together the things that are known. Then people can decide for themselves what kind of man he was.'

Late that afternoon Kincaid met with Julian Thorne at the hotel. 'Here's what I found out,' he said. 'She's not a whore and she's not a gun moll. She's a skinny little farm-kid who never should have left South Dakota. But she was crazy about Dillinger. They lived together for two or three months this past summer. She had no idea who he was till the night he was shot. He told her his name was Frank Taylor. Said he was a labour organizer. He wasn't a boozer, she said. He liked ice-cream and they went to the movies a lot. And he liked to sit around in the zoo and look at the animals.'

'Jesus,' Julian said, 'if that gets out we'll have to scrap the picture. He sounds like Dagwood.'

'He was a clean decent guy she said. At least with her. Shave and a haircut. A suit and a tie.'

'You're fired, Kincaid. I'll get Leslie Howard to play the part. What about the Hungarian woman . . . Agnes Szepy?'

'The girl's scared of her. But she told me a few things anyway. Agnes Szepy has a nice little cat-house operation and Dillinger had a room there.'

'So she knew who he was.'

'I'd bet on it. She introduced him to Sally.'

'But the girl wasn't working for her?'

Kincaid shook his head. 'Like I said, I don't think she's a hustler. She said she's not and I believe her. She really liked the guy and it sounds as if he liked her.'

'Does she think the Hungarian woman set him up the way the papers say?'

'Wouldn't say a word about that. My guess is she doesn't know. If she does she's scared to talk about it. But just before I left her this afternoon, I asked her who picked out the movie they went to see that night. She thought for a minute, then she said, "Agnes did. She's crazy about Clark Gable."'

Julian smiled. 'Put on her red dress, steered him to the Biograph, and then disappeared in the crowd just before the shooting started. Looks like the papers are right. So where does that leave us?'

'I was thinking about it in the car coming back here. I kept remembering something you said when we had our last meeting at the studio, something to the effect that just because we've got a dynamite ending we can't let it throw the whole picture out of whack. Dillinger wasn't Dagwood or Leslie Howard. He was a smart tough son of a bitch. He lived tough and died tough. That's the movie. I don't doubt the things Sally Wick told me about him, but that's not our story and we can't let it be. We don't have to answer all the questions. I think it's better if we don't. Let the audience decide if Agnes set him up. Let them wonder about Sally Wick just as we were doing before I talked to her.'

'So what do we tell Tim and Evan?'

'I'll handle that. I'll tell them she did her best but she didn't know very much. I'll tell them Agnes Szepy is the one who knows the whole story and she's not talking. I think it's the only way, Julian. We can't let Evan get Sally's version of Dillinger in his head. The same with Tim. This is a hard-nosed story and we can't risk going soft on it. No buying bouquets from old ladies or giving an ice-cream cone to a kid.'

'You're right. We'll go with the script we've got through the Wisconsin gun-battle. He disappears, we have a montage about the FBI search, we see some fast shots of him with a moustache here in Chicago, then we have the ending the way it happened. Any dialogue between him and the two women that night will be casual stuff, not giving away anything, while we cross-cut with Purvis and the police setting up the ambush. And the audience says, "Who the hell were those two women?" '

'That's the way I see it.'

Julian smiled, 'And Sam will say to me, "What did I get for my ten thousand dollars?" '

'He'll get a lot,' Kincaid said. 'Because when I'm playing the part – car chases, bank robberies and all the rest of it – I'll know about this other side of Dillinger, I'll know about me and the girl, I'll know that Agnes Szepy would double-cross her mother for fifty dollars, and most important, just before I die, I'll know she fingered me. And when you're supervising the final cut you'll know those same things. You'll see what I'm doing and what I'm thinking, and you'll know what to put in and what to take out. We'll let the audience guess there's something else to this guy but we won't hit them over the head with it. You were right from the start. There is a connection between Ned Kelly and Dillinger. It worked for us in *Bushranger* and it will work this time.'

Thorne walked across the room and poured two drinks out of a whisky decanter. 'I was about to tell you how smart you are for recognizing how smart I am.' He walked back, handed Kincaid a glass, and sat down. 'Then I suddenly remembered my brother's favourite saying. He says the most dangerous thing in this business is an intelligent actor.'

Kincaid smiled. 'You tell Sam what those intelligent actors say. They say the rarest thing in this business is an intelligent producer.'

'Sometimes I think my instincts and my brain live in two different bodies,' Sophie said. 'They seem always to be at odds with each other. But my brain, such as it is, invariably gets the upper hand. That worries me.'

She was sitting at luncheon with Gloria Westerfield, in a green-leather booth in the dining-room of the Bel Air Hotel. The terrace was crowded and lively so they'd asked to be seated in the cool near-empty dining-room.

'You were meant to be born into my family,' Gloria said. 'Reason is everything in the Westerfield clan. Reason and intellect. You dare not come to the dinner-table in my father's house if you don't have a doctorate in *something*. When I was still an undergraduate at Smith my father had doctoral degrees in both Philosophy and Medieval Literature, my mother had a doctorate in Astronomy and my sister in Archaeology. I was not required to say, "Please pass the salt, Doctor", but I did feel more at home once I had my own degree.'

'What was your field of study?'

'Casual and unimportant, I'm afraid, by my family's standards. American Literature.'

'Did you plan to teach?'

'No. I simply wanted to feel welcome at the dinner-table. The irony is that once I had my degree from Brown, I moved to Hartford, then to New York, then to California, and I've never lived at home since. From a place where a high degree was obligatory I've settled in a spot where I must be careful never to mention it. Of course there are educated people out here, there are even some in motion pictures, but it's not something that one boasts about, particularly if you're a woman.'

'Perhaps that's why you're here. A reaction against your background.'

'I hate to think it's as simple as that but it may be. The Chinese say that if you over-react to something that threatens you, then you've already been defeated. In any case I got on this subject only because you were discussing impulse or instinct versus reason or whatever we call it. Much to the horror of my family I seldom make considered choices. I tend to leap right in and try to patch things together later on.'

'I wouldn't guess that about you.'

'Of course not. I know the impression I make. God knows I've been told often enough, particularly by young men who believe that I'd fall limp and moaning at their feet if only I'd let myself. It's impossible for them to accept the fact that my sensory equipment is in excellent working order but it simply doesn't respond to them. They prefer to believe that my mind is working as a sort of governor on my libido. Not true. Men as a group may not interest me but with certain men I am absolutely silly and defenceless.'

'And what sort of man is that?' Sophie asked.

'No way of knowing in advance. There seems to be no formula. And it hasn't happened often. But when it does there's been no resisting it and I haven't tried.'

'Sounds awfully dangerous to me.'

'Of course. On at least three occasions I have been absolutely enslaved by men who were worthless. If I'd been asked to interview them for jobs I would have turned them away without hesitation. But since there was no need to be rational or prudent I wasn't rational or prudent. And on each occasion I paid for it dearly.'

'I can't believe what I'm hearing. If I've ever seen anyone who seems to be in total control of . . .'

'Of my life? Oh but I am. Except when I lose control of it.'

'You told me before that you've never married . . .'

'But that's another matter, isn't it? If I were reasonable and cautious I would have been married long since. I have met any number of men who got high marks as potential husbands. When I was very young and still getting to know myself I even became engaged to some of them. In each case they were absolutely flawless fellows. And there was no question about their feelings toward me. They were ardent and attractive and relentless, all good qualities in a man. They were determined to make me love them as much as they loved me. In retrospect I think that was perhaps the problem. You see, those few men that I really cared about didn't give a damn whether I liked them or not. I can't resist that. Almost all of us are anxious to please. It's a pleasant shock to be thrown together with someone who has no impulse at all in that direction.'

'You're not one of those women who only want men they can't have, are you?'

'Not at all. At least I don't think I am. You see, I've always been able to have what I wanted. I'm just saying that the ones I've wanted most desperately were not men I wanted to keep. Whereas the ones that my head told me were keepable I didn't want at all. If you're about to conclude that I'm a loose woman, I must tell you that I've had very few love-affairs. The last one was with a man more than twice my age who was a hopeless invalid. I lived with him for almost four years and I loved him passionately but we never shared a bedroom or slept in the same bed. He used to say, "I love you, kid, but you got here twenty years too late. Don't believe that stuff about your spirit slipping out of your body. My body slipped away from my spirit." Not long before he died, when he was half-paralysed but still conscious and able to talk, I stood beside his bed and took off all my clothes. I didn't touch him or say anything. I just stood there looking at him. Finally he blinked both of his eyes at me like a double wink and said, "Thanks, kid." Then he closed his eyes and I put my clothes on again and a couple of days later it was all over.'

'How long ago was that?'

'Three years. A little more. I didn't feel sorry for myself. I didn't give up men for ever. But since then nobody else has come along. Like I said, I've met some perfect men, all sweet and clean and eager to please, but nobody I wanted to tie up and carry home.'

'Everyone tells me this is a terrible city for a single woman. Do you think that, too?'

'Rotten,' Gloria said. 'But it's also a terrible place for a married woman.'

'Didn't you tell me you came out here from New York? Would you like to go back there?'

Gloria shook her head. 'Bad memories. One of those guys I told you about. A married drunk who can't tell the truth. But I was crazy about him.'

'New York's a big city.'

'That's right. But he was my boss at AP and I still work for them. Also, my family's there on the East Coast, eager to iron out the flaws in my life and caution me against my dangerous impulses.' She laughed and sipped her wine. 'Actually, there is a chance I'll make a move. They've offered me a job in Chicago. Have you ever been to Chicago?'

'No,' Sophie said.

'It's a good place. A lot of people say bad things about it but most of those people have never lived there. I'd put it number two, after Boston. New York's number three.'

'So you may be leaving California?'

'I'm definitely going to have a talk with the people in Chicago. Then I'll make up my mind, I guess.'

'When will you go?'

'As soon as I can get away. In a week or two.'

'Kincaid's there now, you know. Julian Thorne and the whole company.'

'I know. But I won't be checking in with them. I'll just do my business and come back. At least that's what I'm planning now.'

'You have to promise me you'll have dinner with

Kincaid. They've been murdering him for the last three days in that alley beside the Biograph theatre. He needs somebody to tell him how wonderful Chicago is. At the moment he's not convinced.'

'Why don't you fly out there with me and surprise him? I'm sure he'd like that.'

'Not as much as I would. But I just can't do it.'

'Your brain getting the upper hand again?'

'It looks that way.'

As they walked out through the lobby toward the car-park Burt Windrow came across to meet them. 'Hello, Gloria. And Mrs Kincaid. You may not remember me. I'm Burt Windrow. We met last year at Ronnie Colman's.'

'Oh, yes. Of course I remember you.'

'Be careful what you say to him,' Gloria said. 'Burt writes a syndicated column now. He may put words in your mouth.'

'No one has to put words in Mrs Kincaid's mouth,' Windrow said. 'She speaks very well.' He turned back to Sophie. 'I'm sure you know that everyone in the British colony out here is very proud of your husband. He's a credit to us all.'

'Thank you. He'll be happy to hear that.'

'And you've settled in with your family I understand. Malibu's a charming place to live.'

'Yes, it is. We're quite happy there.'

'Will you be a permanent resident now like the rest of us?'

'No, I'm afraid not,' Sophie said. 'We'll be going back to London when Kincaid finishes his new film.'

He held out his hand and said, 'It was awfully nice to see you again. I look forward to the next time.' He turned to Gloria, 'And I'll be watching your column for the latest news about Mrs Kincaid and her family.'

Gloria gave him a blinding smile. 'Mrs Kincaid's my friend, Burt. I don't write about my friends.'

He switched on a blinding smile of his own. 'That

wouldn't work for me, I'm afraid. I must have a thousand friends out here and they're all in the film industry. If I didn't write about them there'd be nothing to write about.'

When he walked away Gloria said, 'Isn't he lovely?'

'He is rather lovely in his own egocentric way. But I don't think you admire him.'

Still smiling Gloria said, 'One day they'll discover he's missing from the reptile farm and we'll never see him again.'

5

Burt Windrow was not an intelligent man. He was neither perceptive nor contemplative. He was shrewd, however, and quick. When he guessed wrong about something he was able to guess again, several times if necessary, so that little damage was done. In the California gossip industry, of course, he seemed truly intelligent, and because of that perception was despised by his colleagues.

In his favour, however, were his strong white teeth and British accent, features that are often associated, in the minds of fools and social climbers, with gentle breeding and clear thinking.

Since Windrow usually had nothing interesting to say he had learned to present tiny scraps of discarded information with a certain flair and sense of discovery that commanded attention. Particularly from people who seldom listened to anyone or anything, and who noticed little difference between a lorry klaxon and a cello.

With most of the women Windrow met, it made little difference what he said or indeed if he said anything at all. There was a banal undangerous beauty to him and an unsettling lewdness in his eyes and around his mouth that passed for sensuality. So both the innocent and the wicked longed to be in his company. Elderly wives, mothers-in-law, twelve-year-old maidens, and servant-girls were hypnotized by him. *Les vicieuses*, who recognized at a glance that he was available to all comers, studied him carefully and promised themselves to keep the room fully lighted when their moment came to mount his blond magnificence.

Because his mother and his sisters had fawned over him, because women of all ages and descriptions had petted and praised him from the time he was a toddler, he developed a self-esteem that was quite remarkable. Men, however, and boys his own age were either sceptical or envious. His Uncle Cyril growled to himself, 'A lad who's been raised and directed by women is likely to be a bit of a pussy himself.' But Burt surprised Cyril. By age sixteen he had become a street-fighter and a bruising footballer. He was tall and strong and sure of himself in ways that could not be traced to mother-love. At twenty, after two years at a red-brick university outside Cardiff, he joined a repertory company whose actor-manager exclaimed, 'The boy has it all, doesn't he? God knows what he might achieve if he's steered properly. Guided and moulded, one can only guess how far he may go.'

By this time Burt could see the future clearly. Nothing would be denied him. One opportunity would follow another. Some benevolent hand had mapped his destiny. All he had to do was stay beautiful and independent, and continue to select his wardrobe with care. Then everything would fall smoothly and brilliantly into place.

He clung to these convictions year after year, through one failure after another. Every opportunity dissolved in his hands. But each time he consoled himself by saying, 'It wasn't meant to be. I didn't aim high enough. When the moment comes, when I go for the big prize, it will be there for me and no doubt about that.' The big prize continued to elude him, however. And the smaller ones as well. At last, when he was thirty or more, he realized that although the women who had always presented themselves for his approval were still there in substantial numbers they seemed suddenly older to him, less persistent, not so beautiful as others he remembered. And most humiliating of all, they had expectations of their own now, terms to discuss, demands they expected him to meet. When he said to one of them, the youngest and prettiest woman he knew just then, 'It's not equal terms we're talking about, is it? Love isn't a democracy, my darling. It's a monarchy as it's always been,' she replied, 'I've no objections to that as long as it's understood that I'm the person on the throne.' They'd laughed and drunk a great deal of claret that night and they'd had a glorious romp in his bed. But next morning when he woke up she was gone. And no one answered the telephone at her flat. A month later he heard that she'd married an Argentine and gone off to live in Buenos Aires. He sent her a warm note of congratulations and a small piece of Georgian silver.

Burt selected a fiancée himself not long after. 'Not a great beauty,' he explained to Alec Maple, 'but deliciously young and eager to please. Her father's a peer, her mother's a baroness, and the family owns half of Surrey – the better half, one hopes. But whichever it turns out to be we'll muddle through, won't we? When Dicky Wells said he was astonished to hear I was giving up my sexual freedom, so to speak, I said, "I'm giving up nothing, Dicky-do. I'm simply making an acquisition, taking on some real property as it were, and my sweet Ruth Rose, named after each of her grandmothers, is simply a clause in the contract. I will provide her snotty father with a number of grandchildren and he will provide me with the sort of life I am destined for."'

A month before the wedding Burt was invited to a midday meeting with Ruth Rose's father at White's in St James's Street. When he arrived the porter took him to a private reception-room on the ground floor where his host was waiting.

Burt took stage immediately as he always did. 'It may

surprise you, Lord Hixson, but this is the first time I've been a guest at White's. I'm told they put out an excellent lunch. I'm looking forward to it.'

'We're not having lunch. That's why we're in this private room. So I don't have to be seen with you.'

'I don't mind telling you, sir, that I'm surprised to hear that tone from you. I deserve better than that. And since we're to be in the same family from now on . . .'

'We'll not bloody be in the same family. You can be damned sure of that. I've had some enquiries made about you these past weeks and each report I've had was nastier than the one before.'

'Let's be fair about this . . .'

'Fair? I'm not here to be fair. I'm here to give you your walking papers. Short and sweet and nothing misunderstood.'

'I believe you're trying to upset me but I shan't allow that to happen. You're my fiancée's father and I respect you. If we have some differences I think we should put them aside in respect for Ruth Rose. After we're back from our wedding-trip there'll be plenty of time for you and me to sit down . . .'

'That's what we're doing now. We're sitting down face to face and it's an ugly experience for me, I'll tell you that.'

'As I said, I refuse to get angry with you. I think it's important to remember that the marriage contract is between me and your daughter, just the two of us. The announcements have been made, the invitations have been sent out . . .'

'I can't decide if you're deaf or dumb. You must realize that I wouldn't be talking this way to my future son-in-law. In case it hasn't become clear to you, I'm making a wedding announcement to you right now. The wedding's cancelled. There'll be no wedding.'

'With all due respect, sir, I think that's for Ruth Rose and me to decide.'

'There's nothing left to decide. It's been decided.'

'Not to my satisfaction, it hasn't. Not till I hear it from your daughter.'

'You'll hear nothing from my daughter. And she'll hear nothing from you. Her mother's taken her away.'

Among his technical skills as an actor, Windrow had been able to weep on cue, whenever a scene demanded it. He looked down at the floor now. When he looked up there were tears welling. He turned his head slightly so his eyes caught the light. 'Have you considered what you're doing to two young people's lives, mine and your daughter's?'

'I'm *saving* my daughter's life. That's what I'm about. As I told you, I know quite a lot now about the sort of life you fancy. I hate to think what would happen to my daughter if she were dropped unawares into a situation like that. Don't try to look bewildered and heart-broken. You know very well what I'm talking about.'

'Did she know you were planning to see me today?'

'Yes, she did.'

'Did she know what you were going to say to me?'

'Yes. Her mother told her. I won't pretend that she was happy about it. She's taken with you, the poor child.'

'You can't keep her away from London for ever, can you?'

'Of course we can't. And we don't plan to. Ruth Rose is young but she has good sense. She'll realize at last that what we've done is for her own good.'

'What if she doesn't realize that? What if she's determined to be with me?'

'I've considered that. In such a case I would depend on your good judgement. I would expect you to agree with me that it's in your best interest as well as hers to leave her alone. Then she'll be able to meet someone of her own class and have a decent married life. On the other hand, if you fail to see things my way, then other means will be found to persuade you.'

'If you think I can be bought off . . .'

'I expected that thought might occur to you.'

'I assure you that no amount of money . . .'

'I'm glad to hear you say that,' Lord Hixson said. 'Because it never occurred to me to offer you so much as one shilling. I'm not negotiating with you. I'm foreclosing.'

'Threats won't work with me either, sir.'

'If you're implying that I want some physical harm to come to you, you're mistaken about that as well, but since you've brought up the matter, let me make clear where I stand. I have power and money and influence. In my political life I have heard myself described as ruthless. I don't accept that assessment of my character but in this particular instance it is entirely accurate. I mean to say that where the happiness of my daughter is at stake I will stop at nothing to protect her.' He stood up and walked to the door. 'Keep that thought in your mind.' He opened the door. 'I'll ask the porter to serve you a drink before he shows you out. I'm sure you'll never be inside this club again so while you're here think carefully about what I've said.' Just as he closed the door behind him he said, 'And enjoy your drink.'

Not long after his meeting Windrow bought a steamship ticket for America. To his friend, Alec Maple, he explained his decision.

'Once again I've saved myself in the nick of time. I can't imagine how I got involved with that silly girl in the first place. I expect I felt sorry for her. But as I've told you, when I sat in bloody White's that day with her toad of a father, as he explained to me all the hideous opportunities and social tortures that would become available to me once I was his son-in-law, I began to feel like a poor red fox caught in a snare. The old prune spoke to me as though the marriage contract was between him and me, and his odd daughter was simply a codicil of some sort. I began to think perhaps he'd switched over and had some future plans about cornering me in the shower-room.

413

Suffice to say, as we sat there and he kept my glass filled with Remy *l'âge inconnu*, it came to me in a flash that I couldn't be a part of that rotten Hixson clan, that I simply must not spend the rest of my life helping Ruth Rose locate her misplaced spectacles. So I told my future father-in-law that one had suddenly realized there were other fish to fry and other girls to try. I left him stunned in his Queen Anne chair and strode out into the clean air of St James's, feeling as though I'd just skipped away from the guillotine. As I walked up Bond Street it came to me suddenly that the perfect moment had come at last for me to go to California. Half the bloody actors we know are there already. And doing damned well, even the ones who were lucky to have a bed-sitter here in London. The Sandhurst boy, Davy Niven, is working all the time, they say. And Olivier with his strange hair. And Colin Clive, Ralph Forbes and Tony Bushell. Raymond Massey, that stick, as well. And even poor old Karloff, stumbling about and lisping away. So I strolled along Bond Street, and I said to myself, "It's time to strike, old darling. The age of Windrow is about to begin. The critics in South Africa said that Hollywood is the place for me and I've decided they're right."'

California, when he arrived there, seemed made to order. The sunshine gave him an almost instant golden tan and bleached his yellow hair to a gleaming blend of brass and silver. The haberdashers and car dealers, the restaurants and petrol stations, gave him instant credit, and a wealthy dwarf and his wife offered him the use of their six-room gate-house on Poinsettia Lane for as long as he might want to live there. An agent named Fred Nichols, who represented Gable, Franchot Tone, and Colin Clive, took him on as a client, and he worked in two films, one at Universal, the other at RKO, during his first six weeks in Hollywood. People took his picture, he was invited to a party or a première every night, and Justin Gold mentioned him frequently in his column. Winchell called him 'a tow-head heart-breaker'.

If he had been known as a womanizer in London and Bristol and Brighton there was no word to describe his activities in the greater Los Angeles area. Ralph Richardson, who had worked with him in repertory in Manchester ten years before, had described him thus to Sybil Thorndike. 'He's beautiful and available. He has no character, no standards, and almost no talent, but for his chosen line of work those things aren't necessary.' Burt never heard this assessment of himself and would have been offended if he had heard it. But he was delighted to find himself in a community where that precise description applied to thousands of young women. What could be more helpful to an actress's budding career than being seen with a rogue Englishman who drove a white touring-car, was on intimate terms with Cary Grant, George O'Brien, and Jack Oakie, and who had Fred Nichols for an agent?

It lasted for almost a year. Burt worked in eight films, bigger roles each time. Reports from the studios were good. His salary tripled. He was in demand. Until the films he'd appeared in began to be released. Then it became clear that the Windrow love-affair with the motion-picture business had a serious flaw. The camera didn't love him. The self-esteem, the sardonic flair, the sexual energy didn't come through. What the camera recorded relentlessly were his flaws. A slight poutiness to the mouth, something furtive in the eyes, a spoiled child's expression on the face and body of a man. And the clear evidence of sleepless nights. Strong features beginning to blur from gin and champagne. But the greatest flaw was in his failed self-love. Something tentative about him. The voice not quite strong enough, the hands not anchored, the body not at ease. No look of eagles. No firm gaze. Weakness in the moments where strength was mandatory. Was there a trace of fear in his eyes? Hard to say. The camera simply and repeatedly declared, 'This man is not what he is required to be.'

There were no discussions or suggestions or recommendations. No one came forward with an offer to fix things. No one said or did anything at all. His career as an actor in motion pictures simply ended. Fred Nichols, in warm friendship, advised him that some other agent would probably be better for him. The dwarf and his wife told him they were obliged to offer their gate-house to Edward Everett Horton's mother, and all the stores and tailors and rental agencies and restaurants who had freely given him credit were suddenly pressed for cash and needed to be paid at once.

It was at this critical moment in his life that Windrow met Kincaid. At a time when he seemed in danger of losing what little he had managed to accumulate, he had a drink one afternoon at Lucey's with this cool Australian stranger who seemed to have everything. In the past ten years Burt had suffered many humiliations. But he'd found a formula for dealing with them. God's will. Destiny. Greater rewards just round the corner. But lately he had begun to suspect that this California, this business, this Hollywood were his destinations of last resort. 'You keep heading west till you come to the Pacific Ocean, till you can't go any farther, and that's it. You'll meet a lot of people there who feel just as you do. They've failed everywhere else. Maybe things will turn round here. At least there'll be sunshine and oranges on the trees. There's always that.'

As we've seen, Windrow was not a man who examined his experiences and tried to draw conclusions or chart new courses. He simply reacted. Hot or cold. Good or bad. In triumph he felt triumphant. When things went bad he felt painfully sorry for himself and looked for someone to blame. At that particular low-water mark in his life he found Kincaid. The incident that afternoon in a booth at Lucey's tattooed itself on the most sensitive and vulnerable part of his memory and stayed there as a reference point. This sense of failure and the name Kincaid became permanently welded together in his mind.

Every movement, every word the two men had exchanged that day were as clear in Windrow's memory as a page of memorized dialogue.

We discover Kincaid and Windrow in a booth in the bar of Lucey's restaurant.

WINDROW: Ah, well, so it goes. (He drinks.) You still haven't told me what Julian Thorne is up to. Is he truly planning to foist you off on the public as an actor, a man whose only experience is dreary recitation? There are many of us, you know, qualified chaps, who are full-time residents here, working at our trade, struggling for a major opportunity. So it doesn't go down well at all when a new bloke drifts into town with his rich and tender wife on his arm, smelling of money and French perfume . . . (*Kincaid's arm comes up suddenly. His hand fastens on Windrow's throat.*)

KINCAID (*In a husky whisper*): Listen to me, you son of a bitch. One more word about my wife and they'll find you dead in this fucking booth. (*Windrow tries to speak but can't. Red-faced. Eyes bulging.*) Now, I'm going to take my hand off your throat. But if you say one rotten word, if you make one sound, I'll drop you. Do you understand what I'm saying? If you do, blink your eyes. (*Windrow blinks like a child's doll and Kincaid turns him loose. Windrow stares at him.*) Not a sound out of you. You understand that? (*Windrow nods again.*) I don't know who you think I am and I don't care. I only care about your filthy mouth. If you say another word about my wife, if I ever hear that you've mentioned our names, I promise I'll make you wish you were born a mute. Remember how my hand felt on your neck. Then pray to God I never have a reason to put it there again.

From that moment Windrow had been obsessed with the thought of getting even. A year later, after the success of *Bushranger*, that obsession had intensified. When his opportunity came to be a columnist it seemed to solve that problem. His credit was re-established. He was petted and fondled, gifted and catered to by the same people who had abandoned him a few months earlier. His column was a weapon he could use as he saw fit. He hoped that he was admired and respected, knew that he was hated and feared. But no one ignored him. Best of all he was in a position to do damage to Kincaid.

Windrow was shrewd enough to know that a frontal assault was not the answer. Guerrilla tactics, he decided, were better. The whispering campaign he'd organized had not been a total success but seeds had been planted. In his mind the conspiracy with Alec Maple to destroy Evan Tagg's car had been an assault against Kincaid. That was the solution, he concluded, to attack the fringes, to unsettle the people around Kincaid. The confrontation with Sam Thorne and John Corso had been a setback, of course, but even that he had managed to turn to his advantage. Or so he believed. The column was his answer now to everything. Three days a week, in eighty-three papers across the country, he had a platform for whatever praise or condemnation he chose to present. Since that day in Sam Thorne's office Windrow had been generous in his praise of Thornwood Studios, their policies, and their product. The Thornwood publicity department now counted him as a friend, an ally, a supporter. What better position to be in, he reasoned, for his long-range scheme to bring down Kincaid? He outlined his plans in a memorandum to himself.

Don't attack the manor-house. Steal the pigs and chickens. That's the ticket. Smother them all with praise and approval. Gather rose-buds and patiently plan for the day of the thorns. Where is Kincaid vulnerable? Through his wife, of course. His friends. His wife's children. Be alert, fatten the files, sharpen the weapons, and be patient.

• CHAPTER 11 •

1

When Tim Garrigus told Sophie that shooting a film on location was like leading a regiment into battle, he spoke the truth. Troop movements, billeting, supply lines, logistics of food and transport were continuing problems. Fresh terrain and changing camera set-ups demanded new tactics. And always weather was the adversary. And the clock. De Mille said, 'A film-maker's enemy is the clock. Every scene, every take, every script page, is measured in minutes. The work starts before dawn and continues till bad weather, loss of light, or fatigue brings the day to an end.'

The crews and the actors know this routine well. They accept the drudgery, the waiting, the heat, the cold, the dust, the mud, the clash of wills, the shouting matches, because they've learned that all this is part of the work.

The thing that no one accepts easily is the emptiness, the hours between the end of the work-day and falling asleep. After an hour or so of drinking whatever's available and a dinner of institutional food, each individual wanders along the corridor to whatever room he's been assigned, smokes a few cigarettes, looks over the next day's work, listens to the radio if there is one, goes to bed, and tries to sleep.

Evan, although he was accustomed to being by himself, had been unquiet and sleepless since leaving California. Each night when he turned off the light he found he was sharing the room with his mother, with Arthur, or Mary Cecil. He heard their voices endlessly, saw each of them sitting or standing in the darkness beside his bed. They appeared and reappeared each night, like a loop of film feeding through the projector flashing a recurrent image on the screen.

The most disturbing presence was that of his father. Whereas Amy and Mary went on at length about their difficulties and disappointments, Arthur never spoke. He stood, with his hands clasped behind his back, or sat in a wing-back chair staring straight ahead, and said nothing at all. But behind him always, like a soft sound-track, was the sound of Sophie's voice, describing Arthur's bookshop encounter with Margaret in Kensington High Street that summer afternoon.

Just as he had attempted to rationalize that meeting for Sophie so did Evan continue to explain it to himself. But with less surety each time. One night, lying awake and staring at the ceiling, he saw the whole business in one light. The next evening it would look different. As he wished that Sophie had never told him, he concluded that since she had told him, since he knew, he had to make some decision about it, draw some sensible conclusion, and perhaps intercede in some way. But how? Did his father need sympathy and understanding just now or was something more stern required? The child is father to the man and all that. Was Arthur waiting, perhaps, for someone to steer him, to bring him up short, to tell him it was time he got hold of himself? Evan made a dozen separate decisions, then invariably, within a few hours, took a contrary position. At last he sat down, one dreary night in a badly heated tourist cabin just outside Danville, Illinois, and wrote his father a letter of warmth and sympathy. Without mentioning his conversation with Sophie, he hearkened back to Arthur's recent letter to him and tried to respond just to that. When he read what he'd written, however, it seemed insincere and condescending, like praising a wicked child for being less naughty than he was capable of being. Evan put the letter aside, read it through the following evening when he came to his room, then sat down and wrote a second letter.

It's difficult for me to write this letter, Dad. Doubly difficult because the last letter I had from you, while not filled with joyous news, was nonetheless gratifying. As I wrote you in reply I felt as if you'd begun to come to grips with matters that you've needed to deal with for your own peace of mind. I've always thought of you as a strong, unselfish man and I still do, but I've sometimes felt that you were totally occupied with the welfare of others and less concerned with what might be best for you. So, as I say, the tone of that letter seemed very positive to me. It made me feel good.

Since then, however, I've had a long talk with Sophie. More accurately she talked, and I, for the most part, only listened. She told me about the meeting between you and Margaret in the bookshop where you're employed now. It seems that Margaret wrote to her about it in some detail. Sophie was disturbed by her mother's account, and after I'd heard it, so was I.

At first I believed it could not have taken place as Sophie described it. But when I questioned her about certain details she said she was passing it on exactly as her mother had told her. Since I've never known Margaret to be anything but truthful, I have to conclude that what Sophie told me is accurate.

Is it possible that you were as abrupt and cold and unfriendly as Margaret says you were? It's difficult for me to believe that you were. It's even harder for me to see what would prompt you to behave like that.

In all the years you and I spent at the Towers I have never heard you speak of Margaret in anything but the most glowing terms. She was our friend and our benefactor, like a mother to me and a sister to you. When I was nine years old you struck me and scolded me severely, the only time I was ever punished like that. I'm sure you will remember what prompted it. You felt that in some careless nine-year-old way I had not been properly respectful toward Margaret.

Is it possible that my memory is playing tricks on me? I don't think so. Is it possible that your high regard for Margaret was only a part of your working relationship with her and it ended on the day you packed up and moved to London? That's hard to believe.

So I'm back where I started. She says you made her feel like a stranger, a non-person, that you treated her like any other customer. And when she tried to make an arrangement whereby the two of you could meet somewhere, you made no effort to respond. In fact, Sophie said, her mother was made to feel as if she had made an unwelcome proposal.

If all this did not take place as it was described to me I have no idea why Margaret would invent such a story. On the other hand, if it did take place I can't imagine what has come over you. If there's some explanation, please tell me what it is. Otherwise I will be reluctant to contact Margaret when I come back to London. As you know there is no circumstance in which I would not come to your defence. But unless there's some critical fact that I don't know, I can't see how your treatment of Margaret can be defended.

Evan did not expect a prompt reply from his father. Arthur was a conscientious correspondent but a deliberate one. He often said, 'I compose my letters. I don't dash them off.' In this instance however, he apparently sent off a cable to Evan the same day he received his letter.

HOW DARE YOU WRITE ME SUCH A LETTER. HOW DARE
YOU QUESTION MY STANDARDS OR MY BEHAVIOUR.
PLEASE DO NOT DEFEND ME TO ANYONE. I DON'T
REQUIRE SUCH A DEFENCE.

2

Julian Thorne sat in Kincaid's dressing-room caravan
near the town square in Greencastle, Indiana, mid-
morning, a cold November rain slashing down, camera
trucks, actors' caravans, and lighting equipment parked
and scattered all round the court-house. 'I heard from
Rosamund Barwick yesterday. She's in Chicago for a
week or two.'

'I can't believe it,' Kincaid said. 'She told me she never
leaves London. Waits for the world to come to her.'

'Maybe she has new habits. I'll let you know after I talk
to her. I'm having lunch with her tomorrow.'

'I thought you were going to California tomorrow.'

'I am. Four o'clock train. Right after lunch. I have to
find out if you people can make a picture without me.
While I sweat it out in the cutting-room. Try to cover up
all the mistakes you creative freaks have made.'

Kincaid smiled. 'You've seen the dailies. If something
didn't get reshot it's your fault.'

'Don't get me wrong,' Thorne said. 'I've never been
happier with a picture I've made. And we're right on
schedule, bad weather and all. The only major thing
we've got left is the Wisconsin shoot-out. That's the last
thing on the location board.'

'You coming back for that?'

'Wouldn't miss it,' Thorne said. 'Love the smell of
gunpowder. It always smells like money to me.' Then:
'When will you be back in Chicago? Rosamund's going
to ask me.'

423

'Tell her I'll take her to the Pump Room for lunch. Day after tomorrow.'

'She'll be happy to hear it. When's Tim going to turn you loose down here?'

'Later today maybe. Tomorrow noon the latest. Just a few reaction shots and wild lines. Then I'll meet him in Crown Point next Tuesday and we'll pick up some odd shots there.'

'Tim loves it when he can send the actors home and just work with stuntmen and car crashes. So far he's demolished seven Chevrolets and three Buicks. The slicker the roads get, the happier he is. We'll probably have to shoot the Wisconsin stuff in a snowstorm. That'll really make him happy.'

Early that evening when he was back at his hotel Kincaid rang up Sophie. He tried to call her at about the same time every evening. When she answered the phone, instead of saying hello she always said, 'When are you coming home?' This time, as soon as she picked up the receiver, he said it: 'When are *you* coming home?'

'I am at home, you bum. What's your excuse?'

'Home is where the heart is.'

'Don't give me that. Home is where your wife is. How's it going?'

'Things look good,' he said. 'Three more weeks if I'm lucky.'

'What if you're not lucky?'

'Four more years.'

'Not funny, Kincaid. Don't make jokes like that.'

'Julian's going back tomorrow to work on the editing. They're cutting it as we shoot it, and it looks good, he says.'

'They're putting up posters already. All over Los Angeles. You look so much like Dillinger it's scary.'

'Next picture, Julian promised I can look like Richard Cromwell.'

'I love you, darling, but nothing's going to make that happen.'

'Maybe he said Bela Lugosi.'

'That's more like it,' she said. 'Or Lon Chaney. Let's be honest with ourselves.' Then: 'Did you get my last letter, the one about the situation at the Towers?'

'Not yet. What's happening?'

'The same dilemma with my father. But now apparently it's about to be resolved. You'll see the grisly details when you get the letter.'

The next afternoon, when the company driver picked Kincaid up at the hotel to take him to Chicago, he handed him the letter from Sophie. In the section about the situation at the Towers she wrote:

Margaret tries in her letters to put the best face on everything but she doesn't manage very well. There now seems to be (at last) a specific date when the constables will come to escort the Major from the house, and Margaret pretends to rejoice that the situation between the two of them will be finally resolved. But between the lines I read all sorts of conflicting messages. She's very apprehensive, I think, uncertain what to expect. She knows that the situation can't be allowed to continue as it is, but all the same she fears the day of reckoning. I feel dreadfully guilty that I can't be there with her.

We've had a minor problem here as well. Nothing on the scale of what Mother's facing but disturbing nonetheless. You remember the kitchen maid who caused a bit of a problem when she refused to take Homer Tony's meals to him in his little cottage. I'm not sure that you ever knew her name. It's Ursula Martin. She's a pretty little thing. All dimples and pink cheeks and ginger hair in ringlets. Innocence personified. Or so it would appear. Although she didn't say it in so many words one was led to believe that

Homer Tony had perhaps made some sort of advances toward her. Innocence defiled, that sort of thing.

What we've discovered, more specifically what Ruth has discovered, is that little Miss Martin is somewhat less innocent than she seems. In the few months she's been with us it appears that she has provided the grooms, the gardeners, and various tradesmen with a great deal of sexual gratification. The delivery-boy from the Malibu market, for example, has boasted in the local taverns that she joins him in the back of his truck each time he makes a delivery here.

As soon as I heard all this I told Ruth to dismiss her at once but much to my surprise she defended the girl. She said, since most of the staff we hired locally would be made redundant at the end of the year anyway when we all go back to England, why not let Ursula stay on till then. 'I'll give her a stiff lecture,' Ruth told me, 'and then I'll keep an eye on her for these last few weeks. She's dead-set on getting a job in the studios, poor child, and somebody must have told her that passing herself about like a platter of canapés was the way to do it.'

I agreed to keep her on till we close up the house but I'm not sure it's a good idea. I thought it might be wise to sound out Trevor on the subject of Ursula so I made a try but you know how he is. If he knows anything about her he's not about to divulge it. Speaking of Trevor, he's doing splendid work in his art classes. In addition, he's doing a series of charcoal drawings of Homer Tony. Strong, remarkable pictures they are. There's something beautiful about the ferocity in that man's face and Trevor has captured it.

In a postscript Sophie wrote:

You remember I told you that Gloria and I ran into Burt Windrow at the Bel Air Hotel a few weeks ago.

I was afraid he'd write something silly about me in his column but he didn't. Yesterday, however, he had a little item about Sarah. It seems that her drama teacher, Ethel Richmond, had invited some studio people to spend a day at the school to watch the classes and talk to the students informally. Either Windrow was invited or he got himself included somehow. Here's a cutting from his column, the bit he wrote about Sarah.

Someone to watch: we saw a young woman yesterday. Was she sixteen, seventeen, or eighteen? Difficult to tell. But she has beauty and talent and, unless I miss my guess, is destined to be a major actress. Her name: Sarah Kincaid. Studio heads take notice.

At first I was aghast. You know how I feel about all the cheap publicity that floats round out here. But then Sarah rang me up and she was so excited and flustered, near tears, that I couldn't be angry. It struck me suddenly that I can't be so thrilled by the work Trevor's doing and simply turn my back on something that Sarah's equally serious about. It will probably be a passing phase with her as it is with many girls, but meanwhile I must find ways to be supportive. Aren't you proud of me? Never thought you'd hear me say that, did you?

A second postscript:

Gloria took the train to Chicago three days ago. As I told you, she'd planned to go earlier but had to postpone it. She's staying at the Ambassador East. I told her to call you but I don't think she will. If you have some free days in Chicago please take her to dinner or the theatre or the Art Institute. Or maybe all

427

three. I'm glad the picture's going well. And very glad you'll be home soon. And very, very glad we'll be back in London for Christmas.

3

'I'm not a physical coward, you see,' Rosamund Barwick said. 'High threshold of pain and all that. At my age, *soixante-quinze*, I don't feel threatened by anything. But when my comforts are in jeopardy, when someone wants to change the carefully orchestrated rhythm of my life, I get damned annoyed. And that's what I see, what I'm very certain that I see, on the horizon. I've had my differences with Winnie over the years and I've told him so, but I think he's dead right about Germany and their bloody *Luftwaffe*. So I'm keeping my finger to the wind, considering my options. I may decide to close up the house in London and relocate myself and my staff till that simpering maniac in Berlin makes it clear just how much havoc he's going to make.'

'Is this the place?' Kincaid said. 'Are you thinking about moving to Chicago?'

'Lord, no,' she said. 'Not that it isn't a fine city. It's quite a beautiful place actually if you don't wander too far away from the lake. But the weather's punishing for an old person like me. Worse than London, they say. Winds so strong you can't cross from kerb to kerb, weeks on end in winter when the temperature doesn't get above freezing, and days so hot in summer the pavement blisters your feet.'

They were sitting in the first booth, the celebrity booth, just inside the lobby entrance of the Pump Room in the Ambassador East Hotel, waiters in Indian costumes and small black boys in turbans and livery scurrying up and down the aisles from kitchen and bar to booth and back again.

'Noel is plumping for Jamaica, of course. Keen to get me down there. And Auden is determined to trap me in some primitive village in New Jersey. If I know him, he probably has a miserable bed-sitter there and is eager to share it with me. Isherwood now believes that all life begins and ends in California. He's bought a house there, which means he's in love again, and insists that I move into his guest quarters. When I told him I have an irreducible staff of seven he said I could put them in a caravan beside his garage. Gone quite dotty, I think, since he left Berlin. One night in my drawing-room when he was excoriating all of Europe and heaping obscene praise on the California wastelands, I said to him, "I think you're right, Chrissie. Can you imagine what monumental work Goethe and Thomas Mann, Beethoven and Chopin and Velasquez would have done if they'd been fortunate enough to have lived in Pasadena?" He thought it over for a second and said, "By God, Rosie, there's something in that. I never thought of that before." Poor soul. Too long in the sun.'

'So where do you think you'll settle?'

'No decision yet. Waiting for a blinding flash to show me the way. Or so Willy Maugham believes. I'm here in Chicago with him you know. Came all the way from England together. Along with his mean-spirited Chinese companion. If he were a man I'd be frightened of him. Since he's some other sort of ill-defined species he only gives me the tremblies and makes my skin crawl. Fortunately Willy keeps him at bay most of the time, at least during the daylight hours when I see him. Maugham is a genius you know at finding hideaways, usually as someone's guest. And he's done it again. An American planter has offered him a beautiful house and garden in the South – Georgia or Alabama or one of those slave states, perhaps South Carolina – and Willy has condescended to accept the offer, provided a cook and a housekeeper are thrown in. There's a wing there for me, he says, and since I've never experienced the American South I'm tempted to try it. Have you ever met Willy?'

'No, I haven't.'

'Have you read his books?'

'No,' Kincaid said, 'but I've seen several of his plays.'

'What do you think?'

'Not sentimental, I like that.'

'Exactly. Willy's problem is that he writes too much. But his best things are very good indeed. He has a bad habit, you see, of denigrating his own work. Shouldn't do that. It's odd. If a writer says he's a genius, no one believes him. If he says he writes trivial entertainments only, everyone is quick to agree. Willy couldn't write a truly lightweight piece if he tried. He's too bitter. Has a low opinion of all mankind. No man who yearned for happiness or contentment would keep the sort of company he keeps.'

'Why did he bring you to Chicago?'

'Not to make me suffer if that's what you're thinking. As usual he's the guest of a wealthy family, just up the street from this hotel. What they don't realize is that he's using them as a starting-point for his new novel, the best idea he's had yet, I think. Something mystic about it. Something mystic about Willy, too, of course. All that time with the little yellow people left its mark on him. The book, as nearly as I can make out, is about a young man, a child of privilege, who goes to India and comes back a changed man. He rejects the world he's grown up in and becomes in his way, a mendicant. Odd that a man like Willy, who surrounds himself with opulence, who has a Renoir in his breakfast-room and a small Matisse beside his shaving-bowl, would concern himself with a character who longs for simplicity and who sacrifices everything to find it.' She smiled. 'Nothing like you, Kincaid. You've gone from the peasant life to the rococo in two year's time. I hear you've recreated Northumberland at the edge of the Pacific. Have you convinced your beautiful wife that she's travelled thousands of miles and never left England?'

Kincaid smiled. 'I'm afraid not. I didn't expect to do that.'

'Is she here with you in Chicago?'

He shook his head. 'She's in California.'

'Perhaps you made the house too appealing.'

'I don't think so. It's just right. I'm glad she likes it.'

'And how long have you been here in the Midwest? Isn't that what it's called?'

'That's right. We left California about two months ago.'

'I'm an old lady so I can say anything I want to. So I say, why didn't Sophie come with you?'

'We've been on the move a lot. Back and forth through three or four states.'

'No excuse. You've been sleeping in beds and eating off plates, haven't you? I know the answer to that. It's *yes*. So I ask you again, why didn't she come along?'

'Lots of reasons. The house. The children.'

'Her children aren't babies. They don't have to be spoon-fed.'

'You're a valuable lady, Rosamund,' Kincaid said, 'but I think we've exhausted this subject. I don't want to talk about it any more.'

'I don't blame you. Neither do I. But since I always insist on having the last word, here it is. The only good reason I know to get married is so you can eat and drink and go to bed and get up with the person you're married to. If you don't do that, no matter how good you think your reasons are, not only are you missing all the fun of marriage, you're running a big risk of not being married before long. The trouble with being separated is that sooner or later one of the two people involved might start to like it.'

'I don't like it.'

'I'm sure Sophie doesn't either. But it's still a dangerous game. If I were forty years younger, or fifty years younger, and I saw a chap like you strolling round in hotel lobbies by himself, I'd wrap him up and take him home with me.'

'That's only because you have poor taste in men.'

'That may be true. But there are thousands of women whose taste is just as bad as mine.'

After he took Mrs Barwick to her suite Kincaid came back down to the lobby. As he crossed to the entrance where his driver was waiting, Gloria Westerfield came through the revolving door. They were suddenly face to face. 'I'll bet you were just going to a telephone to ring me up,' he said.

'I did promise Sophie I'd call you but I haven't. No excuse. I've been awfully busy these past three days, but as I say, that's no excuse.'

'You have time for a drink or a coffee or something?'

She looked at her watch. 'I'm sorry. I don't. I have an appointment at four in the Loop and I'm really behind schedule.'

'Some other time. How long will you be here?'

'I planned to go back on the weekend but now I'm not sure. I may be held up.'

'Well, I've got a few free days before we crank up again so I guess you're busier than I am. If you have some free time call the Drake and leave a message, and we'll get together.'

'That's a good idea. I'll do that.'

They shook hands, she crossed the lobby toward the elevator and he went outside to his car. He knew she wouldn't call him but he wasn't sure why. He also knew he wouldn't ring her. He did know the reason for that.

4

When Kincaid walked into his suite at the Drake there were five telephone messages on the floor just inside his door. On each of them it said, CALL MRS KINCAID IN CALIFORNIA. URGENT.

As he crossed the sitting-room the telephone rang. It was Evan. He'd just come back from Indiana the day before. 'Jesus, I'm glad I caught you. I've been ringing you every five minutes for an hour.'

'Sophie's been calling me, too. I was just about to ring her back.'

'She got me about half an hour ago. I've got some terrible news.'

'What's the matter?'

'Sophie's all right. It's Margaret. The Major shot Jack Brannigan this morning.'

'Jesus Christ. Is he . . .'

'He's dead. That's all I know. And Margaret's in terrible shape. She's with Clara Causey. That's who called Sophie.'

'That crazy bastard and his guns. Listen, let me try to get through to Sophie. I'll call you back when I ring off from her.'

A few minutes after he placed the call with the hotel operator she called back to say his party was on the line. When the connection was made at last it was Mrs O'Haver on the other end. 'Oh, it's you, sir. Thank God. Your wife's just here.'

As soon as he heard Sophie's voice Kincaid said, 'I already know, sweetheart. Evan rang me a few minutes ago.'

She started to cry then. After a moment she said, 'I'll have to call you back. I can't even . . . I can't talk now.'

Mrs O'Haver came on the phone again. 'Are you at your hotel, sir?'

'Yes. Suite 627.'

'We'll ring you back then when she's got hold of herself.'

Forty minutes later Sophie called him back. Her voice sounded strained but she wasn't crying. 'I'm sorry, darling. I had a trunk-call from Clara. We were cut off for some reason. So if the connection comes through again on the other phone I'll have to ring off with you.'

'How's Margaret?'

'She's in rotten shape, I'm afraid. Clara's doctor came right away as soon as they had the news and gave her a sedative, but she's still in shock. She wants to be taken back to the Towers. She can't believe he's dead . . . I'm sorry, I have to ring off now. Clara's call is coming through again. I'll ring you back as quickly as I can.'

He rang Evan's room then. 'Why don't you come up here. I'm waiting for her to call back. We'll have a drink.'

'I'm three ahead of you.'

'I just poured myself a triple. So we'll be even.'

They sat there by the window watching the sun go down and watching the lake grow slowly black and waiting for the phone to ring. They ordered up a tray of food and ate sandwiches while they drank Scotch. At last the telephone rang. When Kincaid answered, Sophie said, 'Here's what I'm going to do. I'm taking the train east tomorrow morning. Call me in the morning at seven my time so I can tell you exactly when I'll be changing trains in Chicago. You can meet me, can't you, and go with me to the other terminal? I'd die if I had to leave without seeing you. I'll get into New York Friday morning and sail on the *Aquitania* that afternoon. Oliver and Mrs O'Haver will follow me on the *Leviathan* five days later after they've closed up the house. Sarah and Trevor will come with them.'

They stayed on the phone for nearly an hour, Sophie talking almost all of that time and Kincaid asking occasional questions. When they hung up at last, Evan said, 'How is she?'

'Hard to tell. She's not crying but she sounds as if she's been drugged. Like she's reading off a piece of paper. Or reciting something she's memorized.'

He told Evan then about her plans. When he finished,

Evan said, 'I'm not sure I understand what's going on. I know this must have been a terrible blow for Margaret – it was a shock to me and I've never even met Brannigan – but what does Sophie hope to accomplish by dropping everything, pulling the kids out of school, closing the house, and rushing over there?'

'I don't think she's thought about it a lot . . .'

'That's my point. Sophie thinks about everything a lot. I've never seen her go off half-cocked.'

'In this case I think she just wants to be there with Margaret.'

'You said she hasn't even talked with Margaret yet. Isn't that what you told me?'

Kincaid nodded. 'That's one of the things that's making her crazy. She feels that if her mother's not able to talk on the telephone she must be in rotten shape.'

'She's probably right. It just seems to me . . . you know what I mean. What about the Major?'

'That's another thing. When they broke down the door after he'd shot Brannigan, he was sitting on the floor in the corner, babbling to himself and not making sense about anything. Clara says they think he's gone over the edge. They've put him in a psychiatric hospital in Newcastle under police guard. He'll be there till they see if he's able to stand trial. He may be there permanently.'

'Jesus, what a calamity. Margaret has it coming at her from all sides.'

'The Major's a tortured bastard. The first time I ever laid eyes on him I thought he was bonkers.'

'Was that when he tried to bully you out of marrying Sophie?'

Kincaid nodded. 'Out of control. Like a bomb waiting to go off and scatter shrapnel all round.'

'Well, he's done it now. If he felt he had to get even with Margaret, he's done a ruddy good job of it. Did Sophie know any more details about what happened?'

'She seems to know most of the story now. When the

date was set for the confrontation with Cranston, the chief constable asked Margaret not to be at home.'

'Does that mean they weren't surprised by what happened?'

'I'm sure they didn't know what to expect. One of their men had had a long talk with Cranston. I'm sure he saw that the old man was a little chancy. And there's no way to miss all that artillery he had stashed away. So I guess they planned to play it safe. Sophie says they also told Margaret that Cranston might want to put on a show for her if he knew she was in the house. At any rate they asked her to stay with Clara Causey the night before and be away from the Towers when they came to fetch the Major. She objected at first, or so Clara told Sophie, but Brannigan sided with the constabulary. So at last she agreed.'

'But Brannigan didn't go with her.'

Kincaid shook his head. 'There had to be a family member there to witness the proceedings and give the constables whatever authority they might need if Cranston resisted.'

'What was their plan?'

'They'd told him what day they'd be coming as well as the time. Ten o'clock in the morning. They'd bring a van, they promised, to carry away whatever personal things he'd be taking along. He was asked to have his cases and boxes packed and waiting on the veranda facing the west drive.'

'Did he know where they'd be taking him?'

'I expect they didn't want to get into that. The first order of business was getting him off the premises. In any case when they got there, Brannigan met them on the west veranda but there were no parcels or valises belonging to Cranston. When they looked up at the Major's window just beside the portico they saw that it was open and they thought they could make out Cranston standing back in the room, away from the window. The deputy chief constable, the man in charge, called up to him and asked if he was ready to come down. No answer. Then the police officer told him he'd send up a couple men to help him carry down his things. The way I understand it, Cranston stepped to the window then and fired a rifle at the deputy chief. He missed him but hit another constable in the leg. They carried the man inside the house and bandaged his thigh while Brannigan rang for an ambulance. The deputy chief rang his station then and asked for additional men. While they waited one of the constables slipped upstairs and tested the door of Cranston's sitting-room. He reported that it was locked and seemed to be barricaded as well. While they were inside they heard more shots and discovered that two of the tyres on the van had been exploded by shot-gun blasts.'

After the ambulance arrived and took away the wounded constable, after four new men with sidearms were on the scene, the officer in charge consulted with Brannigan. 'It looks as if we have a deranged man on our hands. I'm afraid we'll have to force our way into his quarters and disarm him in whatever way we can. I have my job to do so I'm not asking your permission but I feel bound to tell you there could be some damage to the premises.'

'It can't be helped. I can see that.'

'It's a corner room he's in. With windows on two sides. I'll take a man and we'll get behind the van beneath the window he fired from. I'll have a megaphone and I'll keep talking to him, trying to keep his attention, freezing him at that west window. Meanwhile, we'll send men up ladders to the two windows behind him, and the other men will be waiting upstairs to storm his door when I give the signal. Is there just the one door to that room?'

'No,' Brannigan said. 'There's a door in the north-east corner of the room. It opens on the back stairway.'

'Good, we'll put a man there, too, if you'll show him

437

the way. Though I expect that door will be barricaded as well.'

'Isn't there some way we can talk to him first?'

'We tried that, didn't we? There's no talking to a man who answers with a gun-shot. I've one constable wounded already.'

'But if you try to break into his quarters you may have another one shot. Or more than one perhaps.'

'It's our job, Mr Brannigan. We take as few risks as possible. But we must do what we're sent to do.'

'Maybe I could talk to him.'

'He'll shoot at you as quick as he'll shoot at us, I expect. I'd gamble on that. I could never allow you to go into that room with him, even if he'd permit it.'

'I don't intend to go into the room. But I could go up the back stairs with your man and try to talk to him through that second door. If he won't listen there'll be plenty of time then to storm the place and fetch him out.'

'So that's what they did,' Kincaid said to Evan. 'Everybody got into position, the deputy chief began talking through the megaphone from behind the van, and Brannigan, with a young constable named Morgan, slipped up the back stairs to the second door.'

When Morgan made his report later to the deputy chief he said, 'He's a canny sod. He must have guessed what we were up to and positioned himself just inside that second door. Because as soon as Mr Brannigan began to speak, a God-awful blast from a twin-barrelled pump-gun ripped through the door-panels.'

5

'My God, Kincaid, I can't believe what I'm hearing. We've just had the worst tragedy in the history of my family. My stepfather's dead, my father may spend the rest of his life in an asylum, my mother is surely in a condition I can't even imagine, and you accuse me of over-reacting.'

'Damn it, Sophie, I didn't say that and you know it. I didn't accuse you of anything. I know you want to be with your mother. I'd expect you to want that. I just thought Sarah and Trevor could have been left in school so they could come back to England when I come.'

'You said I was a fool to let the staff go and to close up the house.'

'I've never said you're a fool. You're not a fool. Of course you're upset over what's happened. So am I. But we could have let the Malibu house function till I'm ready to come home. All that didn't have to take place in two days.'

'How can it function without Oliver and Mrs O'Haver? I need them with me. I'd have them along now if I didn't know I was going directly to the north after I dock at Southampton. By the time I'm back in London they'll be there.'

They were in a Thornwood limousine being driven from Sophie's arrival terminal to the railway station in Chicago where New York-bound trains were boarded. 'And as for Trevor and Sarah, I had no hesitation about taking them away from school. Since they would be coming home in time for Christmas in any case, these few weeks earlier won't matter. Frankly, I'll be delighted to see them back in English schools.'

'How do they feel about it?'

'Of course they wanted to stay where they are. I expected that. But that's all the more reason for them to be back in England. A great change has come over both of them since we've been out there, and I'm not sure I like it.'

'They're growing up.'

'No. They're growing away. Sometimes I feel as if I don't know them any longer. They seem to have some sort of secret life and that disturbs me. God knows what

439

Sarah's got herself into there in Ojai. She's like a book without page numbers. I keep losing my place. And even my sweet loyal Trevor has floated off in twenty different directions. I asked him what it was like when he was sitting there for hours drawing those portraits of Homer Tony. "How can you endure those hours of silence?" I asked him. And he said, "There's no silence. I talk all the time. I talk and he listens. I like it and so does he." Doesn't that seem odd to you?'

Kincaid shook his head. 'I do the same thing with Homer.'

'But you two have a lot in common. All the time you spent together in Australia. What can he and Trevor have in common?'

Kincaid smiled. 'You might be surprised. They're both men of the world.'

'That's another thing with Trevor. I think he imagines he's in love.'

'Good for him.'

'I'm not sure it is good for him. I've never met the young lady but I've seen some of his drawings of her. She models in the altogether in his figure-drawing class. She does it to pay for her ballet classes, he says. I'm not sure what she's doing with Trevor but I have strong suspicions.'

'As I said, good for him.'

'Don't try to make me sound like a prude. I know all about adolescence and puberty and the birds and the bees. But Trevor's barely fifteen.'

'He looks eighteen. Hair on his chest and shaves every morning.'

'He's still just fifteen. And I hate to see him base all his sexual standards on . . . you know . . . on something casual. On someone who's not good enough for him. Don't misunderstand me. She may be a delightful girl, as innocent as he is. But all the same I'll be relieved to have him back in England.'

There was a forty-minute wait for her New York train. While the driver looked after her luggage, Sophie and Kincaid went upstairs to a glass-enclosed cocktail-room that looked out on the terminal clock and waiting area just below.

When she came back to their table from the powder-room she said, 'I've washed away the grime from the Los Angeles train. I'm virgin territory now. Ready for the grime from the New York train.'

After she settled into her chair and tasted her drink, she said, 'I'm sorry. I really am.'

'What does that mean?'

'Don't interrupt me. When I apologize, attention must be paid. I was very snotty with you before and I'm dreadfully sorry. I never know for sure if I'm doing the right thing but I try to do what seems best to me. That doesn't mean I don't have doubts. But when you also have doubts about things I do or say or make decisions about, it puts me in a panic. So I strike out sometimes, trying to defend myself, hoping to make you see how wise and courageous I've been. I hate to go back to England like this. All crazy and unprepared. I haven't seen you for weeks and now I'm fixing it so we won't see each other for even more weeks. But what can I do, darling? What in the world can I possibly do under these circumstances but what I'm doing? I hate running away from you. But I really can't face what I know I'll be facing in England if I think you're angry with me.'

'I'm not angry. I didn't say you shouldn't go. I never questioned that.'

'You see, this is what happens to me when I get away from familiar terrain. I'm like a dog who has courage only in his own yard. I'm not going to rail against California. We've had those discussions many times. Too many times, perhaps. But we've found a middle ground. We have our lovely house by the sea now and I promise you we won't have a war in future whenever we have to spend some months there. But all the same I'll never have my feet on the ground there as I do in England. That's not a choice on my part. It's outside my control. I undergo some chemical change when I'm there. I simply don't function properly. I don't like myself as much as I should. I'm also not as likeable. I'm sure of that. But, dear sweet man, I am trying. I'm doing my best. I just feel when I'm there the way an epileptic must feel, not knowing when the next seizure will hit him. Of course it doesn't make sense when one views it logically but it's painfully real for me. When I first had the news about what had happened at the Towers the thought that came instantly to my head was: it never would have happened if I'd been in England. I see you're smiling. You think that's a ridiculous conclusion. And perhaps it is. But all the same I'm sure my father would have been accessible to me. At least he would have talked to me. If he'd seen me standing under his window with the constable he wouldn't have fired his rifle the first time. And if I'd been outside his door I'm certain he wouldn't have killed me with his shot-gun.'

'But you weren't there,' Kincaid said. 'You couldn't be there.'

'It's certainly true that I wasn't there. But I could have been. And I'm tortured because I wasn't.'

6

Sophie's perceptions about Trevor had been correct. Like all young men his age he did have a secret life. More accurately he had secret aspirations, private thoughts and desires and ambitions. Along with his determination to keep all his new-found passions and convictions to himself, he felt an almost irresistible compulsion to share them with someone. Not a parent, however. And certainly not a sister. No one who would try to restrict him

442

or pass judgement. When he began to spend long hours in Homer Tony's cottage, drawing portraits of him, it slowly dawned on Trevor that he had found a perfect confidant. He began to talk as he worked, rambling here and there on any subject that came to his mind, gradually delving deeper into his own thoughts and feelings.

'When I first met you Kincaid told me you were his oldest friend and his best friend. At first I didn't believe him. I thought he was just saying that for some reason. But then, after I saw the two of you together, walking across the fields or up and down the beach, or sitting on the stone wall out there at the edge of the cliff, I could tell that what he'd told me was the truth. You know how I knew you were really friends? Because you never get tired of each other. Does that sound funny? I've decided that's what it means to be friends with somebody. Take my sister, for example. I really like her. She's smart and she's nice to look at, and when she's in the mood or when there's nobody else around she's pretty nice to me. I mean, she's my sister, you see, and I love her. And I'm sure she loves me in her own way. We've spent our entire lives together after all and that must count for something. But all the same I never think of her as a friend, as a close friend, as my best friend. She never could be, you see, because after we're together for a bit she gets very boring. Anything she says is something I've heard her say a hundred times before. And that gets tiresome, doesn't it? But on the other hand, when you have a real friend, they always have something interesting to say. Or if they say the same thing several times it seems interesting. You don't feel like putting your fingers in your ears and running off to hide. I mean, a real friend is somebody you never get tired of and they don't get tired of you. Or if they do, they don't think it's helpful to let you know about it. You know what I'm saying?

'Let's take Kincaid, for example. As I said, there are all kinds of reasons for you two to be friends. You've done a lot of stuff together. You've known each other since you were young chaps. But what chance is there for me to be his friend? No chance at all. Or so it seems. But all the same I am his friend whether he knows it or not. I'm always glad to see him. And ever since I met him the first time, almost two years ago now, I've thought that the two of us would end up as good friends. Not because he's married to my mother. Not because we all live in the same house – at least we do when I'm at home and he's at home – but just because we can talk to each other. The best thing about him, I guess, is that he doesn't say too much. But when he does talk he knows how to do it. He's not just talking to hear the sound of his own voice or to try to make you like him. Did you ever notice that about Kincaid? He never tries to make people like him. You never hear him say anything like, "You may not agree with me and if you don't, I apologize in advance because after all it's only my opinion and I may be wrong . . ." I hate all that namby-pamby beating around the bush, trying not to hurt anybody's feelings, hoping everybody likes you. When somebody gets all wound up on a subject, carries on for twenty minutes, and finally asks, "Don't you agree, Mr Kincaid?", it's very likely he'll get no for an answer. No bloody apologies, no kissing anybody's bum. Just no, I don't agree, and that's that. The reason people get bored with each other is because they know exactly what to expect. When you have a really good friend you don't mind if you get a surprise now and then.

'Here's the problem, however. Most of the grown-ups I've known don't want to be surprised. They never like surprises. My mother, for example. She has things figured out as well as anybody I know but when it comes to surprises she wants nothing to do with them. I expect when she grew up people learned a lot of rules, a rule for everything, and then they were stuck with them. Sophie's not a maniac about it, I don't mean that, but she's not

444

in the market for something new. Tried and true, things I know, articles and ideas I can count on. That's her slogan. There's something to all that, I suppose, but if you carry it too far it can cause a lot of trouble. Let me give you an example. My mum is all excited about my being an artist. She likes paintings and poetry and classical music. Culture. She's a cultured woman. Her mother's a cultured woman. Good books in her library. Classics. And valuable paintings in the great hall. A Van Dyck, a Constable, a Raphael. Serious stuff. So they're not embarrassed to have a painter in the family. Not yet, at any rate. That's because I'm in the learning process, learning my craft, doing still-lifes and portraits and life-drawings, copying old masters, laying a foundation. When anybody sees my work it seems familiar so it's acceptable. There's nothing that requires an explanation or an apology, no reason to turn a picture to the wall when the Bishop comes to tea. But I'm just a beginner, you see. There's no way of knowing what sort of turn my work will take as I go along. Now I'm trying to draw like da Vinci or Dürer or Degas. I can't do it but that's what I'm reaching for. What happens if I end up painting like Soutine or Münch or Modigliani? Art is full of surprises if it's any good. That's what Ben Quigley says. And Grell tells his students the same thing. So how will the family handle it if I start producing work that they think is an ugly mess? Remains to be seen. Chances are they'll hold their noses and look the other way because they're up against something they haven't seen before. Then we'll see what happens when the Bishop comes to tea. We'll see then, won't we?'

Trevor had spent many hours with Homer Tony, had talked his way through countless subjects, personal, familial, and aesthetic, before he edged his way one afternoon into the subject of Lucy Street.

'She's had a complicated life, this girl. Lucy, who I probably mentioned before, the one who models for us in Mr

Grell's life-drawing class. Her parents separated when she was only four years old and her father went off to New Caledonia. And a few years later her mother died of influenza. So Lucy grew up with her half-sister, Grace, who's ten years older. When she told me she felt as if she'd never had a father I told her my dad died three months after I was born. That's when we started to be friends. Like finding out you were born on the same day or your mothers had the same maiden name. Something in common. I expect it wouldn't work out that way if you met an ugly girl with bad breath and she said, "You see we both have warts on our chins." But when it's somebody you want to find common ground with you'll use anything for an excuse.

'The first time I saw this girl, the first time I ever laid eyes on Lucy she was as naked as a cherub. Doing her job. Nothing self-conscious about her, strolling about in her robe between poses, then slipping out of it again as naturally as if she was in her own bedroom. She has the face of a child but I decided that day she must be a girl of the streets, as the old books call it, or she wouldn't be standing there starkers for hours at a time in front of strangers. You see, I'd never seen a naked woman before except in photographs and cheap magazines. I used to see Sarah flipping about on the upper floors in her knickers and nothing else but once she was allowed to wear silk underthings that was the end of it. So there I was, second row from the model stand, staring at this beautiful young girl and trying to draw her picture. But it didn't affect me like looking at pictures of harem girls with my mates at St Alban's. I mean, Lucy was so matter-of-fact about it you couldn't imagine her doing anything personal with a man. She was just a model and we were all trying to draw her picture, and that was that. And once she and I started to talk a little bit between poses and I saw the way she was, serious about her work and trying to train herself for a career as a dancer, it never entered my head

446

. . . I mean, I just looked at her and thought, "She's sure a terrific model and a nice girl", and I always liked it when she turned out to be the model for the day.

'Two or three times we had a cup of coffee together after class was over. She wanted to hear all about England. What life was like in London. All that. She already knew the names of the British ballet companies and the ballerinas and what ballets they were famous for. Then I told her about Wiswell Towers and going to school at St Alban's, and she told me her sister, Grace, works in films as an extra or a stand-in and also does stunts sometimes or gets to speak a few lines. She told me Grace does pretty well because she has a friend in the business who's a famous cameraman. He worked on *Dr Jekyll and Mr Hyde* and *King Kong*. I thought she meant that this cameraman was like a friend of the family or something, till she explained what "friend" meant. She said that was why she and her sister have a nice place to live on *Las Flores* and it's also why her sister sometimes doesn't come home at night.

'Anyway, one day when class got out early I walked home with her and she invited me upstairs to see the flat she shares with Grace. It was a nice place all right, every room painted a different pastel colour, and Chinese rugs on the floor, and mirrors on almost every wall. She showed me her bathroom that had a pink tub and sink, and her sister's bathroom, where everything was violet-coloured. Even the towels and the bathmat. And violet curtains at the window. "Grace even wears violet undies," she told me. I didn't stay very long that day but just before I left we kissed each other. Standing just inside the door at the top of the stairs. It was a very hot day. My shirt was sticking to me and Lucy's body felt warm and damp through her blouse. I held on to her like I was going under water and she hung on to me the same way. It felt like we were wired together standing there in that alcove at the top of the stairs and I wanted to stay that way till

447

I died. Finally she said, "You don't have to go yet, do you? Grace won't be home tonight."

'I wanted to stay all right. God, how I wanted to stay. I wasn't sure what would happen but I was keen to find out. But I'd rung up home when I left Grell's class and told the driver to meet me at the corner of Santa Monica Boulevard and Las Flores at five-thirty. When I looked at my watch it was five forty-five. I told her the driver was waiting and I had to go. So I left and she stood there in the doorway watching me go down the stairs. I felt like a stupid clown but I knew I had to go, not just because the driver was waiting for me but because I was scared to stay. Does that sound dumb? It sounds dumb to me. But I was afraid she'd find out I didn't know *anything*, that I was a stupid bloke from London who didn't know the first thing about women.

'As soon as I was in the car heading for home I knew I'd made an ass of myself. And next time I saw her in Grell's class I was sure of it. She was nice to me, all right. But it was the way she'd been in the beginning. She treated me the same as she did everyone else in the class. And when I asked her to go for a coffee after the session ended she said she was late for her dance class. Then she smiled at me and said, "But at least I don't have a driver waiting." So I knew she was sore at me. And every time I've seen her since she's been the same. Cool and sweet and not interested. And there was another rotten development. I can't draw her picture now. When she takes off her robe and stands up there with nothing on, I get so hard I have to drape something across my lap. My face gets red and my hands get cold and wet, and I ache so much I can hardly sit there on the bench. She stands there on the model stand with a little smile on her face, just looking at me as if she knows what's happening to me and I deserve it.'

Lucy didn't appear at Grell's class for several sessions after Trevor had told his story to Homer Tony. When

Trevor asked the class monitor about her he said, 'We haven't been able to contact her. I guess she's not available.'

When Sophie told him about Brannigan the day before she left for New York and told him that he and Sarah would be coming along a few days later, Trevor began ringing Lucy's number. But no one answered. The next day he slipped away from his school, called a taxi and went to her apartment. No one answered the door. He tore a page out of his school notebook and scrawled a note on it.

This is terrible. I have to go back to England. Leaving Friday. I have to see you or I'll die in the street like a dog. Please ring me. Here's my number.

Thursday morning she rang him at home. 'I was in San Bernardino,' she said. 'I just got home this morning. Are you really leaving tomorrow?'

'I have to take the train at three in the afternoon.'

'I'm sorry I've been so stupid,' she said. 'Can you come here?'

'When?'

'As soon as you can. Now.'

Trevor made no explanations before he left the house. He simply instructed the driver to take him to the corner of Las Flores and Santa Monica. When he got out of the car he told him to pick him up there the following morning at ten.

He also made no explanations when he returned home the following morning. Oliver met him just inside the hall and asked him if he'd be having breakfast.

'Yes, Oliver. I'll have a tray in my room.'

'Joseph says there'll be traffic because of the football match. He thinks we should leave just after one.'

'Thank you, Oliver. I'll be ready in good time.'

Sarah, who had come home just half an hour before

449

Trevor, had also offered no explanations, had felt no impulse to reveal that she was arriving, not from her sheltered school in Ojai, but from Culver City. She had spent the night there, in a bungalow court, with Burt Windrow.

7

When her train from Chicago arrived in New York City, Sophie went directly to the pier where the *Aquitania* was boarding. From the purser's office she rang Kincaid in Chicago. 'I'll bet I woke you up,' she said.

'No. I was up early. Getting my head together.'

'When do you go up to Wisconsin?'

'Some time tomorrow. Rotten weather up there. But we start shooting day after tomorrow, no matter what.'

'You don't sound too happy about it.'

'I'm hung-over. Evan and I held a wake last night for Brannigan. Just the two of us. We found a pub called O'Leary's on Clark Street and drowned ourselves in Guinness and Jameson's.'

'You poor thing.'

'Don't worry about it. I've got a big pot of coffee here and I recover fast.'

'Good. And you mustn't worry about me either. I'm better today. I love you and I'll cable you as soon as I get to Southampton. Then a long letter from the Towers when I'm settled in there.'

Twenty minutes later his telephone rang again. It was Gloria Westerfield. 'I know you're awake and moving around,' she said, 'because Sophie just called. She told me you're hung-over and grumpy and in need of distraction. She made me promise to take you out this evening.'

'That's very nice of you but I think I'll pack it in tonight. We take off for location sometime tomorrow morning.'

'I thought you'd say no but I promised Sophie I'd ask you anyway.'

'I'm sorry,' he said. 'If it was any other time . . .'

'Don't worry about it. I understand. If you change your mind for any reason I'll be at the Stafford Theatre at seven forty-five this evening. *Anything Goes* opens there tonight and I promised a friend at the *Tribune* I'd do the review for him.'

'Thanks again. But I don't think I'll change my mind.'

'I don't think you will either. Good luck in Wisconsin.'

He stood at the window then, looking down at the lake. It was raining, a cold, straight-down November rain, soaking the beach and running deep in the gutters along Lake Shore Drive.

When he turned away from the window he finished a cup of cold coffee, shaved and showered, and got dressed. Ten minutes later, in a long raincoat and tweed hat, wearing the smoked glasses that had become a necessary feature of his public wardrobe, he walked south along the edge of the lake in the rain that had now turned to a cold mist. Crossing Chicago Avenue he went along to Ohio Street. Turning west there he crossed St Clair Street and Michigan Avenue. In a small coffee-shop at the corner of Wabash Avenue he found a table by the window and ordered a breakfast of ham and eggs and potatoes. He sat there for more than an hour eating, drinking coffee, and watching the traffic on the street outside. When he left the coffee-shop the rain had stopped but the wind off the lake was picking up, blowing leaves and papers through the tunnels of the east-west streets. With the wind at his back he walked along Ohio Street to Clark Street, then turned north to Division Street. He found O'Leary's, where he'd been the night before with Evan, and went inside. He hung his hat and coat on a rack just inside and sat on a stool against the wall at the near end of the bar. He ordered a bottle of beer, took off his dark glasses, wiped the moisture off them with a paper napkin, then put them on again.

It was late morning now. Two grey-haired women in coats and shawls and wool hats sat in a booth by a window on the Division Street side of the room, and an old man, thin and wasted, with stringy white hair and a Donegal cap on the back of his head, sat half-way down the bar, nursing a glass of whiskey and smoking cigarettes, lighting each one from the glowing butt of the preceding one.

Just after the bartender, a wiry fellow with no expression on his face, brought Kincaid his third bottle of beer, the old man, stepping briskly, came along the bar and around its corner to where Kincaid was sitting.

'Pardon me, sir, my name is Duggan. I'm a harmless fellow as Richard, the barman, will tell you, so you needn't be afraid that I need a drink paid for or anything of the sort. I've amply provided for my old age so I'm not dependent on a soul. What I'm saying is that there's no act of commerce involved here. I'm neither a borrower nor a lender. Do you mind if I take this stool for a moment?'

'Help yourself.'

'Thank you,' Duggan said. He hitched himself up on the stool and carefully set his half-full glass on the bar.

'Don't annoy the customers, Billy,' the bartender said. 'Leave the man in peace.'

'It's none of your affair, Richard. I appreciate that you're trying to run a decent place but you've no worry about me. You pay half your electric bill with the money I lay out in here. And besides, this gentleman will tell you, if you ask him, that I had his permission before I perched on this stool.'

'Just don't wear him out, that's what I'm saying. Don't take up all the air in the room. Let the man breathe a little.' He turned to Kincaid. 'Am I right, Jack?'

'It's all right,' Kincaid said. 'He's not bothering me.'

'Nor will I do that,' Duggan said. Richard moved away

452

to the far end of the bar and gave his full attention to a news broadcast on the radio. 'However,' Duggan went on to Kincaid, 'there is a question I'd like to ask you if you wouldn't be offended.'

Kincaid turned and looked at him. 'If you think I might be offended you'd better not ask me. I take offence easily.'

'No, you don't. I'd gamble on that. I know your sort. Tough as a nut. Always ready to fight but not eager to start one up.'

Kincaid smiled. 'Not me. I'm no fighter. I'm a fast runner.'

'Don't tell me that. I know a hard-nose when I see one. But you've got some humour about you as well. Show me a man without humour and that's a man I'll never drink with.' He sipped carefully from his glass, savouring the taste, making it last. 'When I heard you order your beer from Richard, just after you sat down, I thought to myself, "Where have I heard that voice before?" So I studied you from where I was sitting just down the bar. No clues came to me. Then you took off those black cheaters you're wearing to wipe the rain off them and I had a good look at your face. That prompted me to come along here and ask you a question concerning your identity. If it offends you in any way just tell me to toddle off and that's what I'll do.' Another sweet sip from his glass. 'I'm sure I'm mistaken about this but on the other hand I might not be. Is there any chance that you might be connected with the movie business in some way?'

'Not me.'

'No chance that you could be an actor, hiding behind those black glasses, looking for a little privacy?'

'No chance.'

'Let me tell you my routine. I come here after breakfast every morning, have a sandwich at lunch-time, and then at about two or three I stroll up to North Avenue to the Jewel Theatre and see the double feature. Sets me back a quarter and they change the programme every day or so. So that's where you'll find me of an afternoon. If they don't change the programme it's all the same to me. That just means I'll see the same bill twice. If business is especially good they've been known to keep the same pictures going for a week. Or if it's one good one and one dog they'll keep the good one like as not and change the other one every day. Now here's what happened a couple of months ago. They had a picture that ran a week or ten days and I saw it every day except Sunday. That's the day I don't go to the movies. The reason is, this saloon's not open of a Sunday and I'm not about to struggle down to North Avenue from my place just to see a movie. On Sunday I have breakfast downstairs at the Greek's while the wife sleeps in. Then I go over to Lincoln Park if it ain't raining and see what the chimps are up to. Do you think you're descended from the monkeys? I don't. Not me. Not for a minute. But as I say that I have to admit there was a great-uncle on my mother's side who seemed to support the theory.' He sat looking at Kincaid for a moment. 'Would you mind taking those dark glasses off again so I could have another look at you.'

'Yes, I would mind.'

'Sorry, then. Just thought I'd ask,' Duggan said. 'That picture I mentioned, the one I saw six or seven times, had a guy in it looked a lot like you. Played the main part. Don't remember his name. Don't remember the name of the picture either but it was an Australian tale. Kind of a cowboy story. About an outlaw. Don't remember his name. What's your name, by the way?'

'Thorne. Julian Thorne.'

Duggan shook his head. 'I guess you're not the guy. You sure you're not an actor or something?'

'I'm sure.'

'Your first name – Julia – that's a woman's name, ain't it?'

'Not Julia. *Julian.*'

'You sure have the look of that actor. The same voice, too. Did anybody else ever tell you that?'

'You're the third person today.' Kincaid gave him an electric smile.

'Well, there you are. Proves I'm not batty. You hear that, Richard? Three other people mistook him for somebody, the same as I did. What's your line of work?'

'Kincaid looked around the bar area. 'I sell napkins,' he said. 'Paper napkins.'

'I'll be damned. Here's a guy gonna sell you some merchandise, Richard.'

Kincaid shook his head. 'I'm here on vacation I work in California. Los Angeles area.'

'That must be why I took you for an actor. You meet many actors out there?'

'I've met a few.'

'What are they like?'

'Some good, some bad, like everybody else.'

'I read in the paper the other day, some divorce lawyer said, what every woman in this country really wants is to divorce her husband, go to California, and be a movie star. You think that's right.'

'I don't know.'

'I can't imagine my old lady as any kind of a movie star. She might get by as a Marie Dressler type but that's about it. Are you a married man?'

Kincaid nodded.

'Is your wife here in Chicago with you?'

'Not this trip.'

'Hear that, Richard? Here's a man gets to travel without his wife along.' He turned back to Kincaid. 'My wife wouldn't let me go to Kankakee by myself. Went to Calumet City with my brother-in-law one time but we came back before supper. When I leave home in the morning, Esther knows I'm heading for O'Leary's here and after that to the Jewel Theatre, and that's all right with her, just as long as she knows where to lay hands

455

on me. But no sashays out of town. None of that. No crossing the Cook county line. She says, "Any place you go, I go with you. That's what being married's all about." She ain't right about most things but I guess she's right about that. If she goes off to Sheboygan for a day or two to visit her daughter I always think I'll have a hell of a time while she's gone. Eating Chinese food out of a carton and listening to the radio half the night if I want to. But by the time she's been gone three or four hours I'm like a jumpy tom-cat. Catch myself listening for her on the hall stairs. Can't wait for her to come back. Isn't that bewildering . . . an old fart like me? But like the fella says: Can't live with 'em, can't live without 'em.'

He finished his drink then and slid off his stool. He leaned close to Kincaid and said, 'You're a pretty good liar, buddy, but not good enough. I knew you was that actor the second you took off those shades. It must be a pain in the ass havin' to slip around some place, tryin' to have a peaceful drink or two without people like me pesterin' you to death. I'm sorry I bothered you but I'm like everybody else, I guess. I had to make sure. I know your name's not Julia, too. I'll look you up in my wife's *Silver Screen* magazines tonight and find out what your name *really* is.'

It was mid-afternoon when Kincaid got back to his hotel. The rain had commenced again. He took off his wet clothes, put on a robe and slippers, and sat in a chair by the window looking out across the lake. After a while he lay on his back on the bed but he couldn't go to sleep. At five o'clock he got up, got dressed, and had some food sent up from room service. At seven forty-five he met Gloria Westerfield in the lobby of the Stafford Theatre on Monroe Street.

Four days after Kincaid went to Iron Lake, Wisconsin, to film the final location sequences of the Dillinger film and one day after Sophie's arrival in England, Ursula Martin, their pantry-maid and kitchen-helper, ran into the sheriff's office in Malibu, near midnight, her blouse torn and bruises on her face. She told the duty officer she'd been attacked. Forty minutes later two deputies went to Homer Tony's cottage, handcuffed him, and took him to the Santa Monica jail.

The story appeared in the next edition of all the Los Angeles papers, along with an angelic professional photograph of Ursula and a ferocious production still of Homer Tony taken during a gun-battle scene in *Bushranger*. One paper printed the pictures side by side on the front page. Over Ursula's picture, one word: VICTIM. Over Homer Tony's picture, one word also: SAVAGE.

The Thornwood company worked late the next day. Thorne had bought an old resort lodge on a backwoods lake eighty miles north-west of Chicago. The plan was to shoot interiors first, the Dillinger gang members inside the lodge, before and during their gun-battle with the government men. The final exterior shots then would show details of the siege, and end with the destruction and burning of the lodge and Dillinger's escape. Great care had been taken in the planning. The filming would be critical because everyone knew that once the buildings were in flames and finally destroyed retakes would be impossible.

When Kincaid got back to the location hotel, Angelo, the production assistant, met him in the lobby. 'Gloria Westerfield's been trying to reach you. She's in Chicago. I left her number under your door.'

Kincaid rang her as soon as he was back in his room. She said, 'Has anyone told you about Homer Tony?'

'No. What happened?'

She told him all the details she knew from the California papers. Also what she'd learned from the Associated Press office in Los Angeles. 'It's awful,' she said. 'The papers are going crazy. They've tried him and convicted him already. If they keep it up there'll be a lynch-mob outside the Santa Monica jail by tomorrow afternoon.'

A few minutes later, when he hung up the phone, Kincaid called Julian Thorne in the trailer they were using as a production office. 'I've got to see you and it won't wait. I'll meet you in your room in five minutes.'

Thorne was waiting in his room with the door open when Kincaid got there. 'Have you talked to the coast today?' Kincaid asked him.

'Half a dozen times at least. Sam calls me every time he makes a bet on a horse.'

'Did he say anything about Homer Tony?'

'Yes, he did. I was going to mention it to you this evening. He's in some kind of a scrape with the police. I knew you'd be upset about it so I thought I'd better not mention it till we shut down for the day.'

'You mean, you've known about it all day?'

Julian nodded. 'Since sometime this morning.'

'Jesus Christ, Julian. What if my wife was run over by a train? Would you wait till we had the last shot of the day before telling me about it?'

'Of course not. But this is hardly . . .'

'Hardly what?'

'I mean, it's not your wife, nobody's dead, and since there's nothing we can do about it from here . . .'

'There's a hell of a lot I can do about it. I'm flying out there tonight.'

'You're not making sense, kid. I know this guy's an old pal of yours but it sounds as if he did something he shouldn't have. Here's what I suggest. I'll call Sam, we'll get a hard-nosed lawyer on this and your friend will be out on bail in two hours.'

'You don't know the whole story, Julian. The prosecutor's already said Homer should be held without bail. They're crucifying the poor bastard. When the papers get through with him he won't be safe on the streets even when he does get bail. Somebody has to be there with him, to talk to him and tell him what's going on. Since I'm the only friend he's got, it has to be me.'

'Who told you all this? About the prosecutor and everything?'

'Gloria Westerfield. I was just on the phone with her. She's been talking to the guys in her Los Angeles office all day. The AP plane is flying from Chicago to LA at midnight tonight and she said I could be on it.'

'Use your head. Have I ever screwed you up? What makes you think I'm going to now? You're disturbed about this and I don't blame you but give yourself some time to settle down and think it over. I'll call Sam right now and tell him to get hold of Ralph Sugarman. He's the best criminal lawyer in California. Let's handle this whole thing by the numbers instead of going off half-cocked.'

'That's exactly what I want to do. Handle it. Tell Sam I'll call him as soon as I land at Burbank. I'll be going straight to the Santa Monica jail from the airport. Tell him to have Sugarman meet me there.'

'You're not listening to me, are you?'

'I haven't missed a word, Julian. But I know what has to be done.'

'All right. Let me try again. I guarantee you, Sugarman can tie this whole thing in knots that will take weeks or months to untangle.'

'And what happens to Homer Tony in the meantime?'

'He'll be at home. Out on bail.'

'You can't guarantee that, Julian, and you know it. But what if he does get out? He's helpless by himself. Do we lock him in a hotel room some place and hire somebody to keep him there? What happens to his head all this time? What happens to *him*?'

'We'll work something out. And before too long you'll be back out there. We'll all be back. Two more weeks, three at the outside and we'll have this picture in the can. A week or ten days in the studio and we're home free.'

After a long moment Kincaid said, 'I thought we were talking about a poor silent bastard who's locked up in a cell trying to figure out what's happening to him. But it looks as if I'm the only one who's concerned about that. You're talking about getting your bloody picture finished on schedule.'

'You bet I am. I'm not ashamed of that. We've got tight deadlines here. You know that as well as I do. Sixty people on the payroll. Weather problems. Time problems. All kinds of headaches we can't even anticipate. A lot of money at stake. My money. Your money. I'm in the picture business. So are you. All of us are. None of us can come and go. We have to stick with it. You know the rules. You know what I'm talking about.'

'That's right. I do. You're talking about a picture that may go over budget if I go to California on that plane tonight. I'm talking about a man who might be dead if I don't.'

'Oh, for Christ's sake, Kincaid . . .'

'I know what I'm talking about. They've got him caged up out there in the same cell with God knows how many derelicts and crazy drunks. He can't be locked up like that. Either he'll kill somebody or he'll kill himself.'

• CHAPTER 12 •

1

In the near-empty tri-motor plane flying from Chicago to Los Angeles, re-fuelling in Albuquerque, Kincaid sat by himself, looking through a small window at the starless dark, a plump lady wrapped in a fur coat sleeping in her bulkhead seat at the front of the cabin, a grey-haired man in the rear quietly tapping on the keys of a portable typewriter balanced on his lap.

Kincaid had gone to sleep as soon as the plane was airborne. But an hour later he was awake, a blanket folded across his legs, the cabin dark and cold all round him, no sound except for engine growl and the gentle tapping of typewriter keys. He felt smothered by puzzles he couldn't solve.

Trying to put these concerns out of his mind, trying to clear his brain so he could sleep again, he found Gloria Westerfield repeatedly coming into focus, heard her voice . . . 'Trying to do too much and trying to do it too fast. Isn't that always the problem? Santayana said – I think it was Santayana – size and speed are the enemies. Make it bigger. Do it faster. Build it higher. Beat the clock.'

After they'd met at the theatre in Chicago, after they'd seen the performance of *Anything Goes*, he had gone to the Associated Press offices with her and waited while she typed up a review of the show. Then they went to a restaurant called Siena in an alley fifty steps below the level of Michigan Avenue. 'You won't have to wear your dark glasses here,' she said as they went in. 'Nobody will bother you. Only Capone's friends wear dark glasses at Siena.'

They drank Bardolino, ate squid and carbonara, salty bread-sticks and *vitello piccata*. And they talked till two in the morning. More accurately, she talked and he listened. 'I get energized when I go to the theatre. Especially if it's a happy show and everything turns out all right. My sister, Ellen, says my mind was frozen at age eight. She thinks I still believe in trolls and goblins and fairies and living happily ever after. And it's true, I guess. Does that mean I'm a simple soul? Probably. The odd part of all this is that I'm a 28-year-old spinster who lives alone in a rented apartment, while my sister has three children, a splendid husband, and a great showplace of a house on twenty acres west of Boston. She does endless research and publishes her views in important magazines while I write a silly newspaper column about one-dimensional people in a two-dimensional business. What I'm saying is that my sister has everything but she's nervous and full of anxiety. By her standards I have nothing. Yet I'm disgustingly content. It doesn't make sense, does it? But it's true. Maybe I am simple-minded. I'm sure that's what Ellen thinks. Or perhaps I'm just lucky. Do you believe in luck?'

'I used to. I believed in bad luck,' Kincaid said.

'How about now?'

'Now I don't think about it.'

'That's odd,' she said.

'How so?'

'I'd expect you to feel lucky. Because you are, you know. You have everything that most people think they want. You're young and successful, you have money and you're famous, you live in a mansion and you have a beautiful wife who adores you. So unless you're suffering from a mysterious illness . . .'

'I'm not.'

'There you are. You're healthy as well. With all that you say you're not lucky?'

'I didn't say that. I said I don't think about luck. I don't.'

'What do you think about?'

'I used to think about survival, how I was going to make it through the next day or the next week. That was all I thought about. I still think about that,' he said. 'You don't believe me, do you?'

She smiled. 'I wouldn't put it that way. I'd say it's hard to believe.'

'You're right. It is hard to believe, I expect. But old habits hang around.'

'Are you saying you're like my sister? Nervous and driven?'

'No. I'm saying I never expect anything to last. I keep wondering what I'll do when it all goes away and I'm back where I started.'

'Are you serious?'

'Sure I'm serious.'

'But it can't just go away. You're in demand. Any studio in Hollywood would be delirious to get their hands on you.'

'I know that. But one rotten picture and I'd be back on the street selling apples.'

'You're putting me on, aren't you?'

'A little bit. But all the same, bad luck never surprises me.'

'So you're a pessimist? Is that the message?'

'Not exactly. I just have a lot of idle time to think.'

She sipped her wine and looked at him over the top of the glass. 'You had nothing before and you could get by with nothing again. Is that what you're saying?'

'Something like that.'

'I think you're just saying that to make me feel good.'

'Why would that make you feel good?'

'I told you I have nothing by most people's standards but it doesn't bother me. You have everything but you're saying it wouldn't bother you if you had to give it up.'

'I didn't say it wouldn't bother me. I'm saying it wouldn't surprise me. And I could live with it.'

'How would you live with it?'

'What do you mean?' he asked.

'You say you think about it a lot. You must have thought about what you'd do if you had to start over.'

'I'm not sure what I'd do. But I know where I'd go.'

'Where would you go?'

'Tasmania.'

'Sophie told me you hated it there.'

'I was a kid. I hated what was happening to me. But I never hated the place.'

'What's it like?' she said.

'Mountains and lakes. And it's as green as Ireland. Small and slow. Nice beaches. Nothing very big. Nothing very fast.'

'My kind of place.'

He shook his head. 'I don't think so. I can't see you in Tasmania.'

'Why not? Don't get me wrong. I'm not inviting myself. I'm just curious. Why would Tasmania be out of bounds for me?'

'Too primitive. It's still a frontier island. Have you ever been to Nebraska?'

'No.'

'Neither have I. But I expect it's a bit like Tasmania.'

'No rivers or mountains or lakes in Nebraska. No beaches. The ocean's thousands of miles away.'

'As I said, I've never been there. Don't expect to be.'

'And I'll never see Tasmania.' She smiled. 'Too primitive for me.'

'It was a horrid crossing,' Sophie said. 'Dreadful winds and high seas. Dishes crashing about in the dining-salon, passengers stumbling round on the decks and in the public rooms. And a surly staff as well. The only good feature was that it helped to keep my mind off the situation here. How are things now? How is Margaret?'

Clara Causey had met her at the railway terminal in Newcastle. They were being driven back to Wingate Fields, where Margaret was waiting.

'It's hard to say. I think it's still too soon to know what the effect of all this has been. One day I come to a conclusion, the next day quite a different one. As you know, your mother is always determined not to burden other people with her woes and troubles. So there's that struggle going on inside her. I wish she could just wail and weep and get drunk and break china and work some of the pain and confusion out of her system, but she simply cannot behave like that. Even when she first had the news, in a circumstance where I would have been hysterical, she was dead silent, almost catatonic. I stayed with her all the time, we slept in the same room, and she didn't even weep at first. Then, the second night after the chief constable had been here to explain to her what had happened, I heard her crying in the night. And the following morning she wept terribly in the morning-room after breakfast.'

'How did she get the news? Who told her?'

'John Trout spoke to her first on the telephone. Then Mrs Whitson. And at last the deputy chief constable was on the wire with her for several minutes. She told him she'd be coming home at once but she collapsed as soon as she was off the telephone. Our doctor came round straight away and gave her a strong sedative. We put her to bed and there was a nurse who stayed with her until two days ago.'

'And poor Jack Brannigan . . . did Margaret . . .'

'She wasn't allowed to see him, of course. When the chief constable came along here, the doctor and I spoke to him before he saw Margaret and we all agreed that no purpose would be served by telling her the dreadful details. She knew of course that Brannigan was dead, that the Major had shot him, and that Cranston himself had been taken under guard to a military hospital outside Newcastle, but the dreadful truth about Brannigan's head-wound, the ugly destructive effect of that shotgun blast, was kept from her. As were the facts about Cranston, who had wet himself and was found whimpering and mumbling military commands, sprawled in a corner of his sitting-room, when the constables broke in. My husband had gone over and taken charge as soon as we had the news, and he was appalled by what he saw. He arranged for Brannigan's burial and a simple service a few days later.'

'Was Mother there?'

'No. The doctor wouldn't permit it. And I stayed here with her. Ned was there, of course, and John Trout and Mrs Whitson. Brannigan was placed in your family crypt and it was all over quickly. No one knew how to locate his children until Margaret was taken off the drugs. She told us then where to find their addresses. So letters have been sent off to them. Perhaps you'll want to send a more personal note yourself.'

'Of course.'

Later, as they came in sight of Wingate Fields, Sophie said, 'I'm trembling. I can't understand it. I've come all this way, I can't wait to see her, and yet I dread seeing her.'

'You'll be surprised, I think, but not in the way you may imagine. I think you'll find her very much her old self. She's not, of course, but she's found a way to cover up. Doesn't refer to the whole terrible happening at all. At least not with me. And when it does come up in some way, she seems almost matter-of-fact about it. Resigned to it.'

'I've seen her like that. When Toby died. She was terribly attached to him, as you know. But two weeks after we buried him she seemed to have put all the memories behind her. It was as though she'd forgotten he existed.'

'But she hadn't, of course.'

'Of course not,' Sophie said.

'You've had some experience with it then so you won't be surprised.'

'Is she eager to go back to the Towers or is she reluctant to go?'

'She's said nothing about it. But I know there's a lot on her mind that she's not letting out.'

'Has all the damage to the house been dealt with? No evidence left of any sort of . . .'

'No. Ned saw to that straightaway. The constables carried off all the Major's hideous arsenal, and Trout packed up his other bits and pieces and stored them away. And Brannigan's caravan was put in the carriage-house out of sight.'

'Then she could go home at any time? Whenever she's ready?'

'Yes, she could. But I haven't suggested it. And perhaps you shouldn't either.'

'I'll have to see about that,' Sophie said. 'Sarah and Trevor will be along soon and I'm sure she'll want to be back at the Towers when they get here.'

'One would hope so. But you'll have to judge that for yourself.' As the car rolled up to the south entrance Clara said, 'One more thing. I know this is a sad occasion for you but if you can hide your feelings from Margaret I think it would be a wise choice.'

'I'll do my best.'

Half an hour later, after she'd freshened up and changed from her travelling-clothes to a jersey and trousers, Sophie went down the corridor to the rooms that were always kept for Margaret's use at Wingate. When she went in her mother was sitting by the garden window with a book. 'Oh, there you are,' she said. She came to meet Sophie and put her arms round her. 'I thought I heard the car on the south drive. Then Clara popped in a few minutes ago and said you'd be along as soon as you'd changed. Come and sit down. The tea has just arrived. A moment before you.'

As they sat in chairs facing each other across the tea-table Sophie said, 'How lovely you look.'

'Rose gave me a shampoo this morning. She said I had to look my best for your homecoming. And she laid out this new frock for me to wear. So if I look nice it's Rose who must take all the credit. Now, what about you and Kincaid and the children? Clara says you had a nasty crossing.'

'Yes, I did, but that's behind me now.'

'Good. Are Trevor and Sarah with you or did you drop them off in London?'

'They didn't come with me. They'll arrive next week on the *Leviathan*. Along with Oliver and Mrs O'Haver.'

'I see. And Kincaid?'

'He'll be here by mid-December, I hope. But not later than Christmas in any case.'

'Then you came alone?'

'Yes, I did,' Sophie said. 'As soon as I heard . . . when I had a cable from Clara.'

'How thoughtful and kind you are. To come all this way. Leaving your family behind.'

'What else could I do? I had to come. It never occurred to me not to come.'

Margaret tested her tea, dropped another sugar in the cup, and tested it again. When she spoke again her voice was quite soft. 'It was a dreadful nightmare. Never in my life did I imagine such an awful thing could happen to me. Or to anyone else. And I can't help feeling I was to blame for it.'

468

'You're not to blame in any way. Daddy was sick. He's still sick.'

'But did I bring him to the point of doing what he did? That's what I keep asking myself? If there was a war between your father and me, why did Jack have to suffer for it?'

'Because he was there. It's as simple as that. Daddy also shot a constable. Because *he* was there. If he'd wanted to kill Brannigan he must have had a hundred chances to do it earlier. He shot through a door. He may not have known Brannigan was there.'

'But he heard his voice, they said . . .'

'It's not your fault, Mother. No matter what. You're not to blame. Disturbed people do wicked, crazy things.'

'And now your father's to be locked up in a room somewhere.'

'That's not your fault either,' Sophie said.

'Whose fault is it then?'

'It's nobody's fault. Things happen. Toby went to war and he died. And Jack Brannigan . . .'

'Jack married me and he died.'

'You have to stop this. What good does it do? Fixing blame doesn't change anything. It's rotten and it's painful, but it's over. Life's not fair. It was never meant to be.'

Margaret smiled. 'Ahh, but for some it's more fair than for others.'

'It is. But there's nothing you and I can do to change that. All we can do is feel bad.'

'And that's how I feel,' Margaret said. 'I'm trying to believe everything you tell me. And I do believe it. My brain believes it. But dear God, how do I change the way I feel? I feel as if I'm the one who died.'

'But you haven't. And you're not going to.'

They sat silent then for a few minutes, each of them fully occupied, it seemed, with her teacup. At last Margaret said, 'I know you came home because you felt

I needed you, and I'm grateful for that. But I wish you hadn't. I wish you hadn't taken the children out of school and disrupted their work. I was hoping we could keep all this from them as much as possible.'

'But how could we ever do that, Mother? We can't pretend the Major's gone off on holiday. We can't say that Brannigan died a natural death. I'm sure everyone in the county knows what happened. It was a police matter. So how can we keep it from Sarah and Trevor?'

'Perhaps we can't. But I wish we could. I'd hoped they could be told later when they came home as you'd planned, just before Christmas. You know what I'm saying. We might have protected them a bit, not made it such an emergency, such a catastrophe.'

'Good God, Mother, it is a catastrophe. It's a tragedy for you and for all of us, for our entire family. And Trevor and Sarah are part of that family. They'll soon be grown-ups. Independent people with their own responsibilities. Of course I don't want to hurt them or upset them if I can avoid it, but when something like this happens they can't be excluded.'

'Perhaps not. But I would have tried, nevertheless. You see, there's nothing anyone can do, Sophie. It's not family business as you say. It's all my sad affair and I have to patch my life back together as best I can. I'm not sure yet how I'll go about doing that but I see very clearly that it's something I must do on my own.'

'Of course there are things that no one can help you with. I understand that. But that's not to say that none of us can be helpful in any way. I daresay Clara has been quite helpful.'

Margaret nodded. 'Yes, she has.'

'And your family can be helpful as well. I can be helpful. That's why I'm here. I'm sure it would be impossible for you to enquire about my father's condition, to find out about his medical profile, and to see what criminal actions may be brought against him.'

470

'I'll never be able to see him or talk to him again,' Margaret said. 'I'm ashamed of the way I feel but I can't change it. To me he's dead. It's odd. I can't believe that Jack is dead and I refuse to believe your father's alive.'

'But that's what I'm saying, you see. You mustn't be put in a position of answering questions or making decisions about him. Or arranging for his legal defence if that becomes necessary. Those are things that I must do, whatever my personal feelings may be. Many such matters will have to be dealt with. That's why I must be here. And there's the Towers to think of. I'll be taking you home now in a few days. But before I do I'll want to spend some time with Trout and Mrs Whitson to make sure there's been no slippage there, that they've put that ugly day behind them and brought the household back to proper order.'

'You needn't be in a rush about that. I won't be going back just yet.'

'Of course not. I expect it will be a week before I have things shipshape for you. But I'd like to see you safely tucked up there before I dash down to London to meet Sarah and Trevor and get things in running order in my own house.'

'I'm not in a rush, Sophie, and you mustn't rush me.'

'Oh, I shan't. Whatever you like. Whatever's best for you. If you prefer to stay here till I come back up from London, then let's do that. Then when you're back home I can stay on with you and we can make plans for Christmas together.'

'I haven't given a thought to any of that. I don't think I want to do a big Christmas this year.'

'I understand that. Neither do I. Just family and whatever really close friends you want to include. Or perhaps we'll have an evening for staff and the family and no one else.'

'I don't want to do Christmas at all this year,' Margaret

said. 'Clara says I can stay on here. Or perhaps I can go to London for a few days with you.'

Sophie ate a watercress sandwich and sipped her tea. Margaret sat with her hands in her lap looking at her. At last Sophie said, 'I think I know better than anyone what you're going through. When Toby died I wished I could die too. But I couldn't and I didn't because I had two small children to look after. And that's what saved me. I forced myself to go on with the details of my life. I kept myself busy. I realized that other people depended on me. I knew I couldn't forget about my grief but I saw that I mustn't let it destroy me.'

'I know you're determined to do what's best for me but I have to decide what that is,' Margaret said.

'I don't mean to preach a sermon, but I think the sooner you put yourself back into a familiar routine at the Towers, dealing with the staff, managing the lands, the sooner you'll start to feel like yourself again.'

'What if I've decided I don't want to feel like myself?'

'I don't know what you mean by that.'

'I mean, I don't like myself a great deal just now. I feel very much a part of all that ugliness you referred to. All of it was related to me in one way or another. It's hard for me to live with that. And I can't imagine that rushing home to all those familiar rooms will make it any easier. As far as my familiar routine is concerned, it doesn't exist any longer. Never before was I an aging widow living alone with her staff. Now that's what I'll be. Through the years, at various times, you and Trevor and Sarah were there, and Toby and your father. And Evan and Arthur Tagg. And finally Jack Brannigan. I love my home. You know that. But I never saw it as a separate thing in and of itself. It was a place where certain people lived. People who were dear to me, close to me, part of me. My life, my days, my routine as you call it, was linked to them. The Towers existed for me in relation to those people. Now it's become a place where I must live by myself. With an old woman's memories and an old woman's nightmares.'

'You're not an old woman. Why do you say that? You mustn't think of yourself that way.'

'Yes, I must. Because it's true.'

'You're only fifty-five, for God's sake.'

Margaret smiled. 'When Jack was alive, I was twenty-five.'

3

Ralph Sugarman was hated by some people, feared by many, and respected by everyone. No one in the film business knew anyone else who had graduated from Princeton. He spoke like an easterner, dressed like an easterner, and lived in Pasadena with his wife and daughters exactly as he had lived in Philadelphia. He loved the conflict and chicanery of criminal law but he never let that love interfere with lucrative fees in other legal areas. His presence and his name, his flawless wardrobe, and his arrogant silence at an adjudication table were considered to be, and nearly always proved to be, immeasurable assets to a nervous swindler or a studio head who had stolen a scenario from a penniless writer.

Sugarman was waiting for Kincaid when he arrived at the Santa Monica jail. After they shook hands Kincaid said, 'I know Sam Thorne put pressure on you to come here but don't hold that against me.'

'Nobody puts pressure on me. Not even Sam.'

'I mean, if you're just going through the motions that's not good enough this time.'

'It never is. But before you get yourself overheated, let me tell you a couple things. I've been making phone calls ever since I talked to Sam yesterday afternoon. I guarantee you, I know more about what happened than you do. Number two, my daughter wrote her Master's thesis on Aborigines. Homer Tony won't be a surprise to me. And I won't be a surprise to him. Today I'll just be listening.'

Earlier that day Sugarman had arranged for Tony to be put in a private cell. He and Kincaid met with him there, Tony sitting on his cot, the other two on stools.

'This man's a lawyer, Homer. He's going to help us. I just have to talk to you for a few minutes. Then we're going to get busy and arrange to get you out of here. How does that sound?'

Homer smiled and nodded his head. 'I'm going to ask you some questions about Ursula Martin, the girl who works in the kitchen for us. The one who used to bring your supper to you every evening. You remember her?'

Homer nodded again.

For fifteen minutes Kincaid questioned him. Sometimes he asked the same question twice. Or came back to it later and rephrased it. After each question Homer Tony soberly shook his head or nodded. Sugarman said nothing. He sat quietly, looked at his hands or the floor, and occasionally looked up at Homer.

When they walked out of the building Kincaid said, 'You weren't looking at him. How do you know how he responded?'

'I don't have to know. You know. No man can think straight when two people are staring at him. Come on. Let's sit in my car for a few minutes.'

'What do you think?' Kincaid said when they were inside the car.

'You know him. You asked the questions. What do you think?'

'He never touched that girl. I'd bet on it.'

'She told the prosecutor she's always been afraid of him.'

'The servants told my wife she wasn't afraid of anything in trousers. Apparently she bounced around with half the workmen who came on the premises.'

'So why would your friend be an exception?'

'That's what I thought,' Kincaid said, 'but he says no, and I believe him. He's not retarded, you know. He's not stupid. Just because he can't talk . . .'

'So he'd be smart enough to lie about her if he knew his ass was on the line.'

'Sure he would but not to me.'

'If he didn't do it, what's the girl's angle?'

'I don't know.'

'I don't know either. It doesn't make sense. But funny things happen out here. I asked a guy in the prosecutor's office how she got from your place to the sheriff's station on the coast highway – that's six or seven miles – and he said somebody drove her there but she was so upset she doesn't remember who. Another thing, not long after she talked to the police her lawyer showed up, a small-time guy from Sherman Oaks named Henry Flanders, and a man named Stuart Teal was with him. Said he was a family friend. Said she'd telephoned him before she went to the sheriff's station.'

'Who's he, do you know?'

Sugarman shook his head. 'My office is checking on him. We're also looking into a few other corners. Let me put things together and call you tonight. Where will you be?'

'At home. Sam knows how to reach me.'

'Good. I'll check in with him in an hour or so. By the way, am I working for him or for you?'

'For me. Sam has his own agenda. I'm not discussing anything with him till you and I decide where we're heading.'

'Good. That's fine with me.'

'What about bail?' Kincaid said.

'The District Attorney's nervous about it because of all the publicity, but I've been after them since yesterday and they know they have to cave in. It's going to be a high figure though. They're trying to cover themselves. They'd like to set an amount so high that nobody will come up with it. But I won't let them get away with that.'

'How much are we talking about?'

'Thirty thousand maybe. Could be more. Fifty at the most.'

'How fast can we do it?'

'No more than forty-eight hours after I put on the pressure at City Hall. How fast do you want him out?'

'I want him out but I want him safe. At least he's in a cell by himself now.'

'That's right. Let's see where we are. Then we'll decide when to pull him out. I'll ring you at home tonight.'

When Kincaid drove up the highway from Santa Monica to his house a uniformed guard stopped him at the gate. 'Sorry,' he said. 'The family's away. Nobody goes in.'

'Do you know who lives here?'

'We're not allowed to give out that information.'

'I live here. My name's Kincaid. I own this place.'

There was another guard sitting in a car at the front entrance to the house. And a third one in his shirt-sleeves drinking coffee in the kitchen. Of the staff, only Ernest, the handyman, and his wife, Bettina, who'd been the cook's helper, were still in residence. They were playing cards in the breakfast-room. They seemed rattled to see Kincaid. 'Nobody told us you'd be coming,' Bettina said. 'There's nobody left here now but us.'

'Just the two of us left,' Ernest said. 'Mrs Kincaid told us we'd be kept here to look after things till further notice.'

'Then you will be.'

'I've been kept awful busy just cooking for all these guards sitting around. They're hard to please, I tell you that,' Bettina said.

'Well, as long as I'm here, you only have to worry about cooking for me. Tell them they'll have to make

476

other plans for their meals. They don't live here. They just work here.'

'They won't like that much.'

'If they don't like it, tell them to talk to me about it.'

At ten-thirty that night Sugarman called. 'Sorry I'm late. My youngest daughter gave a piano concert tonight at Marymount. Damned good, too. So I just got home a few minutes ago. I practically live in my car. That's the price I pay for having a house in Pasadena. Hope I didn't wake you up.'

'Wide awake. Anything turn up?'

'Nothing to put in the bank, but a couple of interesting things all the same. One, this guy, Stuart Teal, doesn't seem to be a family friend. In the first place I don't think he's anybody's friend, and in the second place, the girl's family lives in Ohio. Teal's from the Midwest, too. Came out here from Detroit about five years ago. The police say he was locked up half a dozen times in Wayne County. Nothing heavy. Nickel-and-dime stuff. And out here he's been picked up at least once a year. He's got the Hollywood bug but no way to finance it. Can't seem to decide whether he's a talent agent or a pimp. Mostly he's a small-time con artist, working on young girls who want to be movie stars. The other thing we found out is that the photographs of the girl and Homer Tony were hand-delivered to all the papers in town the same night she went to the sheriff's office in Malibu. It looks as if some of the pictures may have been delivered even earlier. How does that sound to you?'

'It smells.'

'I agree.'

4

The next morning Kincaid met Sam Thorne for breakfast at a coffee-shop on Franklin Avenue. 'How's everything in Wisconsin?' Kincaid asked.

'You know Julian. He weeps and wails and threatens to fire everybody. Then the next thing you know, he's solved his problems and he's all smiles. He's at his best when the shit hits the fan. Why do you think he's riding herd on this picture, wearing his boots and cowboy britches and slopping around in the mud, instead of staying here at his desk and keeping the studio on the rails? Two reasons: one, he loves trouble; and two, he's like all the rest of these studio heads out here – he wants everybody in town to think he's creative. You tell any of those bastards that you liked one of his studio's pictures and he'll say, "Big trouble on that one. The rough cut was a mess. I saved it in the cutting-room." Julian's no different. You gave him a problem when you left Chicago and now he's busy solving it. Changing schedules, checking the weather, figuring out how many days he can shoot without you. And unless you drop dead in the street he'll find a way to bring the picture in on schedule. That's what he's good at. How'd you make out with the lawyer?'

Kincaid told him about his meeting with Sugarman the day before. And their telephone conversation later that night.

'Sounds like a scam to me,' Sam said.

'That's the way it sounds to us. So we've got a scam of our own.'

An hour later, back in his office, Sam put through a call to Henry Flanders. 'This is Sam Thorne, Mr Flanders. Do you know who I am?'

'Yes, I do.'

'Good. One of our producers here at the studio is interested in a young woman named Ursula Martin. We understand you're her lawyer.'

'I am representing her, yes. What can I do for you?'

'We'd like to have a talk with Miss Martin. There's a part in a picture we're planning that she might be right for. Our producer is just here for the day so if she's interested we need to see her this afternoon.'

'I see,' Flanders said. Then, 'Miss Martin has an adviser, a personal manager. You'll have to talk to him first.'

'No, I don't have to talk to anybody else. I'm talking to you. You talk to him. Tell him to be here with his client at three this afternoon. And if he thinks he's doing me a favour, tell him not to come.' Sam hung up the phone then, turned to Kincaid who was sitting on the couch near his desk, and said, 'How'm I doing? Do I get the part?'

Kincaid smiled. 'I'll have to check with Julian first.'

'Screw him. He wouldn't know a good performance if he saw one.'

Stuart Teal and Ursula Martin arrived at Sam's office promptly at three o'clock. He kept them waiting for half an hour while he talked on the telephone with John Corso. When his secretary ushered them in, Sam studied Teal as they took chairs in front of his desk. Teal was short and slender, pale skin and close-cropped dark hair. Like many small men he took long steps and swung his arms, imagining that thus he appeared taller. He wore an off-the-rack dark suit and an expensive tie with a fake-diamond pin. He sat as tall as he could in his chair and forced himself not to stare at the splendour of Sam's office. 'I want to be fair about this,' he said as soon as he sat down. 'Mr Flanders mentioned something about an interview with a producer. Miss Martin will talk to no one if I'm not present.'

Without hesitation Sam stood up and said. 'Thanks for coming in. The interview's over.' He pressed the button on his intercom and said, 'Get me my brother in Wisconsin. Leave a message for him to call me back if he's on the set.' He turned to Ursula, 'Sorry, young lady. You look to me like you could have a future. But you're dead in the water unless you get a new manager.'

'Wait a minute . . .' Teal said.

'I said the interview's over. Now I've said it twice.'

'I don't know what you mean.'

'Then I'll spell it out,' Sam said. 'This is my backyard. I'm the bulldog here. Nobody waltzes in here and starts telling me the rules. I make the rules.'

'I didn't mean to say . . .'

'Who the hell are you, anyway? I know everybody in this town and I never heard your name till today. Who do you think you're talking to?'

'He didn't mean anything, Mr Thorne,' the girl said.

'That's right,' Teal said. 'I just wanted to explain . . .'

'Explanations I don't need,' Sam said. 'Once you opened your mouth I knew all I needed to know about you.'

'I can see you're angry but let's try to work out a solution . . .'

'I already worked out the solution. I want you to disappear.'

'I ain't afraid to talk to somebody by myself,' Ursula said. 'I'll audition or do a screen test or whatever you want.'

'I'll handle this, Ursula . . .' Teal said.

'Maybe I've got a chance for a contract here,' she said. 'I ain't gonna let you screw it up. You're supposed to help me, not get people mad at me.'

'She's smarter than you are,' Sam said to Teal, 'why don't you go hang out at the pool-room so I can talk business with this young lady.'

'I don't know anything about business,' she whined. 'I just want to act. I want to show people what I can do.'

Sam turned to Teal again. 'And you want to show me what a sharp negotiator you are.'

'I have a personal management contract with her.'

'I'll bet you do.'

'He's really smart, Mr Thorne. You'll see. And he won't be trying to make any rules, will you, Stu?'

Teal looked uncomfortable but didn't answer. Ursula smoothed her skirt along her thighs and said, 'Can't I go along and see that producer now?'

'That depends on your personal manager.'

'He don't care,' she said, 'do you, Stu?'

Again he didn't answer. Finally Sam said, 'Why don't we do this? You go along for your interview, Miss Martin, and your friend and I will sit here for a few minutes and see if we can put together a deal. We'll be talking about a seven-year contract. I assume that's all right with everybody.'

After Ursula floated out of the room and down the corridor with Sam's secretary escorting her, Sam said to Teal, 'I think you may have a money-maker on your hands, kid. She's certainly off to a good start with all the publicity she's been getting. Don't misunderstand me. That must have been a rotten experience for her but she seems to have come through it all right. After what I read in the papers I was afraid she'd walk in here looking like she'd been run over by a truck.'

'She wasn't badly beaten. The papers were wrong about that . . .'

'I thought the police report said . . .'

'No. She was just . . . you know.'

'Yeah,' Sam said. 'Terrible thing. But sometimes something bad leads to something good. Here she is, a few days later, talking to a major studio about an acting career. I guess that's what she's always wanted. That picture of her in the paper was certainly a professional portrait. Done by a man who knows how to photograph beautiful women. And you have to hand it to the newspapers: they all had a print of that picture by the time the police picked up Homer Tony. I was talking to Dale Biggers in our publicity department and he said he never saw a news story, a crime like that, get such instant photo coverage. They even had a portrait of the guy they arrested. Biggers said that head shot came out of our files.'

'That doesn't mean anything,' Teal said. 'You can buy any production still you want at Larry Edmund's bookstore on Hollywood Boulevard.'

'Is that a fact? I didn't realize that.'

'Make a copy negative and print as many of them as you want.'

'But how do you suppose the identical photographs got to the papers all at the same time? Who made the copies?'

Teal's eyes hooded over a bit as if he suspected he was being led down a dark street.

'Hard to say,' he said. 'Maybe they weren't there at the same time. Maybe one paper had them first and then the others managed to catch up.'

'Maybe so. But whoever got the job done deserves a lot of credit. That's the kind of operator our publicity people are always trying to hire.'

An angular smile from Teal. 'If somebody tells me how all that happened I'll get in touch with you. Times are tough. Lots of people trying to make a dollar.'

5

Ursula Martin was taken to an empty office in the executive building. While she waited she stepped into the wash-room and inspected herself in the looking-glass. She wore a flowered rayon frock that clung to her plump body, no stockings, and very high-heeled ankle-strap slippers. She fluffed her hair, retouched her lipstick and mascara, and tightened the wide belt of her dress. She studied herself again and opened one more button in front of her dress. Quickly then she unbuttoned the dress to her waist, slipped her arms out of the sleeves, removed her brassière and put it in her handbag. Fully confident then that she looked her best, she went back into the still-empty office. She stood half-turned to the wide window so whoever saw her there would have the impression that she was quite tall.

When Kincaid came in and said, 'Hello, Ursula, I'm

sorry I kept you waiting,' she didn't recognize him at once. Checking her nails and her *décolletage*, she didn't look at him fully till he sat behind the desk and said, 'Take a seat. Let's have a talk.'

'Ohhh . . .' she said, 'it's you. I think I'm supposed to be . . . I mean, I'm seeing somebody else. A producer, they said.'

'That's right. I'll be producing my next picture. I asked to see you after I saw your picture in the paper.'

'Gee, I feel funny. I didn't expect it to be somebody I knew already. After what happened and everything. With that man. And even before that I knew your housekeeper was trying to get me canned because somebody told her a bunch of lies about me.'

'I'm not interested in any of that. The newspapers said you hoped to be an actress. That's why you're here this afternoon.'

She sat down, smoothed her dress, and said, 'It's funny, but a time or two I was tempted to ask you if you could help me get a start in pictures. But I always lost my nerve. Now here we are. I'm sitting here because you asked me to come.'

'That's right. And I'm happy to see you looking so well. No one would guess from looking at you what you've been through.'

'Well, the newspapers exaggerated part of it. It wasn't exactly the way they said. And besides my manager, Stuart Teal, says we don't want to talk to the press or anybody about all that. He says it's a bad image for me. He sees me doing parts as an innocent young woman. At least at first. Girl-next-door. You know what I mean. Like I really am.'

Kincaid nodded. 'I want you to know that I'm very sorry all this happened to you at my home, while you were working for me. I feel responsible for people on my staff. And in this case, of course, the man involved also worked for me. He's a man I've known since we were boys together. I was shocked to hear it.'

Suddenly she looked uncomfortable. 'I was pretty shocked myself.'

'I heard before that you were frightened of him, that you refused to take meals to him in his bungalow.'

'I didn't refuse exactly. He just looked awful queer to me. I never seen anybody that looked like him before.'

'Had he ever tried to touch you before? Was that why you were scared of him?'

'He didn't exactly do anything till this time. I just kept thinking he would. And finally he did. I wish you wouldn't ask me any more questions. My manager says I'm not supposed to tell anybody nothing. Not till after the trial.'

'He's right. You're lucky to have a good man giving you advice.'

'He's got plenty of ideas all right.' She smiled. 'Stu says we're going to be millionaires. Isn't that a hoot?'

'Well, I hope he's right. Sounds like an ambitious fellow. How long has he been your manager?'

'I just signed papers with him a few days ago. But I've known him for about six weeks.' She giggled. 'And he's been giving me advice since the first day I laid eyes on him. He's a handful, all right. You talk about smart, he's smart. Got an answer for everything.'

Kincaid got up then, walked round the desk, and leaned against the edge just in front of Ursula. 'Let me tell you about this project I'm working on,' he said. 'When you find out about it you may not be interested.'

'Oh, I guess I'll be interested no matter what,' she said. 'Beggars can't be choosers. Stu would murder me if he heard me say that. He says I should always act like I don't give a darn whether I get a job or not. But I'm not like that. When I want something, I want it. And I've wanted to be an actress since I was ten years old back in Ohio.

I guess I'd do just about anything to get to the top and be somebody.'

'Most actors feel that way, I guess. As long as they don't have to break the law or do something that hurts somebody else.'

She blushed suddenly. 'Why'd you say that. About breaking the law? I didn't break any law. Not that I know of. I'm a victim. That's what the papers said. Big print, right over my picture.'

'And they said Homer Tony was a savage. Do you think he's a savage?'

'I don't know what he is. I don't want to talk about him.'

'I can understand that. That's why I thought you might not be interested in this film I'm planning. You see, it's about a young woman your age who goes to the police and tells them she was raped.'

'I guess I'm an expert on that, ain't I?'

'She identifies the man just as you did, but when the trial starts the man's lawyer tries to prove she wasn't raped after all.'

'I guess a girl would know if she was raped.'

'You'd think so,' Kincaid said, 'but the writers have done a lot of research on this and there are hundreds of cases where the jury has decided that the defendant hadn't raped the woman, that she'd been a consenting partner, as they put it. And in some cases they've decided that she hadn't been touched at all, that she just made the story up for some crazy reasons of her own.'

'Who would tell a story like that if it wasn't true? It's embarrassing. Having your picture in the paper. Being recognized by people in the street.'

'That's a good question. But you have to remember that some people would do almost anything to have their pictures in the paper and be recognized wherever they went. Everybody in my business wants to see his name in the paper. They think it's necessary. And maybe they're right. Look at you, for instance. You and I wouldn't be talking like this, and your manager wouldn't be talking with Sam Thorne, if your picture hadn't been in all the papers. I must have seen you a hundred times at my home but I never thought of you as an actress till I saw your picture on a news-stand.'

'You've got me all mixed up now. I don't know what you're getting at.'

'I'm trying to find out if it would be awkward or embarrassing for you to act in a movie that seemed almost like a part of your own life. Would it?'

'Life is life and acting is acting, ain't it?'

'I think so. But a lot of actors haven't worked that out yet.'

He walked back to his desk chair and sat down. 'I know you're not an experienced actress but I'll bet you know a lot about how movies are made.'

'I sure do,' she said. 'I read all the magazines, especially the ones that have screenplays in them with a part for me that I can read out loud. And I've read books about cameras and lighting and all the technical stuff. I always told myself that when my big break came along I'd be ready. I can even do make-up. I can make a cut or a bruise on somebody's face so it looks like the real thing no matter how close you get.'

'Good. So you know about auditions then. Doing readings for casting people or directors.'

'I sure do.'

'All right. That's what you and I are going to do. I have some pages here from the scenario for this film I've been telling you about. It's just a first draft. The character's names aren't even decided yet. It just says *lawyer* and *girl*. The girl is the one who says she's been raped and the lawyer is the defence attorney. Don't try to act or be theatrical. Just talk to me the way we've been doing. When I'm speaking you listen carefully, and when you talk say it as if you mean it.' He reached across the desk

486

and handed her four or five pages of dialogue. 'This lawyer has been questioning the girl for a long time. They're both tired and he's angry. He's trying to make her admit she's lied and he's being pretty rough on her. This is what we call a cold reading. No rehearsals and no cameras. The important thing is for us to make contact with each other, for you to feel what's going on, to realize what the lawyer's saying to you and what it means. Are you ready?'

'Yes.'

Kincaid came round the desk again, leaned back against it, looking down at her. Reading from the script, he spoke very softly at the beginning. 'I've been questioning you for some time. I've asked you a great number of questions and you've answered them all. The judge has heard those answers, and so has the jury. What would you say if I asked you now if you've answered truthfully.'

'I did. I told the truth,' she said, reading from the script.

'What if I said you're lying, that you've been lying since this trial began.'

'That's not true. I'm not a liar. I'm not.'

'What if I told you that I have proof that you've lied? What if I produced a witness who swears that the man you accused was in another part of the city when you said the attack took place?'

'Who says that? He *was* with me. I mean, he wasn't *with* me exactly. He surprised me. He . . . he did everything I said.'

'All right . . . let me ask you this. You've heard the defendant testify. Do you think he's a liar?'

'I didn't say he was a liar.'

'If you were a member of the jury hearing him testify, do you think you'd say to yourself, "That man's a liar"?'

'I didn't call anybody a liar.'

'But if you say he attacked you and he says he didn't,

487

then one of you is lying. You've sworn on the Bible that you're telling the truth so he must be lying.'

'I'm not telling any lies, I'm sure of that.'

'Then the defendant must be lying.'

'All I know is what he did.'

Kincaid turned to the next page of the script. 'How long have you known the defendant?'

'I don't know exactly. A few months, I guess.'

'If I said it's been exactly fifteen weeks would that sound right to you?'

'I guess so.'

'You worked together . . . is that correct?'

'Not together exactly. We worked for the same company.'

'So you saw each other every day?'

'There weren't so many people working there. We all saw each other all the time.'

'Did you talk to the defendant? Did you have conversations together?'

'We talked once in a while.'

'Did he ever ask you to go out with him?'

'No. I wasn't interested in him that way.'

'Did he ask you questions about yourself or tell you things about his own life?'

'No.'

'Did he ever hold your hand or try to kiss you?'

'Gosh, no.'

'So as far as you could tell he wasn't interested in you at all.'

She shook her head. 'I guess not. He never said anything.'

'Then all of a sudden one day he attacked you. That's what you've sworn to in this court.'

'That's what I said and that's what he did.'

'Did he say anything to you that day, at that time?'

'I don't remember. I don't think so.'

'Did he seem angry? Do you think he wanted to hurt you?'

'No. He just wanted to . . . like I said.'

'Did you kick him or scratch him or try to fight him off?'

'I don't remember.'

'And as far as you remember he didn't say a word to you?'

'I don't think so.'

Ursula's face was flushed now and her voice was fainter. She stumbled over the words as she read. Twice she dropped a page of script on the carpet and had to retrieve it. 'Are you all right?' Kincaid asked, and she said, 'I guess I'm just nervous.'

Kincaid studied the scenario for a long moment before he started to read again. 'I don't have much more to ask you. Just a few more minutes. Why do you think the clerk asks you to put your hand on the Bible when you swear to tell the truth?'

'So you'll know it's serious.'

'That's right. Most of us are taught that it's a sin to lie. To lie after you've sworn to God to tell the truth is even more serious. Do you believe that?'

'Yes.'

'Then there's the legal aspect of it. On the witness-stand everyone is required to tell the truth. When a witness lies he can go to jail. When he knowingly accuses someone of a crime they didn't commit, the punishment can be even more severe. I'm sure that's been explained to you before.'

Ursula looked up from the script and said, 'Do we have to read this whole thing, Mr Kincaid? I thought maybe you'd heard me enough to . . . you know what I mean . . . to see if I can . . .'

'Are you all right?'

'I'm awful shaky but I'm not sick or anything.'

'Let's just go on to the end then. We're almost finished.

489

You don't have any more lines but it's important for me to see your reactions to what the lawyer says.'

He looked at the script again and started to read where he'd left off. 'In cases like this where there's no real physical evidence, where it comes down to one person's word against another's, strange things can happen. A jury must decide who's telling the truth, the plaintiff or the defendant. Perhaps this jury has already made up its mind. So what happens if a man is falsely accused and the jury believes his accuser? The defendant in this case, for example, has never been arrested before. He's not a law-breaker. But if the jury believes your story his life will be changed for ever. You insist that you've told the truth, and if you have you've simply done your civic duty. But God help you if you haven't. If you've lied under oath either an innocent man will go to jail or you will.'

She sat staring at him. The script pages slipped to the floor beside her. Her face had gone suddenly white. 'I'm scared,' she said. 'I'm scared to death.'

6

The next morning Kincaid met Sugarman at his office in Beverly Hills. When they sat down Sugarman said, 'As I told you on the phone, and as I explained to Thorne last evening, that telephone conversation and this meeting between the two of us are ghost events. They never took place. If this case ever goes to trial, and I don't think it will, the information you're about to give me and what Thorne told me yesterday will be useless to me. If what took place at Thorne's studio came out in court I'd have to withdraw from the case.'

'I understand that. What I don't understand is why you think the case won't go to court.'

'Let's hear what you have to say first about your

meeting with the girl. Then I'll tell you how I see it.'

Kincaid told him in detail exactly what had happened when he'd talked with Ursula, when they'd read the script pages that had been prepared for the purpose. When he finished Kincaid said, 'I think it was a good idea. I was all for doing it. But I felt like a bastard when it was over. She's a poor dumb kid trying to make a score any way she can. And that bastard Teal has her tied in knots.'

'All right,' Sugarman said. 'Let's see where we are. Both you and Thorne think this whole thing was engineered. Either Homer Tony didn't go near her, or she served herself up on a plate in front of the poor bastard and he took what was offered. Teal picked her up and dropped her at the sheriff's station. Then he contacted the papers and saw to it that they all got photographs. Without ever showing his face. Is that the way it looks to you?'

'That's right. Something like that.'

'Your friend's innocent so there shouldn't be any problem getting him off. You've got an expensive lawyer and all the facts. And justice will be served. Right?'

'I have a feeling you're about to hit me on the head with something.'

'I am. I'd bet a year's income that Homer Tony's innocent. But the facts haven't changed, the charge hasn't changed, and the courts don't pay off on instinct and divine revelation. This is still a case about a young pretty girl who swears she was raped and a man who can't deny it. He can only shake his head. It shouldn't matter that he looks like something out of *National Geographic*, but it did matter to people who saw his picture in the papers and it will matter to the jury when they see him in court. There are a lot of Bible-thumpers out here in California and they love to be on juries. Those people think any fornication deserves six months' hard labour. Give them a shot at a guy who looks as if he should have a bone stuck through his nose, who's accused of preying on a blue-eyed girl from Ohio, and they'll vote to burn him at the stake in Griffith Park.'

'But if we believe Homer Tony's innocent,' Kincaid said, 'then can't the case be presented in such a way that the jury will believe it, too?'

'I'm supposed to be pretty good at that. And maybe I could pull it off this time. But so far I haven't found the weenie. In this country you're innocent till you're proved guilty. Everybody knows that. But sometimes it doesn't work that way. Our friend, Mr Tony, was convicted in a lot of people's minds the day his picture appeared in the papers. When a pretty girl sits on the witness-stand and points to a man and says he raped her, and that man can't even go on the stand and say she's lying, there's a real problem.'

'Isn't there a chance she might change her testimony?'

'Why would she do that? I'm sure Flanders and Teal are telling her they're home free. Flanders is no genius but he's not stupid either. And I guarantee you, Teal can't wait for the trial so he can drum up some more publicity for her.'

'You don't think I scared her with the perjury business?'

'I'm sure you did, but she's in a corner no matter what she does. If she comes clean now and admits she was lying – before the trial, I mean – she beats the threat of a perjury citation but she makes a public ass of herself and wrecks whatever chance she thinks she has to be an actress. I guarantee you, Flanders has her coached already. As soon as she's on the witness-stand she'll point her finger at Tony and then she'll start to cry. And she'll keep it up till the jury starts crying, too. Anything I ask her, she'll say she was so upset she can't remember. And Flanders will jump up and say I'm badgering the witness.'

'Sam had a couple of ideas. Did he tell you about them?'

'Sam has a thousand ideas. Most of them would land

me in the penitentiary. Or I'd end up practising law in the Fiji Islands under an assumed name.'

'He said he'd offer the girl a contract if she agreed to tell the truth. On the level. Guaranteed for a year.'

'That's his best idea. But very dangerous. If she got on the witness-stand and said Thornwood Studios was trying to buy her off, Homer Tony's goose would be cooked. Teal could say that already probably, based on his meeting with Sam. But I don't think Teal wants to go near any courtroom.'

'I don't think she'd blow the whistle on Sam. She'd cut her mother's throat for a screen test.'

'You're probably right. But still it's a risk. Because if it all blows up Tony's the one who suffers. He's in a no-win situation anyway, even if a miracle happened and he got acquitted.'

'How do you figure that?'

'Because of me for one thing. People who don't know any better think a high-powered lawyer can talk you out of any corner. So a lot of red-necks who saw those pictures in the paper and decided Tony was guilty will still think so. He'd either have to leave town or stay home all the time. And even then some motorcycle cowboy might decide to put a torch to his place some dark night.'

'How can these bastards get away with it? I hate to see people picking on a poor son of a bitch who can't defend himself.'

'How do you think I feel? I haven't been working on this mess because it's going to make me rich.'

'Is it really as black as it looks?'

Sugarman made a gesture with his hands. 'I'm not Jesus Christ. I could be wrong. But usually when I'm wrong it's from being too optimistic. When I'm pessimistic about a case it almost always turns out as bad as I expected. Sometimes a lot worse. But listen, never mind what I think. You're a smart guy. Forget what I've been saying. How does it look to you?'

'I thought if we convinced ourselves that it was all a put-up job, we'd be able to convince anybody. You see, I don't see him the way other people do. I don't notice the way he looks because I know what he's like inside. And that's what's killing me. He's a crazy bastard who only knows about horses and cattle and dogs and being outdoors all the time. Every time I see him in jail he seems to be a size smaller. For him, being locked up is like having the blood sucked out of his body. A quart every day.'

'Have you told him what we've been trying to do?'

Kincaid shook his head. 'I stay off that subject. I just bull-shit him and try to cheer him up. Talk about other times, when we worked together in Australia. He twisted a wire off the bed-spring and scratched the word *home* on the wall of his cell. I pretended I didn't see it. I don't know if he means my place up the coast or the cattle station where he's spent most of his life.'

When he left Sugarman's office Kincaid drove to Santa Monica and spent two hours with Homer Tony in his cell. Just before he left he said, 'Not tomorrow but the day after, I'm coming to take you home. Right after the middle of the day I'll be here to get you. How does that sound?'

Homer smiled, a wide grin, and patted Kincaid on the shoulder.

From the jail Kincaid drove down the Colorado Street ramp to the coast highway. He drove north, away from the pier, for a few hundred yards, then turned into a paved area at the back of the beach and parked, facing the ocean. He stayed there for more than an hour, slumped down in the driver's seat watching the gulls wheel in toward the pier and back out to sea in great careening circles.

When he started the car at last and pulled out into the afternoon traffic, he drove slowly toward Hollywood along Santa Monica Boulevard. When he came to Vine Street he turned north to Franklin, then up

Beachwood Drive to Thornwood Studios.

After he told Sam about his meeting with Sugarman, Sam said, 'That's what I hate about lawyers. They've got a sad-assed view of life. All they do is tell you what's impossible, then send you a bill for two thousand dollars.'

'He's right this time, Sam. I have to stop thinking about what's legal and what's right and try to do what I can for Tony. Sugarman pushed through the bail proceedings yesterday, I'll give them a certified cheque tomorrow, and the day after I'll pick up my buddy at the Santa Monica jail.'

'Then what?'

'That's what you and I have to talk about.'

7

Before she left Wingate Fields to go down to London, Sophie sent off a telegram to Arthur Tagg.

LUNCH ON WEDNESDAY. NO EXCUSES. I'LL FETCH YOU.
WE MUST TALK. URGENT.

She took him to a small restaurant on Half Moon Street. After they were shown to their table and brought drinks, she said, 'It's grand to see you. Seems like forever since the last time.'

'Yes, it does.'

'Many changes since then.'

'Yes, I suppose so,' he said.

'Have you heard anything about . . . I mean, are you in touch with anyone at the Towers?'

'I'm afraid not. No credit to me. Haven't been good about writing. Not keeping a good schedule as I used to. I work at the shop, have a bit of supper, listen to the wireless sometimes, then fall asleep. A new life. New habits.'

'I hope you're feeling well. You look awfully thin.'

'You think so? I haven't noticed. Don't think much about that sort of thing.'

'Shame on you. You must look after yourself, you know.' When he didn't answer she said, 'I hate to be the bearer of sad tidings but I'm afraid I have some frightful news to tell you.'

'Nothing about Evan, is it?'

'No. Evan's fine.' She told him then about what had taken place at the Towers, about Brannigan's death, Cranston's collapse, and the effect it had had on Margaret. 'She's lost her will, it seems, except in a negative way. She has no notion about her future. She's only firm about what she won't do. She refuses to go home.'

'Good Lord. What a shock she's had. Going through all that. Thank God she wasn't there at the time. But all the same I can see that she'd be reluctant . . . I can imagine her feelings about going back. Being alone there.'

'Everyone understands how she feels. That's why she must be helped. Trying to start a new life in Provence or on the Algarve is no answer.'

'Is that what she's thinking of?'

Sophie shook her head. 'Nothing so positive as that, I'm afraid. But that could be the next development. Those are places she knows. She might be tempted to go there.'

'Maybe that's the answer then. Perhaps she wants a change.'

'She's had a change,' Sophie said. 'That's the problem. The solution is not for her to isolate herself by the sea or in the country somewhere, surrounded by strangers speaking a strange language. Nothing warm or familiar to her. None of her family nearby. What she needs is to get back to what she knows and loves, to her own home, her staff, her animals, her gardens, and her friends. She has to find herself again, not try to create a new self.'

'Have you said that to her?'

'Of course. Many times since I came back.'

'And she doesn't respond?'

Sophie shook her head. 'She has a blind spot about it. I've never seen her like this. She usually thinks so clearly. When everyone else is confused and stumbling about she's the one who has the answers. But not this time. She seems to see the Towers as a cold deserted place where she'll be alone with nothing but ugly memories.'

'What can you do then?'

'I have to do something positive to show her she's mistaken. And I think I can do it. But only if you help me.'

'What can I do? There's almost nothing I wouldn't do to help. But just now . . .'

'I know that,' Sophie cut in. 'That's why I'm counting on you.'

'. . . in these circumstances,' he went on, 'I'm afraid I'm as helpless as you are.'

'But I'm not helpless, and neither are you, Arthur. I want to go to Margaret and tell her you're coming back to the Towers, to manage the lands and the tenants and the financial affairs as you did for so many years.'

He shook his head. 'No, you mustn't tell her that. I'm afraid that's out of the question.'

'No, it's not. Why do you say it is?'

'Things have changed. A great number of things have changed.'

'Of course they have. But other things have not. Margaret needed you before and she needs you again. In the same way. That hasn't changed. Now she needs you more.'

'Did she say that?'

'No. I haven't discussed this with her. She doesn't know I'm talking to you.'

'Then you may be making assumptions . . .'

'Damn it, Arthur, I'm not making assumptions. I know what the situation was and I know what it is now. Of course she wouldn't mention your coming back. Since she saw you that day at your bookshop . . .'

'You know about that?'

'Of course I do. She was bewildered by the way you treated her. Stunned.'

'I was awfully surprised to see her that day. Just there suddenly. Standing before me. I know I behaved badly. I expect she was angry about it.'

'Not angry. Bewildered, as I said. And hurt. She couldn't believe, after all the years you've known each other, that you'd suddenly treat her like a stranger. Like a customer.'

'I don't understand it myself. I just know it's something that happened. Unfortunate. But it's another reason why I could never . . . it wouldn't be appropriate . . .'

'Oh for the love of God, Arthur, we're not talking about manners or table-settings, we're trying, at least I'm trying, to help someone I care about, someone who's in terrible trouble and desperately needs to be helped.'

'I appreciate that. And I would help as well if I could. But I simply can't do what you're asking.'

'Why not? That's what I don't understand.'

'I have my reasons.'

'Oh, I see. Things you and I can't discuss. Is that it?'

'It's just that I've made certain choices and certain adjustments.'

She sat looking at him, stern and silent. Then she signalled to the waiter and they gave their luncheon orders. After the waiter moved away Sophie said, 'I'm going to be blunt, Arthur. You'll probably be angry with me but so be it. Do you think I don't know why you left us after more than twenty years and came down here to London? You'd had a silent war with the Major ever since he left military service and came home to live. But still you stayed on. When he accused mother of having

498

an affair with you and said he was suing for divorce and naming you in the action, you still stayed on. But when you found out about Margaret and Jack Brannigan, *then* you decided to leave. Margaret didn't want you to go, nobody wanted you to go except the Major and by then it was plain that he was the one who'd be leaving. So why did you feel compelled to leave a good situation in a place that was truly your home?'

'As I told you . . .'

'I know,' she said. 'You had your reasons.' Then: 'Did you imagine that your feelings for Margaret were stronger than her feelings for you? Don't you know that she'd have left my father years ago if she'd had any indication that you wanted to take his place?'

'I don't think these are matters that you and I should be discussing.'

'Maybe you're right but you must be patient with me because I'm quite desperate at the moment. If you think I'm trying to act the role of Cupid, you're mistaken. I'm simply trying to clear your head so you'll see that the important thing is not what happened years ago or didn't happen, not how everybody felt then or feels now – none of that. We're not concerned with who was married to whom and for what reasons and for how long. The question now is how we can help Margaret, how we can help her get right again, living in her own house, surrounded by her own things, doing her work, being herself. That's what we're talking about. That's all we're talking about.'

'But how can anyone help,' Arthur said, 'when she seems not to want it.'

'Because we must. I must do it because she's my mother and my best friend. And you have to help because you owe it to her. You don't want to hear that. I can tell from your expression. But I'm being blunt again. You owe it to her because she helped you. When you came back to England from America with a small son, no wife, and no house of your own to go to, she gave you a job and she gave you a home. She treated Evan like her own child and she treated you like a friend. I said she was my best friend, and she is. She's also your best friend. Any ideas you have in your head that have made you forget that are ideas you have to get rid of. You must help her, Arthur, because *she helped you*. She *needs* you, whether she admits it or not.'

8

Middle of the afternoon, cruel white sunlight and an off-shore wind coming in: a grey limousine pulled into the car-park behind the Santa Monica jail, with two young men in dark suits in the front. One of them stepped out, opened the door to the back. Ralph Sugarman got out and walked into the rear entrance of the building.

The man who'd been sitting in the front leaned against the side of the car and smoked a cigarette. He finished a third cigarette before Sugarman came out, Homer Tony walking beside him. The back door of the limousine swung open again and both men climbed in. Kincaid was waiting there, invisible from the outside through the tinted glass. Tony sat beside Kincaid, and Sugarman sat on the jump-seat. 'You're all set,' he said. 'Signed, sealed, and delivered. Just remember what I told you. Don't get out of the car. You're not here. You won't be in San Pedro. Your name wasn't on the bail-bond.'

'Does that matter?' Kincaid said.

'Everything matters. It's one thing for you to blow the bail money. It's something else if they see your finger-prints on the next step. I'd rather you didn't go to San Pedro at all.'

'I'm going,' Kincaid said. 'I have to go.'

'All right. But stay in the car. Let Corso's two social engineers handle things down there. And call me at home tonight.'

Sugarman got out of the limousine then and walked across the parking area to where a taxi was waiting.

'I told you I'd get you out of that cheese-box, didn't I?' Kincaid said to Tony. 'You get in trouble. And I get you out. Just like the old days in Glenrowan. How do you like this car? Pretty fancy, eh?'

Tony smiled and nodded his head, and Kincaid said, 'Nothing too good for a horse-thief like you.'

All through the long ride Kincaid kept talking. Old stories, old escapades, old jokes, as the limousine followed Olympic Boulevard to the east, then angled south on Sepulveda to Manchester Avenue, due east through Inglewood to Figueroa Avenue, and straight south through Gardena and Torrance and Wilmington to the docks at San Pedro. Guards stopped them at two control gates there but the driver showed a card in his wallet and they waved him through. One of the guards gave him a sloppy salute and a grin.

The car rolled along the wharfs slowly, through cranes and tractors, bundles and bales, trucks and cartons and stacks of oil-drums. And squads of men loading and unloading freighters. At last the car stopped, away from the edge of the dock. A medium-size, well-worn freighter was moored there flying an Argentine flag, its gangway down and secured to the timbers of the dock, its name, *Rio de Plata*, rusting away but legible on the prow.

As soon as the driver turned off the engine, the other man in the front seat got out carrying a slim brief-case and walked up the gangway to the deck.

'Listen close to me now,' Kincaid said to Tony. 'We don't have much time and I want you to understand what's going on. I know you didn't do anything bad to that girl. And Mr Sugarman knows it too. But we don't want to put you through a long trial while we try to prove it. You know what a trial is. Like what they did to me in *Bushranger*.'

Tony nodded, very solemn now.

'And there's a chance we could never prove it. Then you'd have to go to jail and stay there for God knows how long. I don't want you to do that and you don't want it either. So I'm going to send you back to Australia, give you a nice boat-ride to Sydney, then to Victoria. Back to Glenrowan. McBride knows you're coming. He'll meet you in Sydney and take you to the cattle station. He's got a bunch of young horses that need to be broken. How's that sound? You've got a long face on you. Did you think I was gonna let you hang around my house for ever, stinking up the place and pissing on the rose-bushes?' He cuffed him on the shoulder and they both laughed. 'You'll have some good stories to tell now. About how you were in the movies and hung around all the actresses with red hair and big titties. You'll be a hero in Glenrowan. Till I get there and tell them the truth about you.'

The young man came back down the gangway then. He got into the front seat, slid the glass partition back and said to Kincaid, 'The captain's got the money, the passport, and the papers. That's him, waiting at the top of the gangway. He knows all he's supposed to know and he's not nosy about what he don't know. I explained to him how pissed off we'd be if anything went wrong.'

Kincaid turned back to Tony then. 'OK, Baby-face, we've got you all taken care of. You see that bird up on the deck. He'll keep an eye on you. He's gonna like you a lot because you're the only bloke he's ever met who's uglier than he is.'

Tony laughed and pointed his finger at Kincaid. 'Not me,' Kincaid said, 'you're the ugly one.' He put his hand on Tony's shoulder. 'Until you get to Australia your name is Bill Moore. Can you remember that? That's what they'll call you on the ship. After McBride meets you in Sydney you can be Homer Tony again. You got that? *Bill Moore*. When you hear that name you smile and wag your tail.'

Tony put his hand on Kincaid's shoulder. 'All right,' Kincaid said, 'get the hell out of here and get on board. They'll be pulling out pretty soon now and I don't want to be stuck with you.' Just before Tony opened the car door Kincaid said, 'Stay out of trouble on the boat. Stay in your room. No fights and don't get drunk.' Then: 'You know why you have to go, don't you?'

Tony nodded.

'You know I don't *want* you to go, don't you?'

He nodded again, then got out of the limousine, crossed the wharf, and climbed the gangway, carrying the canvas bag he'd brought with him to California. When he got to the deck the captain led him away and out of sight.

'Do we go or do we wait?' the driver said to Kincaid.

'Let's wait.'

They sat there for forty-five minutes, watching the dockside work, the men and vehicles coming and going, and the *Rio de Plata*'s gangway being cranked up. At last after a lot of shouting and swearing, whistles blowing and the grind of metal against metal, the hawsers were freed, the engines rumbled and complained, and slowly the ship eased away from the dock, guided by tugs, made its way to the interior channel, and headed for the ocean.

When Kincaid tapped on the glass partition, the limousine backed up to a wider part of the dock, turned round, and crawled through the harbour clutter toward the highway.

9

Kincaid got home from San Pedro early that evening, the sun still glowing orange above the ocean; he found a cablegram in the entry-hall from Sophie.

ARTHUR'S COMING BACK TO US. MARGARET'S HOME AT
THE TOWERS. ARE YOU PROUD OF ME? I'M PROUD OF
MYSELF. HURRY HOME.

He went upstairs then to their bedroom. The day he'd
arrived from Chicago, Bettina and Ernest had removed
the dust-covers from the bed. The other chairs and pieces
of furniture in the room were still covered, however,
formless and shrouded. Dead-looking. The furniture in
all the other rooms was also in grey-white cover-cloths,
phantom shapes in a shades-drawn house that seemed to
have been unoccupied for months. The paintings had
been taken down, the pieces of sculpture draped, the
crystal and china and vases and silver and framed
photographs locked away. The windows on the ground
floor had been boxed-in on the outside by great slabs of
plywood so the rooms were dead-dark until the lights
were switched on. The floors were as bare as the walls,
the carpets having been rolled and sent away to storage
before Oliver and Mrs O'Haver departed with the
children and surrendered the keys to the security office.
Sophie's flower-garden, too, outside the morning-
room, seemed unkempt, as though the gardeners
had misunderstood the instructions for continued
maintenance.

Just before Kincaid went upstairs Bettina had
appeared in the lower hall, wringing her hands and con-
fessing that she'd prepared nothing for dinner. 'We didn't
expect you, sir. If you said you'd be here for the evening
meal, it wasn't clear to me. Perhaps I could put together
a nice plate of cold sausage and cheeses for you. Would
that be satisfactory?'

'That's fine,' he said. 'And ask Ernest to fetch a bottle
of Sancerre from the cellar and send that up as well.'

'Oh, I'm awfully sorry, Mr Kincaid, but the liquor's
been locked up and no key was left for us. Perhaps the
security people have the key.'

504

'Never mind. I'll just have a pot of coffee.'

'Very good. I promise I'll cook a fine breakfast for you first thing in the morning.'

'Just coffee will be fine. I'll be leaving very early.'

After he ate the food she brought upstairs he tried to ring up Sugarman at his home but no one answered. He packed his bag, the one he'd be taking with him the next day, then he stood at the window, looking out at the sea, only a greenish streak of light now marking the clean horizontal edge where the sky disappeared beyond the water. He stood there for a long time till the horizon line grew faint in the greyness and the wind began to bend the branches and rustle the foliage of the trees that bordered the garden.

At last he put on a jacket and a cap, went downstairs, and out through the garden doors. He crossed the garden, passed through the gate in the wall and walked down the slope to the stables. The doors to the tack-room and loose-boxes stood ajar and the empty stalls hadn't been cleaned or set right after the horses were taken away. He walked along the path to Homer Tony's cottage. A light burned over the entrance. He could see that the padlocks the police had put on the door were still in place.

Angling away from the house then, the fields turning silver from the dim moon and reflected light from the sea, he walked directly across the wide meadow where the sheep had been kept, through the groves of eucalyptus and oak, to the farthest southern border of his property. When he reached that point he turned west toward the ocean, following the dark shadow of the wall till it ended at right angles to the old stones marking the edge of the bluff. In the soft dark everything seemed abandoned.

He turned back toward the house, following this second stone wall as he'd followed the first one, stopping frequently to look round him, his eyes accustomed now

505

to the gathering darkness. When he came near to the house, he sat on the wall at the spot where it had been reconstructed, where the gap had been when he'd seen it the first time, the strange Aborigine opening that had unsettled Sophie, that had been filled in later so the wall would be solid, so no questions would present themselves as to why that space had been left open when the original wall was built.

While he sat there in the silence, the two security guards at the house went off duty and two others came to replace them. He heard their voices floating rough down the slope from the driveway where the arriving car and the departing one sat for a few minutes beside each other.

The house was a heavy shadow now in the general darkness. Only a veranda light at the south portico burned. And the light he'd left on in the second-floor bedroom where he'd eaten his scraps of sausage and cheese among the jumble of ghost chairs and tables.

Once the guards stopped talking there was no sound. No voices, no dogs barking, no clump of horses hooves in the stables. He felt like the last survivor in a world gone mute.

It was very late when he went upstairs to bed. Early the next morning a studio car came to take him to the airport. The sun was just up in the east when the tri-motored plane took off and started its climb at the edge of the dark ocean, then circled north, and at last settled in on its eastern path to Chicago.